Joinings

CARIN LOCKHART

TRAFFORD

• Canada • UK • Ireland • USA •

Note for Librarians: A cataloguing record for this book is available from Library and Archives Canada at www.collectionscanada.ca/amicus/index-e.html
ISBN 1-4120-9228-0

Printed in Victoria, BC, Canada. Printed on paper with minimum 30% recycled fibre.
Trafford's print shop runs on "green energy" from solar, wind and other environmentally-friendly power sources.

TRAFFORD
PUBLISHING™

Offices in Canada, USA, Ireland and UK

Book sales for North America and international:
Trafford Publishing, 6E–2333 Government St.,
Victoria, BC V8T 4P4 CANADA
phone 250 383 6864 (toll-free 1 888 232 4444)
fax 250 383 6804; email to orders@trafford.com
Book sales in Europe:
Trafford Publishing (UK) Limited, 9 Park End Street, 2nd Floor
Oxford, UK OX1 1HH UNITED KINGDOM
phone +44 (0)1865 722 113 (local rate 0845 230 9601)
facsimile +44 (0)1865 722 868; info.uk@trafford.com
Order online at:
trafford.com/06-0982

10 9 8 7 6 5 4 3

This book is dedicated to the women in my family: Mom, Brittany and Grandma Edith. I love you all.

Special thanks to everyone who read early versions of the book and provided me with invaluable feedback, and to Eli, my coach and editor, who fearlessly trudged through each version with his trusty black pen. I couldn't have finished this without your input and encouragement.

~ Table of Contents ~

The Sodalicium

~ *1* ~

The moment it is all revealed to me happens, appropriately enough, on Christmas Eve. The living room ambiance is apt, light wavering across the walls, the flickering glow emanating from the mass of white candles placed throughout the house, remnants of the Christmas festivities earlier. Her hand cool and steady, Grandma is lifting my chin, her striking eyes probing me, assessing me. "Sweetheart, you have a gift. Or, as we in the family like to officially call it, a bequest – a sensory power that lets you experience something more intensely, more deeply, than other people."

I've always thought of myself as oddly receptive to art and people's hand-writing, but figured it was just a personal quirk. I learned at an early age that it makes people uncomfortable, and so I generally try to hide it, usually avoiding art in public places altogether. But its pull on me has always been strong, not something I can deny for long.

"Let me explain." She pauses, her graceful neck tilting to one side and her lashes obscuring her eyes. I observe her, marveling as I have many times since coming here, how alike our features are. The same vivid blue eyes, heart-shaped curve of our faces, pale complexions that always necessitate sunscreen – even our builds are the same, both of us tall and slender. But while my hair is still a deep auburn color, Grandma's has transformed over time to an equally brilliant silver. Her name, Grace, is perfect for her, embodying so much of her looks and her character.

"There is a secret in our family that goes back throughout time," she finally continues. "Every firstborn child in every generation of our family is a girl, and her firstborn is a girl, and so on and so forth. And each of these first born girls is blessed with a gift, a sort of sixth sense, called your *bequest*. Not the whole commercialized psychic thing, but more like there is one thing that we are especially in tune with, that we can feel or understand in a way different than other people. Something that most folk, for whatever reason, can not sense, but is visible to us, in a very real way. Do you understand?"

I nod, frozen.

"For me, darling, it is the weather. I can feel things in the air, draw in information from clouds, in rain, things invisible to other people. I am connected to these things emotionally in ways difficult to describe." Grandma's voice trails off, her gaze vacant.

Incredible.

"Your mother," she continues on in the same dreamy voice, "could always sense things about people she touched, usually something that had happened, or occasionally, something that was about to happen. It is part of the reason she became a lawyer. Funny, no? She felt she would always know the truth about a case and know which side deserved to win. But it was a hard bequest in other ways, as it is very difficult to know things about people you care about, especially sad, or dark things."

Numbly, I find myself nodding again. Can something that causes so much pain be called a gift, when it had driven my mother to forsake me to the care of strangers? The precious journal she left for me before she died – the only real thing I have of hers – is full of loving words and tender passages, yet still she abandoned me to be raised by others. *"Why?"* I think.

"I don't know, sweetie." In her uncanny way, Grandma has just answered my question, without it ever being asked.

"I have always," I say, "been abnormally sensitive to the messages contained in art. Writings and paintings and sculptures all seem to communicate with me – not only what the artist wants to let me know, but more: I seem to be able to jump right into the art and watch them as they work, understand their state of their mind. I mean, I can see them, plain as day, looking at their computer, or holding their paintbrush, or staring at a blank canvas. But I always thought that was just me."

"That's your gift, honey." She leans forward, her voice suddenly energetic. "The key is to not let it overtake you and try to fight it, but embrace it, letting the feelings run through you. We call the experience *iunctum*; a joining, a melding of souls. It can throw you off-balance, but I can help you master it, teach you how to flow with it, maneuver through it."

A silence falls. I incline my head towards the picture before us, a large, framed piece that Grandma recently brought out of the basement and placed before me. "So the print. Who painted it?"

"I think you know. Why not dive in?"

I can't think of the last time I purposely sought out art, with the full intent of extracting its secrets. My feet, suddenly heavy, slowly traverse the oriental rug that covers the expanse between me and the painting. Uncurling my tightly fisted fingers, I wipe my sweaty palms on my trousers before kneeling down, the art now tantalizingly close. Reaching out, I touch the canvas with my fingertips, the sensation fluid and porous, as if I could sink my hand into it, melding with it in a magical way. The picture comes alive, the colors blending, mixing, forming a tunnel and pulling me in, whispering, absorbing me. It takes great effort to speak. "This was painted by my Great Grandmother, your mother. She was very sick at the time – cancer – and knew she would never see her grand-daughter grow up. She is painting this picture to freeze the memory, to create a piece of herself, to crystallize her love for her grandchild."

"Ah, that's very good; you're quick," Grandma's voice sounds far away, coming from a dimension different from that I now occupy. "My Mother painted that when she was in her seventies and already knew she was fighting cancer. She passed away a year later."

The trance is enticing, consuming, holding me in its grip. I am unable to back away, despite the warning bells, developed long ago due to self-preservation, that are madly ringing in my head. I go further, free-falling, a cocoon of liquid warmth surrounding me. "She has white hair and intense blue eyes, the kind of eyes that can penetrate straight through you, see more than what you intend to expose. Just like yours. She is hungry as she paints, her tea and toast having grown cold, but the walk back to the house would take too long, be an in-terruption to her work, the girl, the setting, just as she wants them, this moment in time perfect for the picture she wants to capture. She has argued with the girl earlier that day about putting a band-aid on a scrape, the girl afraid it will stick on and never come off. She is a bit distracted by a hang nail on her left thumb. The butter on her toast tastes odd today, a bit like the cow has been eating mildewed hay. The wind is pick-ing up, ruffling her sketches that are sitting on the small table beside her." Random streams of information flow towards me, carrying bristling packets of emotions, images and data.

I feel hands on my shoulders, from where I am not sure. Slowly, I grow conscious that it is my Grandma, her steady and insistent touch pulling me from the warmth, extracting me from the scene. I experience a sudden chill, the withdraw-al complete.

As I sit back, the ordinary, but still beautiful, one-dimensional picture of a girl standing amidst the tall grasses on a hill, returns to focus. I feel temporarily drained, as if part of my energy has chosen to linger behind in the pastoral scene. I can't remember ever going this deep into a painting before. I've felt hunches, invitations, flashes of insight, but never this. "What was her gift? Great-Grandma's, I mean. Does it have something to do with food?"

"Well, yes!" says Grandma, looking pleased, "Did you pick that up from her painting?" I nod. "She had a connection with food that was truly… incredible," she continues. "She understood how spices and herbs mixed together in ways that went beyond a mere ability to cook. The food she made seemed to reflect that, full of unique tastes, so harmonious and balanced. Whenever she sampled something that someone else had cooked, she could list every ingredient and even tell you how they had blended things together, down to the type of spoon – wood or metal. It was really quite something."

"And other people. Didn't they think you were weird?" I ask.

Grandma cocks her head to one side. "Do you think you are weird, dear?"

Before I can answer, she says "Different, maybe. And as I like to think of us, *distinctive*. It's true that others do not always understand us, but we are a family of women specially endowed, chosen, really, to carry gifts that can have great impact in this world. Remembering this helps you see beyond people's reactions."

Ella! For the first time since the conversation began, I think of my three-year-old daughter. If this is something that passes from generation to generation, then that means my little girl has some kind of bequest too? "What about Ella?"

"Of course she has a gift, of that I am certain. As for what, well… I'm afraid I can't answer that. We will just have to watch for signs as she grows. Usually, you can start seeing clues when they are still fairly young. It is important to watch and coach them when the time comes, because sometimes it can be a bit overwhelming, even scary. Plus, their gift can often lead them straight into pure trouble. We must nurture Ella's gift so that she isn't afraid of it and learns to master it. We must work until she reaches the moment of discernment, that point in time where she truly understands the power she holds and how to wield it properly."

I focus on the silver ring I am twirling on my finger. It is time to ask the question that has been throbbing in my head for months – if not years – just below the surface. "Why would my mother give me to strangers when she knew all this? I mean, she knew I'd be different and no one would understand. Why? Why would she do that?" I am pushing against the floor, straining my muscles, feeling the sudden heat of ancient heirloom rage.

"I don't know," Grandma speaks quietly. "I can only believe that she knew something, and that she was somehow trying to spare you pain, either due to her gift, or something else."

"I thought you said there was great joy with the gift."

She flinches. "Yes, that is so. There is great joy," she entreats me with her voice. "But to understand great joy, you must first understand great sorrow. That is the human condition, darling. And Katie's gift, especially the occasional ability to see into the future, was often bittersweet."

"But what if I don't want this gift?"

"Ah child, don't say that." Candlelight is moving across her face, its motion obscuring her expression, but her voice is earnest and clear. "It's our family legacy, our destiny. It's called a bequest and not a curse for a reason. You must let me help you understand it, become comfortable with it. Give it some time."

"This *gift* has caused me to be an outcast my whole life, and now I find out my mother fully understood what would happen, but put me through it *anyway*? To spare me how exactly?"

Grandma sighs, raising her palms as if to express a loss for words. "I know she loved you, dear one," she says softly.

"I'm glad *you* do. That makes one of us." My voice is bitter, small. A hot pang sends tears pouring down my face. Leaning forward, I rest my head in her lap.

"Now, now," she says in a soothing tone, holding me close with one hand, drawing slow, wide circles on my back with the other, "everything will be revealed to you in its proper time."

For a long while we simply stay locked in our embrace, a feeling of peace spreading through me, and then Grandma asks softly, "So, can I see your star?"

I am taken aback. My star? My mind races backwards, trying to think of a time when I might have accidentally exposed it, but I am very careful and the chances are remote. I pull away, backing up to meet her gaze.

"Don't be frightened," Grandma says, a twinkle in her eyes. Slowly unbuttoning the top of her white silk blouse, she exposes the small, perfect shape, tucked right between her breasts, the same place as my own. Hers is a deep rose, a little darker than mine, but not as intense, I notice, as Ella's. All of them, however, are flawless five-pointed stars, as distinct as if crafted by an accomplished tattoo artist.

Continuing to stare, I pull down the neckline of my black knit shirt, exposing my own symbol, an exact match in every way, but a bit lighter. "Why?"

"The mark," Grandma says in a faraway voice, "says you are part of the Sodalicium. The sacred trust."

"And Aunt Emily?"

"No. No bequest, other than her finely tuned mothering

skills." She buttons her blouse, pulling her jewelry out and re-positioning it around her collar. "And we can never discuss this with her, as it can only be shared with the firstborn daughters. It has been passed down from generation to generation, with the expectation that no one share the secret. I am not sure if it comes from the fear of being accused of witchcraft in earlier times, or if it would end the magic if the bonds of silence were broken, but none of us has ever felt it was worth taking that chance." She pauses a moment, looking like she is about to say more, but instead claps her hands on her legs. "But tonight grows late, and it's time for bed."

My limbs heavy, I know she is right. But my head is whirling with thoughts and unasked questions eagerly waiting to be answered.

"We have lots more to do to help you along with your discernment, but don't worry, we'll get to it all in time." Grandma is moving gracefully from candle to candle, extinguishing them with seemingly nothing more than a light brush of her hand over the flames. She turns to me and smiles, "The hand motion is really more for the comfort of those outside the trust. I suppose with you, I can skip that little show." Suddenly, all the candles flicker and go out in unison. "It's just a bit of a trick with the help of the wind."

With only the full moon now to light our way, we head up the stairs, the wood creaking softly under our weight. "You know, I wanted to tell you on Christmas Eve because I wanted you to remember this day always. Working towards your discernment is a special time."

As if I would ever forget this day, even if it had happened on a mundane Monday, I had a gnarly math test and my period had just started? I could have heard this news in any of the many linoleum and fluorescent-lit shelters I've frequented over the years, and it wouldn't have lost an ounce of its impact.

Lying in bed, I know my only hope for sleep is sheer mental exhaustion. I'd arrived here seven months earlier, staggering into their lives from a threadbare seat on a greyhound bus. An exhausted nomad, I'd been traveling from shelter to shelter, my infant daughter in tow, until I'd finally gotten up the nerve to seek out my Grandmother. I've been incredibly happy here, but now the bright packages and adornments of the holiday are overshadowed by the enormity of all I have just learned, and the anticipation of what is to come. And as I do many nights, I fall asleep thinking of my mother, my mind flowing back into the past to try and catch her as she moves forward, out of my life.

Grace let out a muffled scream, struggling for breath, the urge
to climb out of her own skin so strong she almost thought it
possible. She held her pillow against her face, the flannel case
damp from perspiration. Focusing hard, she tried to force the
foreign entity away, willing it to leave. She didn't have many
uninvited visitors, and those that she did were normally fine,
genuine folk, either looking for help or perhaps simply a brief
companion. There were few here on earth with whom they
could actually communicate – she might be the only one for
all she knew – most folks experiencing them simply as a wave
of gooseflesh or a sudden chill on the back of their neck. And
then there were the visitors like this one; angry, bitter and re-
vengeful. Knowing they would be taking a different, more
permanent path, never to pass this way again, they seemed
to want to vent on someone, using her as their whipping boy,
frustrated that they were unable to change the course of the
lives that had brought them to this point. Visits like this were
extremely rare – especially during the Christmas season, when
good tended to prevail in the spirit world just as it did in the
human one – but when they happened, they took their toll on
her, draining her, and troubling her heart.

She felt the spirit trying to invade her core, his foul stench
almost tangible to her nostrils, his mission evidently to force

her to feel all of the dark, pent-up wrath that had swallowed him, changed him, broken him over time. Grace fought. She would not succumb, and while she might be an old lady with precious little skin covering her bones, she was a tough old bird after all these years. She'd met others just like him, and today would not be the day that the likes of his kind overtook her. Her beautiful hair was in total disarray, matted strands of it plastered to her face, and she was breathing hard, panting with the struggle, small whimpers intermittently escaping from her lips.

He seemed to be fairly young, maybe in his late twenties, and it was clear that he'd committed murder – more than once. During an *iunctum*, or joining, the name used to describe this sort of spiritual melding, she normally saw everything the presence allowed, but this time her resistance to him was strong, and she wanted to know nothing – especially not his name. He probed in every passage, looking to invade her, while she, eyes squeezed tight, fists balled, her body curled tight, straining, pushing and resisting, did her best to seal herself shut.

Suddenly a gust of wind came into the room, frisking the curtains and bringing with it another presence, this one entirely different, its' essence strong and pure. As suddenly as it had come, the wicked presence was gone, much like a weight being lifted, evidently banished by the new arrival. Her hero was unfamiliar to her, definitely not one of the Sodalicium, but Grace was certainly grateful all the same. She lay still, slowly unwrapping the protective layers of tension from her body, opening the inner valves to let the world back in. Soon the room was empty again, leaving her lying amidst a damp tangle of covers, spent from her ordeal. She tried to catch her breath, to slow things back down, the fluttering in her chest more than a bit disconcerting.

Slapping her forearm over her eyes to block out the mental

images in her head, she groaned, frustrated to be awakening on Christmas morning feeling like bloody hell. Why couldn't she have had a joining with Oliver, her late husband, or Katie? That would have been a fine Christmas gift, infinitely preferable to *this*. But instead she was laying here, her heart doing back-flips, worrying about whether she could even muster the strength to get out of bed.

Through the window, the first hints of pale dawn light were stealing in, and she remained still, fervently willing the odd fluttering in her chest to stop. Drawing from what had helped in the past, she turned her thoughts towards peaceful images, fond memories she had stored up for use on occasions such as this. Today's choice was a cherished memory of her husband Oliver and her daughter Katie walking hand-in-hand down the lane in front of the house they had lived in for over thirty years. It was fall, the golden blots of leaves were falling from the trees, lying in mounds along the side of the dirt road. An occasional gust of wind sent them twirling, ruffling the skirt of Katie's plaid school uniform, blowing wisps of dark hair loose from her long braid and stirring Oliver's roomy trousers.

Eventually sleep overtook her, and when she awoke, she found that dawn had come and gone, morning well underway. Testing her stiff joints, she'd eased herself out of bed, slowly making her way towards the adjoining bathroom. Resting her hands on either side of the cool porcelain sink, she peered at her reflection in the mirror, gingerly touching one of the puffy circles under her eyes. Damn! I look like hell, she thought to herself, disgusted with the whole situation. She felt much too old for all this – what other seventy-three year old women would have the fortitude to put up with this constant stream of voices, spirits and ethereal babble? She bathed, trying to wash away the tell tale signs of her ordeal. The last thing she needed was for her sister Emily to begin fretting over her, concerned she'd had another "heart episode" and annoyed when she received only paltry half-answers to her inevitable questions.

With sure and steady strokes, she brushed her thick, silvery hair away from the prominent widow's peak at the crest of her forehead, closing her eyes for a moment, enjoying the tingling sensation rippling along her scalp. The cloudy feeling in her head started to clear, thoughts of the spirits fading into the background, her focus turning to Lucy. What would her granddaughter be thinking after their difficult, important exchange last night? She picked up her pace, impatient to find out.

Dressed and ready to leave the room, she glanced back, noticing her tousled bed. Ugh. She could care less about the messy bed, but knew Emily would feel compelled to straighten it, fussing with the throw pillows and refolding the throw blanket carelessly tossed over the arm of a nearby chair. What's more, her sister's keen eyes might see beyond the clutter, causing her to suspect that Grace had experienced another one of her 'incidents'. Beloved Emily had carefully been kept in the dark these many years. Heading back into the room, she tidied it herself, silently cursing the fact that she had to be a neat freak in her own house.

Walking along the corridor, she was unsurprised to find the rooms were empty, everyone evidently already downstairs. Typically not a late sleeper, she still rarely awoke before Emily, who routinely rose early to let out the family terrier and to spend time alone in the kitchen, reading the morning paper and nursing a stiff cup of coffee.

The living room was awash with sunlight, but equally uninhabited, her great-granddaughter's bright red Christmas stocking emptied of its contents, a telltale candy wrapper discarded on the polished wood floor nearby. A clutter of cheery paper, bows and boxes were scattered underneath the Christmas tree, left-over from last night's gift exchange, but other than that, the large expanse of the cozy, lodge-style main room was in its usual neat state. The dusky reds, greens and blues of the furniture and throw-rugs, combined with the honeyed pine of the log walls, gave the space a warm, inviting ambiance. Tall bookshelves were nestled between the long, floor-to-ceiling windows, displaying the family collection of hardbound books along with artwork collected from all over the world. Suddenly the tinkling sound of Ella's laughter floated towards her from the direction of the kitchen, firmly establishing the location of the rest of her small family.

The little girl was visible in profile, as she stood on a small stepladder, helping her aunt at the counter, the two of them rolling out dough for what would undoubtedly be her sister's famous orange sticky buns. While the toddler's sleeves were rolled high and her favorite red apron was securely in place to protect her clothing, flour covered virtually all of her exposed skin; her hands, forearms and face all lightly dusted in the fine, white powder.

Grace smiled as she shook her head, still amazed at the change that had overtaken her house in the last year. After her husband died three years ago, and Emily came to live with her, she'd assumed that the remainder of her life would unfold uneventfully, save the steady stream of activity due to her gift. But then the most extraordinary event of her entire life occurred: she discovered a granddaughter and great-granddaughter she had never known existed until they appeared one day, apparently out of nowhere, on her very own front porch.

It had actually been Chloe, the family terrier, who had alerted them to their visitors on that fateful spring morn. They'd found a pale, disoriented young woman curled up sleeping on one of the deck couches, her small daughter snuggled up tightly against her. Lucy, who had barely turned twenty at the time, her three-year old daughter at her side, had softly, but

unwaveringly, told them her identity. Grace was able to readily accept the news, what with her looks and the star she'd
glimpsed on the child, but it was something that her sister
Emily had adjusted to in time, requiring the proof of Katie's
journal and Lucy's birth certificate. Lucy had initially seemed
ill at ease, obviously wanting to stay, but equally afraid of
letting down her guard. So while Ella had quickly adjusted,
happy to claim Grace and Emily as her own, Lucy had eased
into 15 ½ AL more gradually, exposing herself in bits, each
glimpse something to be treasured. Grace was curious about
the story surrounding the child, but had never felt compelled
to ask, figuring Lucy had been subjected to enough judgment
and mistrust to last a lifetime, and would, in time, share the
story with her on her own.

Sensing her presence, Ella turned towards her, a broad grin
lighting up her impish face. "Nana!" She scrambled down
from her perch, rushing over and hugging her great-grandma
around her knees. "Happy Christmas," she chortled as she
gazed up at Grace, her dark head titled back, her thick-lashed
blue eyes round, looking as mischievous as ever. She ran her
tongue across her lips, no doubt tasting some of the sticky
substance that had been left behind from whatever was in the
abandoned candy wrapper.

And then, with a giggle, she scampered off, evidently
having stood still for as long as she was able. Rushing back
towards the counter, she gave Chloe, her inseparable canine
companion, a loud kiss on the nose before climbing back up
on her stool to self-importantly resume her cooking duties.
Grace looked down and shook her head, a band of white now
visible across the lower half of her grey pants. Easing herself
down next to Lucy at the rustic wood table in the center of the
room, she brushed off her legs with a nearby dishtowel as she
gauged her granddaughter's mood.

The girl's beautiful face was impassive as she sat watching

the flurry of activity in the room. Her dark hair was capturing the light, absorbing it and throwing it back with a fiery, red glow. Her heart-shaped face had an elfish quality; a slight point to her chin, large blue eyes framed with coal-black lashes, her lips full and sensual. Everything about her was willowy, her limbs long and slender, with a slight softness about her that kept her from being a little too angular, a little too knobby. She exuded a quietness, a sort of reserve from everything going on around her. But over time, that seemed to slowly be changing. Finally she noticed Grace's gaze and smiled, the emotion not quite reaching her eyes.

"Ella Kate!" cried Emily, the soft-hearted house disciplinarian, "How many times do I have to tell you not to feed Chloe people food?" She sighed loudly, shaking her head.

Furrowing her tiny brows, Ella pouted, her small arm reaching out behind her back to offer her canine buddy access to the moist dough covering her right hand.

"I can see that, little missy!" Emily affected a stern look, which didn't seem to fool the toddler. From the table, Lucy merely watched the exchange. Grace knew that on any other day, her increasingly outgoing granddaughter would be laughing along with them, trying to correct her errant daughter instead of playing spectator. But today she seemed pensive, withdrawn.

Grace began to idly smooth out the cloth napkin sitting next to her. Perhaps, she thought, she had jumped the gun in her zeal to bring her into the fold. Maybe it had been too much, considering everything she'd been through. Most girls within the trust would have been well-trained in their gift by the age of ten or so, having celebrated their discernment with their mother and grandmother, and having written in the Diurnus for the first time.

Emily washed off Ella's hands, the flesh on her round arms jiggling with the rapid motion. The little mischief maker chortled in delight, an accidental burst from the faucet leaving them both wet and dripping from the neck up. Emily muttered something about monkeys.

"Grandma." Lucy's hand stilled her Grandmother's fidgeting.

"Yes?"

"You're looking at me like you're afraid I'm going to run away. But everything's okay. I just feel quiet, you know?" Lucy maintained eye contact for a few moments, and then looked away as she withdrew her hand, tucking her hair back behind her ears, and returning to her former pose, elbows on the table, her chin resting on her palms, staring into the middle distance. Both her and her daughter, Grace thought, shared the hereditary Carlson looks, the only differences being the light dusting of freckles across Ella's nose, and the slightly more determined set to the lines of her jaw.

As Grace watched her, she couldn't still her own worried curiosity. What is preoccupying her: the bequest, or thoughts of her own mother? Incapable of understanding herself why her own daughter, Katie, would have given birth and then offered the child up for adoption without telling her, Grace could certainly understand her angst. She hadn't had a joining with her only child, who had been living in the afterlife for a good eighteen years now, in some time. She was fairly sure that Katie was avoiding her to postpone explaining about Lucy, and she had a laundry list of questions ready for her daughter the next time they met.

"Nana! Wanna see me dance?" Ella shifted her weight from one foot to the other as she leaned against Grace's knees, dramatically tilting her head to one side, grinning broadly. Despite herself, Grace laughed.

"Bathroom first?" Her grandmother knew the signs.

"Noooo! I can hold it! I am a big girl!"

Lucy sighed, finally offering up a small, albeit real, smile.

"Okay little miss, come on." Scooping up her protesting daughter, she headed off in the direction of the bathroom, small little feet incased in white tights and black Mary-Jane's flailing wildly on either side of her.

Grace watched them retreat, then turned to find her sister leaning with her back against the counter, watching her. A morning of watching it was. Her silvery eyebrows arched quizzically, their harsh angle at odds with the rounded softness of her body and the cluster of curls atop her head, she appeared to be waiting for something.

"Yes?"

"Are you going to tell me why you have dark circles under your eyes, why Lucy is so quiet, and why you two seem to be thicker than thieves about something or another?" Her arms crossed in front of her chest, she peered down at her sister over the top of her black-rimmed reading glasses.

Grace racked her brain, frantically searching through her list of possible explanations. But over the many years, she'd grown used to this. And today's cover-up was larger, weightier than usual.

"Oh never mind! Geez, don't mind me. I'm just the kitchen help! No one ever tells me anything. Our whole lives, no one tells me anything!" She turned back to the sink, vigorously scrubbing a baking dish, her temper evident in the harsh scratching sounds filling the room. "I just take care of you, with your heart condition, and the rest of the world in the bargain! Why should today be any different?"

Grace blew out a long stream of steady air, knowing that she had no explanations for any of it – at least none that she could voice. Somewhat saddened by this, she did the only thing she could, standing up and embracing her sister's sturdy form from behind, laying her cheek on her shoulder. "I love you Em, I hope you know that."

The scrubbing paused for a moment, then resumed, but

her sister's shoulders had relaxed a bit, and the scrubbing was a little less fierce. "I believe I do."

~3~

And then, before anything else can happen – wouldn't you know it! I get sick. I swill a particularly noxious red liquid medicine which keeps me in a perpetual haze, my brain fuzzy, as closed off to fresh, clean input as my nose. Barely venturing downstairs, I hug my bed, surrounded by a growing mound of crumpled tissues and discarded dishes. Grandma and Aunt Em have been the hardest hit, probably due to their age, and so Margie, our closest neighbor, has been spending most of her time trying to keep them comfortable, on top of helping me by looking after Ella.

By the fourth day, I re-enter the world, carefully descending the stairs, my head still feeling a little woozy. My hair pulled back into a pony tail, and my nose red from constant blowing, I am hardly stylish, but it feels darn good to see the first floor again.

"Mama!" Ella comes running towards me, hammering into my shins. I kneel down to hug her, as bending over might start the whole head-spinning thing again. A hint of her delicate musky-sweet scent manages to make its way through my clogged nasal passages. Her slender little body feels good; a mass of tiny limbs in constant motion, vibrant and alive.

Margie is watching us from the couch, looking the epitome of health, her white hair neatly pulled back in a clip and her face lightly tanned from the out-of-doors. "We were wondering when you'd make an appearance," she says good-humoredly, and deftly folds another small garment from the laundry pile beside her. "Ella and I were going to head out to watch Jack fish this morning. Want to come?"

Jack and Margie are our neighbors, sort of caddy-corner to the northeast. Except for owning the trendy local coffee shop, "The Drip", they are for all intents and purposes retired, the two visible many mornings out in the meadow, Jack's fly line forming lazy snake patterns in the air above the stream, and Margie reading a book in her folding green camp chair. Both of them are tall and lean, have been athletic all their lives, and seem to thrive in the out-of-doors.

I readily accept her invitation, and along with Chloe, we head out into the crisp, Rocky Mountain air. Before coming to Colorado, I always pictured the place as a kind of year-round snowfield with mountains. But the weather is surprisingly mild – mysteriously so. No matter how much snow falls, the high-altitude sun makes quick work of it, and the weather can be warm and inviting, even in January.

Our short little street is called Alpine Lane, better known as 'AL' to its small number of inhabitants. With only three houses to its credit, AL barely qualifies as a street, and is merely a small extension off the main drag, Harrison Avenue, which is the only thing separating it from the meadow and majestic peaks beyond. While all three homes are distinctly Victorian, two are vintage, and ours, oddly numbered 15 ½ because it faces perpendicular to the others, is obviously new. Large, with a timbered porch surrounding it on all four sides, it seems grandiose compared to the small ranch home I grew up in, but I am slowly settling in.

Our other neighbors, Fern and Gus, are also retired, but spend much of their time cruising about the country in their gigantic motor home. Sometimes they return in the spring, eager to enjoy the beautiful Colorado weather, along with the rest of the tourist crowd, but often a more tempting offer comes their way, and they heed the call of the road, traveling to wherever it takes them. Inevitably dressed alike in jeans and chinos, the pair thrives on travel, their occasional letters inevitably bearing the postmark of a town or burg unfamiliar to me.

Margie and I pick our way across the street, carefully avoiding the occasional puddles in the graded dirt road. Ella, of course, takes the opportunity to jump in them with her shiny red rubber boots, relishing sending muddy water spraying everywhere. The rest of us scatter, giving her a wide berth.

Waving at us from the front porch, Jack heads towards us, his favorite tan fishing cap – complete with a somewhat pungent odor and an assortment of lucky flies – on his head, and a thermos of steaming coffee in hand. His face is wonderfully weathered, the lines and grooves near his eyes and mouth indicating his propensity for smiling, the silver of his eyebrows arching above warm brown eyes. He pauses at the bottom of the steps, giving a few farewell pats to Sammy, their twelve year-old black lab. Completely blind, the dog sits on the grass, his heart willing, but his body no longer able to maneuver down by the river. The two finish their exchange, and Jack heads down to meet us at the front gate, a cleverly crafted contraption made from a collection of old skis, where the rest of our supplies lay waiting. We all grab something, even Ella, who is delighted to carry the wool lap blanket, and head off in the direction of the stream.

It is a year round brook, brawling and big in spring, and shrunk to a sluggish flow in winter. Just now, it is moving at an unhurried pace, evidently in no rush to reach its destination. Ella, trailing her blanket, runs past me, obviously happy to be outside after having been cooped up for the last few days. She rushes to the grassy bank and teetering forward, peers intently at the water. "No!" Margie and I shout at exactly the same time.

With Ella safely upright again, she and I stroll along the river bank while Margie sets up her chair, settling in with her current, dog-eared novel, and Jack steps into the river, ready to cast his first fly of the morning. I follow along next to my daughter, watching as she runs her hands over the grass, crouches low to inspect a shiny black beetle and exclaims in delight when a hawk flies overhead. Even with the meadow dormant, she manages to locate small signs of life. Her ability to find even the tiniest animals amazes me; perhaps her talent is due to her sheer nearness to the ground.

"Mommy, who's that?" asks Ella. She looks around, then pauses, standing perfectly still, her eyes blank. Even when the wind tousles her dark auburn curls about her face, she is oblivious, maintaining her perfectly frozen pose, still as a statue.

I listen, hearing only the gurgling of the stream, the clicking sound of Jack's fly reel and the breeze fluttering the leaves in a nearby aspen grove. The merest sound of a page being flipped in Margie's book, Chloe's panting, but nothing else, certainly no *one* else. "I don't hear anything sweetie."

"Mommy, *shhh*." Her tiny dark brows furrowed, she concentrates, her gaze now directed towards the water. She starts towards the bank, pulling me along beside her. We are about a foot away from the water when she stops, and dropping my hand, crouches down, evidently looking at something, completely mesmerized. If we are playing make-believe, I feel dense, because I don't understand the game.

Seemingly completely unaware of my presence, she shifts, lying down on her stomach, her head resting on her hands. Chloe lies down beside her, and I am mildly surprised to notice their poses are identical. Apparently as engrossed as my daughter, Chloe, too, peers into the stream.

An eerie feeling creeps over me. Except for the bright sunshine bouncing off the glossy mantle of the water, there is nothing visible, save a leaf lazily making its way downriver. Having no better idea, I sit slowly down behind the pair, resting my head on my knees, watching.

Ella looks as if she is in conversation, but without the words. She makes occasional hand gestures and laughs, sometimes looking towards Chloe, as if sharing a thought or seeking accord. Dressed completely in red today, she is a vibrant swatch of color against the otherwise neutral landscape.

Suddenly she glances over her shoulder at me, her eyes merry. "Mommy, did you hear what he said? Isn't that funny? Chloe and I think it's really funny!"

Despite my growing sense of unease, I try to act casual. "I didn't hear him, honey, what did he say?"

"That he eats bugs! They all do!" She went off into peals of laughter. Fighting a rising panic, I slowly crawl forward on my hands and knees, the brittle grasses crunching under my weight, until I am directly alongside her.

At first I see nothing, just the same dancing rays of sunshine. Then a cloud drifts in front of the sun for a moment, obscuring its glow and allowing me to see below the surface. I am stunned. There, about two feet out in the stream, a large number of fish, maybe ten or so in all, are paused in the water, barely moving, their gills slowly swaying in and out, apparently peaceful and unconcerned. Huddled in a group, they look directly at me as though awaiting instructions. Neither facing upstream, nor looking for food, nor darting about in the ripples of the water, these usually skittish creatures are resisting the current, remaining perfectly still, and staring directly at us with something approaching friendliness. As I watch, open-mouthed, more fish come to join the assembly, some politely filling in on the outer edges and others jostling to push their way in amongst those already gathered.

Holy crap!

Before I know it, instinct kicks in; grabbing her around her middle, and hoisting her up, I am walking as fast as I can in the opposite direction. After the initial shock wears off, she begins screaming, drawing Margie's startled gaze in our direction.

My heart beats so hard that it feels like it is coming out of my chest. I collapse down on the ground, Ella in my lap, Chloe beside me. I hug her tight, as tight as I am able, shielding her, protecting her, from what I now, with dread, can recognize will be her destiny. She is finally quiet, more from shock than anything else.

"Mommy, did I do something bad?"

I shake my head. "No sweetheart. You could never do anything bad."

Margie has made her way to us, her usual long, sure strides covering the distance in short order. She stops a few feet away, slowly kneeling, her long flannel shirt now touching the ground. I frantically rack my brain for something to say, not wanting my daughter to hear me tell a lie. Margie waits, never one to be uncomfortable with silence, knowing an explanation will eventually come.

"We were playing a game, that's all." I am quickly fabricating a story, even as I speak. "Ella is a fairy princess, and I am saving her from an ugly prince who eats bugs." I look down at Ella, who is eyeing me with interest. "Right honey, eating bugs is icky!"

I am deeply thankful when my rosy cheeked daughter simply nods, choosing this once to say nothing more. *Thank you,* I whisper to myself, and hug her tight, sending her a silent message of gratitude.

"Well, okay then. I thought someone had been mortally wounded there for a second." Carefully pushing up on her knee for balance, Margie stands back up. "You two coming? I brought some of those granola cookies Ella likes."

Ella starts to squirm, obviously in favor of Margie's suggestion. I am unsure if my shaky legs will hold me, so I wait until the pair have turned away before I make an attempt to follow. Do I want to make sense out of what has happened this morning? I am probably overreacting, I tell myself. But even as I think this, a small voice in my head calls my bluff, reminding me that deluding myself is a conscious, cowardly choice, and that the inevitable has just taken a giant step forward into my life.

~*4*~

Their faces seem blurry to me now, and I can no longer remember the exact color of their eyes, or the shape of their noses. It's more like they are simply sensations, or a collection of feelings, than anything else. I can remember little things they did; things that made me feel special, and things that made me feel small. I vaguely recall how they smelled, how they moved and yet when I think about them, I feel sort of empty.

I don't dredge through my past often, since the memories are stale and the feelings they evoke unpleasant. And there is something else unsettling about my memories: they're all cast in black and white. I don't know if it's like that for everybody, but it's always been that way for me. If I am absorbed in a piece of art, the world around me glows with intense, rich hues, but the vignettes from my own life, memories of my adoptive parents, consist of drained and endless shades of gray.

When I was in grade school, I observed my classmates, noticing that some of them had lives very different than my own. Orchestrated like clockwork, their days were segmented into a series of neatly planned events; school, music lessons, play dates and recreation time. Their moms were the ones applauding madly at school plays, traveling along with us on field trips, bringing in trays of carefully decorated cookies at school parties and taking videos of them getting on – and off – the bus their first day of school. Those kids always seemed a little more complete, a little more vital than the rest of us.

I belonged to another, lesser group – those who had to figure things out for themselves – scrappy, independent kids, who grew up without the benefit of music lessons and hovering moms. True, my adoptive mother and father, Janet and Carl Harrison, looked like the quintessential parents: a stay at home mom who dressed in neatly-pressed blouses and slacks, her hair always fashionably styled, and a father who managed the local grocery store, always smelled of Old Spice and played golf on the weekends. Sure, I was clothed, fed and sheltered. They taught me not to not to cross the street when there was traffic. They instructed me that getting good grades in school was important and that I should always clean behind my ears. But there was always something elemental missing from my life, and that void only worsened as I grew older.

It's not that I was unlovable, but more that I was an extraordinary child interjected into a family that strived to be ordinary. No doubt I appeared normal as an infant, save the star marking on my chest. And clearly they meant well, adopting what they thought was a sweet baby girl, rosy-cheeked and charming, the perfect addition to round out the family they so desperately craved. There was every reason for them to expect that the three of us, living in a pretty little white house on a wide, tree-lined street in a small North Carolina town, would get along just fine.

But as time went on, I became myself, a girl who could see more than was intended in the things people created. It all started fairly innocently, like the time I inspected the writing on a small brown box and informed the mailman that the contents had been packed by a smelly lady with a large wart on her armpit. Or when I scrutinized the drawing of a fellow kindergarten classmate and blurted out to everyone that he habitually sat in his tree house picking his nose and eating his boogers.

And my list of strange 'episodes', as my adoptive parents termed them, only increased over time. They had laughed stiltedly, passing it off as impetuous when, as a young toddler, I'd advised the visiting minister that the choir could smell him when he farted during church, a fact I picked up from reading some sermon notes tucked in his Bible. When I was five, they had sent me to timeout – a common occurrence by then – for reading a gift card on a Christmas package and announcing to all of our holiday party guests that the green ear-muffs inside, a gift from my cousin, were ugly, and had been bought from the thrift shop downtown. But then one day I crossed the line forever. I will never forget the look on their faces that hot summer day, when, in front of the ice cream parlor, with half the town present, I accused Mr. Jenkins, the proprietor, of having lustful thoughts about my mother, of imagining her naked with a maraschino cherry stuck in her belly-button. The horrified look on my parent's faces as they backed slowly away from me is etched in my memory forever. My mother's visage was pale and distraught as she clutched my father for support, while his features were closed, hard, lined with disgust. The desolate emptiness I felt in the pit of my stomach as they whispered to each other, forming an inner circle to which I no longer belonged, was the harbinger of hard, lonely times ahead.

After that, things changed. I realized at the age of six, after having read my adoptive mother's grocery list, that she was embarrassed by me, that she actually feared me and wished I'd never come into her home. On more than one occasion I entered a room, only for her and my father's hushed conversation to draw to an abrupt halt, the two of them eyeing me skeptically, as if trying to decipher what made me tick. I heard snippets of conversation about doctors and tests and special schools, but in the end, they elected to simply treat me as a visitor in their home, pretending to the outside world that all was normal, and simply ignoring me when we were alone.

On my tenth birthday, despite their reservations, they honored a promise they'd made to my mother before I was born. After celebrating with a small, store-bought cake and a carton of strawberry ice cream, my adoptive father trudged up into the attic, returning with a dusty brown cardboard box. Setting it in front of me, he flatly informed me that it was mine from my birth mother, and I could do with it as I wished. Aware that I was adopted, but having heard little about my real mother, I was instantly intrigued. Wanting to explore the contents in private, I hefted the large thing up to my room and set it in the middle of the pink flowered rug. Carefully wiping off the lid with a dishtowel, I opened the container, and was immediately captivated by the rather large book inside, the massive thing bound in leather and boasting a small, sparkling pink jewel on its cover. At first, I could only decipher bits and pieces, many of the words unfamiliar to me. But soon, armed with the family dictionary and fierce tenacity, I was able to read it cover to cover, and I found myself enchanted with the discovery that I had another family, one in which I belonged.

Under the dark cover of night, I spent hours underneath my sheets, flashlight in hand, reading and re-reading the tender messages penned by my real mother. I gingerly touched the precious, faded photos of women who looked much more like me than anyone I lived with, their beautiful, long auburn hair wild and untamed as my own. There were only brief references to my father, a medical student who had left to join the Peace Corp, never to be heard from again. But still I studied each entry that mentioned him, imagining the feel of his strong hug, the sound of his deep voice. The book was only partially filled, the bulk of the latter pages empty. My mother had abandoned it, albeit not by choice, when she'd been killed in a car wreck, only three years after my birth. But despite its lack of contents, it seemed to contain more than just ink, paste and photographs. When its pages were opened, I could feel an intimate sense of belonging and comfort that was missing from my everyday world. My bond slowly transferred from the Harrisons to the journal, a strange embodiment for a mother, but I was grateful for it nonetheless.

When I was eleven, Janet and Carl finally, and unexpectedly, were blessed with their own naturally born child. From the minute they learned Janet was pregnant, a glow was visible about them that had been missing before. But the glow didn't reach far enough to include me in its warmth, and when they brought her home from the hospital, tightly wrapped in pink flannel blankets, they had sat me down and explained, their faces hard, that I was not to get too close to my sister, that I was different and not a good influence for Paige. And so I spent my days going to school, reading novels and sometimes, when no one was about, indulging my curiosity by analyzing people's handwriting and gazing at whatever artwork I could get my hands on. Hidden deep in my closet, the smell of moth balls and cedar surrounding me, I would turn on the desk lamp I pulled in with me, and lose myself for hours, simply living in someone else's world. My favorite piece was a note written to a classmate, Mary, by her mother, and placed within her lunch bag. The note itself was short: *Mary, I've put two brownies in for you today. Remember I love you as far as the ocean is wide.*

True, the words themselves were sweet and loving, but what drew me was the real emotions and sense of family I could feel whenever I absorbed myself in it. Security, devotion, a pretty pink room done up with antique stuffed rabbits, painted toenails, frilly homemade dresses, family vacations… the list went on.

They say the opposite of love isn't hate, but rather indifference. Maybe that's why, oddly enough, I am not angrily bitter, but rather dispassionately disappointed. Maybe that's why I allowed myself to float away, leaving behind my old world and searching for my Grandmother, choosing to affiliate with the beautiful, but unknown, women in my journal, finding them intensely more appealing than being a fringe member of a commonplace, replacement family.

I suppose the person who haunts my memories the most is someone whose face I have never seen in person, but rather only in a single picture pasted in a time-worn journal, and now through photographs throughout my Grandma's house. She is the one woman from my past who I love enough to hate.

~5~

It's Friday, the house has finally settled back into its usual rhythm, and I am firmly established in my favorite chair, reading a bit of Thoreau for my American Lit class, one of four courses I am taking remotely this semester from the university down in Boulder. Now fifty pages in, I find myself regrettably stuck. I've been staring at the same page for well over ten minutes, my mind seemingly more bent on cataloguing the snack foods in the downstairs refrigerator and wondering exactly what the discernment process entails. *Sigh.*

My heart does a guilty but hopeful leap when my bedroom door creaks open, the tantalizing possibility of escaping the world of transcendentalism palpable. Grandma's head pops around the corner, a sly smile on her face. Stylishly dressed in her favorite black wool coat, matching hat and leather boots, she is obviously planning on heading out somewhere. "Come on, we have things to do." Without saying more, she walks in, takes my book and, after setting it on the nearby desk, offers me her hand. I take it. My Aunt Em simply nods and smiles as we pass through the kitchen, evidently already aware of our mystery outing and in charge of watching Ella while we are out.

An elfin air of conspiracy crinkles Grandma's face as we drive up Harrison Avenue, the town gliding past outside my window, splotches of vibrant color, an appealing contrast to the white, dormant world of winter. A red-faced jogger in a canary yellow jacket, a lovely Victorian in plums and blues, a snowboard propped against a fence, bright green with a silver peace symbol. Then there's Grandma's profile, possibly more striking to me than the rest, not because of any garish color, but more due to the compelling harmony of her features, and the sense of an inner light, illuminating her from within. Her appearance is classic, everything about her simple, yet undeniably elegant, the kind of nonchalant perfection that ladies with money try to achieve with expensive cosmetics and spa treatments, but that invariably eludes them in the harsh light of morning.

We pull up in front of an old red brick building identified by its rectangular white wooden sign in front, "Community Art Center." Ah, so that's it. This must be part of the discernment process, as Grandma calls it. We have our pick of parking spaces since the small lot is virtually empty.

Grandma smiles at me, inclining her head towards the door. I can not help but laugh, her mischievous mood a good indication that she is indeed feeling better, the only remaining sign of her cold an occasional cough. Crunching on the squeaky white snow, making our way to the sidewalk, I hold on to Grandma's arm, steadying her, our mingled breath forming cloudy puffs that whisper, dissipating away into the crisp air.

The grand front door of the building is a monstrous thing, crafted of walnut and boasting a beveled glass window. The bell on the handle alerts our hostess, a cheery white-haired lady, small and wiry, her fluttering movements bird-like. "Welcome young lady. You must be Lucy." She takes my hands in her own, her eyes darting over my features as if thoroughly inspecting an incoming piece of art. Apparently satisfied, she pats my hands then releases them, turning her attention to Grandma.

"Yes, this is my Granddaughter." Grandma pulls off her leather gloves, placing them in her pocket. "How are you Teddy?"

"Fine, fine, fine." The words popping out in rapid succession. "So, you have the place to yourself, just as I'd predicted. I'll be in the back if you two need anything." Teddy hands us each a brochure outlining the current pieces on display and briskly heads off towards the rear of the building, disappearing through a doorway marked "office."

The building is divided up into a handful of airy rooms, the combination of brick, white walls and high ceilings perfect for showing off art work. There are skylights in the ceiling and unobtrusive white track lights focusing warm light in just the right places. The warm honey-colored wood floor smells of pine cleaner, as if Teddy has recently cleaned it, and sports bright woven throw rugs placed strategically for added color. The whole image looks too pristine to mar with slush and dirt, so I shed my shoes, placing them under the bench near the door.

I immediately begin picking up vibes, a subtle undercurrent mixing in with the new age jazz that is playing melodically in the background, evidently intended to lend the proper ambience to the room. Rubbing my arms, I try to dispel a sudden chill. I am dying to practice my gift, but the long-formed habit of carefully avoiding places like this holds me in its grip.

Grandma comes up right behind me, her cheek close to my ear and her hands on my shoulders. "I feel your fear, but there is no one here for you to worry about." My shoulders slump, relaxing. "Let's just take it slow. Do you see anything that draws you, appeals to you?"

Scanning the room, I let my eyes blur, trying to minimize visual distractions. Through slitted lids, I make out mosaics of color, accompanied by pulses, beats, muted throbs. Walking slowly towards the source, the throbs grow louder. The painting giving off this energy is about three feet wide and four feet tall. It is a piece of modern art, the colors a mixture of vibrant purples, pinks and oranges mixed with more muted shades of white and yellow. Some are flat, laid down in bold, clean strokes, and others have been applied such that they form a lumpy texture on the canvas. Now standing directly in front of it, my Grandma by my side, I feel its naked, brutal force. The throbs are louder now, deafening, primitive; I press on my temples, feeling my pulse against my fingertips.

Blood rushes to my face and through my limbs; a vibrant tingling awareness filling my senses. I can barely grasp Grandma's words, arriving as if from a great distance, "*Feel* it, then take it apart… what can you pick out?"

The pulses coalesce, recombining into images. I am *seeing* in sound. Bodies emerge. A man and woman, she in her forties, he a bit older. Her hair, long and flowing, smells of vanilla. She is painting in a large sunroom, facing the windows, her view that of a mountain range. Nature's palette fills her canvas. The rose of the early morning fog, the vibrant blues of the sky, the grays of the shadows, and finally the warm, soft oranges of the setting sun. It is spring and the woman is yearning for something… someone… her son. He is in the army, away overseas in Iraq. She is fearful, yet proud. She needs to feel connected with the mountain… to feel its stability and enduring strength… to feel the cycles of life.

Pressure. My Grandma is gently squeezing my shoulder, calling me back out of the scene. I feel disoriented, off-balance as I back away. Turning to her, I wipe away the moisture that has gathered in my eyes, the imagery having touched me with literal force. I describe what I've seen, the woman, her yearning, and Grandma eyes me closely, nodding every now and then.

"Okay. Good," she says. "And now I want you to go back in, further this time." She thinks for a moment, her fingers to her lips. "I know – tell me the son's name. And this time, try to pull yourself out once you've got it."

I nod, and give it my best shot, focusing hard. But the shaft of concentration feels dull. And where before there was penetrating clarity, now my forward motion of mind simply produces a blur of crowded images, and I find myself unable to get past the first phase of immersion in which the art itself blurs and floats away, exposing its real soul underneath. Frustrated, I look at the floor for a moment, gathering my thoughts. Grandma stands by patiently, her steady, unhurried presence encouraging.

I try again, this time relaxing and letting myself simply flow into the piece. Finally, the curtain of colors opens, and I re-locate the woman, sitting in front of her easel. Moving in closer, the sensation feels almost like swimming, the air dense and warm, as if I can feel the sun as it streams into the room. The woman's eyes come into view, blue, with tiny flecks of grey. Reading her thoughts, I can feel the glow of her mood emanating from her, the color an electric blue. I listen, not with my ears, but with some part of me hard to define, something deep, perhaps my soul. Slowly, I start to pick up on remnants of her thoughts… she has to get to the grocery store before it closes… she worries her husband isn't as interested in sex as he used to be, worries that he is losing interest in her… there's been no letters from Brian in over a month. Ah, so that is his name, Brian. I start backing out, detaching. Little by little, I move further away, floating out of the picture, the scene growing distant, until it disappears altogether, the painting obscuring it, snapping back into focus.

Straightening, I turn towards Grandma. "Brian."

Her face relaxes, the lines in her forehead disappearing.

"Ah, well done, well done! Did you know you were out, so to speak, for almost ten minutes?"

Shocked, I absentmindedly shake my head, for the first time wondering how often this has happened before. Thank goodness the place is empty.

"Let's try something harder." Grandma starts eyeing pieces about the room. "Pick out a piece that speaks to you in a different way, a bit darker perhaps." She watches me as I retune to the sensations coming from the artwork, listening, standing perfectly still, the energy in the room dancing around me in sparkling waves.

I spot a sculpture in the corner, its chant primitive, the light surrounding the piece murky. I slowly move towards it, idly noticing Grandma has moved to a nearby bench, her eyes following me.

Okay, this work is very different. Outwardly, it is a sculpture of a mustang, rearing up onto its back legs, its mane and tail blowing in the wind. Sculpted out of a dark rock, it is majestic and proud. But there is so much more. Reaching out, I trail my fingertips along its smooth, cool surface, until its borders slip away, and I see beneath its hard rock shell, my fingers now touching an invisible, humming, permeable barrier. Having attained this critical point, I let myself float down, making the transition from this reality to the one suspended before me, a realm delicately protected in its clear, fluid shell.

This time the artist is a man, handsome, with coarse blond hair and deep-set brown eyes. He is fairly young, maybe early thirties, his skin unlined, but his eyes keenly knowing. Dressed in a white t-shirt and jeans, his chin showing no evidence of a recent shave, he looks disheveled, his eyes bleary, as if he's stayed up all night working, or possibly whiled away the hours drinking, considering the stale smell of his breath; I back away. Following his gaze, I examine the crude beginnings of a horse taking form in the hard rock in front of him.

His sculpture doesn't really represent a mustang, but more a wild yearning inside of him, a desire to burst out, break free. From what? An uncomfortable feeling takes hold of me, the persistent drumming starting to grate on my nerves as the timbre changes, the sound now like screeching winds, pulsing, howling. Tim – I catch his name as it passes by – is bound, restrained in his relationship with his wife in such a way that it is literally bearing down on him. The Pressure! She is putting pressure on him to change, take a different job, have kids. He is resisting, fighting an internal war, wanting something different, something that touches his heart. Oh! I reel backwards as the force of his anger hits me like a fist inside my chest. He resents his wife with a bitterness previously unknown to me. He is tightly ensnared in her love, attached and unable to break free. Hostility surrounds me, swirling, an ugly, dark thing. It takes hold and I am unable to pull away, to separate myself. Something is tugging at me… it seems faraway, but it is growing stronger, and I eventually register that Grandma is yanking, quite forcefully, on my arm and repeatedly calling my name.

Slowly disentangling myself, pushing, rising out of the invisible scene, I turn to her, blinking my eyes in an effort to focus. The worried expression on her face makes my stomach knot. "Its okay, I'm okay." I stand for a moment, with one hand on Grandma's arm to steady myself, regaining control, willing my breathing to return to its normal state. When I am able, I describe this connection, so different from the first. As I speak I catch sight of the clock, surprised to see I have been absorbed for a good twenty minutes this time.

"It scares me, the force of it, and the way it pulls me in and won't let me go." My hands shaking from my experience, I tuck strands of hair behind my ear, all the while trying to avoid eye contact with the sculpture. "If you weren't with me, who knows how long I might have been standing here."

"That's one of the things we have to work on – being able to truly see and feel all the information that might be useful, and then be able to break the connection when you are ready. It's easier when the work isn't intense or dark." She is looking questioningly at me, as if trying to decide something. "Do you want to try and go back in, this time picking a point and coming back out when you've hit it?"

I let out a long breath. Can I go in again? If I do this, will I get swept away, becoming part of the desolate scene forever, a permanent formless presence, destined to simply hover there for eternity? But I must learn to master my gift, controlling it instead of the other way around. "Yeah, I'll try it."

I can do this. Shaking out my arms and twisting my head from one side to the other, it occurs to me that I must look as though I am limbering up for some type of physical confrontation – perhaps I am. Consciously controlling my breathing, I wait until I am ready, then I head back in, this time with a plan to come out when I've catalogued the visual elements of the room.

Breathing in deeply, I gaze at the piece, letting my eyes blur until the dark stone slowly lifts away and I find him again, sitting in front of an old, wooden table, the mustang sitting half-finished before him. Floating down, I join him in the watery orb, readjusting as I grow accustomed to the space. He stares at the art before him, his eyes obviously unfocused, his thoughts turned inward. I survey my surroundings, looking around the confines of the small room. Sketches, clay, brushes, jars and rags are everywhere, the smell of turpentine drifting through the scene. A plate of half-eaten food – a bologna sandwich – sits near him, along with a chipped glass that looks like it contains red wine. The gloomy walls of the dark space are painted forest green, but the dozens of sketches pinned up with thumb-tacks give it some relief. Only a single small window exists to offer light from the outside, but it is covered with a broken wood blind, the ends carelessly left crooked and its slats fuzzy with dust. A small bulb dangles from the ceiling, no shade adorning it, casting harsh shadows throughout the room.

I am drawn to this man – Tim – as he seems so despondent. Could his wife be as bad as all that? Maybe I'll try and get just a bit more before backing out. I ease in, his bristly chin now only inches in front of me. Waves of thoughts are now visible, swirling around him, their glow very different form the woman's; more a muddy, dull brown color. I intercept the stream, letting the tide pass through me, sifting through the flow. Sad, he is sad... the pulses intensify and I feel the anger towards his wife again, the feelings of entrapment... oh! His wife, she is... dead! Mary... she died in childbirth and the baby along with her.

The sadness that engulfs me is like none I have known, the thing a physical presence, a parasite, invading my core, determined to overtake me. His bonds with his dead wife are like heavy metal chains, dragging him under, pulling him back. Remorse, guilt. His wife's face, soft, glowing, her devotion to her unborn child obvious. His own smile false, his affection manufactured. He doesn't want this child. And while she sees their simple home as rustic and charming, he sees it as crude and inadequate, his skills as an artist insufficient to provide the type of home he feels she deserves. More guilt, so much guilt! Like a quickly moving tide pool, the mass of emotions pulls me in, helpless, unable to fight it off. From somewhere I feel the familiar tugging, a part of me knowing it is Grandma, and that she is calling my name, her breath next to my ear. I feel like I am floating, in limbo, between two realities, but it is more pleasant now, almost like being weightless. She pinches me! Hard! The suction of air releases, expelling me and almost throwing me backwards. I grab onto Grandma, squinting, the light hurting my eyes, almost as if I'd actually been in the dark, green studio.

"Well, that didn't work so well." A mixture of humor and concern in her voice, Grandma wraps her arms around me to lend me her strength. The room is spinning and my knees feel unsteady. Leaning against her, I let myself adjust. Finally, when I am able to stand on my own, we sit down on the near-by bench.

"Wow," I say, stretching out my limbs, "I meant to just look at the room and come back out, but he was so sad, and I wanted to find out why, and... you pinched me!" Glaring at her, I run my hands over my face. "How am I going to, you know – get out – if you aren't here? The digging in and finding out stuff isn't too difficult, but the getting out part– it's really hard!"

"Well, we'll keep working at it. I'll see what ideas I can come up with." The bell at the entrance tinkles as a young couple comes through the door, a gust of cold air accompanying them. Grandma leans towards me and whispers. "Come on – let's head over to The Drip." I readily nod, eager to escape the constant flow of pulses and feelings bombarding me. Shrugging on my coat, I glance up, my heart lurching as I spot Teddy, only part of her visible as she peeks around the office door, her sharp eyes piercing me with a probing look.

~6~

It was just a little thing, but it was such an *odd* thing. Certainly a curious thing, and one that warranted further mulling. It could be nothing, but this was a blood star child we were talking about, and Grace was beginning to believe that perhaps she should start taking any potential signs more seriously. It probably wasn't time to alarm Lucy yet, and thankfully she'd been down in Boulder attending an art history lecture being given by a visiting professor when the event had occurred.

Seated at the kitchen table, she'd been idly watching Emily and Ella mixing peppermint cake batter, the two of them forever baking something. Ella had the wooden spoon firmly grasped in both hands, and was moving it around the perimeter of the sunny yellow bowl with great effort, her features crinkled in concentration and her tongue peeking out between her lips.

"Don't forget the edges, like I've shown you dear." Em peered over the child's shoulder, inspecting her work, the chains holding her reading glasses swaying merrily. "Hmm. Yes, that's better. Get all that flour mixed in there now." Holding the salt at the ready, she watched her little assistant chef closely, her lips pursed together. Her face full of soft curves and gentle padding, framed by a riot of short, white curls, she made a cherubic chef, dressed in her cheery red and white checked apron.

The child paused in her stirring, looking over her shoulder for guidance. Em nodded, then poured out a measure of salt in Ella's palm, the white granules quickly tossed in with the rest of the sticky pink mixture. Ella returned to her stirring while Em headed off to fetch a small mixing bowl from the cupboard. "You keep stirring that Ella Roo, and I'll fetch the eggs."

A queer look passed across her Great-Granddaughter's face. The stirring stopped, her hands still wrapped around the spoon. "Auntie Em?" Em paused on her way to the refrigerator, looking over at Ella, the bowl suspended in front of her. "Are they chickie eggs? Like the ones in the book?"

"Well, yes, they are chicken eggs. They make the cake rise." Em continued on her path to the refrigerator, grabbing the handle.

"Noooo!" Ella jumped down off her chair, sending it crashing to the floor, and ran straight at Em, clutching her around her legs as far as she could reach. "Noo! We can *not* eat little chickie eggs!" Her eyes squeezed shut, Ella clutched Em, her small arms visibly straining.

Luckily Em had the appliance handle for support, as in spite of her closeness to the ground and sturdy frame, she appeared to be teetering a bit, probably more from Ella's outburst than from the impact of her comparatively tiny body. "But honey, we have to put eggs in it, or it won't rise."

"No! We can't eat baby chickie eggs!" Ella screamed, whirling around, sliding past Em, her back now against the refrigerator, her small arms extending out as far as she was able. "I *won't* let you."

Grace gazed at the girl open mouthed, as perplexed by her sudden outburst as Em appeared to be. She watched as Em backed up, her bowl clutched protectively against her chest.

Taking hold of a nearby kitchen chair, her sister lowered herself into it, a few feet away from her adversary. The two contenders took stock of each other.

"Ella, you know how cakes get kind of puffy when they cook in the oven?" Em leaned forward as much as her girth would allow, her face at Ella's level, the tone of her voice soothing.

Ella shook her head, a lock of hair falling across one eye, her cheeks rosy from her sudden burst of temper, and her blue eyes glittering.

"Well, the eggs make it puffy. It's a perfectly normal thing. Everyone uses eggs in cakes."

Em smiled hopefully, despite Ella's already fiercely shaking head.

"No. Eating baby animals is bad. Bad, bad, bad." Maintaining her pose, the child turned towards her constant ally, who was currently sitting under the kitchen table. The terrier perked her ears, the two maintaining eye contact for several seconds before the small dog trotted over and stood next to Ella, her rump firmly pressed against the refrigerator, her stance as determined as the girl's.

Grace was unsure whether to laugh or reprimand the child, the whole thing was so outrageous. And the fact that the dog was now involved was starting up a whole host of warning messages in her brain that she didn't have time to dwell on. Em looked at her with pleading eyes, but frankly, she had no better ideas than her sister. Clearly they needed another tack, something that would help Ella see reason. But why the sudden upset over eggs? She adored animals, so perhaps this outburst was simply an extension of that? True, if you thought long enough about the origin of an embryo, it was unquestionably a disgusting thing to put in a deceptively pretty pastel confection, but did toddlers really philosophize to that level? Grace decided on another approach. "Ella, honey, the eggs in the refrigerator are different than the chickie eggs in the book." So far so good, as Ella wasn't shaking her head yet. "They aren't fertilized, which means they can't ever turn into baby chickens."

Ella's stance relaxed a little, her eyes narrowing. "What does ferd-a-lized mean?"

Grace's mind whirled around for explanations that might make sense to a three year old, but nothing came to mind. It was a bit early for a talk about the birds and the bees, and equating the whole things to magic fairy dust seemed demeaning, even to a child. She looked to her sister, but Em simply shrugged.

"Do they come from the same Mommies as other eggs?" asked Ella, both she and Chloe's eyes trained on her, the fate of the cake in Grace's hands.

Even before she started to answer, she suspected she'd lost the battle, but she didn't want to lie. "Well, yes, they…"

"Then NO! We can't eat babies!" Ella's limbs became rigid once again, her shoulders squaring. Looking down at Chloe, the two locked gazes for a moment, some type of curious communication passing between them. Then, evidently having jointly decided on a course of action, the two turned towards Em and began barking. Barking!

Em's bowl went crashing to the floor, small pieces of shiny white china scattering across the kitchen in a dramatic display. Her eyes round as saucers, she watched the show amidst the cacophony of sounds, the chorus of woofing continuing on after the final piece of bowl had settled to lay silently on the floor. Her face strained, she took a deep breath, throwing her arms across her chest. "Well! I never!"

Grace groaned, slapping her hand to her forehead, the chaos in the kitchen rattling her nerves. "Ella! Stop barking!" She yelled, trying to be heard above the din. The child stopped, but maintained her pose, her chest visibly rising and falling. Suddenly, an idea occurred to Grace. Granted, it was sneaky and less than honest, but she had no other options. Rising from her chair, she walked gingerly, but determinedly, around the broken pieces of china. "You know Em, we could call Margie." She caught Em's gaze and winked.

"Hmph!" Em was still visibly trying to settle down. "I suppose we could," she conceded, watching Grace, waiting for cues.

"Yes, we could have Margie do her special magic. That would make the cake rise." Grace nodded briskly for effect, looking at Ella with what she hoped was a resolute look. "Em, you clean up the bowl and I'll go into the living room and ask Margie to come right over."

Her sister nodded numbly, making her way to the pantry to fetch the broom. Ella and Chloe maintained their post, the commanding officer's pink dress with rosebuds seeming an oddly feminine uniform for a small rebel.

Explaining the situation to Margie over the phone, Grace found herself smiling at her Great Granddaughter's spunk. But as she waited for Margie in the living room, she couldn't help but wonder about the oddness of the whole scene. If it was any other child, well, that would be one thing. But this was a child of the trust, one with especially strong powers, given the intensity of her star marking. Could it be?

Margie knocked on the window before letting herself in through the seldom-used living room door. "So, where is the budding vegetarian?" she asked. Grace rolled her eyes, knowing that being a vegetarian herself, Margie would love nothing more than for Ella to follow in her footsteps. But for now, the fact that she was a vegetarian, and the fact that the child knew that she didn't eat animals, was in her favor. She led her into the kitchen, where everything was as she'd left it, save the pieces of broken bowl now piled in the dustpan.

"Hello Ella. I hear you want me to use my special cake magic so that Auntie Em doesn't have to put eggs in the batter. Is that so?" asked Margie, her eyebrow cocked, looking down upon Ella from her considerable height. The child meekly nodded. "Well, okay then. You must leave the kitchen, because otherwise I can't do my secret magic."

Ella slowly lowered her arms, looking to Chloe as if for guidance. Eventually, she nodded, a smile emerging on her face, and after grabbing Em's hand in her own, she happily skipped off towards the living room.

Grace turned to Margie, the raised eyebrow still in place. "How should I know?" said Grace, beginning to worry that she in fact did know more than she was telling. She looked around, making sure that not only was Ella out of sight, but Chloe too, before she headed over to quickly add the necessary eggs to the batter, stirring swiftly.

I know they were talking about me. I could feel it the whole time they were here, Teddy and her friends, sitting in the L-shaped booth over in the far corner of The Drip. It had been a busy morning, and I'd been occupied running the espresso machine, but I could still sense the invisible wave of curiosity that was stirring up the air, a mischievous rippling current, carelessly tousling about peoples' personal business like tempting bits of gossip, devoured with gusto by the deceivingly frail-looking white-haired biddies. Grandma and I had tried to be cautious over the last few weeks during our practice sessions at the art center, keeping an eye out for Teddy, but I swear she could see through walls, her curiosity a finely honed laser directed squarely at me.

The Drip is usually one of my favorite places, a homey creation of hardwood floors, oversized chairs in purples, blues and rusts, and hand painted scenes decorating the walls. The lights are all different, as are the tables, adding a chaotic charm to the place. Blackboards done by local artists in chalks contain the menu, listing the array of espresso drinks, smoothies, sandwiches and pastries in neat rows, with pictures of skiers sloshing down the sides and mountain peaks jutting up behind. A couple afternoons a week I run the place by myself, but on busy mornings, I work alongside Jack, and he and Margie's son Noah, both of whom I like.

But this morning everything feels different. Instead of gabbing with the regulars at the counter, I've mainly kept my eye on the group of biddies across the room. And when they paid by credit card, I'd slipped the small receipt in my pocket to analyze before putting it in the register. I've been waiting for a good half-hour, but things have finally slowed down enough for me to sneak out back for a few minutes, in a place where I won't be watched.

So now I am standing in a small clump of aspen that border the dumpster. Sliding down against the rough red brick of the building, I sit on my personal rock, an oversized hunk of granite perfect for taking a quick break on a busy day. When I squint at the bold signature, I find it has been signed by Teddy herself, Theodora Hemmings. Practically jumping about in my hand, the small slip is emitting waves of information, the torrent literally lifting off the page and streaming towards me. Before long, the signature dissolves into small black dots, the loosened mass hovering above the surface, allowing me to pass beyond it, down to the hidden thoughts lurking underneath. She fed her cat Irmal earlier... her blue, floral underwear is uncomfortably hiking up in back... she worries she hasn't put enough water in with the pot roast this morning. Hmm. Interesting, in a weird sort-of way, but not what I am looking for. I visualize myself, trying to locate a connection to me in the midst of the random collage of thoughts. At first the only images I pick up are of me serving her coffee earlier, but then reaching further, I discover deeper thoughts, perceptions, emotions.

Ah, *better*.

She is working at the museum this afternoon and wonders if I will be in, feels that my Grandma and I are an odd pair, both of us sometimes prone to bizarre spells, continually babbling about imaginary people. She wonders if Grandma is already slightly senile, and I am humoring her, in which case I am a devoted, but misguided, Granddaughter. She is jealous: of our striking looks, our hip clothes, our air of confidence. We intrigue her, like colorful, exotic birds co-existing in a flock of wrens. But at the same time, we are unsettling, different, a disruption to her world of ordinary, familiar things. She's told her friends about us – just the weird part. They are going to keep an eye on us, try to figure out what we were up to, try to determine if we are out to infiltrate the Methodist church.

Should I laugh or cry? This is Leadville, Colorado for crying out loud, where being eclectic is not only acceptable, but in vogue! If I can't blend in here, I have absolutely no chance of blending in anywhere. This small, mountain town is one of those places that hasn't succumbed to the atmosphere of the posh ski resorts, the kind that boast luxurious mountain summer homes, trendy restaurants serving five star cuisine and residents that mill about in designer leggings with fur trimmed parkas to match. The two thousand or so Leadville-ites are a down to earth bunch, more inclined to decorate their front lawns using discarded junkyard collectables and gad about in oversized hand knit sweaters, loose elasticized pants and sturdy water-proofed hiking boots. They have loads of style, they simply choose to define it as opposed to having it defined by others.

Within thirty seconds I bet I can compile a list of at least ten people who either dress or act weird on a daily basis. Let's see, there's smelly Bob, who thinks that dressing, and smelling, like a mountain man is still trendy; Jill, who wears berets and chain smokes while regaling her listeners with the ills of the government; and Marnie, who while she is in her eighties, still dresses in black leather every day and rides a Harley. Okay, that's like five seconds and I already have three names.

No one thinks *they* are out to undermine the church on the corner! I guess I've lulled myself into a false sense of security, feeling naively safe here… until now. But then again feeling "safe" has never been a luxury I could afford.

Rising up to head back in, I brush off my jeans and straighten my black apron.

"Hey kiddo, I wondered where you ran off to." Jack opens the door and smiles, removing his baseball cap for a moment, running a hand across his thinning, silver hair.

"Yeah, I was just taking a quick break. Beautiful day, you know?"

"Yep. Good day for fishing," he says, winking.

I raise my eyebrows as I pass him, a silent acknowledgement that *I* know that *he* knows that *I* know that he always says that, no matter what weather.

He chuckles. The place has cleared out a bit, so I grab the damp white rag from the oversized stainless-steel sink and head out to wipe down tables. The chairs are all helter-skelter, newspapers and napkins left abandoned beside them, a sprinkling of crumbs over it all, like snow. I wipe down the large top by the umbrella stand and cringe as my rag skids to a sticky halt. Obviously Janie was in with her twins, Dylan and Ryan, aka, The Honeydrippers.

The bell hanging at the entrance rings. Noah, battling to hold the door open with his leg, wrestles in a very large, brown-paper encased package. I drop my rag and jog over to help. "What's this?"

"Aaah. This monstrosity happens to be a very special piece of chalk art I found at an art sale last week in Denver." He is smiling, dimples showing, his dark, whiskery chin looking as if he hasn't bothered to shave in the last few days. Tall and healthy-looking, just like his parents, he somehow always manages to look both masculine and boyish at the same time.

I eye the walls, wondering where there are enough

contiguous square inches of space to hang this thing. It looks like it is as tall as Noah, who towers over me.

He sets it on its edge, ripping off its protective wrapping. "Ah, now that's my beauty. Come to Papa!" I head around to stand beside him. It's not at all what I was expecting. The art itself, which is against a cardboard backing, is almost paper-thin, with some type of tough, hard coating over it. Gently, he slides it down onto the floor. "See! Its one of those sidewalk pieces they do that looks 3-D."

The image is breathtakingly vivid; a colorfully dressed mountain climber on a jutting rock, bright sunshine forming reflective beams that bounce off the shiny metal of his carabiners and spikes. The sheer rock face looks as if it sinks into the floor, the climber hanging off its vertical face, the dense forest far, far below. And the piece is obviously an original, based on the vibes that are rushing towards me, the familiar pulsing in my head. I try not to stare – I know what problems it can get me into – but there is something…

My mind is weaving into the art, separating the colors and diving deeper, closer. The lively fresh cold beats of data, their pitch playfully varying, seem to be beckoning me, inviting me in. The messages are light and easy; the creator is indeed an outdoor enthusiast, having in fact climbed one of the peaks, Mount Elbert, that is visible from my very own window on AL. He is in his late twenties, loves fly fishing as much as Jack and is on an intramural soccer team. I can see his house, an attractive little bungalow on an established tree-lined street, his mountain bike on the front porch at the top of the steps, leaning against a white pillar, bits of dirt and mud still stuck in the tires. Nothing dark, just simple, warm images streaming my way. I should back away, but it's way too late.

And there he is! Standing over the artwork, critically eyeing it for any needed touch-ups. He is gorgeous! Dark hair, a tuft on top standing straight up where he's unconsciously been running his hand through it while he mulls, pensive grey eyes and a chiseled face. His name is Scott and he is chronically messy. A vegetarian with over twenty-five plants in his house. He has a tremendous sense of humor and is slow to anger. A bit of a dreamer, he is almost always late to appointments, but can bowl people over with his charm. His parents, both doctors, are disappointed, wishing their son could get serious about something besides art. He has dated several women, but has only been close to marrying once. Uncertain, he shied away too long and she gave up, ending the relationship in fear that he would never commit. As for his current dating life… *what the hell*? I have to get out, sheer shock helping push me back. I frantically disentangle myself from the image, closing myself off to the stream of information surrounding me. Changing my focus, I will the colors to snap back into place, to form a solid barrier over the scene. When I can, I close my eyes, eliminating the picture. Breath, damn it! In, out, in, out. Okay, I can do this. I open my eyes.

Crap. Noah and Jack are staring at me from no more than two feet away, their expressions a mixture of curiosity and concern. I have seen this look many times before in my life. I have certainly seen worse, though. "Are you all right?" Jack touches my arm. "You're as white as a ghost."

Yeah, and they've probably been wondering how long I was going to stand there in some kind of mental trip. I glance at the clock, but since I didn't know the time before, I can't tell how long I was out, so to speak.

"Phew!" I say, putting my hands to my cheeks. "No, I'm fine. No worries. Really. Just a little dizzy there for a minute." I force a smile, walking slowly over to the table where I left my dishrag. "I like the picture Noah – it's awesome." Well, they are still staring at me, but what else could I do? I had to look. But how can I possibly tell them the truth about what I've just seen?

Warm milk. That's what they drink in movies when they can't sleep, and I've seen Aunt Em with it on more than one occasion. I head downstairs in my robe and slippers, peeking in on Ella briefly as I pass, her heart-shaped lips partially open, a bit of drool visible on one side. The moon is full, lighting my way, and I think to myself, as I often have since coming here, how quiet it is at night. It's not like the city, where there is an entire symphony of background sounds that you've grown used to and just don't hear anymore. Here it is truly quiet, just the simple duet of sighs and whispers played by the wind and the river.

When I return to my room, I notice a small bit of light from under Grandma's door. Company sounds good, considering my wakeful state – wakeful ever since I saw Noah's new piece of art. "Grandma? You up?"

In the room, only a small bedside lamp is on, throwing most of the space into shadows and making it difficult to see anything but vague outlines and shapes. She doesn't appear to be here, but the French doors are open to the balcony, the curtains blowing gently in the breeze. What would Grandma be doing outside on such a chilly night? Setting down my milk, I make my way towards the opening, the moon like a beacon in front of me, the tops of the peaks gently outlined in silver.

She is standing on her deck overlooking the meadow, her nightgown billowing gently out behind her and her hair alternately lifting and falling with the breeze. Circling around from behind her, I am able to see her profile. The look on her face is pure contentment, serene joy, her eyes closed and her lips slightly parted, curving with the hint of a smile. Her hands rest on the railing, enabling her to keep her balance, but she looks far away, all but unaware of her physical surroundings.

The sound of the mountain breeze is different tonight, more keen, more fraught than usual. As if in harmony with the night, her slender body is like a string on a cello, poised to vibrate at the musician's touch, to quiver ever so slightly, emitting a note, perfect in its clear, pure tone. Her oneness with the night reminds me of diving into a painting, becoming absorbed in a realm other than my own, visiting another time and place without the encumbrance of my physical shell. What does she see? Clearly what is happening is something far beyond someone simply enjoying a beautiful night. But despite the fact I feel like an intruder, I am compelled to stay, to experience, if only on the fringe, whatever is happening. Thoughts race through my head as I slide down against the house, my warm flannel robe draped over my feet. Is this part of talking to the wind? Despite the chilly air around us, the air on the balcony is relatively pleasant – a good twenty degrees warmer than the air beyond the railing.

Time stands still as I watch her, the scene too amazing to disturb. She stays exactly as she is, seemingly held captive by a song that only she can hear. Her body seems to quiver slightly, as if her muscles are undulating under her skin, expanding and contracting, testing the confines of their flesh encasement. The air around her ripples in waves, her silhouette outlined in an electric blue glow. Finally, the tone of the wind changes, the breeze begins to cool, and she awakes from her trance. She slowly blinks her eyes, taking in the beautiful star-dotted sky and the dark peaks in the distance, a radiant smile on her face as she leans back, supporting herself via her outstretched arms. Throwing her head back, she sighs deeply, letting her breath escape in a long, steady stream.

The whole balcony seems to hover in silence, and I sit un-moving, reluctant to break the spell. Eventually, however, she seems to sense my presence and turns towards me. "Lucy," she smiles, and stretches out her hand, indicating that I should rise and join her. We walk inside and she closes the French doors, pausing for a moment to look back towards the sky. We sink into the pair of yellow chintz chairs in the bedroom, and she sits silently for a moment, eyes closed, her breathing measured.

When she opens her eyes, her face looks relaxed and con-tent. "You've just witnessed the most wonderful part of my gift. It's hearing the voices; the spirits that travel in the wind." She pauses, taking the nearby throw blanket and placing it over her lap. "When I first understood what my gift was, I was somewhat disappointed. I mean, knowing what the weather will be for the foreseeable future is interesting, but it isn't re-ally as grand and impressive as some of the other gifts that our ancestors have had." She sips her tea, now tepid, from the nearby night stand.

"Then when I was about ten, I began to have very differ-ent experiences. I'd be standing outdoors and I would slowly begin to feel things – beings – in the wind. It's hard to ex-plain, but more than just feeling in tune with it, like I always had, now I was seeing and sensing spirits as they passed by. It wasn't exactly like hearing their voices, but more like hav-ing them pass through me, being able to experience them, un-derstand them and communicate with them in a non-verbal way. Mostly it would be one person, but every once in awhile, two."

She seems so complete in this moment, so utterly unto herself. I love the woman she is. "This is, well... I don't know, *huge*," I say. "What is it like?"

"It is kind of overwhelming at first, very intimate, you know?" She rests her head against the chair. "Imagine penetrating directly into someone's thoughts and feelings, knowing almost everything about them, like a simultaneous merging of selves rather than a back-and-forth volley of information."

"Who are 'they'?"

She sighs. "Just people, some good, and some bad. From what I can tell, most of them are good folk, passing by on their way to check in on their loved ones still here on earth. I think they are always in touch with the happenings here, but every so often, they get to come and be very physically close to the ones they love. You know how you get goose bumps when you sense that someone you love, but has died, is nearby? Well, it is probably because they are." She smiles as I hunch my shoulders, a shudder passing through me.

"On the other hand," her face falls, "there are those who are definitely *not* good." She hugs herself, arms across her chest. "They are very different. They aren't traveling to see anyone, they're fighting to stay here. They won't get to come back and visit, and they are angry, bitter souls, looking to lash out, trying to cling to this world."

My head hurts. I raise my fingers to massage my temples. "Why didn't you tell me about this before?" I ask.

She sighs. "I just wanted to be careful, not flood you with things so fast you couldn't process it all. The discernment process takes time."

"You knew whoever was here tonight, didn't you?" I ask.

Her eyes widen momentarily, a smile lifting her lips. "Yes." She raises a finger across her lips, watching me. "It was your grandfather, my Oliver." Her eyes become moist, and she wipes her hand across her cheek. "It's a very special and rare occasion for me to get to be with Oliver or Katie. You see, these joinings – which are similar, but more intense than what you experience with your art – take quite a toll on my heart, especially the dark ones, but even the joyous ones. I think they are very mindful of that."

"Is Grandpa still here?" I try to sense a presence in the room, but everything feels still.

"No, not in the same kind of way. I can tell when he is close, sometimes feel him in the wind. But he is gone for the evening," her voice sounds slightly melancholy.

I fiddle with the sash on my robe. "When did you talk to Mom last?" I am embarrassed to hear my voice break.

She leans forward, her hand on my knee. "Not in a while, sweetie." Taking my hand between hers, she begins gently rubbing it. "She is a bit afraid to confront us, I think. She has been withholding something, and now I understand what."

I pull my hand away, my fingers willing themselves into fists. "Why? Am I so horrid that she has shunned me completely? Now I know that she can still talk to you, her own mother, and yet she has never mentioned me? Why?"

It's as if the room is closing in; my chest is tight, my breathing hard. The rejection is complete, and utter. It's like being plunged into oblivion, no thumbprint, no name, not even a reflection in the mirror. It's like not being.

"I want to read the journal." At the beginning of my discernment process, I gave it to Grandma to keep until I was ready. "I want to know why." Turmoil plays across her features.

"No." She sits quietly, having come to her decision. "You are not ready, and you are angry. Now is not the time."

"I've been practicing for almost two months! When *will* I be ready?"

"You have more practicing to do, the Diurnus to read and the percepta-orum." She watches me in that patient way of hers. "You, Lucy, are not ready to read that journal."

"I'll be twenty-one next week! How old do I have to be before I get to know why my mother dumped me with two dull people who could never love me? She knew I'd be a freak! And yet she cared so little about me that she's been able to effectively erase me from her life? I think I deserve some answers, don't you?" I can't control my breathing, my anger a living thing, hot, fiery, burning my senses and consuming me. I barely hear Grandma's response for the ringing in my ears.

"Yes. I think you deserve answers." I am surprised to see she has grown angry as well. "I think we both do."

~*9*~

Her head leaning against the window frame and her breath leaving a small circle of condensation on the glass, Grace concentrated, watching as her granddaughter's form became a dot on the horizon, occasional flashes of her red sweatshirt still visible. The meadow was mostly brown, with just the beginnings of new life evident, lime green sprouts heralding the imminent arrival of spring. Lucy had headed out on a run along the path that led out towards the peaks before winding its way North, following along the edges of the spiky, dark pines. Whether she ran towards or away from something, Grace was unsure.

Letting go of her tightly maintained focus, Grace let her eyes blur, taking in everything else: shimmering halos of light, some traveling quickly, others on a more leisurely course, and then there was energy, pure and unformed, radiating in both waves and beams. Outsiders, including Em, always assumed she was a daydreamer, constantly staring into space, seemingly unaware of her surroundings. But oh, how wrong they were! She saw so much, too much. It was excruciating at times to try and act like everyone else, completely ignoring the streams of sensory input. But today was relatively calm, and none of the travelers seemed to be channeling in her direction. One glow, however, was different than the others, flickering, hesitant, content to stay in the distance, close to the jutting peaks. Grace was intimately familiar with this beam; it was her daughter Katie.

Mad as hell at her only child, Grace couldn't believe she had done this, depriving Lucy of roots, leaving her to fend for herself. And the fact that she'd managed to deprive Grace of her only grandchild for twenty years wasn't sitting well either. She had sensed Katie nearby more than once lately, but her daughter had yet to venture quite this close, or linger this long, since Lucy's arrival. The force of Grace's anger rippled above the meadow, slamming into the beam and sending it faltering backwards, the light sputtering for a moment before it eventually steadied itself, a bit softer than before. But it was persistent, tenaciously maintaining its post, refusing to be forced away.

Standing in the quiet, Grace felt a fluttering in her chest, a sensation that had become unsettlingly more and more familiar recently. Clumsily moving to a nearby chair, she sank down into the cushions, her hand over her heart. Damn! She had too much to do yet and needed more time. Focusing on her breathing, she closed her eyes, the darkness soothing. The fluttering slowed, her heart returning to its normal rhythm.

Em and Ella come into the room and, assuming she was asleep, headed upstairs to put clean sheets on the toddler's bed. Grace was grateful she had escaped notice, not wanting to upset her sister with worries about her health, nor wanting the careful attention that would inevitably ensue. The metronome that maintained the tempo and balance of the house, Em seemed to move about with quiet precision, the dependable force that kept their daily routine moving forward. Eventually Grace's head emptied of conscious thought, sleep no longer an act but a reality. Thoughts turned to dreams, a swirling puzzle full of portent whose meaning seemed to vanish upon wakening.

~*10*~

As I stare at the stars, reflecting back on the day, I can not help but think that there are times in life when joy intermixes with sorrow in such a way that the intensity of both emotions is heightened and finely tuned, each remaining markedly discrete, rather than one diminishing the other. As joy can not be experienced without first understanding true sorrow, the contrast is vivid when the feeling of emotions at both ends of the spectrum is simultaneous, bringing life to its most fundamental state. And ironically, the day had started out so normally.

March. It isn't an eventful month really. The weather nondescript – boasting only grey skies and wind – everyone simply going about their business in hopes that spring will hurry up and come as scheduled, bringing an end to this dreary, monotonous month. And then, as if I don't have enough things about me that are freakish, fate decided to launch me into the world during this bleak, final stretch of winter, insuring my birthday would never be filled with pool parties or volleyball games, but rather indoor activities that never seemed quite as festive.

But this is my twenty-first birthday, my first birthday since coming to AL. Maybe here, instead of feeling like everybody is dutifully celebrating the day out of a sense of obligation and guilt, my blood family will be genuinely excited, truly happy I exist and eager to celebrate with me. No one will be waiting to see if I have one of my 'odd' moments, as my adoptive parents always did. Their constant fear that I would react to some type of writing or artwork was especially high when there were guests in the house. I suppose it was understandable after my fourth birthday party where we had all created finger-paintings and I broke into laughter after seeing a girl's picture, announcing to everyone that she wet her bed most nights. After that, they'd stopped letting me have birthday parties altogether, deciding it was just too risky, preferring instead to have quiet celebrations at home.

I'm awake earlier than usual, my stomach knotted from an odd combination of anticipation and dread. Rolling over to check the bedside clock, I read the hands on the illuminated face: 6:17 am. It will be a little while before Ella wakes up, so I lie thinking in the quiet, enjoying the sensation of moving my feet between the colder sheets at the outer edges of the bed and the cozy warm spot in the center. It is wonderful to have my own private space, especially after the many months I spent in shelters and bus stops during my pregnancy with Ella and the first couple years after her birth. My expansive, yet cozy, room is more than I'd ever hoped for, which I guess is pretty much how I feel about most things since coming to AL.

Ella is rustling in her bed across the hall. The wood floor is chilly on my bare feet as I quietly make my way into her room. She smells delicious, a scent delicate and musky all at the same time. Her small, dainty face is so perfect, like that of a porcelain doll, her dark lashes fanning her rosy cheeks. Smoothing her auburn curls back from her temples, I once again marvel that she is actually mine. I blow softly in her ear until her lashes flutter, her eyes turning towards me, a smile inching along her lips. Climbing in with her, the two of us are cocooned in the pink flannel teddy bear sheets that adorn her bed, whispering in the quiet until we hear morning overtake the house.

We run through our morning rituals, the process always taking almost an hour, regardless of whether we try to hurry or not. The smell of pancakes is wafting up the stairs, definitely an incentive to rush things along. Hanging my head upside down as I blow dry my hair, I gaze down at Ella lying on the floor, grinning up at me. Her vibrant deep-blue eyes are merry as she makes a game out of grabbing locks of my hair as they sway to and fro. It seems like eons ago that getting dressed was a simple process, a one-person activity as opposed to a team sport.

Finally, we are making our way into the kitchen, where pecan pancakes are piled high, the syrup pooled on top, forming lazy rivulets as it spills over the edges, making its way towards the white china below. Grandma and Aunt Em are grinning at me like fools, practically squirming in their chairs. They are definitely in on some kind of a shared secret, eager to spring it on me as soon as the moment is right. Ella and I slide into our chairs, my daughter licking her lips in anticipation.

"Morning." I shovel in a mound of pancakes and enjoy the sensation of them dissolving into sugar in my mouth.

"Yummy! I *love* pancakes Auntie Em!" Ella places a finger in the syrup, watching as she pulls her finger slowly away, the sticky brown connection stretching before finally breaking apart.

Aunt Em smiles at her above her glasses before turning to me. "Good morning dear."

"Yes, and happy birthday." Grandma is watching my every move, apparently having all but forgotten her own breakfast. "Did you sleep well?"

"Uh-huh." I had long since noticed that with the senior generation of AL, questions about your sleep, health and meals were pretty routine, often the mainstay of conversations. "And you?" I encompass them both in my gaze.

"Oh fine dear."

"Yes fine."

I nod, shoveling in more pancakes. I wonder how long they can stand it, the tight white curls on Aunt Em's head practically vibrating, her entire being tense and alert. The only sound in the kitchen is that of Ella's fork clattering against her plate, an occasional popping sound coming from her lips.

Finally, I eat the last bite of pancake. Aunt Em lets out a long breath of air and turns to Grandma, "its time."

"Yes, I believe it is. Lucy," she turns towards me, looking very formal, "we have a little birthday surprise for you. Look in the sugar bowl."

Aunt Em is rubbing her hands together, her expression expectant. I notice a strange clanking sound as I lift the delicate antique. Inside is a set of keys – car keys. A hot stroke goes through me, and now I am the one shaking, barely able to contain my excitement. Car keys! Unbelievable! Incredible! But to what?

"Well, go look outside already!" Grandma barely gets the words out and I am up and running, grabbing my chair before it goes sailing to the floor before heading out the door.

Parked in the street, shy, white and beautiful, is a brand new SUV. "Oh my gosh! Oh my gosh! I can't believe it! This is really all for me? Oh, this is way too much. I can't accept this, can I?" It feels glossy and smooth as I run my hand over its pearly white hood, sister of the black one parked inside the garage. My mind reeling, I realize I have no ready-made category under which to file this in my head. The word *overwhelming* comes to mind.

Grandma seems to read my thoughts, "Lucy dear, we felt you would need a car, for getting back and forth to Boulder and for toting Ella around. Your driving has really progressed and you have your license now. And besides, if I can't spend my money on my family, who can I spend it on?"

I hug her tight, my entire body shaking, struck dumb by the enormity of her generosity.

"Well, so go ahead and get in," says Grandma, beaming.

The leather seats smell like brand new gloves. The car's insides, engineered for sleekness and comfort, are full of gauges, knobs and buttons. I see a car seat for Ella in the back, and another special belt for Chloe. Grandma smiles at me and waves, she and Aunt Em backing up, obviously expecting me to take the car for a spin.

It fires up with quiet precision, my fancy steel steed. I drive slowly down AL, afraid to really let loose, hesitant to let go and trust fate with my brand new car. Turning onto Harrison, I actually let the speedometer inch above thirty. Another mile and I am out of town, the needle steadily moving up to fifty… sixty!

Aaaah! Incredible! The word cherished, which I never understood until now, is definitely not overrated. The puzzle pieces of my life have always been in disarray, only a few ever being neatly aligned and in place at any given time, but now it is as if they have all come together, the picture they form a reflection of myself that, while I can't seem to believe it, I actually like. Granted, it's taken the bulk of my life so far to find someplace where I am actually accepted, where there is someone who doesn't think I am a freak of nature or something. And things could still blow up in my face, but today, well it's glorious! It's mine, and I'm taking it!

The rest of the day is spent either in the car, admiring the car from the outside, or in the house talking about the car. I occasionally try to change the topic of conversation, but my mind seems to readily return to thoughts of the beautiful automobile outside, despite my best efforts.

The residents of AL converge upon us after dinner, everyone festive and bearing gifts and food. As if a new car and

Aunt Em's dinner spread aren't enough, they've brought more. It feels like overindulgence of the worst sort. I so wish I could store it up to dole out slowly, savoring it over the course of weeks instead of cramming it all into a single twenty-four hour period.

But then, somewhere amongst the reading of cards and the opening of prettily wrapped boxes, a fissure rips through my false sense of security, breaking though the gaiety and bright colors, exposing the baser, monotone side of life. The envelope looked innocent enough, the mint green parchment color-co-ordinating with the gift bag beside it. My lips smiling, words of gratitude for the last gift coming out of my mouth, I slit the paper open, pulling the card out from within.

I look briefly at the picture on the front – a cute little bull-dog dressed in a bumble-bee costume – and then I open it, to read the message inside. But instead of seeing words, I see a blinding flash, an image of a woman, her head bald, save a few clumps of ragged looking hair. Dressed in a hospital gown, she is retching over the toilet, shaking as she holds the tank for support, her arms pale and frail. She runs the back of her hand across her mouth, her head hanging, either from exhaustion, nausea, or a combination of both. She slowly makes her way to the sink, leaning over it, catching her breath, and then looks into the mirror, her eyes sunken, dark circles smudged beneath them.

I really look at her face for the first time and truly see her. The card flutters unheeded to the floor. I rush to the bathroom, unaware of anyone or anything around me, and find myself in the same pose as the women, retching the remains of Aunt Em's spaghetti dinner into the clear water below. The tears are flowing, and I really don't care. This feeling is not unfamiliar, but for the person to be someone so close to me is making the entire experience way too intense. Damn it!

Things were going so well. Grandma would understand,

but what would everyone else think? Just great. Now what? What I am supposed to do with all this. Why can't I have a regular birthday for once like everybody else? She has to be okay – she can't be sick! These people have come to mean so much to me. I can't let this happen to her!

Okay, I've got to steady myself, get cleaned up and go back out there. The longer I am in here, the weirder it'll all get. Wiping my eyes with the available toilet paper, I rinse out my mouth and splash water on my face, trying to reconstruct my former appearance. My complexion looks extremely pale against my dark hair, so I pinch my cheeks and bite my lips to add a little color.

Just as I suspect, everyone is looking at me with a certain uneasiness. "I'm okay, just some kind of stomach thing all of the sudden." I give Margie a hug to thank her for the gift, finding myself holding on a little too tightly for a little too long. They partly buy my pathetic attempt at a smile, and the evening continues on. I am eager for everyone to leave, eager to discuss this with Grandma, to figure out a plan.

My brain swirls for the remainder of the night. This is bad, very bad. Why hadn't I seen this at Christmas when we'd looked through the Christmas cards? Probably Jack had written the notes in the cards. Yes, that was definitely it! I remember the handwriting, and it was completely different. So here was my first real test since coming to AL, and my most intense image to date. What the heck am I going to do?

Eventually the house is empty, and the dishes are put away. "Well dear, did you have a good birthday?" asks Aunt Em, pausing as she wipes her hands on the dishtowel, then refolds it neatly before returning it to the counter.

That was a question worth pondering. But except for the things Aunt Em doesn't know, it was absolutely the best twenty-first birthday I can imagine. "It was totally awesome

Aunt Em. I can't believe my presents and everyone was so nice. I feel like a princess."

"Well, good. Every girl needs to feel like a princess now and then. Even girls my age," she smiles, playfully elbowing me in the side.

My forced smile is the last I have in me for the day. After a quick check on Ella, who is sleeping peacefully in her canopied bed, I head to my own room, only to find my Grandma already there waiting for me.

"Grandma, I have to talk to you. But you already know that, don't you?"

"Well, I kind of figured you might after that reaction you had to Jack and Margie's birthday card. What's up?" she looks at me intently, quietly sitting in her robe and slippers, her silver bobbed hair tucked neatly behind her ears.

"Well, I suppose I could be wrong, but I feel very sure there is something wrong with Margie." I can feel my eyes welling up with tears just thinking about the image I'd seen earlier. "I'm not sure what exactly, but I am pretty sure she is sick – like really sick."

Grandma sighs, "Oh dear. I wasn't sure what you sensed, but I had hoped it wasn't something like that." She sits quietly for a moment. "I know it will be hard, but I think it might help if you look at the card again and concentrate. See if you can decipher more."

I groan. "Oh Grandma, it just hurts too much. I can feel it, really *feel* it. It's like knowing things that you shouldn't know. And it's so sad."

"I understand dear, but we can not help if we don't know as much as we can. I took the liberty of bringing the card upstairs – it's over there on the window seat. Are you up for giving it a try?"

"No! I can't do it! It's too hard… too painful!" She takes my face in her hands, leaning close to me, peering at me with that intense look again. "You can do this Lucy. You have to. It's for Margie."

I swallow the lump in my throat. She is right of course. I have to do this, I have to! I would do anything for these people, these wonderful people who are the first family I've every truly had. But God, why does it have to be so hard? I nod.

Picking up the card, it now almost feels like a living thing, no longer a simple creased piece of cardboard with whimsical sayings, but instead an ominous missive that I alone can read. Opening it, I slowly unlock my eyes, realizing for the first time I have clamped them firmly shut. There it is, the image, the feeling of utter despair. I can feel my stomach start to knot again, and the tears start back up, leaving droplets of moisture on the words. Sometimes I have to concentrate to see the hidden message in things, but with this, it is practically jumping from the page.

"I can't do this! It's too hard!" I have to look away before I start throwing up again and completely lose it. Grandma takes my shoulders in her hands.

"Luce. Look at me." She waits until I make eye contact, her eyes boring into mine. "I understand – yes, I really do! Now. Tell me what you see."

"I see Margie. She is in the hospital, and she is really, really sick. God, she is so sick! Her hair is missing, and she is vomiting, and her face looks like someone punched her in both eyes. It's awful!"

"Okay. So we know she is sick." Grandma thinks for a minute, her fingers tapping rhythmically on the chair arm. "We need to know what she has. You must re-look at the card, this time focusing on her body, trying to figure out where it is dark, where the disease lies. "

I look again. This time I am able to look without feeling physically sick. Better. I look over her body, but I feel nothing.

I hear Grandma's voice, "as you look, feel your body as if it is hers. *Feel* the disease."

I let myself feel, the bile rising even now. I try to think past it, starting in my belly and radiating outward. My stomach is nauseous, but otherwise it seems okay. My liver, my kidneys, everything is okay. I move upward, feeling my heart – okay. I move outward – wait, something isn't right. My breasts… they are gone.

Pulling out, I gather myself together and deliver the sad news. "It's her breasts, Grandma. Margie has breast cancer."

Grandma slumps back in her chair. "Well now, that is something we can work with. It's not good, but it's something to work with." She sits still for a long time, staring at the wall behind me. "So. We must find a way to get her to the doctor for a mammogram."

"How are we going to do that?"

"Leave that to me."

~11~

"A Mammogram bonding party! Have you lost it entirely?" Margie snorted and took a sip of tea, shaking her head all the while.

"Absolutely. Why not? We are all like family anyway, we have all admitted we are overdue for one, and what better time than the present?" said Grace, plastering an enthusiastic smile on her face, determined to make the idea seem both important and adventurous enough for everyone to buy in. She'd invited Margie over to join she and Em for afternoon tea, and had waited until they were well into their second cups before pitching her idea. The three of them were sitting at one end of the large antique harvest table, prettily made up with linen placemats, and set with the pink and blue Carlson china, the atmosphere and conversation both decidedly feminine. Sleeping soundly, the small white canine of the household occupied the hearth, the rock slab still warm from the dancing flames that had been crackling in the fireplace during breakfast.

"Well, I am not sure I'd call it a *party*, that's for sure. I absolutely hate that nasty machine. Men just don't know how easy they have it! They think prostate exams are bad. Try smashing devices, speculums and childbirth," Margie shook her head, her nose wrinkled.

Em laughed. "Well, it is probably a good idea; I'm sure

I'm overdue." Suddenly she paused, her tea cup in mid-air. "I know! We can start a new and trendy group, like that red hat society! We can call ourselves the *Busty Mamas* or something."

"Or we could be the "Smashing Pumpkins." That's more like it," Margie grimaced as she took a bite of her lemon scone.

"I think there is a band with that name already, so we probably can't have that one. Besides, mine are more like plums than pumpkins, so I vote we go for smaller fruit," Grace raised a silvery eyebrow, smiling mischievously.

"Humph. Fine, we can go by whatever name anyone likes, but we are only holding a single annual meeting, because I am *not* doing this more than once a year," retorted Margie.

Em's eyes lit up and she rubbed her hands together. "Oh, Oh, how about the "Pink Scarf Society? We could all wear pink scarves in support of the association for fighting breast cancer."

"That's the spirit!" Grace kept up her enthusiastic approach. "So it's settled. We will head out tomorrow at 8:00 sharp."

Margie rolled her eyes. "I clearly need to get new friends." Her cup clattered as she set it back on its saucer, the delicate china protesting the mistreatment.

"Oh, now there's no need to get catty," said Em, reaching over and patting her arm.

Grace smiled at the interchange. Her sister made an interesting picture sitting alongside Margie, Em so fair and round, and Margie so tan and lean, even her fingers and facial features having a slender appearance. It seemed impossible that of the three of them, it is Margie with the life-threatening disease. She felt her smile fade as the sobering thought reminded her of the reason for this gathering. Sitting back, she contented herself with watching the easy banter of the others, her own mind too occupied to contribute any meaningful conversation.

Em was more animated than she's seen her lately, she and Margie sharing an easy camaraderie that was foreign between the two sisters. Ever since they were small, there had been the secrets of the trust forming a chasm between them, and while they loved each other, their relationship had a formality to it that they'd never overcome. For most of their adult lives, Em had been occupied teaching at Berkley and Grace had lived hundreds of miles away, busy with her small family, their chances to visit each other few and far between. Grace had hoped their relationship would deepen when Em had moved in with her a few years ago, and things had indeed improved for a while. But then her episodes had picked up, Grace having only paltry, half answers that didn't adequately explain away the sweaty bed covers strewn across the floor, her extreme reaction to sudden bouts of wind, or the way she could stand in a trance for almost an hour, her body quietly twitching.

"Nana!" The side door banged open against the wall as Ella exploded into the room, running pell-mell around the kitchen table before finally hurling herself into her grandma's arms. Cheeks rosy from the chilly air outside, her eyes were wide with excitement. "Nana, look! I painted a pony!" she said as she lifted up a finger-painting, the corner crumpled where it had been clutched in her small hand. "Isn't he pretty?" She cocked her head around to admire the pale blue pony alongside her Grandma.

Grace beamed at her, rubbing her back. "Why sweetie, that's such a pretty pony! Did you do that all by yourself?" She ran her fingers through the girl's soft auburn ringlets, her baby fine hair feeling like silk.

"Uh-huh. Ms. Wilson said I did a real good job," she rolled her tongue across her lips, her small legs wiggling as she held onto Grace's knees. "I like his tail. Did you see his pink tail Nana? Do you want to see his pink tail Auntie Em?" As suddenly as the butterfly had landed, she was off to her next stop, eager to show off her prize, her small white companion rushing after her, tail wagging.

Grace looked up to see Lucy standing in the doorway, trying to catch her eye in the chaos. She nodded at her slowly, assuring her that all was well, and their plan underway.

~

After everyone had finished their tea, Em accompanied Margie across the street, the two of them, both gardening enthusiasts, out to check on Margie's recently bloomed new peach tulips. A first peek at spring's lush floral color palette, the hearty bulbs had courageously pushed up through the melting snow, determined to make a timely appearance despite the high altitude and frigid nighttime temperatures. They would soon be joined by the purple crocus, yellow tulips and pink hyacinths planted in Em's wooden flower boxes that lined the porch railing, the fusion of hues lending a festive, joyous air to AL.

"Look Mommy, Chloe has hard hairs under here." Ella lay on the wood floor, looking up under the terrier's chin, her fingers probing deep into her white fur. "They feel funny."

Lucy smiled as she sat down next to Grace on the couch, the three of them alone in the living room. "Those are her whiskers honey. They are supposed to feel that way."

"Why?" Ella asked, her heels clicking as she used them to propel herself in circles on the well-polished wood floor.

"I don't know sweetie," Lucy looked to Grace, shrugging her shoulders. "I didn't realize how many things I don't know until Ella started her why stage." Lucy sat still for a moment, before turning towards Grace, leaning forward, elbows on her knees. "I've been wanting to tell you something for a couple days, but it just hasn't seemed as important as everything else that's going on." She turned away briefly to look at Ella, evidently making sure she wasn't getting into mischief, before continuing. "When I was down working at the Drip the other morning, a couple things happened. The first was that Teddy and her friends came in and I could sense that she was telling them about me. Well, actually, I was pretty sure, but then I analyzed her signature on the receipt, and I was positive of it."

Grace's expression turned serious. There are certain things that are just not done, but of course, she hadn't discussed the percepta-orum with the girl yet, so how could she possibly know? "Well, I'm not happy to hear she is talking about you, and I can guess what she is saying, but we must discuss when it is and is *not* appropriate to use your gift to obtain information."

"She can talk about me and spread rumors, but there is some rule that says I can't find out what she is saying?" Lucy sat up straight, looking indignant. "Well that kind of sucks, doesn't it?"

Grace chuckled. "Well, I suppose it does suck. But gift or no gift, we are not sinking to her level. We'll worry about Teddy and rules later. What else happened?" She could sense that Lucy was saving the more important news until last, a suspicion that was confirmed as Lucy began fidgeting with the edge of her striped sleeve.

"Well, I don't know, the next thing is kind of weird." she said, her gaze directed at the floor, a hint of a smile on her lips. "Noah brought in some artwork he bought down in Denver, a really cool 3-D sidewalk piece. So I looked at it – you know, really looked at it – and I saw something," she finally met Grace's gaze. "The artist, Scott, is supposedly going to be my husband someday." She put her hands to her face, but not quite quickly enough to hide the blush that was engulfing her cheeks.

Grace sat back, considering this momentous announcement. "Well." What words were there for something like this?

"I know!" Lucy cried. "I'm not sure what to think! I mean, I've never seen something prophetic before, and I'm not even sure I believe in fate." She stood up, pacing the width of the wide area rug, her arms folded across her slender form. "I just don't know. Maybe I just *wanted* to see it. But that doesn't make sense, since I'm not looking for anyone, and I don't even know this guy!"

The jarring transformation and surge of emotions associated with truly embarking on a new romance were tumultuous enough; Grace could only imagine the keen anticipation that the elusive promise of knowing the identity of your true love must evoke. "So, what's he like?"

Lucy paused. "Well, he is... perfect really. His name is Scott, and he is funny and messy and has incredible dimples. I don't know!" The pacing started up again. "So do you think it's true?"

"That's a tough one," said Grace, as she assisted Ella who was climbing onto the couch alongside her. "As far as I know, the bequest is usually quite accurate."

Lucy groaned. "So fate has already decided to foist me upon this poor guy? He probably won't even like me!" She pulled her long hair back from her face, her stunning profile causing her grandmother to doubt her words.

"So maybe it's simply that fate knows what choices the two of you will make, not that it's being decided for you. Maybe fate, or God, can simply see further ahead than you."

The front door moaned as it was pushed open from the outside, Em making her way in from the North porch. "So! What's everybody up to?" She rubbed her hands together, smiling, her nose pink from the wind.

"Oh! Um, nothing really," Lucy answered as she looked

awkwardly at Grace, swiftly switching gears, before turning to Em and producing a smile.

Em's gaze narrowed as she eyed the two of them, suspicious. "What were you two talking about before I came in here?"

"Nothing really, Lucy was just telling me about some new art they got down at the Drip." Grace hugged Ella close, trying to act as casual as possible. She knew this look, and knew that Em's instincts were telling her that there was something more happening, some secret that she was not in on. And as usual, she was right.

"Oh Grandma, that's not true! Mommy was telling you about her husband Scott!" Without thinking, Grace's hand quickly clamped across the child's mouth, her heart skipping a beat.

"Oh?" Em looked from Lucy to Grace, her brows angry white slashes above her eyes, her lips pressed together. "So. What's up? Another secret that I can't be in on?"

Grace opened her mouth to voice an explanation that had yet to form in her head, while Ella worked to pull her hand away from her face, her small fingers surprisingly strong. "Oh Em, no. We were simply-"

"Just forget it! I'm so *sick and tired* of all this!" Tears welled up in her eyes, and she wiped them away with her fingertips, her shoulders slumping forward.

Her sister's crumpled face pulled at Grace's heart. This wonderful woman, who took such good care of them all, was being torn apart, yet again. She took a chance, leaving Ella to sit by herself on the couch, and made her way towards Em. Lucy was merely standing frozen, her face white, her expression horrified, obviously unable to assist in any way. But just as Grace got close to her, Em jerked her arm away.

"Don't touch me! Don't you *dare* try to pacify me." Em headed towards the stairs, walking straight past Lucy without looking at her. Pausing at the landing, she stood facing away from them, her curly head bowed. "Is there something wrong with me?"

Grace's heart fell with a thud, the dejection in Em's voice igniting a dull numbness throughout her body. "Oh, God no Em." She watched through her tears as her sister slowly headed up the stairs, never looking back, her whispered rejoinder hanging in the air, "Then *why?*"

~12~

The dark clouds were suspended low in the sky, obscuring the tops of the peaks and forming a dense grey mantle over the meadow, its underside occasionally drifting off in wispy strands, intermingling with the quiet drizzle before being washed away. Spring in the Rockies could be an unpredictable mess, some days full of dark and heavy clouds, laden with white snow destined to be deposited on everything in sight, leaving the landscape looking kind of like a lemon pie covered in meringue. Other days were grey and rainy, everyone coming into The Drip carrying umbrellas which they lay dripping all over the purple mat placed by the front door for just that purpose. Still other days, most days, the sky shone a brilliant blue, pristine and vibrant, the kind of sky that brought visitors from all over the country. The famous Colorado saying was "if you don't like the weather, wait a minute, because it'll change."

Margie watched from her enclosed back porch as Sammy trudged down the gravel drive, his sightless eyes unable to help him in maneuvering the growing mass of puddles forming in the dips and crevices. Her heart went out to him, able to commiserate with his helplessness. She stood, her arms crossed tightly about her waist, trying to keep warm despite the chilly, damp mountain air. She knew the routine; Sammy would walk slowly until he got to the gate, then he'd bump it lightly before reversing directions, finding his way back to the door. She always watched though, just in case he needed some help. And today she was armed with a plush oversized towel, ready to rub him down before he could shake himself, a process that would no doubt cover her clean glass windows with millions of tiny clear droplets.

She wiped away a tear, interrupting its descent down her cheek, thinking it ironic that she and Mother Nature seemed to share a similar mood today, both of them shedding their sorrows in the form of tears. She'd known about her cancer for less than twenty-four hours, and still felt dizzy, as if she'd been spinning and couldn't quite regain her balance. One day they were having a mammogram party, the next she was getting a call with news that would change her life. She'd notified Grace and Em of the results, but now felt the need for solitude, not yet ready to see their inevitable piteous looks, harsh reminders of a reality she wasn't yet able to face. Kneeling down, she intercepted Sammy, rubbing him hard, her head leaning against his, tears streaming down her face, the exertion feeling good, real. She led him inside, steering him towards the hearth, where a crackling fire was blazing, built by Jack before he'd headed out to pick up her new list of prescriptions.

Sinking into the couch, she stared straight through the flames, her mind reeling, thoughts swirling out of focus, nothing seeming real or normal on this damp, April Fools Day. It couldn't possibly be true. Cancer. This was a remote, apocalyptic thing you read about in articles, and donated money towards for research in hopes of finding a cure. Okay, so she was sixty-seven years old and things like this were going to start happening. Her body was falling apart. Shit. Was she going to be one of those people with their Monday through Friday pill cases, a handful of tablets for each day, looking deceptively cheerful with their bright colors and varying shapes, but all really talisman telling you that you were just plain old?

And of course, all that was the bright side, assuming she could beat this thing, assuming it didn't just devour her breasts, then her hair, then her energy and finally, *her*. The next year ought to be just full of joy. She didn't want part of her body to be removed. Okay, it's just a shell, right? Not really her, just a casing, an armature. Maybe, but she was damned fond of this armature! She wanted to leave this world with everything she'd come with! On the other hand, why did she care? It had totally let her down, deciding on its own to become weak, to let this thing invade it. Or could she have stopped it if she'd actually been better about doing self checks and mammograms? Maybe *she'd* let herself down, maybe her body had been trying to tell her something for a long time and she hadn't been listening, fully preferring denial.

Margie felt inside her layers of clothing, finding the lumps easily now that she was aware of their presence. Shit, shit shit. She was scared. There was way too much left to do in life. She had The Drip, the kids, grandkids, Lucy, Ella, Sammy. And of course, Jack. Big tears rolled down Margie's cheeks. Her Jack. He loved her no matter how grumpy she was, no matter what she looked like, no matter how irrational she could become. He didn't deserve this, this taking care of a wife who was going to be on an emotional rollercoaster for the next year. Plus she figured she'd lose her hair and become ugly besides, one of those women wearing bandanas on her head and trying to look avant-garde about it. Was she strong enough to keep herself from leaning on him too much? She had to try. She didn't have enough energy to try right now, though. Maybe she would tomorrow, or next week. She'd have to get over feeling sorry for herself first.

Margie patted Sammy, who was now leaning against the couch, sensing that she needed companionship. "You can

hang out with me when I am feeling bad, huh Sammy boy,"
Margie gave him a quick kiss on his damp nose. Then she
laid her head back and closed her eyes, thinking of days gone
by, when she'd lived in Vail, working in the ski school with
Jack. Bright blue skies, the swooshing sound of skis speeding
down the mountain, and her younger self, racing, healthy, in-
vincible. It felt back then as if she was simply moving too fast
for disease or old age to catch her, as if she wasn't quite real,
but more a snow goddess, impervious to mortal woes. What
happened? Maybe if she'd kept moving fast she could have
outrun this thing. Maybe she'd let her guard down and cancer
saw she was a ready and waiting victim. Maybe this was just
the start of her entire body going to hell. No! She wasn't going
to let that happen. No way, nuh-huh! She could beat this! She
could!

It all just hurt too much. She decided to think about nothing. Crap, even in yoga class she'd never mastered thinking
about nothing. What was nothing? If the color white was really the collection of all colors, then was nothing really the
sum total of absolutely everything?

Margie snorted. This was useless. She would think of Jack,
fishing in the meadow at sunset on a warm summer day. The
backlight making the world glow around him, bugs flying
through the air looking like lit up fairies sketching curves on
the sky. The calmness of the rhythm, the sound of the river, and
the wraparound moist air. Ahh, now that's better. She had this
to look forward to in a couple of months, when the meadow
was lush with wildflowers, the river running full, its waters
heaving against its banks. The snow was great, and it used to
be the season invented just for her, the time of year in which
she gathered her strength. But now, in this stage of her life, she
found herself longing for the warmer days, especially those
when you could walk outside and the temperature was so utterly perfect that it was neither hot nor cold, but absolutely

right, as if you were so one with the world that you simply existed, an integral element perfectly bonded and absorbed.

The crackling of the fire drew Margie out of her reverie, reminding her of the current season, and of the fact that the fisherman playing the starring role in her daydreams was actually still out in the ever-intensifying storm that controlled the weather beyond the cozy confines of the house. Margie walked to the window and looked out, seeing that the drizzle had turned into sheets of snow, the visibility almost zero. Damn. Where was he? He should have been home a while ago and now, seeing the weather, Margie was beginning to worry. Well, there was certainly enough to worry about, wasn't there? And none of it things she could control. At least figuring out where Jack was would happen within the next few hours as opposed to the rest of it, which would take months to unravel.

Margie began to pace, unable to sit any longer, the emotions in her head too much to handle without some kind of physical outlet. Jack was fine and he'd be home any minute, she told herself mentally over and over. The wind picked up, lifting the snow and flinging it horizontally against the house. Sammy seemed a bit agitated as well, whining every once in a while, standing on the chair nearest the window, his snout pointed upward, his nostrils quivering.

Needing more to do, Margie headed into the kitchen and decided to bake something. Baking had always been a soothing pastime, the routine measuring of ingredients and a bit of new age music playing in the background a combination that never failed to relax her. Granola cookies were often the result of these moments, a recipe that she hoped she was continuing to refine over time. She didn't usually follow the recipes to the letter, often simply eyeing the smaller measurements instead of using a measuring spoon and frequently throwing in uncalled for ingredients that sounded like they might be interesting. If she came up with something really delectable, she usually repeated it, making sure she wrote down any recipe deviations so she could pass it along for use at The Drip.

After putting on a Cusco CD and adjusting the volume so the music, while still subtle, could be heard over the snow outside, Margie retrieved her favorite crockery mixing bowl and wooden spoon, measuring out ingredients one by one and adding them to the mix. The mundane normalcy of it all was the balm she'd hoped for, something routine in this new reality that seemed anything but ordinary.

Sammy headed into the kitchen, veering towards his water bowl. Taking a long drink, he lifted his face, large water droplets dripping from his chin, leaving a wet trail behind him along the floor's wood planks. Margie looked at him and simply shook her head. On another day she might have been a bit frustrated and taken out an old towel to dry the wood floor and clean up the mess, but today she simply observed the event, as if from some other place, already consumed with other thoughts and having that distancing sense that she had little control over the day's events anyway. The puddles of water were left to evaporate unabated.

Long after the cookies had been taken from the oven and cooled on the rack in the kitchen, their warm scent still permeating the air, the phone finally rang. Margie fumbled in her rush to pick it up, and was greeted by Mac, the local mechanic, who was calling to tell her that Jack had slid off the road and into a telephone pole. He'd sat in his car a bit until Mac had come along, towing another stranded car, and had waved him down. Jack had a gash on his forehead, so Mac had taken him to the hospital to get it stitched before bringing him home. That's where they were now, so it'd be a bit before they made their way back to AL. Hands shaking, Margie placed the phone back in its cradle.

Uninvited, tears began to weave trails down her cheeks, their journey unhindered by tissues or hands. The outlet of emotions was comforting, preferable to simply feeling numb. She pictured him, sitting dazed in his car, bright red blood a vibrant contrast to the world of white surrounding him, hiding him. That he was alone and in need was agonizing; her dear Jack. Every line, every crease, the topology of his face was intimately familiar to her. Imagining it changed, marred because she needed some silly pills was unbearable.

Still the tears came. With everything topsy-turvy – her breasts, the storm, Jack – she felt more than justified simply giving in to their therapeutic balm. Her shoulders shook, as she gave herself to the emotional tide, simply bowing her head and folding her arms across herself, holding on for dear, dear life. Eventually the tears ran their course, and she rinsed her face, knowing that her eyes would still be puffy and red, but at least she'd feel a bit more herself.

Inspecting her reflection in the mirror, she tried to picture herself without her hair, hating to have to admit that she was rather prideful of the thick, glossy, white tresses. Her features were ordinary, she knew, and with age having set in, she had her share of laugh lines, the thin creases like gentle tracks along the slopes of her cheekbones. But they were *her* features. She was attached to them. Smoothing her hands down her chest, she skimmed along the reassuring fullness of her breasts, the curves feeling familiar, right. She tried to imagine herself flat, without nipples, a hard, angular plane where soft roundness used to be. Damn. When would Jack be home?

Another hour passed before Margie finally saw Mac's big truck making its way up the road. The massive thing rumbled to a stop in front of the house, splashing through the large puddle at least six inches deep that had already formed in front of the gate. Carefully making his way down from the high cab, Jack slogged his way slowly through the snowy, wet mess, trying to avoid the worst of it, and finally made his way to the front porch, where he stomped his boots before opening the door. She was waiting for him.

Her eyes darted across his features, taking in the swath of white where the wide, white bandage covered the bulk of his forehead and right temple. Already a purplish blue hue was spreading across the right side of his face, a deeper bruise visible across his dear, straight nose. Slowly reaching her hand out, she gently fingered his cheek. So cold. Lovingly, she cupped his face in her hands, lending him her warmth. Her kiss was slow and trembling, her fear still intensely real.

She helped him shed his coat, hat and gloves, leading him over to sit down next to the fire. They sat in silence, he in the chair, she on the ottoman, both of them looking at each other with a mixture of worry and love in their eyes. Margie climbed carefully up against him, nestling under the strength of his arm. Her tears wet the warm flannel of his shirt, the very shirt she clutched tightly with both hands. He held her tight, resting his head atop hers.

Spent, Margie knew she could be content staying like this forever, protected and cherished, impervious to life's foes. While others often saw her as matter-of-fact, the practical realist of the group, with Jack she showed another side, a more vulnerable side. She gained much of her strength from simply being near him. They'd been married too long to need words, the comfort of each other the best treatment for any of life's serious tragedies. Nestled close to him into the comfortable oversized chair, the relief of finding him at last and the effects of over twenty-four hours without sleep combined to ease Margie into a gentle slumber without the aid of the pills sitting in a crumpled white bag next to them on the side table. Jack smiled and laid back his head, the two staying huddled in the chair until well into the evening. The storm was still ranging, its duration and final impact unknown, but at least they had this moment, this time.

~13~

As I prop her pillow, a sense of guilt overtakes me, thinking about the number of times I've daydreamed about a catastrophic event happening to me, something that would jar my adoptive family out of their stupor, forcing them to realize how much they loved me, and how much they would miss me if I was gone. I never picked anything that would seriously disfigure me though, or that would leave me in a handicapped state. Of course it wouldn't have worked anyway, as they'd been eager to send me away once they'd discovered I was pregnant, and had never once tried to contact me since I had left.

Her pretty snowy-white hair fanning across the pale blue pillow, Margie lay quiet, the medication dripping slowly into her IV having a sedating effect. I feel reassured to see her chest rising and falling, and feel compelled to feel the softness of her cheek, to smooth back her hair, the fact that she is asleep overriding my usual inhibitions. With the bandages, her chest still seems the same, their artificial bulk giving her a familiar fullness under her gown. My eyes grow moist as I think about what Margie has lost. It's funny, in an odd way, since breasts are not a part of our bodies that we feel or use most of the time, how much they play a part in defining our femininity, the subtle, soft curves that mark our sex.

I trace the small freckles and age spots that are sprinkled across the back of her hand. It's interesting the changes that overtake our bodies as we age, the added details that perhaps mirror the accrued wisdom within, so much more varied and interesting than the smooth, blank slate of childhood. I don't fear growing old, having never enjoyed my youth, and preferring the often less judgmental and interesting company of people my grandma's age to that of my peers. Margie simply has to come through this okay, her solid presence having become a source of strength for me. I find myself anxious to analyze her handwriting to get a better feel for her health.

I turn as I hear footsteps, Grandma and Aunt Em returning from the cafeteria with lunch. Things have been somewhat strained since the confrontation the other day, but with everything going on with Margie, no one seems to have enough emotional reserves to deal with anything else. I head over and take the tray from my aunt, leaning down to kiss her cheek as I do so, putting forth my best effort to smooth things over. She smiles, the sentiment softly visible in her eyes, a sign of steady improvement, her spirit continuing to slowly heal and return to its normal, cheerful state. I place it on the small visitor's table, removing the tan plastic covers from the plates, exposing the steaming grilled cheese sandwiches and tomato soup underneath.

"Well, I better get down to the Drip so Jack can come back over. I promised I'd be there by one." I grab my coat and backpack from the nearby counter. "Plus I want to check in with Annie and see how Ella is doing," I say. Annie, a friend of my Grandma and Aunt Em's from church, had volunteered to watch Ella for the day so that everyone else could look after Margie.

Grandma comes over to give me a hug, "Okay dear, you go ahead. We'll take good care of her." I eye our patient over my

Grandma's shoulder as we embrace, wishing I could stay, but knowing my help at the Drip is vital as well.

I call the sitter on my cell phone as I walk through the corridors, my conversation seeming loud and harsh in the quiet, echoing halls. Satisfied that everything is fine, I shrug on my coat and don my sunglasses, the bright sunshine particularly intense after having been inside. The drive back to the Drip takes little time, and Jack looks relieved to see me, eager to return to his wife. He has spent almost all of his time at the hospital, and we had thought that shooing him off to the Drip for the morning would be a nice break, but as I see his agitated state, I am not so sure.

Tying the short black apron on around my waist, I scan the place, looking for anything that needs straightening or tidying while I wait. Evidently Jack's worrying had found a natural outlet in the form of cleaning, since everything looks particularly spic and span. A few patrons are still sitting at the four top by the window, lazily drinking their espresso, their quiet conversation occasionally punctuated by laughter. I plunk myself down onto the tall stool behind the counter, settling in to wait for my next customer. I am not sure whether I am relived or disappointed that Noah has left the sidewalk art splayed in front of the counter, the vibrations coming from it wreaking havoc with my concentration. The thing is a constant temptation, and I'd caught myself in limbo more than once, jerking myself back from the dangerous, albeit fascinating diversion.

Mornings were vibrant and alive, filled with daybreak coffee drinkers, looking for their "fix", their unbridled need for caffeine evident in their impatient fidgeting and blank, vacant eyes. The place would be crazy, regulars everywhere, visiting, reading and, of course, drinking coffee. But afternoons, well, they were created for the more casual drinker, wandering tourists or locals simply looking to relax, rest their feet, and enjoy a warm comfort drink before either returning to the shopping fray, starting the drive back to Denver or heading home from a trip to town. Lulled by the gentle hum of the coffee maker and the ebb and flow of the conversation across the room, I lean my chin on my hands, almost, but not quite, able to forget the picture on the floor that is partially hidden from view by the counter.

Eventually the welcome chime rings, two men walking in through the front door. The sound reverberates through my head, drawing me out of my pleasant reverie and causing me to jerk suddenly, knocking the pen designated for signing credit card receipts to the floor. I mumble to myself as I bend to retrieve it, wondering if Jack has misjudged my ability to actually run a place of business.

Standing up, I place the pen on the counter. "May I help you?" I look up and find myself frozen. The man standing in front of me, oblivious to everything but the artwork which he is studying, is my mystery artist and future husband. Having no idea what to do or say, I simply squat back down, hiding behind the counter.

Oh my God! Now what? If I stand up, I'm going to look like a complete idiot! It is altogether likely my voice won't even come out right, and as for the ability of my brain to actually formulate words and transfer them to my mouth right now? Pretty chancy! Lets see… option two is pretty much to just stay here, crouched near the floor, cowering behind the counter and pretending that he might simply go away and not recognize me if we meet, as we most likely will, in the future. Also not an attractive option, as my knees are already killing me. Option three… well, never mind option three, since he's now leaning over the counter.

A dark head is peering down at me from above, his grey eyes curious. I stand up slowly, feigning concern over something on the floor, smoothing my apron to give my hands something to do.

"Everything all right down there?" asks Scott, or at least the person who will be Scott once I am introduced to him. His gorgeous eyes crinkle at the edges as he tries to contain a smile. I can't help but think he looks as if he should be on the cover of one of those outdoor magazines, his face tanned, a bit of stubble along his chin and his short hair in disarray.

I realize the silence is lengthening and try hard to concentrate, finally mustering a small smile. "Oh, yeah. Everything is fine. I just dropped something, that's all." I stand for a moment, suddenly remembering the business at hand. "Oh! Would you like something?"

When he smiles with those dimples screaming boyish sex appeal, it makes me feel like I would give him anything he wanted, if he would just stand like that for, well, *forever*. "We'll take two Fourteeners, black," says Scott, using the term designated for large-sized cups of steaming brew.

Still not trusting my voice, I simply nod and gratefully turn around to grab the cups, appreciative for something to do. Unfortunately, it doesn't take very long, and I am again standing face to face with Mr. Hunk. "That'll be $5.67," I say, ringing the sale into the register, the rhythmic beeps familiar and reassuring, dropping a bit of reality into the otherwise surreal scene.

The sight of my husband's hands unnerves me as he extracts a ten dollar bill from his wallet. On automatic pilot, I hold out his change. "Thank you." I croak. "Let me know if there is anything else I can do for you."

"Thanks." says Scott, and then looks at me a moment, quizzical. "I know this sounds like a line," he says, "but have we met?"

"No, I don't think so," I try not to stare, flirt, or say any of the hundred outrageous things crowding the forefront of my mind. The Drip is cool, but suddenly I realize I am sweating heavily.

He picks up his two brews off the counter. "Wow, you sure seem familiar." He remains standing at the counter, drinks in hand. Not knowing what else to do, I smile. A strange, deep, enveloping feeling of calm is stealing over the two of us. Suddenly he shakes his head, like someone waking from a trance.

"I guess I better go deliver these before I drop them on the floor." Still shaking his head, he backs away from the counter, pausing briefly to eye the floor before heading towards the table where his companion sits. I would love to follow him, grab him by the shoulders, kiss him wildly. But I tell myself that fate has this all under control – it has brought him to The Drip, hasn't it? – so maybe I should just trust it awhile longer.

Another small wave of customers arrives, providing a distraction to keep me from simply leering at him from over the counter. But I am pretty adept at this, and ten minutes later, I've finished everyone's drinks and I'm back to sitting on my stool, trying to distract myself with the slight bustle of customers lounging around the shop. I allow myself to look his way every now and then, but no more than I am looking at anyone else. I wonder if he feels it is sacrilege that people are walking on top of his creation, or if he is used to it by now. If I didn't already know something about his character, about his total lack of ego, I would be surprised he didn't mention it when we spoke earlier. He and his friend are lounging back in their chairs, reading the paper and occasionally talking.

The next ripple of customers enter the shop, interrupting my study of my future. I like the challenge of making each request exactly right, not a small feat considering the precise orders rattled off by new-millennium coffee connoisseurs. Practically no one simply orders espresso drinks exactly as they are listed on the neatly lettered, chalkboard menu board above the counter. Oh, no, they all want a tincture of this, a dollop of that, low-fat or no-fat, decaf or triple shots, soy or skim, extra hot or room for cream. The number of folks who simply order straight coffee is small, and somehow the fact that Scott is someone who doesn't need his drink personalized, but is content with basic brew, coffee in its purist form, makes me feel close to him.

I look up from handing an elderly woman her change and my heart leaps as I see Scott and his friend no longer occupy their table. I quickly look around and am relieved to spot him over by the trash bin, throwing his cup away. My breath catches as he turns and heads in my direction, his stride long and casual.

"Hi. Can you tell me if there is a hardware store nearby?" He looks a bit sheepish, and I am flattered that perhaps he is simply asking as a ruse to talk to me again.

"Sure," I point to my right. "There's one two blocks down the street."

"Great. Thanks," he says, pausing, obviously looking for something to say to extend the conversation. "I still can't get over how familiar you seem. I know that sounds corny, and I can't explain it, but..." His voice trails off.

I decide to help out my valiant Prince Charming, "well, maybe you've seen me around Boulder? I take courses at the university electronically, and sometimes go there for lectures and things. Are you ever in that area?" Even before I finish my question, his eyes light up at the word Boulder.

"Ah, that must be it. I don't know where we've met, but I live in Boulder, so that probably explains it." He looks pleased, making me wonder what he is thinking. "So what's your name?"

"Lucy Harrison," I smile, feeling more confident now that

the interest appears to be mutual. I extend my hand, "and you are…"

"Scott. Scott Edwards." His hand is warm, his grip firm and most importantly, his palms are nice and dry, a relief as I have always hated guys with sweaty hands. Does he feel the electrical current pulsing between us? "It's nice to meet you Lucy. Perhaps we will run into each other soon."

I love the way he says it, more of a factual statement than a question, delivered in distinctly masculine vernacular, with the dashing dimples making one more quick appearance. I say my appropriate line, "I'd like that." And then watch, a bit outside my own body, as we exchange smiles, his stride as he leaves marked by a hint of a satisfied male swagger. He didn't even gloat about his art. Is there such a thing as a perfect man? Hell yes!

Percepta Orum

~ *14* ~

Grandma leans towards me, her eyes bright and alert, despite the fact it is almost midnight, and we are stealthily tucked away in her room. "So, it is time," she whispers, her soft, blue silk robe draping about her form, adding to her mystical quality. "Tonight we move onto the next step in the discernment process: the percepta-orum."

Capturing my full attention, she walks over to the bed and reaches underneath, pulling out a large wooden box that is as deep as a shoebox, but twice its width. Made of a dark wood, the whole affair looks rather nondescript, save the intricate brass lock holding its contents securely within. Placing it on the bed, she lovingly runs a hand over the rough lid. Reaching into the pocket of her robe, she extracts an intricate brass key, a five pointed star on its handle, along with a scrollwork letter S. She slowly turns the lock and, lifting the lid, she smiles as she looks inside.

I move from my chair and kneel down beside it to get a better look, and my initial suspicions are confirmed; the box is empty! Confused, I look up at Grandma. She gently nods her head, then leans close to the box and, closing her eyes, blows softly into it, the long, steady stream forming a hazy mist within the void, white fog slowly filling the box until it is floating out over the edges, spilling out onto the bed.

Opening her eyes, she watches intently as the mist begins to clear, the box no longer empty, but instead containing something sparkly; hundreds of tiny colored jewels reflecting the lamp-light, their collective brilliance forming a beam of light that extends to the ceiling, illuminating the room in glistening white light.

Reaching inside, she carefully extracts what appears to be a very thick book, rough handmade paper bound with strips of leather, the front and back covers made of leather as well. Over five inches thick, the uneven, worn edges of the parchment pages look velvety smooth, the thick cream paper aged to a warm honeyed hue. Suddenly, I realize I have seen a version of this book before; the journal my mother gave me is an exact replica, save that it has only a single, pink jewel on its front cover.

I follow her as she carries the book over to her small velvet chaise lounge, sitting directly beside her, barely able to contain my desire to touch the beautiful object. I look to her for permission, and when it is given, I reverently run my finger over the magical cover, the mass of gems feeling warm and alive. The room feels suddenly vibrant, the air an animate force, wisps of current lifting strands of my hair, the edges of my nightgown and brushing against my cheek.

I am startled when she speaks, even though her voice is only a whisper. "This is the Diurnus, the journal kept by the women of the trust. It dates back well before Christ, and contains the story of each woman in our family." Her face serene, she gently puts her hand over mine, lifting it off the book and setting it in her lap before turning her gaze towards the cover. "Each woman in our family places a jewel on the Diurnus when her firstborn daughter comes into this world. Everyone picks something different, sometimes a birthstone, sometimes a favorite color. There is one here for all of us."

I suddenly feel hollow, confident there is not one here for

me. She extracts my index finger, and passing it over the journal, places the tip on a radiant pink jewel.

"This is yours."

When I seek her gaze, I see there is a single tear in her eye. "Yes, your mother put it there, evidently when you were born. I noticed it about fifteen years ago, but thought, with all the other gems, I was mistaken and had simply missed it before," she smiles. "When you came to me, with a Diurnus of your own, boasting a single pink jewel in the identical location, I knew exactly who you were. *My* granddaughter."

A swirling mix of emotions fills me. I am mesmerized by the exquisite book, the collection of gems conveying a powerful legacy, one of which I am a part. *Me.*

"I took the liberty of picking a jewel for Ella," she holds out a small, brilliant ruby, its fire shining separate from the rest. "Our Ella is a blood star, something I will explain in time, and she is so strong and independent that I felt no other color would suffice. Do you approve of my choice?"

I nod, still trying to take it all in.

"Then it will be so. I will teach you how to add a sister to the Sodalicium, or sacred trust." Holding the key by the long stem, she places the small gem on the handle, directly over the letter S. Carefully balancing it, she transitions the key and jewel to me. "Now, you must say the words "Accessio sodalist Ella", then breathe of the spirit." She turns to me and smiles, probably noting my befuddled expression. "It's not so hard really, just a bit of Latin and some hot air. So. Try the words on your tongue, Accessio sodalist Ella."

I swallow and repeat the words, requiring three tries before I have it exactly right.

"Okay. Now for the breath of the spirit. You must reach down inside yourself, and while you expel a long, steady breath, you must merge with it the essence of you; your spirit, your sense of legacy, your uniqueness. Shall we try? I will coach you through it."

I nod hesitantly, unsure if I can do what she asks of me. I close my eyes and say the words, "Accessio sodalist Ella." I blow gently on the key, trying to find myself within the blackness. Nothing. A void.

"Keep your eyes closed and listen to me. I love you Lucy, so very much. Can you feel it?"

I find a single warm light flicker on within the dark. I nod.

"You are my Grandchild, and I am very proud of you. You belong to me, with me. We are a family. Can you feel it?"

The warmth extends, the light brighter. Tears stream down my face, and an odd sensation begins to radiate through my chest, a tingling rush of heat swelling inside. I nod.

"You are exquisitely beautiful, tall and willowy, your face like an angel's, your hair vibrant and lovely. You are kind, funny, generous and caring. You are intelligent and creative. You are a wonderful mother. You amaze me sometimes with the depth of your thoughts. You are unique. You are *special*. Can you *feel* it?"

The light is brilliant now, having overtaken the darkness, its warmth extending through every part of my being. I nod.

"Then *breathe*."

I do. The breath sustains itself long past the ability of my lungs to produce air. The sensation is glorious, complete, truly as if I am sharing a part of me, something deep, something I hadn't known existed until this very moment. And when I open my eyes, a mist swirls about the key, the gem gone, having joined the others, the light coming from it brighter than the rest.

She embraces me, my wet cheeks dampening her shoulder. "I knew you could do it," she whispers. "I am *so* proud of you."

Incredible. Glorious.

"There is so much to tell you, to share with you." She eventually leans away, her eyes meeting mine. "But we must take it in chunks. I think tonight we will cover just the percepta orum. You'll be needing them, what with Teddy, Margie and Scott." She opens the journal carefully, exposing the inside front cover. There, the set of rules, written in Latin, are carefully hand-scripted in black ink. "I know you don't read Latin, but with your bequest, I believe you'll be able to get the gist. Give it a try."

I transition through the familiar stages, always easier with handwriting, and quickly decipher the first rule. "Never use your bequest for evil," I say it out loud.

She nods and pats my hand. "Yes, exactly so. You must never use the gift to cause someone harm. And," she crooks an eyebrow, "that includes meddling in Teddy's escapades. There are other ways of dealing with her sort. Okay, how about the next one?"

I go back in, the feeling of gravity streaming towards me. I mull the second one, pulling out when I have it. "Never use the bequest for selfish gain."

"Precisely. No trying to win the lottery, trying to outwit someone, that sort of thing. I don't worry about you on this score. Okay, let's read the last one."

The final rule is the hardest to extract, the meaning cloudy... I find myself struggling. "I can't seem to get this one," I turn to her and find her smiling.

"Yes, this is the hardest one, for some reason," she sighs. "The third rule is that you must never mix the bequest with love. No forcing someone to love you, impressing someone, or delving into your true love's feelings. Trust me; it will only cause you heartache in the end."

We sit in silence for a bit. She runs her hand over the leather, slowly closing the cover. "There is so much to teach you, but I think this is enough to absorb for now. You should spend much time thinking about the rules of the percepta orum; even though they seem simple, they are not always easy to employ. And now that you are aware of them, you must honor them," her look has grown serious.

I try to force my thoughts towards the three rules, but mainly I find myself preoccupied with the wonderful magic permeating the room, and the small pocket of warmth that still lingers deep inside me, an indefinable feeling that wasn't there before.

~15~

Ten shiny, candy-apple red toenails, peeking out from beneath the covers at the end of the bed, their gay tint a brilliant splotch of color amidst the plain white sheets. Margie and I inspect them critically, the small budding pedicurist watching us, waiting patiently for our assessment. "Absolutely lovely," Margie cocks her head to one side, admiring them from another angle, graciously ignoring the fact that some of the bright polish extends onto the toes themselves. "I don't believe I have ever had my toenails painted before. Feels like absolute decadence, but as I am laid up today, why not?" She lays her head back on her pillows, which are piled high against the beautiful cherry headboard of her bed.

Smiling, Ella carefully climbs up beside her, careful not to disturb her wet toes. "You look like a princess, Auntie Margie. Princesses always have pretty ladies to paint their nails." Her eyes beginning to droop, Ella lays her head down next to Margie's, producing a rather large yawn. She curls up tight, laying on her side, her white anklet dangling off her left foot and her shiny pink barrette sliding down her locks.

"Princesses, huh," Margie turns towards me and whispers, "I think I'm a bit crinkly and grey to be a princess, don't you?"

I smile and shake my head, thinking that perhaps more

princesses should be real women like Margie; women who had been softly sculpted by life's experiences, their form beautifully molded to reflect their rich inner character. Dressed in a pretty nightgown with tiny yellow rosebuds and her hair pulled back into a short ponytail, she looks utterly feminine, despite the fact that the folds of her gown fall unimpeded down her chest, no soft curves visible underneath. Her complexion pale, her large blue eyes seem even more vivid than usual, the dark circles underneath saddening me when I think about what she has yet to endure.

I shift in the big upholstered chair I have dragged close to the bed, pulling my feet up alongside me. Ella and I, comfortably dressed in sweatshirts and pajama pants, are sharing the bright April day with Margie, watching over our patient who underwent radiation treatments again this morning. "I think she is asleep," I say.

Margie turns and lifts her head to inspect the child next to her, the pale blue terry cloth of the little girl's sweatshirt rising and falling with her rhythmic breathing. "That looks like just the ticket. Perhaps we should join her," Margie sighs.

I go to the bottom of the bed and, after testing to make sure the polish has set, reposition the bedclothes over Margie's feet. Evidently lost in my thoughts, I am startled when I hear her voice, "Can I ask you something?"

"Sure. What is it?" I sit back down.

"Can I hear the story of Ella?"

A cold rush of dread washes over me before I remember where I am, who I am with. I swallow hard.

"Honey," Margie reaches out and touches my knee, "You don't have to tell me if you don't want to, but I've always wondered, and since you've never mentioned him, I assume the story isn't all sunshine and roses. Talking about it might even help." She watches me, leaving her hand where it lies.

Lying before me is a woman that I know well, not only

because of what she has shared with me on her own accord, but because of ill-gotten information gleaned from a birthday card she gave me as a *gift*. I can see intimate, personal details of her life, anytime I choose to look, yet she knows little about the major pieces of my history. The gift, well, that is a sacred trust, but Ella's father… talking about him is difficult and painful, but it seems a fair confidence to offer her, considering.

I've never told anyone the whole story, some things too messy to drag out and expose, even to yourself. I grip my hands together and begin. "Well, my friends and I went to a party at a fraternity house one night. Mary was dating a college guy, even though we were only juniors in high school, and she wanted to go see him." As I talk, I can feel the night, the trees on the UNC campus having just leafed out, the world new and fresh, the air smelling of cherry blossoms, the students having recently returned from spring break. It was rare that I did things with other kids my age, but heading out to a party with the two girls I worked with at the bookstore on such a gorgeous night sounded much better than sitting cooped up in my small, colorless room at home.

"I've always been sort of a loner I guess, and so Mary and Andie were off drinking and talking to people and I was pretty much just hanging out, waiting for them in a quiet spot by the door." I recalled the oversized armchair, done in a gaudy green and blue plaid velvet, that was in the living room, partially hidden by a large hat tree oddly decorated with baseball caps, tennis shoes hung by the laces, jackets, strands of Mardi Gras beads and a discarded pair of boxers. "And then this guy came over and asked if I wanted to go out for a walk."

He'd seemed wholesome enough; a nice smile, short, spiky hair, a clean long-sleeved green t-shirt tucked into dark blue jeans. And going outside had seemed preferable to sitting and listening to the deafening music. "His name was Rick.

He was a junior majoring in business at another college, and he seemed really nice." He'd been an easy companion, asking lots of questions, smiling and nodding, appearing to be listening attentively. Hands in his pockets, he'd been nothing but casually friendly, never even attempting to hold my hand.

I continue on, "So we walked around campus for a little while, and then we headed back to the party. I told him goodbye and went to look for my friends, but they were rather occupied." The two were making out in the dimly lit dining room, their partners guys I had never met.

"Since I couldn't exactly go interrupt them and ask when they'd be ready to leave, I went back to sitting in the chair After a while, Rick came by and asked if I wanted to go upstairs and watch a poker game that was going on. So I went." I am suddenly cold to the bone, telling the story. But I must finish it.

"But of course, there was no poker game. We went into a room, but there was no one else there," my voice has faded to a whisper. Margie is gazing intently at me now, her eyes dark with foreknowledge. I place her hand against my cheek, feeling my own tears forming. "He... he closed the door and grabbed me... said he'd just done a line of coke, and he didn't want to waste it." Using my sleeve, I try to staunch the flow from my eyes and my nose. "He shoved me on the bed and... he raped me."

I recount how my screams were muffled by his hand, by the blaring music. I tell of the forceful slap across my face, a knee shoved between my legs, my underwear being ripped away, pressure, his entire weight spread on top of me. The sharp pain, my struggle futile as his limbs seemed to be everywhere at once, restraining me, invading me. I bit his hand, hard, and he yelped and elbowed me in the face, a blinding pain ripping through my head. Finally he grunted, the act complete. Rolling away from me, he stood up, and with his back to me, straightened himself; tucking in his shirt, fastening his pants and running his hands through his hair. He left, without looking back, without seeing the blood on the bed, without seeing the broken mess he'd made.

Margie is holding me in her arms now, her breath hoarse in her throat. We rock back and forth, the motion comforting I think, to us both. "Oh, sweetie, how terrible," Margie croons, clutching me tight.

But somehow, as painful as it is, I want – no *need* – to get the rest out, to have told the whole thing… finally. "I never saw him again. I just left, walking the whole way home." Limped was more like it. And when I got there, I stood under the warm shower spray for over an hour, scrubbing my skin until it was raw, trying to rid myself of every touch, inside and out. "I didn't tell my adoptive parents, because even if they'd believed me, they wouldn't have supported me in fighting it. It would have been too messy, too… real for them." I look at my daughter, a gift so precious, despite the circumstances of her conception. Why does destiny play so with feelings? "When they discovered I was pregnant, they just wanted me out. I tried to explain, but it didn't matter. They just couldn't deal with it."

"My God Lucy, I had *no* idea." Margie takes a tissue from the box on the nightstand and gently wipes my face, even as her jaw settles into a hard line. "Where did you go?"

"Well, at first I went to a home for unwed teens," I say. "It was in a big old house, and the lady who ran it was pretty decent really. I took summer school classes and was able to graduate from high school. Once Ella was born, we kind of stayed in shelters and things." Going into more detail seems pointless. "Until I found my Grandma and came here."

"Oh, child." says Margie. Her gaze reflects my pain, and I fall back into her embrace, closing my eyes, the contact safe, reassuring. "It wasn't your fault, you know."

I consider her words. "I'm not so sure. I mean, why me?" My heart beats faster in my chest. "How did he know that he could do that to me? There were probably fifty girls there, but he chose me. Maybe I'm stupid, or pathetic, or... I don't know. Maybe I'm just... defective."

"Do you really *believe* that?" she says, watching me.

I know I am supposed to say no, but somehow I can't, so instead I say nothing.

She takes my face in her hands, "What he did, what your adoptive parents did, well, that was about them; not about you." She searches my features, looking for something. "Do you see that girl behind me? That independent, self-confident, beautiful child? And her mother who is here hanging out with me on this beautiful spring day? That's about *you*." We stay locked this way, staring at each other. Finally she releases me, settling back in the bed.

But I can't handle the tenderness in her eyes, the raw emotion there too painfully close to my own. "Ice cream?" I ask, eager to move about back into the normalcy of today. She nods, curve to her lips.

Unfolding my legs, I slowly rise, stepping over Sammy and heading downstairs towards the kitchen. I run my hands along the old-fashioned chair rails, feel the rough wallpaper in the hallway, allow myself to touch my fingertip to the sharp edge of a brass picture frame on a shelf. Real. And so far away from my past, a time that I have worked hard to leave behind.

My stocking feet feel slippery and smooth on the polished wood floor of the kitchen, the place deserted, the only sound that of the old mantle clock looking down from above the oak cupboards. As I grab the refrigerator handle, I notice a grocery list, written in Margie's hand, posted on the door with a magnet. Should I look? It must be okay, since I am looking out of concern for Margie and not for myself. Tunneling in, the words become hazy, the letters relaxing, swaying in front of me. But the image is still there, Margie going through chemo, her hair gone, her skin sallow and drawn. But the intensity has lessened. I burrow deeper, feeling it in my body, my breasts. I can feel them missing! It is a foreign, uncomfortable sensation. The sinister patch of disease, black before, is now a dull grey, still lingering around my chest area. And Margie... as she writes this, she is worried... afraid. I am going in too far! I hurriedly back out, at least relieved to see that the cancer has diminished significantly, even while it still hovers nearby, it's remaining forces weak.

~16~

The recent May shower had left the town looking like a newly finished watercolor set out to dry, its colors more vibrant than usual and its detail crisply outlined, the artist having lovingly filled in each shade and hue. As Grace breathed in the scent, fresh and intense, she felt rejuvenated herself, the tangy bouquet of pine and the light perfume of the budding plants in the nearby flowerbox mixing together to form a delicious combination. Holding tightly onto her hand, Ella danced alongside, her swirling pink skirt swaying, the strange mismatch in her chosen outfit – a pink velvet and tulle princess dress, blue and purple striped tights and a short, red wool jacket on top – an oddly endearing combination.

"Let's walk down to the antique store. Want to?" said Lucy, holding the child's other hand as the little monkey picked up her feet, dangling happily between them. Standing outside the Drip, coffee in hand, the trio faced south, the length of Harrison Avenue stretching before them.

"Sure. Sounds good," Grace replied, waiting until Ella's black Mary Janes were firmly planted on the sidewalk before moving.

Their progress was slow, as Ella felt the need to stop and touch the bright red tulips and purple pansies growing along the walkway in the halved, dark-wooden barrels. Her enthusiastic zeal left a path of petals in their wake, the rough grey cement a bit more festive than before. As they crossed a small side street, the Lake County Courthouse loomed before them, the large red-brick building sitting back a bit from the thoroughfare, a healthy expanse of lawn and a row of flowerboxes gracing its front. Halfway down the block, Grace paused. Something was moving quickly towards them, racing down the street from the north.

Lucy lifted one hand above her brow to block the sun from her view. "What the heck?"

As the dark spot took form, Grace could see it was a dog. The canine looked ragged; a large white pit-bull, its coat matted and dirty, a dull film of brown mud clinging to his fur despite the recent rain. About a block away now, it was still moving rapidly, its path helter-skelter and its expression angry.

Harvey, an elderly gentleman who long ago gave up and now simply indulged his alcoholism, was sitting on the street bench at the far end of the block, a bottle encased in a paper bag dangling from one hand, his inebriated state leaving him only partially aware of what was taking place around him. Dressed in an overcoat, its color indistinguishable, a hat with ear flaps, brown trousers and old army boots, he was a familiar sight, usually blending in with his surroundings. But the canine seemed alert to his presence, his course generally progressing in the drunk's direction.

As the dog drew near to Harvey, Grace and Lucy moved in close to Ella. They watched as the canine ran up to him and, stopping abruptly a short distance away, growled menacingly, approaching him more slowly now, apparently waiting for some movement that might justify retaliation.

Eyeing the dog from beneath his half-mast lids, the drunk seemed to only partially understand the potential threat. While sitting perfectly still seemed like the easiest and smartest choice, Harvey, who was three-sheets to the wind, unfortunately choose a different course of action. Extending a hand towards the dog, he slurred "hey li'l feller, how ya doin?."

Taking his words as an invitation, the "li'l feller" lunged at him, viciously biting and ripping his hand before resuming his hell bent race down Harrison. Harvey let out a pathetic howl, pulling his bleeding arm protectively against his chest. And then, before Grace could even react, Ella pulled out of her grip and ran towards the dog.

Gasping, she lunged for the girl, losing her grip on her coffee cup, the dark liquid forming an arch before splashing onto the sidewalk. Stumbling to her knees, clutching her chest, she kneeled, transfixed, horrified, left to watch the frightening scene unfolding before her.

"Grandma!" Lucy's terrified face appeared above her. She reached towards Grace, even as she tried to catch a wisp of her daughter's bright skirt that was rapidly fluttering out of reach. But her fingers grasped air, and she was left kneeling beside Grace, both of them frozen with fear.

The canine was now racing directly towards Ella, a low snarl coming from his throat. And just as Grace was sure he was about to maul the girl, the strangest thing happened: the dog raced within two feet of her before skidding to a grinding halt, and then stood, teeth bared, uncertainly before the girl. Without taking her eyes off the scene, Grace held tight onto Lucy, the two of them managing to stand up, despite their shaking limbs. Clutching each other for support, the women moved cautiously towards the pair.

It was like nothing Grace had seen before. Small, bright orbs of light, her kindred Sodalicium sisters, were rushing in from every direction, all of them hovering around Ella, forming in a protective shield. Usually traveling in small numbers, appearing in mass only for special occasions, their collective presence was rare. The object of their protection was standing with her hands on her hips, back rigid, her pink skirt floating out behind her in the breeze. As Grace came along beside her, she saw that instead of looking terrified, the girl was angrily staring the beast down, her brows drawn together, her lips a thin line. Grace's eyes wide, her hand rose to her mouth. She should have known. Catching Lucy's gaze, she put a finger to her lips, urging her to keep her silence.

Afraid to break the spell, Grace stood perfectly still, watching. Ella's little face was stern, her eyes still capturing the dogs in an unblinking stare. She raised her finger and pointed at the beast. "Bad dog!" she said repeatedly, with enough silence in between each declaration for him to think about his actions.

Grace watched, astonished, as the dog drooped, laying his head down on his paws, looking up at Ella, the whites of his eyes showing. "Humph!" The child waggled her finger at him, towering directly over him, continuing to maintain eye contact. The orbs maintained their position, their glow a bit dimmer than before.

Grace turned to Lucy, eyes twinkling. "Most excellent," she whispered.

Lucy looked perplexed and unsure, but she kept her silence, turning her attention back to her daughter.

A few folks started tentatively towards them, evidently having heard the commotion and decided to come out either to satisfy their curiosity or offer assistance. Chuck, the deputy sheriff, emerged from the café across the street, his walk slow and steady, his hands hovering over his gun and billy club. As he drew near the animal, his features transformed into a dumbfounded expression; Ella's visage unyielding, she was clearly holding the large animal at bay. Shaking his head, Chuck bent down and, taking his belt, stretched forward to fashion a makeshift muzzle on the beast. The dog lifted his head and turned towards him, snarling.

Ella, arms folded across her chest, jutted out her chin, shaking her head in disapproval. The canine immediately stopped growling, placing his head back down on his paws with a disgruntled look of resignation. Chuck took full advantage of the moment and moving quickly, fastened the temporary restraint in place. Radioing in on his walkie talkie, he requested backup, all the while kneeling next to the perpetrator.

With the dog temporarily contained, bystanders ventured in even closer, some to watch the fascinating exchange happening between the little girl and the dog, and others to help Harvey, who was still sitting on the bench, bleeding and confused.

"What is she doing?" Lucy whispered close to Grace's ear, her face drained of color.

Grace smiled, squeezing her hand. "I believe our youngest member in the sisterhood is showing off a bit."

"I knew it! I just knew it! You are witches! All of you!" Teddy hissed, as she stood at the edge of the small crowd, her eyes fiery, her crooked finger pointing at Grace and Lucy. "They tried to hurt Harvey." The gathered assembly murmured. Through narrowed eyes, Teddy stared at them, a smug smile on her face.

Grace was ready for her. "Theodora, are you actually suggesting that a three-year-old in a fairy outfit was trying to convince a dog to attack an old man?" Standing tall, eyebrows arched, Grace relied on all the dignity she could muster as a silent rejoinder.

"Shhh, Teddy, you sound ridiculous! She's just a little girl." A woman named Mary took hold of Teddy by the arm, doggedly pulling her away.

Grace leaned towards Lucy. "Go get Ella." And as she waited for her Granddaughter to convince the toddler to leave her post, she watched Teddy, who was being escorted down the street by two determined women, the old bat occasionally looking back over her shoulder in their direction, muttering. Some of the Sodalicium had evidently decided that Teddy was as much an adversary as the pit bull, a small number of them following her as she departed.

Townspeople were helping Harvey. The picture of defeat and apathy, he appeared more stunned and confused than anything else. His hand carried a large bite mark, the flesh torn and mangled, bleeding and in dire need of stitches. Dorothy, the owner of the town's vintage clothing store, braved the foul stench surrounding him, wrapping an old shirt around his wound, and sitting down next to him to hold it in place.

"I can't believe she stopped a pit bull in its tracks!" Lucy came up behind Grace, supporting her arm and leading her to a nearby bench. "How is she doing it?"

Grace eased herself down onto the slatted supports. "I believe it's more through thoughts than actual words, but I am not completely sure myself."

The sound of sirens became louder as the ambulance and animal control vehicles came into view. The medics helped Harvey onto a stretcher, insisting that he leave his alcohol behind, a decision that evoked more emotion from the drunk than the bite had. The canine was quickly leashed and given a tranquilizer shot, Ella watching the process with an unblinking stare, her dusting of freckles standing out along her abnormally pale cheeks.

Ella squirmed in close between her Mother and Grandmother, looping her arms around her mother's neck and tucking her head beneath her chin. "He's a bad dog, Mommy," she whispered, her small frame shaking. "I didn't know animals could be bad." She seemed truly frightened now, ironic, considering the feat she just performed.

It is agony, this waiting. My stomach is tied up in knots, and I am sweating, despite the fact that I've put deodorant on four times already. It's pretty pathetic, considering he's not even due to arrive for another ten minutes, and I know he has a propensity towards being late, but I have never been on a real date. My anxiety has been building since Wednesday, when Scott called and asked me out, having wheedled my number from Noah down at the Drip. I guess I could dust one more time, but the furniture is already glowing – more like on the border of being downright greasy – and Grandma and Aunt Em laughed at me during the last round, swearing they were all on a lemon-oil high.

I feel shaky, so I grab a banana from the bowl on the kitchen counter. I try to ignore Grandma and Aunt Em, both of them smiling at me as they play gin rummy at the kitchen table, Ella along with them.

"You know, you will survive this," Aunt Em looks at me over the rim of her glasses.

A groan escapes my lips as I vigorously peel my banana. "Yeah, right." I am halfway through it when I spot a silver Prius coming down the street, knowing immediately it is him. "Oh crap." The lump of moist banana suddenly feels like cement in my mouth. Rushing to the sink, I spit out the brownish-yellow clump down the drain. Grandma chuckles near my ear.

Leaning close, she whispers, "Calm down dearheart. Best to approach these things with a clear head." She runs a finger down my arm, tiny shivers following in its wake. "Your gift... well, just go slow." Her voice is conspiratorial; I turn, perplexed. But with a raise of her eyebrow, the moment is gone.

Two quick knocks sound from behind me. He's there, divided into hundreds of tiny sections by the screen door. But the mass of small black wire does nothing to diminish his impact. Dressed in a loose navy sweater over his white t-shirt and faded Levis, his tanned face sporting the suggestion of whiskers and his short hair stylishly tousled, he looks... *perfect*. I push open the screen door and he grins at me, the gorgeous planes of his face and the subtle scent of his aftershave doing nothing to calm my nerves. I introduce him to everyone, noticing his slight surprise when I get to Ella, who eyes him quietly, bright-eyed, over the back of her chair.

Grabbing my purse from the living room, I check my appearance in the mirror one more time. My trendy white blouse is new, the little beaded black vest and pants things I picked up at a store in Boulder on the Pearl Street Mall. I worry I look too young, too matching, too *something*. Leaning towards the mirror, I check my teeth for seeds before popping in a peppermint.

Too late in the season for skiing, but too early for much else, we head towards nearby Breckenridge – nearby at least by mountain standards – where Scott's friend's rock band is playing at a local hangout. Fussing with the long straps of my bag, I take in his car: clean, recently vacuumed, a collection of change in one cup holder, a small note with my address and telephone number in the other. Oddly persistent, the small yellow paper practically screams at me, almost demanding that I decipher its hidden thoughts. Resisting, forcibly dragging my eyes away, I peer instead at the majestic peaks speeding past the window, jumping a bit when he breaks the silence with a question.

"How old is your daughter? Ella, right?"

"Uh, yeah. Ella," I twirl the strap tighter around my finger. "She's almost four." Watching his face as he drives, I try to divine his thoughts. "Maybe I should have mentioned her…"

"Hey, no problem," he meets my gaze, "I was just a little surprised, that's all." And while I enjoy the deep sound of his voice, the way his muscles are moving along his jaw and neck, I can't help but wish I had my mother's gift: the ability to discern the truth of his words.

Swallowing hard, I ask "so do you travel a lot? With your art, I mean?"

"Yeah, usually a few times a year," he wrinkles his brow, "Whoa, you know about my art?"

"Yeah. I sort of…" my mind searches for the right phrasing, "looked you up after I saw the piece of yours that Noah bought for the Drip."

"Really?" he glances my way for a moment. "That's cool."

Left watching his profile again, I wish real driving could be more like movie driving, where people can take their eyes off the road for huge expanses of time and remain indifferent to oncoming traffic. "I really like the piece. I'm actually studying art history myself."

"No *kidding*?" he says. "Wow, that's quite a coincidence!" And the conversation takes off, now that we are on common ground. He tells me about his pavement art, and his tours in Europe where he and others move from town-to-town, decorating walkways and streets in colorful 3-D scenes. We talk about my studies, my professors, and what I thought of the recent guest lecturer. And while we agree the man's art is passable, we both laugh over his exaggerated facial expressions, especially one particularly dramatic raised eyebrow display that had shifted his toupee just a bit.

Surprised, I glance at my watch to find that almost an hour has passed and we are nearing our destination. Nestled in a valley, Breckenridge is a colorful mix of old and new. Mature homes hug the hillside to the east, and the sleek condominiums and posh vacation homes extend up the hill to the west, interweaving with the ski runs; long green swathes cutting through the pines and ending at the chair lifts situated along the bottom of the hill. It is dusk, the sun already behind the mountains, and the town is cooling off quickly. The main street, which extends north to south, is slowly coming alive with twinkling lights, the long line of shops gaily boasting a variety of wares: mountain bikes, handmade crafts, real estate offices, souvenir shops and restaurants.

Having parked the car, we make our way along the sidewalk, the street fairly empty this time of year, the mountain town in-between seasons. I carefully avoid looking into windows with artwork, since my jittery nerves seem to be making me particularly susceptible to their pulsing call. Picking out a pizza joint, we maneuver through the dimly lit interior, sliding into a corner booth. Face-to-face for the first time, I feel oddly comfortable with him, as if we'd grown up together in the same paddle pool and played on the same little league team. But to spite the familiar feeling, his presence seems to ignite an extraordinary, new chemical reaction in me; every nerve in my body feels wonderfully alive, yet my stomach is churning the fruit I ate earlier into complete mush.

"I can't believe you drew on the sidewalk in front of the Louvre." I say, both hands pressed on the table top. "That's incredible! You were right there alongside Michelangelo, Da-Vinci, Monet… I can't even imagine." Compared to my life, his seems glittering, fabulous, remote. He's like Rick Steves with a chalk case.

He laughs, "Yeah, but my work will be washed away with the next rain."

"Forgive me, but it's still kind of awesome."

"If you insist," he shrugs modestly.

I sigh, leaning back against the booth, a subtle drumming sound echoing in my ears, probably from nerves "You'll think I'm just some provincial girl, but I've never been anywhere outside the states, and nowhere further west than here."

"Really?" he considers for a moment. "Well, then its clear that some travel is in your future. Travel is my school, my world, my muse."

"Your muse?"

"A figure of speech," he turns his attention to the menu.

Left alone, I idly run my finger across the table top. I feel deep grooves, and even before I look down, suspect what I will see: crude carvings in the honey-colored surface, hundreds of names and drawings engraved by previous patrons. The drawings are obviously the source of the humming, the whispering susurrus swirling just above the marred table like a tide-pool, misty, inviting. Mesmerized, I gently lift my hand off the table, slowly running it through the energy, feeling the prickly, electric sensation on my skin.

"Lucy?"

When my head jerks up, I meet his gaze, two blue eyes quizzically scanning my face.

"Sorry, I was just admiring the art."

"The art, eh? I'm not sure I'd go quite that far as to call it art?"

"But look at this one here," I point to a small dog, one that I know has been crafted by a little boy, with a bit of help from his father. "It is so wonderfully childish, like something Ella would draw. And isn't childhood the basis for all great art?" Gently fingering it, I can't resist adding, "See there? It has wings on its back, and I think these fluffy lines are clouds. What we are seeing," I announce, "is nothing less than a portrait of a dog that has died and gone to heaven."

Scott cranes his neck over the table, inspecting the drawing. "Wow. I would never have figured out those were wings, but I think you're right," he says, grinning at me. "Hey, you really *do* have an eye for art."

Soon the waitress returns with our pizza, and the clutter of dishes and utensils help cover up the etchings, dimming their clamor. I feel my cheeks grow warm as Scott's beautiful eyes watch me as I eat. "So, tell me about your family. How is it you live with your Grandma?"

Munching my way through a mouthful of stringy cheese, I consider my reply. "Well, I grew up with an adoptive family, and my birth mother is dead. After Ella was born, I decided I wanted to find my real family, and so I came to Leadville. To my Grandma's house."

"Hmm. And that was… ?" he asks.

"A little over a year ago," I say. "She and Aunt Em have been great to me. And to Ella. I am very lucky." I can tell by his face that he wants to ask more, but refrains. My eyes are drawn to a scar along the side of his neck. "Where did you get that," I squint and point towards the small imperfection.

He touches it with his fingers. "Oh, this old thing," he rolls his eyes. "I kind of got into a fight with a chicken."

"A chicken?" I grin, eyebrows raised. "Like a rabid chicken, or something?"

I feel a thump against my shin under the table. "No, not a rabid chicken, smart ass. Just a regular, old, ticked off bird." He tells me the story about the time he was six, and he visited his Aunt Edith and Uncle Clarence in Kansas for the first time. Sent out to gather eggs in the chicken coop one morning, he'd met up with one hen who didn't quite like the way he'd fumbled underneath her, an obvious novice, searching for an egg. He couldn't exactly remember what had happened during the scuffle, but knew the scar was the result.

"So basically, you're saying you're hen-pecked," I say laughingly.

He leans forward, a glint in his eye. "No way. This is a mark of honor. It means I am definitely *not* a chicken!" He sits back with a grin, proud of his joke. "So. I think this means you have to cough up a story."

Ugh. Picking through my memories, I search for one that isn't too depressing, and that doesn't involve my gift. There are few left. Fortunately, the large clock overhead saves my bacon. "Oh, look at the time," I cry, pointing upwards. "I think we better get moving, don't you?" Grabbing my shoulder bag, I slide out of the long wooden booth and stand up, eyeing him with an expectant look.

"Humph," he looks at me, making no move to leave. 'Well, I'll get one out of you eventually."

The outside air feels cool and crisp. Along the dimly lit street, everything is relatively quiet, save the distant sound of music, which grows louder as we near our destination. The place is teeming with a throng of devoted fans, everyone swaying to the music, beer bottle in hand. Hazy, smoky light from the stage gives everything a softened, muted touch, colors and sounds blending together. "Wanna beer?" asks Scott, grabbing a hold of my hand and leading me towards the bar.

Offering me an icy bottle, he leads me back into the throng, towards a high table near the wall. Ascending the worn, tall stools alongside, we share the space in companionable silence, the music and beer slowly drawing us into the communal mood. The heavy bass feels glorious, the beat for once not coming from art, not something I have to protect myself from. My feet tapping on the chair rung, my senses pleasantly muddled from my half-empty beer, I watch Scott when he's not looking. Eventually the dance floor thins out a bit and he stands up smiling, offering me his hand.

We are immediately enveloped into the energetic throng,

a giant mass of swaying bodies. With barely any space to move, we are simply part of the larger whole, flowing with the music in our small, allotted section of the scarred wood floor. Beer, sweat, musky cologne and floral perfumes blend together, wafting their way through the nooks and crannies. I lift my arms above my head, abandoning myself to the glorious, pounding experience of it all.

~

What happened next was this: on the dance floor, swaying to the music, beer bottles in hand, we kissed – but that simple word doesn't come anywhere *close* to doing the act justice. Perhaps I haven't dated much, and granted, my experience is limited, but when our lips met, it was *amazing*. It was as if we were fusing together – the sensation just like when I dive into a painting – me suddenly moving past his outer layer, diving deeper, the two of us tightly connected by invisible bindings, the mass of them drawing us closer, *closer*. And the throbbing, the jungle-like beat that was going through my head! We couldn't pull away; my fingers were enmeshed in his sweater, holding on for dear life, and his were tangled into my hair, his fingers grasping my face as his lips hungrily ravaged mine.

It took a rather jarring collision from another, uncoordinated dancer to pull us apart. Backing up, our eyes met, his looking almost accusatory, as if I'd put him under a spell or something. Me! Me who has been worried if I can even *have* a normal physical relationship, given my only experience so far has been a brutal act of violence. If I hadn't been completely mortified I think I would have laughed. But who could blame him, as the whole thing reeked of the supernatural, or more specifically, of the *Trust*! When we'd escaped outside to get some air, he'd folded his arms across his chest, his look guarded. But I couldn't explain it either! Not really, anyway. It certainly isn't normal for me to go around kissing anyone, much less practically ripping their sweater off in public!

He'd kissed me again outside in the dim glow from the parking lot lights, and it had been the same mind-shattering melding as before. Like raw passion in its purest form, just a kiss enough to set off mind-blowing, cataclysmic sensations. *Dangerous.*

Neither of us knew what to make of it, and I find myself both terrified to explore it further, yet equally terrified I might not get the chance. Afraid to touch, we'd driven home separated by little more than a couple feet of space and the emergency brake. And when we arrived home, he'd simply clasped my hand, and the pulsing had started up again. Looking down, his brow furrowed, he'd said quietly "I can feel it again." Then he'd looked up, eyes wide with wonder, "can you?"

"Yes," I'd breathed, expelling the breath I've been holding, "Oh, *yes.*"

He'd left shortly after, leaving me in a tightly-wound state of quivering nerves. And all from a couple of kisses in public! Lying in bed now, I know I should try and figure it out, make sense of it all. But instead, I find I'd rather simply revel in the delicious sensations, the intensity, the heat. It's as if I am one with the night, everything fluid, like I have melded into the air around me, like I understand something new and deep. Something so very different than what happened on that night long ago. But my mind reels with questions and reservations that I can barely keep at bay. Somehow this *must* be related to my bequest. Sigh.

The stars outside my window twinkle, their stable, timeless presence making my worries feel small. I wrap my arms above my head, revealing in this feminine feeling so new to me. No matter what happens tomorrow, I have tonight. I am wonderfully, marvelously awake, even after I eventually fall asleep.

"Ella is a Blood star. That is the strongest star of them all. Very powerful," said Grace as she pointed out the colored symbol on Ella's page in the Diurnus, her name and birth date the only other markings on the blank sheet so far.

Lucy groaned, "That can't be a good thing. You said I was a rose star, and that's, what, like two or three shades below hers?"

"Two shades. Here, look," Grace carefully rearranged the journal, exposing a page in the front that showed five stars in varying colors, light to dark, with names written beside them in both Latin and English: blush, rose, ruby, blood and cerise.

Tucking her silver hair behind her ears to keep the gentle early-summer breeze from tousling it about her face, Grace watched her Granddaughter as she studied the page. The two of them had the house to themselves for a few hours while Emily and Ella went to a birthday party for Ella's preschool friend Jenny. It was glorious to be sitting with the Diurnus on her lap, for once not under the cloak of darkness, but rather in the middle of the afternoon, under the vibrant, blue Colorado sky. The usual host of sisters were in the vicinity – she could see their bright orbs hovering all around – but her mother and daughter were not among them. Sitting up on her bedroom deck, she could see for miles, and with the aspens having finally leafed out, the landscape was a symphony of greens.

Reclining back on her deck chair, she breathed in the crisp, alpine air.

"So you are a ruby, I am a rose, and Ella is a blood star," recited Lucy. "But there is one more that is even darker than hers – the cerise. What's that one mean?"

Grace sighed, "Cerise is different. It doesn't really mean that your sense is stronger, more that it is uncommon."

"My mother's mark was cerise, wasn't it," Lucy stated her question as fact, her voice flat.

"Yes." Grace eyed her granddaughter through her sunglasses. "A cerise mark means that in addition to whatever your bequest is – which will be as strong as that of someone bearing a blood star – you will also have the ability to foresee your own death. Usually a Cerise can also see the deaths of those around them, but only a few days before they happen."

Lucy gasped, "That's awful! It's like a curse!"

Grace had expected that response. "Well, I know it seems that way at first, but think about it. If you knew that information, there is much you could do with it, possibly for the good." She carefully scanned through the heavy book, looking for the entry of Sylvia Fletcher. "See, look here. Sylvia was also a Cerise, and she was able to keep her father in-law from traveling on the Express, a steamer that capsized off Chesapeake Bay."

Lucy read the passage. "So people have the choice to choose and possibly change destiny?"

"Well, sometimes. In the case of your Great-Grandma, she'd had cancer for a long time before Katie saw her death." Grace remembered the horrid pallor on Katie's face, a sure sign that her mother's time was near.

"Can we read my mother's page?" asked Lucy.

Grace shook her head, "Let's wait a bit longer. Much of it is in her own hand, so I still worry what we will find."

Lucy expelled an exaggerated sigh, "Fine. Then can we see some of the other gifts women have had?"

"Absolutely." Grace turned back to the front. "Here, look at this page. It lists all the women of the trust, or Sodalicium." She pointed at the first entry, "See there, the first account goes all the way back to 151 BC. We believe there were entries prior to that, but the journal was somehow lost or destroyed. Over the years, the Diurnus has had an uncanny way of surviving floods and fires, so whatever happened to it probably involved foul-play. The jewels on the front are thought to protect it, even a single one missing leaving it vulnerable."

Lucy scanned the names on the first page alone, looking at the various gifts her ancestors had possessed. The registry contained many entries with things like telekinesis, varying abilities to read other's thoughts, healing powers through herbs, the ability – like Lucy had – to divine things about someone through art or fingerprints, and the list went on. "Wow, look at this one… someone named Agnes was able to communicate with plants?"

"That's one of my favorites," said Grace as she searched for the associated page number. "Page 56." Lifting the heavy sheets she carefully spread them apart at the correct spot. "There you go."

Lucy curved around the journal, carefully deciphering the scrolling script, reading out loud. "My name is Agnes Ruth Lockhart, born 1508 in Edinburgh, Scotland. My bequest is the aptitude for conversing with foliage. This talent manifests itself primarily in the ability to unmistakably understand their desires and thus, as I am able to endow them with what they require, I am rather a distinguished gardener." She turned towards Grace. "Oh wow, this is really something!"

Bending back down, she continued reading, this time silently. Grace smiled, completely understanding her enthusiasm, and remembering her first exposure to the Diurnus as if it were yesterday. She'd been eight years old, and her mother and grandmother had brought out the magical book on a cold winter night while her father was away on a business trip.

The wind had been howling outside, the snow swirling up from the ground in long, gyrating white ribbons outside the windows of their Vermont home. She'd sat covering her ears, the sound of the voices deafening, most of them staying outside the confines of the yellow clapboard walls, battered about by the storm, while others ventured inside, whispering, their collective murmur a disturbing din. Grandma Min sat beside her, trying to coach her through it, offering words of encouragement and chamomile tea, the comforting brew being her Grandmother's favorite answer to most of life's more distressing moments.

Grace remembered looking up and seeing her mother coming down the stars, looking like an angel in her flowing blue velvet wrapper, her fiery mane trailing halfway down her back in soft, heavy curls, her face like that of a fine porcelain doll. She was carrying a box – *the box* – in both hands, as if she were carefully balancing a tray of fine china. Grace recalled thinking it didn't look like much, but that the feel of the room changed, the dark haze of voices replaced by a warm glow, the sound now much more pleasant, almost melodic.

Her mother had set the box down in front of her on a low walnut table positioned in front of the chintz floral couch where they sat. Then, sitting next to Grace, she'd taken her hand and placed it gently on the lid. Instantly she'd felt something alive, pulsating from within the box. Startled, Grace remembered quickly withdrawing her hand. Her mother had smiled over her head at her grandmother, and then taking the long brass key from her pocket, she'd unlocked the box, explaining to Grace that the S engraved on the handle stood for the Sodalicium, or sacred trust. Looking into the box, Grace remembered feeling every bit as confused as Lucy had when she'd discovered it empty.

And when her mother had blown out a long slow breath, adding Grace's jewel beside its sisters in the soft, aged leather, the magical mist had covered the table, mixing into Grace's tea and curling along the edges of her bare feet. The jewels had practically hummed, seeming to gather light unto themselves, and the brilliance of it all was one of the most wonderful memories she'd ever had. Her jewel, a deep blue sapphire, radiated from the top right side, almost the same shade as her mother's robe. She felt so complete, so connected, so enclosed by the legacy. Safe. She felt safe. And sitting now beside her own granddaughter on this sunny afternoon, she couldn't help but wonder how much more powerful the feeling must be for her, who had been deprived of it for most of her life.

"I like where Agnes writes that she felt compelled to help out the plants of friends," Lucy said, "and that she was aghast when she'd go for tea and they'd complain of being under-watered or in need of sunshine. I mean, I can totally picture her skulking around while they weren't looking, moving plants and watering them... look here, it says one of them called to her across the room during a tea party and said it needed a bigger pot because its roots were pinching!"

Grace chuckled, "That would be something, wouldn't it?" She took a sip from the tall glass of iced tea sitting on her right.

"But Grandma?"

"Yes."

"Can we look at entries of people who could communicate with animals?"

Grace was surprised. "So you're sure that is Ella's gift too?" Lucy nodded. "Well, I guess it's pretty obvious after the little canine incident we all experienced the other day by the courthouse." She maneuvered backwards to page 53, having already checked out the two related entries many times during the last few weeks.

"Ella's gift is evidently fairly rare, only two of us having possessed it over the last two-thousand years," she revealed, "The first one is here." She tapped the name on the page, Mary Elizabeth. "Lets see... there is a confession here about tampering with a horse race by talking to the steed prior to the competition – she did it to win money to save the family farm." Grace scanned the page attentively, pursing her lips. "Oh, here is the part I thought was interesting. She had an ongoing issue with animals wandering close to her house, evidently drawn to her because of her gift. One of them, a brown bear she visited with regularly, attacked a man. Poor Mary Elizabeth took the blame for that. The townsfolk thought she was casting spells and they were afraid of her from then on. She and her husband ended up moving away," said Grace as she looked at Lucy, her eyebrow arched, "No wonder our ancestors have lived in so many different places, huh?"

Lucy nodded, "Is there anything else interesting in that one?" She slid close to her Grandma, reading alongside her.

"Just that she tried to free all the animals in a circus once. And *that* didn't go over well, as you might imagine. Oh, and she discovered that mountain goats are one of the more philosophical of all animal species." Grace and Lucy exchanged looks of amazement. "Humph."

"Here, my dear," Grace shuffled back to an entry dated in the 1100s, "is the second one. Sivernia Olofsdotter. She lived in Sweden, right after it was unified. The entry is written in Swedish, so I've been waiting for you to read it to me."

"Whoa," said Lucy. "You think I'll get most of it?" Grace nodded. "Okay, here goes." Her granddaughter shifted the book onto her lap, her eyes getting the familiar vacant look. Grace waited patiently, studying her profile while she read. Her hair was pulled back in a long ponytail today, the mass hanging over her shoulder to one side, strands of it being picked up by the breeze and wrapping around her slender arm like a vibrant web. Suddenly the muscles in her arm tensed, and Grace's gaze shifted back to her face, wondering what she was seeing. She worried the entry might expose something distressing, regretting now her decision to let Lucy venture into information she herself hadn't deciphered beforehand.

"Bees. I'm getting bees. Yes, she saved a cousin from angry bees, and her kinsman revered her as something of a bee charmer. Also, she convinced the rabbits to stop eating Mrs. Svenson's lettuces, and trained an eagle to notify her when visitors were approaching by making a special squawk. But that's the tame stuff," said Lucy, turning to Grace and pausing for effect.

"Her kindred spirit was a doe named something akin to Hernell," she said calmly, "and the two of them were, um, kind of in love with each other."

Grace gasped, "You're kidding!" Lucy giggled and shook her head.

"Nu-uh. And did you notice I said Doe? Sivernia was a lesbian."

Grace was shocked. "They didn't…"

Lucy laughed so hard she snorted. "No! But they were very much in love… Ouch," she squealed, looking to her left. "What is that?"

Grace could see a bright yellow orb of energy bouncing around Lucy, pelting her in the side. No bigger than a grape, the feisty ball of light was crackling, sparks flying off in all directions. Sivernia, no doubt. "I think Sivernia feels you are telling more than is necessary," said Grace, grinning at the incredulous look on her Granddaughter's face.

"So I am not imagining it," Lucy squinted towards the sky, trying to see them.

"Absolutely. The sisters like to come close when the Diurnus is open. Can't you hear them as well?"

Lucy closed her eyes, her dark prinked lashes resting on her sun-reddened cheeks. Slowly, as she listened, she began to hear the faintest humming. It seemed as if the air itself were gently vibrating. "Yes."

Grace nodded, but then her brows knit in perplexity. "But wait," she asked. "If she were gay, how did she end up married, and how did our family line continue?" The determined bright sphere of energy bounced in her direction, the crackling sound intensifying. Grace put up her hands in submission. "Don't get all fired up, just this one last question!" The orb hovered, humming and quivering in front of her, embers of bright light flying off in every direction.

"Well, first off, her marriage was arranged," explained Lucy, her arms raised, ready to protect herself in case of another onslaught. "And I think you know the other reason," she peered at Grace from under her arm, eyebrow cocked, "a reason that *someone* should have told *somebody* before they went on a date!"

"Ah. So you discovered *that*, did you?"

Lucy snorted. "Well it certainly wasn't hard. You could have warned me!"

Grace looked contrite. "Yes, I suppose I should have said something. I just didn't think you'd experience the Orexis so soon. Was it strong?"

"Are you kidding me?" Lucy's eyes were wide, "We were practically ripping each other's clothes off on the dance floor!"

"Oh dear."

"What exactly is this *Orexis*?" Lucy leaned forward, brow creased.

"It's an experience of absolute raw passion, desire. Every one of us feels it, usually incredibly strongly before we've had our firstborn, then to a lesser degree after that. Some sisters think it is an animalistic response built into each of us and our lovers to ensure the line continues," her lips curved into a knowing smile, "and others think we are blessed, able to experience sex in a way unknown to others."

"Great. Just great," Lucy thumped back in her chair. "I can't imagine anything stronger than what we felt last night. Just a *touch* set it off. Why do you suppose that is, since I already have Ella?"

Grace paused before answering. "It's hard to say. I only know that it is experienced by each sister differently, very strong for some, and not quite as much for others. Some feel that it is stronger when it's a good match."

"Ah," Lucy nibbled on her lip. "So, were you and Grandpa a *good match*?

"Absolutely," Grace looked smug. "And from what you saw in the painting and experienced last night, I'd say you and Scott are a *good match* too."

$$\sim 19 \sim$$

It is love at first sight. She has him literally eating out of the palm of her tiny hand, grinning merrily at him all the while. Granted, she is only three and a half feet tall, and he is over sixteen hands, but the connection is definitely there. "Mommy, isn't Tali the prettiest horse you've *ever seen*?" says Ella, her entire body wriggling with excitement as she feeds him another slice of red McIntosh apple.

"Yes, he is definitely the most handsome horse here, sweetie," I say. Tali, short for *Tanners Talisman,* is a black English Jumper that Grandma has insisted on buying Ella for her birthday, explaining that perhaps an equine companion would provide a channel for her gift. A four-year-old stallion with impeccable breeding, he seems almost too aristocratic to be showered with kisses by a wee girl in a lavender party dress.

After spawning this horse idea a week ago, directly after we'd finished reading the Diurnus out on the deck, Grandma has been on a mission. She'd contacted an agent, Stella, to hunt down potential equine partners for a "young rider with massive potential." Stella had sent us tapes, and when we read the horse's names written on the side in black magic marker and found that one was named Talisman, Grandma knew it was a sign. She'd tossed the other videos to the side and never looked back. Stella thought it a bit of an odd way to select a horse, but she was being paid an obscene commission, so the horse was sent from its home in Kentucky without further ado.

Walking underneath him, Ella raises her hands, running them along his fuzzy underbelly. She stops midway, standing on her tip-toes, putting her ear up close to his sleek belly. "Grandma, Tali likes oats. We need to get him oats."

"Absolutely dear. We will get him all the oats he can eat," says Grandma, appearing thrilled with the reaction to her gift. She has confided numerous times over the last week that she is sure this will be a wonderful outlet for Ella's need to communicate with animals. Her feeling is that while Ella can be close to Chloe and traipse around the meadow with her, she can't experience the joint sense of accomplishment that will come from riding.

Ella holds onto Tali's front forelegs, leaning forward, poking her head out from underneath his belly, her dress trailing in the hay. "Grandma, can I ride him now? Please! Please! *Pleeeeease!*"

"Well, you can't very well ride him like that, now can you?" Grace offers a hand in the child's direction. "We'll let your Mommy and Auntie Em keep him company while you and I go get you into your new riding outfit. How's that sound?"

"Yippee!" Ella turns to give Tali one more hug before skipping away alongside Grandma, holding her hand. I bend down to pick up the items left in the small princess's wake: a purple satin hair ribbon, a velvet Hello Kitty purse, her white knit sweater and a small tube of glittery pink lip gloss.

Aunt Em gives me a skeptical look. "We are crazy. We are *all crazy*. What if she gets trampled, or falls off and bashes her head, or... I just can't think about it," she says, slumping down on the bench, grasping her head between her hands, her white curls springing out like coils between her fingers.

"I know it seems odd, but they've assured us girls her age

ride," I jerk as Tali paws the hay in his stall, a gust of warm air blowing against my face. "And you have to admit, she has an uncanny connection to animals." All I hear is her murmuring something about 'crazy' again as she shakes her head, apparently unconvinced.

Maybe it does seem like a nutty idea, but somehow I know in my gut that this is meant to be. I look up into Tali's big brown eyes, petting his nose, smoothing his black forelock away from one eye. *Take good care of her, okay?* I silently plead.

A few moments later, Grandma and Ella return with Cindy, the riding coach Grandma has recently secured. A fairly young woman, probably in her late twenties, she is petite and slender, her fine blond hair caught back in a stubby braid, a worn straw cowboy hat on her head and dusty, battered riding boots on her feet. She appears ready to seriously dig in for the afternoon. But do I trust her with my daughter? Her references are impeccable and she has a long list of competitions under her belt, but is she prepared for Ella? At least, I tell myself, she doesn't look the sort to spook easily.

Her cheeks rosy with excitement, Ella is now dressed in black riding pants and boots, a pale blue t-shirt and a black velvet riding helmet, her mass of dark tresses hanging down her back. After the introductions are made, Cindy walks my daughter through the process of getting Tali ready to ride. First, they clean out his hooves, removing any mud or hay. Next, they painstakingly discuss every piece of tack – and there is a lot – before carefully putting each one on the horse, adjusting everything until it is just so. Almost an hour later, I nudge Aunt Em softly in the side to awaken her from her nap. It is time to ride.

We head to the indoor arena, the place empty save a woman working her horse on a lunge line at the far end. The light is muted, drifting in through the high windows and filtered by a thin haze of dust, the earthy smell of horses, dirt and manure permeating the air. My daughter looks strangely at home here, holding onto Tali's lead and practically bursting with pride. Grandma, Aunt Em and I head over to sit on a small section of dusty risers set off in one corner, Aunt Em making tsking sounds as she wipes off the aluminum with a tissue from her pocket. Grandma and I are in jeans, but I was unable to coax Aunt Em into anything less casual than her favorite black cotton trousers.

"Okay. So first you must learn how to get up on Tali," Cindy talks loudly over her shoulder as she starts off towards the corner, where a stool leans against the wall. "I have a special bench that you can use to get up high next to him."

Ella turns to Tali, searching his face. He swings his head around, looking back at her, and gives a quick snort. The next thing I know, the massive animal is lowering himself down to the dirt. By the time Cindy turns around with the bench in her hands, her student is sitting atop the saddle, and Tali is slowly raising himself back up. The bench slides out of her hands and her jaw drops. I now know what the phrase 'white as a ghost' means. Aunt Em is rolling her eyes at the ceiling. Grandma puts a hand over her mouth to hide her grin. "I know she shouldn't have done that, but I'm so proud of her I could just burst!" she whispers fervently in my direction.

To her credit, Cindy leaves the bench where it lies and heads over to her charge. "Well Ella, *that* was certainly something I've never seen before. Perhaps we won't need the bench," she says. I notice, however, that her voice and legs are shaking, but who can blame her? She adjusts Ella's stirrups as Grandma excitedly knots her hands together while Aunt Em continues shaking her head.

They start by simply walking around our corner of the arena. Ella, her tiny form straight as an arrow, sits proudly atop the glossy, black thoroughbred, his muscles rippling under his sleek coat as he walks regally along the ring. Suddenly, he tosses his long mane as he snorts out a breath of hot air. Giggling, Ella pats his massive arched neck, then leans down to shower him with kisses. "Ella, you need to concentrate," instructs Cindy from the center of the ring. "You must show Tali you are in charge." I think that a better approach might be to send the child and her horse to couples therapy so that they can discuss each other's needs and how to partner together, but I figure I should just keep my mouth shut on that bit of advice.

Another rider has joined us in the arena, posting as her horse trots gracefully around the loop. Her movement fluid and smooth, she effortlessly rises and falls in perfect rhythm with her horse's gait. Ella's head continues to swing in her direction, her fascination with the rider obvious. "Ella, you need to *focus*," Cindy reminds her for the fifth time.

"But I want to try that," Ella declares excitedly. "Can I try *that*?"

Cindy shakes her head in resignation and walks closer to the girl. "Ella, I'll let you try, but it takes a lot of work. First of all, you have to learn to ask Tali to go from a walk to a trot."

Ella's brow furrows, "Can't I just ask him?" she asks. Uh oh. I lean down, holding my face in my hands, looking out through my fingers.

Cindy laughs, "Well, it's not as easy as that, Ella. You have to ask him with your legs and hands." Cindy begins explaining the process to Ella while Grandma and I exchange worried looks.

"Well, I told her she's pretty imaginative, that she has some wild idea that she can talk to animals." whispers Grandma. "We'll see," she shrugs.

"Uh-hum," Aunt Em scowls at us, "I'm here too, remember?"

Grandma puts a hand on her knee, "Sorry. Just worrying." Aunt Em seems only slightly appeased.

Cindy is backing away from her small rider and horse. "Okay, let's give it a try. Start walking, and then ease your knees into him and loosen your reins." She walks backwards a bit more, critically watching her rider's every move.

Ella and Tali walk for about three feet before breaking into a lovely trot, heading out towards the far side of the ring. By midway, Ella has progressed from bouncing along atop the saddle to something that at least resembles a rhythmic post, her vibrant hair floating along behind her. As she comes back towards us, she lets go of the reins, lifting her hands into the air, a look of sheer exhilaration on her face.

Cindy removes her hat, wringing the brim in her hands, staring along with the rest of us. Ella and Tali draw to a stop a few feet in front of her, Ella bending down to give her horse yet another hug. Raising her head, she asks, "Did I do okay? I didn't use my legs though. I just asked him."

Cindy turns on her heel and strides purposely towards us, her face set tight. Grandma and I straighten in anticipation. When Cindy comes to a halt a few feet in front of the bleachers, hands on her hips, she begins shaking her head. "Okay. Either she has ridden before, or this is totally psycho." she says. Aunt Em snorts from the other end of the bench. Cindy continues, "I have no doubt I don't know the whole story, but one thing is for certain; this child was born to ride a horse. So I'll train her, because I selfishly want to be a part of this. But I'm not stupid." She turns, striding back towards Ella, her fists firmly clenched at her sides, her back ramrod straight, bits of dust flying out behind her.

Fair enough, I think, finally letting go of the breath I have been holding.

~

Later that evening, Grandma and I tuck Ella into bed, Chloe

curled up next to her, her head on the pillow beside her. Ella absentmindedly runs her fingers through Chloe's soft white fur as she talks excitedly. "Wasn't it so neat? Isn't Tali the best horse ever? Can I go ride him tomorrow? Can Chloe come too?" Ella shoots off questions in rapid succession.

I smooth her hair back from her brow, her widows peak prominent, like mine, "We'll figure all that out tomorrow, sweetie. For now, there is something Grandma and I want to talk to you about." Ella fiddles with the ear on her tattered stuffed bunny while she waits.

"You know how you can talk to animals, just like people, but without having to use words?" I ask. She nods, so I continue. "Well, not everyone can do that. Not even Grandma and I. Just you."

She looks curious, asking "They can't?" I shake my head. "Why not? It's easy."

I look to Grandma for reinforcements. "Well, it's easy for you, because you have a gift." says Grandma.

"I do?"

"Yes," Grandma takes her small, smooth hands, with their peeling purple fingernail polish, into her own. "It's a special gift, and it's a secret only you, your Mommy and I can know about."

"Not even Auntie Em?"

Grandma shakes her head. "No, not even Auntie Em."

"Why?" my child asks. I roll my eyes, that question asked at least six or seven times a day.

Grandma struggles to keep a stern look, the creases of her laugh lines giving her away. "We can't tell Auntie Em, because it would make her sad. And we can't tell other people because if they know, they may be angry or scared, and they might be mean to you."

Ella pouts. "That's not very nice."

"No, it's not very nice," Grandma pats her hands. "But

sometimes when people can't understand something, it scares them, and they do strange things."

"They might think it's really neat," says Ella.

I sigh, "No honey, they won't. It'll be like if another girl got a really big present like Tali and you didn't. You would just feel bad." I wonder if the words are sinking in at all.

"Think of it like you, Grandma and I are princesses, but we have to keep it a secret, cause if we don't, the magic spell that lets you talk to animals will go away." I can see I am making progress with this tack, her eyes round and focused on mine.

"Promise me you will keep it a secret?" I say, putting on my best mother look, peering into her innocent eyes.

She looks from Grandma to me, twisting her lips around, "Well, okay, I guess." Her eyes downcast, I can't tell how sincere she is.

"It's really important honey," I say. "Promise me you will try." She nods, her four-year-old brain off somewhere where I can't follow.

~20~

I feel small, the inanimate, electronic device holding more interest for me today than the people living and breathing around me. Ella asked me earlier to braid her hair, a usually routine task, but the part down the middle ended up looking like a drunken sailor had attempted it, the two plaits so dissimilar that even my four year-old daughter felt compelled to undo them, taking her brush and disgustedly trudging off in search of Auntie Em. And then there'd been the laundry, and that small red shirt of Ella's that I'd thrown in with the whites. Oops. Sure, if one of them required CPR, I'd probably awaken from my stupor, but it would take something pretty drastic to divert my attention from the shiny cordless phone nestled snugly in its base on my desk. *Ring, damn it.*

Scott left a message yesterday while we were at the stables with Ella saying he'd be driving up to Leadville today, as he'd finished the project he was working on. Just hearing his voice on the phone had elicited an eruption of goose bumps across my skin, the thought of having him within touching distance simultaneously thrilling and utterly terrifying. *What's happening to me?* We've talked on the phone several times since our date in Breckenridge, many of our conversations turning back to the surreal physical attraction we experienced at the concert that night. Hell, it was more like a cosmic chemical bonding!

He thinks maybe it was a one time thing, one of those freaky full moon incidents you read about in the paper. But I can tell by his tone that just like me, he secretly hopes that it's more.

So now he is coming up to spend the day, surrounded by everybody on AL, both of us hoping their presence will keep this new physical fascination at bay, give us a chance to get to know each other. God, I don't know if I should laugh or cry. Two single adults afraid of becoming lost in some kind of sexual frenzy.

Looking in the mirror, I see the volcano-zit I've felt coming on for the last few days is finally about ready to erupt on my chin. *Great.* I head to the bathroom to grab some cover-up, which I promptly drop when I look out the window and see the sun bouncing off the hood of a familiar silver Prius.

Moving into warp speed with the small tube of make-up, I accidentally squirt out enough to cover the entire upper half of my body, and then forget about the zit altogether as I worry about simply cleaning the stuff off my hands. Checking my reflection in the mirror, I guess I look passable; the sides of my hair are pulled away from my face, which has now lost most of the sunburn I acquired on Grandma's deck. I am wearing one of my favorite tops, a peach cropped t-shirt that comes within about an inch of my low-rise denim shorts. I remembered to shave my legs this morning – what about my armpits? I pull up my shirt and check, but they seem fine. So what if he can't even see them? I'd know, and it would make me nuts all day. I slide on my Birkenstocks, wondering if I should have trimmed my toenails while I had the chance. Oh well, I am as ready as I'm going to get. I feel like a dessert getting dressed up in fancy toppings and being drizzled in chocolate just to be put on a plate and possibly devoured.

As I reach the kitchen, I hear Grandma and Aunt Em through the open window, the two of them talking to someone with a distinctly masculine voice, something not common in this house; the inquisition has evidently begun.

"So, you've lived in Boulder for how long?" Aunt Em has positioned him in the dark wicker loveseat, she and Grandma in arm chairs on either flank, the two of them resembling well-seasoned CIA operatives, patiently extracting information from their subject. Ella is sitting in her small personal chair alongside Chloe, eyeing Scott from the far side of the coffee table as she slowly chews on a chocolate chip cookie. But I see they've made him tea – how nice.

"I moved there from San Francisco about four years ago." He spots me and smiles, the kind that makes my stomach knot, and then turns to look at Grandma as she serves up the next question.

"So you grew up there?"

"Uh-huh. My parents are doctors there. Mom's a general practitioner and Dad's a cardiologist."

Ella perks up. "Do they make you stick out your tongue with one of those big sticks?" She demonstrates, eyes squeezed tightly shut, her mouth open wide and her pink tongue curling out. "ahhhhhhh."

Scott tries not to laugh, "Only when I am sick." He clears his throat.

"So Lucy tells us you're an artist?" Grandma crosses her long legs, settling back into her chair. My mind completes the picture, filling in the slender, silver mechanical pencil in her right, flawlessly manicured hand, its mechanism making a sharp click as she pushes down the lead, about to write on her small tablet of note paper, routine accoutrements in the investigatory trade.

"Yeah, I suppose so," he says. "I do sidewalk – pavement – art, plus I contract to marketing firms." Scott spots me walking around the corner from the kitchen door, our eyes locking. "The sidewalk art lets me travel and the contracting pays the bills," he says, his eyes still riveted on mine. Leaning against the porch railing, I tune into my internal antenna, testing my surroundings. From here, the pull is manageable. Not gone, but manageable.

His attention turns back to Aunt Em, and I let go of my tensed muscles, relaxing against the warm wood. Aunt Em's flower boxes are behind me, overflowing with annuals in pinks, purples and whites, all tumbling over the edges, forming a lacy border around the entire house. Carefully arranged groupings of wicker and chintz patio furniture are tastefully scattered along the redwood-planked deck. In front of me sit three women, dressed in floaty pastel fabrics, sporting a smattering of curls, ribbons, perfume, jewelry, painted nails and makeup. Even the soft, white and fluffy terrier is female, wearing a pink and black plaid collar around her neck. The whole thing is a giant feminine collage, with probably enough estrogen floating around to suffocate a weaker man. But there sits my Scott in the middle of it all, dressed in a no-nonsense white t-shirt sporting a Moosehead Beer emblem, khaki hiking shorts and flip-flops, his arms and legs covered in dark, wiry hairs and his face looking enchantingly bristly.

"… and I only required five stitches." says Scott. "I've been pretty healthy since then." My mind races trying to recreate the question that prompted such a response.

"Hellloooo!" I turn behind me and see Margie and Jack heading our way, my heart panging as I watch Margie inching along, holding onto her husband's arm, her usually healthy glow replaced by a grayish pallor. She recently finished her radiation treatments and was scheduled to start chemo on Monday. I feel myself shudder just thinking about it.

"Lucy? You okay? You're whiter than a ghost." says Scott, the crew on the deck all staring at me.

"Oh. Yeah, I'm fine, no worries. I'm going to go help Margie." Jumping from my perch along the railing, I head down the steps, eager to make contact, to reassure myself that she is alive and well.

Jack grins at me, scooting his wire-rimmed glasses up his nose just a bit. "Ahoy, Mate! May we come aboard?" Sporting a polo shirt with fish all over it, his face tan save a band along his scalp where his fishing cap normally lay, there was little mystery as to his favorite pastime. He leans close, whispering, "Came to check out the boyfriend." He winks, grinning broadly.

"Now Jack, don't start teasing the poor girl already," Margie playfully jabs him in the shoulder. "We'll try to behave. Really," She croons, producing her most sincere look, the effect a little too overdone to be believable.

I snort. I am fairly certain no one is overly worried about behaving. They are a pack of uninhibited seniors with years of life experience under their belt, intent on brandishing their wiles on Scott, genuinely eager to meet him, but not above having a bit of fun with him either.

So now my "young man," as Grandma calls him, is surrounded by an audience of five humans and one dog, while I resume my post along the railing, the spot offering both a safe, discreet vantage point and easy escape route for us both if things get messy. It's amazing how much I learn about him through the course of the questioning, like the fact that his second toe is a tad bit longer than his big one. Or how he has an impressive ability to maintain eye contact with people when he talks to them – none of that staring at the ceiling or the floor thing. Or how he uses few hand gestures, apparently more comfortable to casually rest one arm along the chair, the other along his leg. Okay, so his answers to the questions themselves are interesting too, but more because they confirm discoveries I have already made, mostly through his art. It's like meeting the character of a well-cherished book, so familiar and yet so refreshingly *real*.

I smile, the volume level moving up a few notches when the topic turns to fishing. It was only a matter of time. "Really, you've fished up in Canada?" says Jack, slapping his knee. "Woo, I've heard there is great fishing up there. One of those guide-run places I suppose? How big are the salmon up that way?"

Scott leans forward, his arms resting along his legs, his face animated. "Yeah, it was a guide run place – real nice too. They took us to some fantastic holes, and my friend Sam caught one over twenty-four inches long."

The two are hooked. They trade fish stories, discuss the technical elements of nymph fishing and speculate on the best fly choices for the river running near our house. Evidently Jack has recently had luck with a simple size 16 Parachute Adams and a small Double Beadhead Prince nymph dropped about a foot lower. Fascinating.

Ella glowers at them the entire conversation, but doesn't seem to completely grasp all they were saying. Thank goodness, since then I'd have a small fish advocate protesting madly. Somehow I sense we are years away from her accepting the catch and release concept, if ever.

Aunt Em, who'd disappeared a short while earlier, strides up to me with a small backpack, stuffed full. "So. I've packed a picnic lunch for the three of you and a few treats for Chloe dog. Why don't you steal him away for a bit?"

Crap. Is one four year old enough of a distraction to keep Orexis at bay? "Thanks," I say, with what I hope sounds like enthusiasm. "That sounds great!" I give her a kiss on the cheek and see Ella behind her jumping up and down and chanting *pic-nic, pic-nic*. We start our goodbyes, with promises of being back soon, and eventually extricate ourselves from the porch a good five minutes later.

Ella starts out skipping along between us, Chloe scampering at her heels. She chatters away about the small insects and bugs we are passing and asks Scott pointed questions, often moving along to her next thought without waiting for his reply. A butterfly attracts her attention and she is off, the beautiful Monarch fluttering about her fingers.

"It's great to see you again," Scott takes advantage of the lull.

"You too. Sorry about the inquisition."

He chuckles, "Well, we said we wanted company, right?"

"We did." I raise a single fingertip, slowly extending it towards him. Raising his own, he meets me halfway, our fingers silently making contact, even as the jolt of electricity shoots through us. Almost immediately, the drumming begins, softly, but growing in intensity, the primitive beat throbbing through me, willing me to seek its source. When I meet his gaze, I see the same passion displayed in his features, his breathing rapid. Suddenly, Ella returns, pulling our fingers apart and frowning, forcefully claiming my hand for her own. The intensity subsides, but the link is there, invisible, palpable.

A short while later we stop at Ella's favorite spot, a big old boulder perfect for picnicking, and sit down to eat the lunch Aunt Em has packed. Scott takes up residence on a smaller rock directly to my left, and Ella positions herself next to me on my right. Every time he smiles at me, she takes my face in her hands, pulling it in her direction and pouting furiously. Increasingly distracted, I hit on a compromise: talking to him about Ella.

"So, I told you about Ella's new horse Tali? She met him for the first time yesterday, didn't you Ella?" I say.

"Yeah," my daughter mutters. The horse, the only topic that has been discussed in our house for the last twenty four hours, has been reduced to a single word?

"Tell Scott about Tali, honey," I give her a pointed look.

She produces an exaggerated sigh. "He's my horse," she

says, as if dully repeating lines from a script, plopping her head onto her hands.

Still game, Scott leans towards her, saying "So I hear he is a jumper?"

My precocious daughter spins her head away, resting her head on her knees.

Just great.

I send him an apologetic look and shrug, mystified myself.

"Come on Chloe, let's go talk to the caterpillar," says Ella, sliding down off the rock and trudging a short distance away. Crouching low, she begins giggling as she pets the spiny bug.

"Lucy," Scott says softly from beside me, "Its still here, isn't it."

I know before I turn towards him that he has moved slightly closer; there's a subtle change in the feel of the air and a tingling sensation has started skipping along my limbs. "Yes. It's still here."

Closing his eyes, he sits perfectly still, absorbing. "It's weird... like I can feel you, like I know everything about you," his eyes open abruptly, "Even though I know almost nothing. Fact-wise that is."

It's not fair, of course, considering I can uncover almost anything about him from just a phone number jotted on a scrap of paper. "So. What would you like to know?"

"Mmm. What's your favorite movie?"

That's an easy one. "Sweet Home Alabama. You?"

"I'm an American History X fan myself. How about your favorite food?"

I recline along the rock, propping my head on my hand. "This incredible lobster dip that Aunt Em makes. Oh, and of course, chocolate *anything*. You?"

Squinting, he mulls, his face clearing up once he's decided. "At the moment, I think its spicy pad thai with tofu. But in my memory, it's Spaghettios. The bummer is that I had a can once a few years ago, and they tasted horrid; nothing like what I remember."

"I know what you mean – I liked those too," I look over my shoulder at my daughter, satisfied to see she is still prattling away to small creatures along the trail. Turning back, I watch him, awaiting his next question. He looks so at ease in this outdoor realm, lounging against a tall aspen, his fingers entwined behind his head, elbows flopping out on either side.

"I know," his foot starts to tap, "what's your favorite band?"

Biting my lip, I think. "I guess maybe Abba." His eyebrows raise and I rush to explain, "I know its weird, and they haven't been around in forever, and their stuff is the musical equivalent of pre-chewed food, but I've just always liked em."

"Wow. I can't believe you picked them. I really like them too. I like practically all music, really. Any disgusting habits? Vices? Sexual proclivities?"

"Not that I plan on sharing."

He unfolds his arms and leans towards me, arms resting along his thighs. "Okay then, how about a harder one? Tell me about Ella's father. Is he still in the picture?"

I hesitate. "No. Definitely not in the picture."

"Why not?"

"Because you have to be *in* the picture to go *out* of it," I say, taking a deep breath. "I was raped when I was seventeen."

"Oh God, I'm sorry… What a stupid-"

I interrupt as I struggle to sit up, "No, its okay. Really." We sit, engrossed in our own thoughts. "It's been a long time ago now. It was someone at a fraternity party, and, well, it was a different part of my life."

"Wow. I assume the guy's in jail now."

"No, not exactly," I say, watching as a confused look spreads across his face. "My parents didn't believe me, and it would've been kind of tough to fight the battle on my own. Please," I raise my hands in supplication, "its *okay*. It's a closed chapter… or at least I try to keep it that way. And I have Ella." We both look in her direction, watching as she alternately spins in circles and talks with Chloe.

"Have you dated anyone since then?" he asks quietly.

"No."

He blows out a long stream of air. "How do you feel about all this? I mean, this physical connection we seem to have? After what happened to you…"

His face registers emotions I don't want to see there – fear and pity. I want to be normal, a woman. "It's different, you know? I mean, that was violent. This is, well, I'm not sure I'd call it romantic, but it's definitely intense and, well, *hot*." I blush, hiding my face in my hands. "God, I feel like some kind of slut or something!"

"Luce." He comes over and sits beside me. "You're definitely not a slut. I'm as confused by all of this as you are. But I like you. A lot." He smiles, "and it doesn't hurt that you make me feel horny as hell."

I groan.

"But are you ready for this? Is it too soon?"

"No," the word comes out more forcefully than I intend it to. "No. It's not too soon."

"So," he brushes his hand over mine, "lets back up to something less personal."

"Okay. But if you want answers to any more questions, you'd better move back over to *your* rock." The throbbing is picking up to an intensity that leaves me unable to concentrate.

"Hmm," he pauses, evidently checking out the connection himself. "Yep. You have a point there." He tortures me with a slow, cheeky grin, a foot from my face, before slowly moving the four foot distance to his small granite perch. "So. Do you have any questions for *me*?"

"Yes," I squirm a bit as I phrase my question in my mind. "Would we be on a second date if we hadn't found out we have this, um, connection?"

"Yes." The speed of his response is gratifying. "We would definitely be on a second date. But considering our *connection*, as you call it, let's take it slow today, okay?" I nod. "Because you know," he cocks his head to one side, his eyes pulling me close, "I personally would like to explore whatever this thing is between us a lot more closely. *Soon*."

~21~

Chemo*therapy*. It seemed odd to Margie that while other types of therapy left you renewed and invigorated, this one was actually trying to kill off parts of your body. Bad parts, true, but it was on a killing spree nonetheless. There was massage therapy, which had always left her feeling incredible, sort of like a warm heap of Jello, every muscle relaxed and content. Then there was aromatherapy, which she'd only tried once, and it had been pleasant as well, leaving her feeling like someone had cleaned out her senses with a vacuum cleaner. There were costly day spas and resorts that specialized in these various therapies involving everything from vegetables to mud, none of them intended to leave you feeling and looking worse than when you arrived.

But this… well, it was not for the light of heart. Her stomach was nauseous, clenching and spinning, its contents long since flushed down the clean white basin in the adjoining room. She had a nasty headache, but couldn't seem to keep the pills down long enough to numb the pain. At this point she was lying on her side in her bed, dizzy, and lacking even the energy to get up. Everything was in bloom, vibrant color all around her, yet here she lay, feeling monotone and crappy, as if someone had revoked her membership privileges in summer.

"I hate seeing you like this," Jack looked as miserable as she, sitting on the edge of their bed and brushing her hair back from her brow, awkward, bereft of something useful to do. "Do you need anything?" She didn't have the energy to take care of them both, and so a light hand on his leg was all she could muster in response.

"Some fresh air?" Jack asked. She nodded, and so he rose, opening the large bay windows that overlooked the forest the bordered the meadow. The sound of the river came rushing in, the clean scent of real pines a welcome change from the cloying phony-pine reek of antiseptic and the sickening smell of vomit.

A knock sounded on the screen door below, followed by a tentative "Hello?"

Jack walked back to her side, "That'll be Lucy, I suspect. Shall I tell her to come another time?" Margie knew that while she didn't have the energy to entertain visitors, Lucy simply needed to see her, feel reassured by her presence. She didn't quite understand why, but she knew her recovery was crucial to the girl.

"It's okay," she said, the words a whisper. After giving her a kiss on her forehead, Jack headed down the stairs, opening the door for Lucy and talking to her in muted tones.

With a welcome energy, her youthful, tanned face popped in the door, her tentative smile quickly replaced by a worried frown. She hurried over to the spot Jack had just vacated, scooping up Margie's free hand. "Oh Margie, I'm so sorry you have to go through this," she said, her eyes quickly swelling with tears. Standing up, she turned away, wiping a hand across her face. "Let's see what needs to be done around here."

Evidently needing to transfer her emotions into some kind of physical activity, Lucy moved about the room, straightening the velvet crazy quilt atop Margie, picking up some discarded clothing and dumping it in the nearby wicker hamper and fastening the curtains so they wouldn't blow in the breeze. "Would you like some fresh water?" she asked from across the room.

Without waiting for a reply, she came over and picked up the half-full glass, toting it off towards the bathroom, the creak of the faucet turning and the sound of running water audible above the stream's gurgling.

Looking for a place to set the glass down near her patient, Lucy appeared mesmerized at the sight of a small notepad on the bedside table, the thing sandwiched between a small vase of wildflowers and the phone, and partially covered by a tissue. It wasn't the first time Margie had seen the girl ferreting out notes and letters, which seemed odd, considering she didn't seem nosey or overly curious in other ways. Moving the tissue aside under the guise of placing the glass on a coaster, she quickly scanned the note, her gaze taking on a vacant look. Then a sudden smile spread across her face, odd, as the only words on the paper were "Dr. Martin, 6-29 10:30."

~22~

The month of June is behind us and summer is in full swing, the days long and the temperatures hot, especially down here in Boulder. Today is the Fourth of July, and the Pearl Street Mall is jammed. A long, multi-block street lined with trendy and eclectic shops and restaurants, the store fronts form a colorful row of aged brick mixed with new age chrome, the space in-between paved with stone and boasting planters and sculptures. Bustling with street entertainers, special interest groups and tourists, the mall's visiting throng is a throbbing mass of scantily clad humanity smelling of coconut suntan lotion, ice-cream, sweat and purchasing power.

Scott's piece is straight ahead, a striking work showing a hawk gliding through the sky over a wide, amber meadow. He'd sketched it from Grandma's deck when he'd been up, but the black and white concept drawing is nothing like the vibrant, colorful finished product. Standing alongside it, he is talking to a couple who've stopped to admire his art, the silver-haired pair dressed in red, white and blue t-shirts, an assortment of shopping bags hanging from their arms. He looks up and sees me, smiling and motioning me over.

"Luce. I'd like you to meet the Sandersons. They're visiting from Maine. They have a picture of my work from a show I did in Vermont," he says, sliding his arm around my waist. I smile and look at the photo the man is holding out in my direction. The picture shows a chalk drawing of a fish jumping out of a bubbling stream.

I look up only to see myself reflected in their sunglasses. "Wow, that's great!" The couple smiles, bobbing their heads in unison. I wonder if they have grown to look more like each other over the years, simply by spending their lives together. Both of them have pleasant, curving lines about them, their faces slightly plump with matching furrows and grooves. And their faded blue eyes, round with sincerity and kindness, suggest they have weathered life's challenges gracefully.

"Well, we'll leave you kids to it, but I have to get one more shot before we go," says Mr. Sanderson, backing up and waiting for a dark-haired, teenaged boy eating a snow cone to lumber past before snapping a picture with his expensive-looking chrome digital camera.

Scott waves as they leave, then bends towards me and plants a quick kiss on my cheek. "More of that on your lips later, when it's safe. So did you make it down to the end of the block? Did you see Mike's piece – the one with the wizard?"

I nod, "Yep. I think I've seen them all now, but I still like yours the best."

He squeezes me, saying "Now that's what I call true love." My mind jerks to a stop. Love? He said love. Does he mean love as in *I am not seeing anyone else but you*? Or, love as in *she's a girl and we date each other occasionally*? I flex my fingers as I try to resist the urge to dive into his art and find the answers I am looking for. I can almost feel Grandma's disapproval, a vivid mental image of her scowling and shaking her head flashing by. But what if I just take a peek – nothing too in-depth, just a quick look to see what he thinks about me? That wouldn't be too bad, would it?

"Want some lemonade?" he asks. I am glad my eyes are covered by my sunglasses, sure that otherwise he would read my guilty expression in an instant. I nod. "K. Back in a second." I sit down in one of the two green folding canvas chairs to watch over his supplies, grateful we are positioned under a shady tree.

I tap my fingers on the wooden chair arm, trying to avert my gaze from the picture in front of me, instead watching the group of children huddled around the balloon man on the far side of the street. One of them, a small boy about Ella's age, is standing on a bronze statue of a pig, stretching high, trying to get a better view. The object of his attention is sweating in the hot sun, rapidly twisting the long, thin, multi-colored balloons into an intricate crown for a small, blond-haired girl, impatiently waiting alongside him, a crisp dollar bill clutched in her hand.

I wonder what Ella, Aunt Em and Grandma are doing right now, their itinerary for the day including Ella's riding lessons, a picnic in the meadow and fireworks later in the evening. It seems odd to be here by myself for the weekend; excitingly grown-up, but at the same time a little incomplete, my daughter at home without me. A momentary pang of guilt shoots through me as I realize the thought of being alone with Scott tonight has consumed most of my mental energy today. Or at least it did until a couple minutes ago, before this current obsession with diving into his art.

The dang picture is practically screaming at me now. Ahh! Okay, I will go in, but just for a minute. I slouch down low in my chair, closing my eyes to half-mast and moving through the steps, the warm, lazy feel of the day making it easy, fluid. As I sink beneath the particles of chalk, the small dusty specks float up in a rainbow-like fog, exposing a circling current of thoughts, memories, sensations. Is he dating anyone else? No... I don't sense the presence of any other woman recently in his more romantic thoughts. Is he attracted to me? Whoa! The whole orexis thing is as strong for him as it is for me!

Following its current, I pick out other discrete thoughts; he does in fact want to make love to me... the sexual fantasies he's been having about me are enough to arouse me just sitting here! Loads of images... my hair, my face, my body... what about *me*? I feel a warmer, mellow current of thoughts streaming by amidst the more vibrant physical memories and quickly shift, riding along its wave. This is better... fragmented traits and facts about me... smart, funny, solid, comfortable, mystical, glowing. The current around me is pulling me in, and I yank myself back before I go too far, hoping that my transgression is minor. I open my eyes, a soft, satisfied feeling permeating my core.

"Wow, you look happy." Scott startles me as he comes up from behind my left side, two clear, plastic cups with iced pink lemonade in his hands.

"Oh... yeah. I like the Fourth of July. It's my favorite holiday."

"That's funny; its mine too," he smiles, and I realize I didn't know that about him. He hands me an icy cup, the chilly plastic refreshing. I take my hands, wet with condensation, and pat my hot cheeks.

We spend the rest of the afternoon sitting and talking, mostly with each other, but often times with people who stop to admire Scott's art and ask questions. And while I thoroughly enjoy the day, a reckless anticipation takes hold of me when the sun eventually sinks behind the mountain with the jutting red rocks, called the Flatirons, to the west, and everything is doused with the muted shades of twilight. The promise of night.

The crowd thins as they descend on local restaurants, ready to collapse in the air conditioning and relax before the fireworks begin. Scott and I pack up the chairs and supplies, stowing them in his car, and head over to the Boulder Café, a restaurant right on the mall with plenty of vegetarian choices.

The crowd is thick, so we order wine and sit at one of the high tables in the bar to wait.

"If you want to, we can watch the fireworks from my roof. You can see them really well from there." Scott waves at someone he knows across the bar before leaning close. "You haven't changed your mind about staying, have you? God, please say you haven't, because I might have to embarrass us both by handcuffing you to this chair!" His expectant, hungry look confirms he is in the same state as I.

"No worries, I'm not going anywhere," I chuckle self-consciously. "I'm not sure I could, even if I wanted to. It would be head against heart and hormones."

He grins, "As long as it's not just me. So, your Grandma and Aunt are okay with you spending the night? I'm just curious."

"Aunt Em called in a reservation for me at one of the local hotels, but Grandma just stood behind her mouthing *do whatever you want*."

"It must be hard, everyone knowing what you are doing all of the time."

"It's not so bad." As I say the words, I realize how much I have depended on that security, the cloak of real family wrapped snugly around me all that I required. Until now. His expression changes and I realize he is reading more in my eyes than I want to expose. I breathe, shifting my gaze and surveying the bustle around us.

Our name is called, and we follow the young waitress with several body piercings to a booth by the window. As I slide in, the credit card receipt from the previous patrons catches my eye. There is something about the signature. The waitress goes to pick up the slip of paper, and I rush to stop her, staying her hand with mine.

"Is something wrong?" she asks, staring at me as I read the signature. Crap. I let go of her hand.

"No, nothing. Sorry, I thought I recognized the name." I sit back and sift through the images racing through my head. Whoever James Schultz is, he is very, very sick. Terminally sick. Does he know that? Should I do something? What would I do if I could? He isn't even from around here – I could tell he is from someplace in the desert – so I couldn't find him if I wanted to. When I look up, I realize that Scott is staring at me, a perplexed look on this face.

"You are white as a sheet."

I am mortified that I am exposing my gift like this. "Oh, its nothing. I just thought…" I have no idea where to go from here. "It's nothing. It just reminded me of someone I know who is sick. So, what do you recommend?" Burying my face in my menu, I focus my attention on the list of choices printed neatly underneath the laminated covering.

I can feel his curious eyes on me as he speaks, "I'd vote for the fondue."

"Is it good?"

"I guess so," he says. I look up, curious, and am surprised by his sly expression. "I was really recommending it because it's *fast*."

Something bubbles up inside of me, something complete and utterly silly, perhaps the result of my jittery state, or merely, perhaps, because of my need to wash away my recent mortification about the credit card slip. Whatever the cause, his words suddenly seem so hilarious that I am laughing uncontrollably, tears streaming down my face. I grab my napkin to stem their flow, and am mortified when I let out a loud snort.

When I finally regain enough control to actually look across the table at Scott, I find him leaning back against the booth, arms crossed, smug. "Wow. And I wasn't even trying to be funny."

I simply wave my hand dismissively at him as I blow my nose, not trusting myself to speak yet. The waitress returns and eyes me as if I am perhaps a mental patient only let out for the day. We order the fondue.

~

The drive to his house seems to take forever, even though its only eight blocks; he only brought the car to haul supplies. The breeze comes in the window, winding through my hair and bringing with it the festive mood of the night. A small boy runs past with a red sparkler clutched tight in his hand, illuminating his freckles and two missing front teeth. Across the street an older couple sits in their folding chairs, blankets over their legs. The young boy's mother calls him from his front lawn, urging him to return.

Anticipation. I never really analyzed the word, nor understood its meaning, until now. We slow in front of Scott's house – I recognize it immediately – and drive into the carport. He turns off the ignition, yet doesn't move. I feel his eyes upon me in the quiet, the only sound that of a resident cricket. "Fireworks?"

"I have no doubt," I say. Turning toward him, I am taken aback by the hot light in his eyes. He moves closer, and, eyes open, I meet him halfway. Like sparking a flame, the kiss is instantly intense, carnal. My body throbs.

"Luce," he speaks, his voice hoarse as he kisses a trail down my neck, "should we go inside?"

Are we still outside? My muddled brain tries to clear, "Okay."

Stumbling out my side of the car, still kissing each other, we gradually make it to the side door. Fumbling in his pocket for the keys, he moans as I kiss his ear, running my fingers up him, underneath his shirt, through the bristly field of hair that covers his chest. Once he pushes open the screen, we fall across the threshold, neither of us noticing the unforgiving wood floor beneath us. We are in a place of our own making, a dark, warm, fluid fantasy where we exist as one. My body feels like a harp, his touch setting the strings quivering. Skin on skin, it's as if the pitch of each nerve has been heightened, every place he touches eliciting a beautiful, clear tone, the song reckless and sensual, almost too beautiful for human ears. He is hard where I am soft. His scent is tangy and musky, the thin film of perspiration now covering us causing his skin to glow softly from the light of the street lamp shining through the kitchen window; he reminds me of some kind of Greek god. Abandonment of all inhibitions, it's as if my body was made for his, its mate in form, its equal in passion. Pleasure and need intermingle, my body seeks release as the song becomes faster, its tone intense, almost discordant. Feeling and sensation blends together, the timbre heightening until we reach its source, its final sweet vibrant display.

Panting, we lay in each other's arms, noticing for the first time our surroundings, which are currently covered with the ghosts of our clothing. Two clogs lie yards apart. A shirt has puddled on the floor. A tossed belt winds like an alligator through the carpet. And on the fruit bowl, my pink and white stripped panties hang like a flag of lust.

"That was... well, it was..." he falters.

"*Amazing*," I say.

"That," he says, still somewhat breathless, "is one of the many words that comes to mind."

"At least we made it indoors."

He chuckles as he runs a finger between my breasts. "Yes," he says, and for a moment his fingers slow to a stop atop the small, red star. "What's this?"

I shut my eyes and hold them tightly closed. "Believe it or not, it's a birthmark."

"Why are you making a face?"

"Am I? I didn't know."

Sliding down he examines it at closer range. "Wow. That's something! It's a perfect star." When he traces it with his fingers, I am surprised to find his touch setting off the pulsing again, its intensity growing again already. I feel the warm waves, starting low and radiating out across my chest.

"Luce?"

"Yeah?"

"Are you, I mean, would you be offended –"

I clasp his head, bringing him towards me, "Yes, I'll absolutely be offended if you don't make love to me again right *now*." Our lips join with even more passion than before, our entire bodies already exposed to each other's touch. Dragging my swollen lips away for an instant, I manage to whisper, "Scott?"

"Hmm?"

"Can we at least see if we can make it to the living room this time?"

And so we manage to scoot ourselves so that we were at least partially on the carpet before we climax. And eventually, well into the night, we clamber exhausted into bed.

~23~

Cindy, Ella's trainer, checked over the girl's saddle, making sure the leather girth was comfortably snug before shifting her attention to Ella's stirrups, repositioning them one notch on either side by yanking up on the leather straps, adjusting the buckles and then settling the shiny metal loops back into place. Ella tested the change by rising up in a mock post, then sinking down into the saddle, experimenting with the fit of her leg against Tali's sides. Because of her small stature, her limbs seemed to barely extend beyond the saddle, but somehow she knew when it all felt just right, producing a confirming nod for her trainer.

Sitting tall and straight atop her stead, she exuded confidence, not a timid bone in her body, especially when it came to riding Tali. And outfitted in her black velvet helmet, riding breeches and tweed show jacket, she looked quite the consummate equestrian, even if she was the smallest rider there.

Since the afternoon they'd bonded with each other on Ella's birthday a month earlier, the girl and her horse had shared a daily riding ritual, Ella's technique developing rapidly. She'd become a familiar sight at the stables, seeming to thrive in this environment of horses, dust and leather, her small form moving fearlessly among the massive beasts, her elemental bond with riding a curiosity to other riders, many of them often eying her with envy. Even to Grace, who understood the root of her bond with animals, her great-granddaughter was a continual source of amazement, her budding gift both terrifying and awesome to watch.

She looked so perfect, her small form executing an effortless post as she circled the ring, her face radiating a curious mix of contentment and total absorption. It was as if she were within the bonds of a spell, existing in a place that only she and Tali understood, a constant flow of communication passing silently between them. And when they cantered, she smiled, their fluid motion one, a smooth rolling rhythm, Tali's tail streaming behind. And when they galloped, Ella grinned, throwing her head back and laughing with sheer, raw joy.

Within the small window of time she had been training, Ella had already mastered small cross-bar jumps and was constantly asking to try something higher. But she was limited by what the adults around her could stomach, their fear for her a constant, living thing. Even knowing Tali would always protect her, Grace found herself flinching every time the pair sailed over a jump, Ella looking like a mere doll in the dark leather saddle. And the fact that Cindy constantly told them, inevitably while shaking her head, that the child was attempting things not normally recommended for months, wasn't doing much to ease her fears.

The small group of spectators that had gathered for the show, all of them perched atop the hot metal risers positioned along one side of the outside ring, were following Ella's progress, eyes hidden by sunglasses, but their murmured whispers and obvious interest clear indications that Grace's great-granddaughter was already somewhat of a celebrity. She caught a snippet of one couple's interchange, "..must be certifiably *insane* to let such a small child ride..." Her back grew rigid, her ire tweaked by the insinuation that they would do anything that might harm their precious Ella. But that was the way it had always been for those within the trust; they were judged as often for what they did do as for what they didn't. While Grace was still sure that her decision to gift Ella with a horse had been the right one, she worried about all this attention. But then, it came with the territory. She had struggled with it her entire life.

Lucy, Scott and Em returned from the car carrying five bottles of water. Sliding in next to her, Lucy opened one of the containers, a quick pop audible as the plastic gave way, and handed it to her.

"So. Did we miss anything?" she asked, adjusting the sunglasses on her nose, the movement bringing the warm scent of her spicy perfume towards Grace's nostrils.

"No. She has simply warmed up a bit," Grace smiled, then leaned close. "But even that seemed to impress the crowd."

On the other side of Lucy, she saw Scott and Lucy exchange an intimate look, the two obviously becoming ever closer as the summer progressed. With the orexis coming into play, it was a foregone conclusion. She was happy for her, of course, but hoped it wouldn't stifle the budding self-confidence that her Granddaughter so desperately needed. Lucy had recently told her, during one of their walks in the meadow, about Ella's father. So many things were coming together. They would read Katie's journal soon – she sensed it was almost time – and who knew what emotions and information that might reveal?

An announcer introduced himself over the loud speaker, the initial discordant twang of the electronic device drowning out his voice and drawing groans from the spectators as they covered their ears.

"Sorry, folks. We'll get the kinks worked out here and get started." The cheerful voice boomed forth, becoming slightly more tolerable as the volume was adjusted. 'There. So, today we will start with the beginner's division..." Grace listened as he proceeded to describe the course and objective for the riders. She sought out Ella and saw she was receiving instructions from Cindy, every now and then stopping to bend down and whisper last minute instructions to Tali. Being just beginners, the pair's task was to demonstrate walking, posting, cantering, and the ability to maneuver four small jumps.

Ella was competing with many girls twice her age, but Grace knew that despite her novice status and youth, she had the edge nonetheless. Lined up with her fellow beginner riders outside the railing, she looked quite official, with a large "17" pinned to her back. Tali, standing tall, his freshly brushed ebony coat shimmering, appeared massive and regal, ready and eager to take his turn in the ring.

The first rider was a girl who looked to be about seven, riding a pretty chestnut. She did well on the course, but knocked the bar off the last jump, her face crumpling with disappointment as she came to a stop before the crowd. Grace's heart went out to the young girl, devoid of magical powers to help guide her horse over the low rail. Someone ran out to re-position it just as Ella entered the ring. She cast a quick look in their direction before making her way to the middle of the arena, gracing the judges with a dignified nod before beginning her routine.

The pair walked to the far end of the course before turning and breaking into a trot, their graceful rhythm belying their short training tenure. Circling the perimeter they reached the midway point and, right on cue, transitioned gracefully into a canter. Grace had learned to ascertain if Tali was on the right lead during this critical transition, and felt herself expel a quick breath when she saw that he was. She stole a glance at Cindy and saw the well-disciplined trainer allow herself a brief smile before her student started into the four small jumps, the more challenging work for most of the contenders. Ella took the first jump like a pro, Tali keeping his stride as he trotted out of it and around to the next gate. The second and third gates were placed close together, the first a low cross-rail followed by another small single. The pair approached the set, Ella again posting, easily maneuvering the first and then the second obstacle without mishap, a small smile beginning to spread across her face. Perhaps she was feeling over-confident, for on the fourth gate, she faltered a moment, and Grace saw that Tali had to adjust for her a bit, as she slid to the left in the saddle. A quick gasp arose from the crowd, but she was swiftly righted again, and continued on to finish the course without incident.

When she rode to a halt, she grinned up at her spectators, her face flush with excitement. She returned to the waiting area, wrapping her arms around Tali and pressing her cheek against his withers, obvious adoration in her eyes. Cindy joined them, and squeezed Ella's leg, her look a mixture of pride and astonishment. Grace knew that she continued to marvel at her young pupil's progress, her well-grounded horse-sense often wavering when it came to Ella, the girl's progress defying everything the seasoned trainer had come to regard as fact. Many times over the last month she had sensed that Cindy was on the verge of asking her more about Ella and her strong connection with Tali, but the trainer always refrained, even once after she had already opened her mouth to speak, instead simply shutting it again and shrugging with a rueful smile on her face. Perhaps she sensed that she would not receive the answers she sought. Or perhaps she was afraid that if she knew the truth, it might somehow take away the magic, disappointing her and ridding her of her prize pupil.

In the end, Ella took second, but it had taken an eight-year old girl with two years of experience to beat her. She sat as regally as royalty on Tali's back as they walked up and gracefully accepted their red ribbon amidst wild cheering and a couple of loud whistles from Lucy. Several camera flashes went off, one of them belonging to a woman reporter from a Denver paper. She leaned against the railing, taking a close-up of Ella accepting the small gold-colored cup from the President of the riding club, a well-dressed, official-looking gentleman with neatly combed silver hair and a top hat, his father-of-the-bride meets circus-ringmaster look seeming out-of-place in the rustic mountain setting.

Ella, with Cindy walking alongside, exited the ring, riding out well beyond the arena where the next division was gathering. Grace slowly maneuvered her way down the bleachers, carefully holding onto the risers with one hand and Lucy with the other as she descended to the ground.

"I swear those bleachers put permanent indentations into my backside." said Em. "But it was worth it to see our Ella." With Scott's help, Em had made it down as well, and was working the kinks out of her limbs and emitting a satisfied groan as she arched her back with a lavish sound of cracking and popping.

As they drew near, she could see that Ella was wiggling, hardly able to contain her excitement. The reporter from Denver was coming up along beside them, looking eager to intercept them for a moment.

"Could I get a few words from you about your daughter for the paper?" asked the reporter. She wasn't much older than Lucy herself, and dressed in her blue jeans, a button down shirt, and sensible shoes, she looked approachable and friendly. Lucy agreed and the two were immediately encircled when the rest of Ella's entourage moved in to add their two cents.

"Psst! Grandma!" Grace glanced down to see Ella tugging on her blouse. It was hard for her to bend down, but she leaned down as far as she was able, her muscles protesting a bit. She eyed her exuberant young granddaughter, cheeks rosy and eyes sparkling, curious to hear her request.

"Grandma, will you come with me and Tali?" Ella whispered, her hands cupped dramatically about her mouth.

Looking around, it did appear that neither would be missed, so Grace nodded her head, backing out of the group and walking alongside her great-granddaughter as she led her steed towards the stables. It was probably ludicrous to say she led him, considering he could do whatever he desired, but he was amenable to the arrangement, and seemed content to comply with whatever Ella asked. He was at ease, his tail swishing occasionally, his neck arched as he kept his head low, his nose routinely turning towards Ella, his nostrils quivering as he picked up her scent.

When they got to Tali's stall, Ella ushered him in, making sure there was hay waiting, and that his water trough was full. Grace sat on the wooden bench right outside his quarters, amazed by the bond that had formed between the two in such short a time. She could hear Ella chatting away to him, patting him all the while. "You were so good, Tali. You are the bestest horse in the whole world." The stable hand came over and helped her remove his bridle and saddle, placing the tack on hooks and shelves along the wall. Normally Ella would have brushed him too, asking him to lay down so that she could reach him, but not today, as she appeared impatient to talk to her Grandma first.

Grace patted the space beside her when Ella came around the corner. Climbing up, she sat close, her feet dangling over the edge. "Grandma, it was so neat," said Ella, her eyes wide and her face still aglow with the excitement of it all. She tucked back a strand of hair that was coming loose from her ponytail. "Tali, he was *so* good! Did you see him?" Grace nodded, smiling.

"He does everything I ask him. He is the best horse ever, isn't he Grandma?"

Grace nodded again, wondering where this line of questioning was going. She suspected that Ella had pulled her away to do more than expound on Tali's virtues. Plus the girl was holding her hand, something she sometimes did when she particularly wanted something, something she was fairly certain she could not have.

"Well, don't you think Tali should get to be the bestest horse and do the bestest things?" Ella paused, and then smiled when her Grandma nodded. "Well, then can't I use my magic – just a little – so he can do special tricks and stuff?"

Grace smiled, but didn't nod this time. She inclined her head, silently signaling for Ella to sit up on her lap. Squirming into position, Ella craned her neck so she could look up at Grace's face, resting one hand against her grandma's cheek, her dimples looking particularly mischievous as she smiled beguilingly.

"Sweetie, you can always talk to Tali, and you can ask him to work together with you to jump and ride, but you can *not* ask him to do something a horse wouldn't normally do."

"Like what? What is *normly*?" asked Ella.

"Well, normally means things he would do on his own, if you couldn't talk to him," explained Grace. "Pretty much anything besides walking, running and jumping is *not* okay. The things you see other girls do with their horses *is* okay."

"But why?" asked Ella, her dimples disappearing.

Grace fought the urge to smile, "Because you can't let other people know about your gift. Remember, your gift is special, and it's a secret."

Ella pouted, her pretty lips puckered and her brows furrowed. Crossing her arms, she spoke without looking at Grace, "What good is a gift if I can't tell anybody!" Grace chuckled, hugging her arms around her and resting her chin upon her head.

"Ah, little one. I know it is hard to understand. But others – those without a gift – they don't understand us. Instead of thinking we are special, they would just think we were odd. Bad."

"Nu-huh! Ella turned her pleading eyes towards her again. "They would think we were really neat and want to put us on TV and stuff."

"No angel, it would not be good, trust Grandma." Grace turned as she saw Lucy walking down the aisle, evidently looking for them.

"There you two are! We were wondering where the star of the show ran off to," said Lucy as she stopped to pet Tali's nose, which was leaning out over the stable door.

"You came just in time," said Grace. "Ella was wondering why she can not use her gift to help Tali do tricks."

Ella began sulking again. Grace knew she was aware that Lucy was even more stern about this topic than she.

"Oh, honey. Grandma is right – you mustn't show off your gift. It is a special secret," Lucy said as she looked at Grace, hoping she would be able to sway Ella on this topic, knowing that they constantly ran the risk of her getting herself into trouble.

Grace nodded, "That's what I told her all right. Ella roo, just listen to me for a minute, okay?" She waited for a moment before she felt Ella's little head moving against her chest, nodding her agreement. She took a deep, considering breath. "I know you think we are special like princesses," she began, "like fairies and angels and famous people on television. But we are different than that, special in a different way." Ella's face was now lifted in careful attention. "We have been chosen to know something, to see something, that other people can not. And we are to use this gift to help people, to help animals." Ella started to talk, but Grace put her finger to her lips. "And no, we can not help people better if we tell them our secret. They would be angry and jealous because they didn't have the gift too."

"But how do you know? How do you know they would not like us?"

"Because it has been that way for a long, long time, darling. Many women in our family have been persecuted – not liked – because of it."

Ella thought about her next question. "But maybe they would like me. And Tali."

"Ah, honey, I know it seems like they would, but they probably would be scared, just like the others."

Lucy rubbed Ella's back. "Your Grandma is right sweetie. My own family – my adoptive Mommy and Daddy – didn't understand, and it made them very sad."

Ella sighed, sounding unconvinced. But then she spied her entourage coming down the aisle way, and she jumped up and ran towards them, intercepting her Aunt and hugging her about her legs.

"Auntie Em, did you see me? Did you see Tali and me?"

Em laughed, and nodded, smoothing the girl's hair back from her face.

Scott leaned down alongside her until he was at eye level. "You were really good Ella, and so was Tali."

She stared at her feet, still holding onto her Aunt Em, not quite sure how to treat this person who liked her Mommy. "Thanks."

"Do you suppose I could help you brush him?" Scott asked. Ella's eyes shot up, a smile lighting up her face as she enthusiastically nodded. She was game for anything that involved people paying attention to Tali and doing nice things for him.

She rushed into the stall and grabbed two soft brushes from the low shelf, put there specifically for her. Handing one to Scott, she motioned him back towards the corner. Then she simply stood, looking at Tali intently. Slowly, he knelt down, groaning a bit in the process, until he was down on the floor directly in front of them. Ella turned and smiled, taking a perplexed Scott's hand and leading him forward.

Grace looked on and shook her head, realizing that they had a long way to go. Soon, she hoped, Ella would understand what it meant to keep her gift a secret. In the meantime, she silently asked the good Lord to watch over them.

"It totally sucked!" I moan. "There I was, just looking at the painting, and the next thing I knew I was literally yanked in. Someone eventually touched my arm, asking if I was okay, and maybe it was the physical contact that triggered it, but I was able to pull out. I looked at my watch, and from what I could tell, I'd been standing there like a freaking zombie for almost ten minutes. Oh, my face was soaked, so evidently I had been crying too. What am I going to do?" I ask Grandma. "I have to be around art – it's my major for heaven's sake – without freaking out all the time."

Gazing at me warmly, she touches my hand. "Oh dear, that does sound frustrating. Were there many people around when it happened?"

I sigh. "Oh, there was only three, but one of them was Scott. He was looking at me like I had two heads. "

"Mmm. Not good." Grandma turns to look at me, her eyes more tired tonight than usual, the delicate skin underneath them slightly puffy and gray. Maybe because she is so ethereal, the harshness of fatigue seems particularly misplaced on her lovely face. "Did he say anything later?"

"No. But I could tell he was thinking about it and wondering how to even broach the subject. But after Ella and Tali, and now this, he probably thinks the whole family is nuts."

Grandma clicks her tongue, "Well, thanks to the orexis, I doubt he'll run too fast." She chuckles as I glare at her, then says, "That aside, he seems pretty taken with *you*, so I wouldn't worry just yet." We lie silently, staring at the ceiling and thinking. I am analyzing the wooden beams that run length-wise along Grandma's ceiling and wondering how long it might take for Ella to warm up to Scott when Grandma's voice breaks into my thoughts, "Dear, I might have an idea that will help you from getting pulled into art." I turn my head. "But first, tell me about him."

I blush, confused. She is looking at me with a knowing smile, her beautiful face relaxed. "I know about *that*," she says, "Tell me about *him*. What's he like?"

A moment passes while I gather my thoughts. I begin, "He is very smart – he knows about all kinds of things – and he loves art as much as I do. He likes to mountain bike and play soccer and… mmm… he likes plants. He's kind of laid-back and he doesn't get mad very easy. He's really easy to talk to…"

When I turn and look at her, Grandma is shaking her head, one eyebrow arched. She sighs and looks away from me, her gaze directed at the ceiling. I wait.

When she finally speaks, her tone is quiet, reflective. "Oliver looked absolutely perfect in a nicely starched, white button-down shirt with the top two buttons undone, his neck looking strong and tan, the muscles moving in such an elemental way when he talked, ah, well, he could mesmerize me for hours. His eyes looked as if they saw straight through to my heart, as if he understood things about me that perhaps I didn't even know myself. He was strong, solid – always the dependable one, always loyal to family. Practically always on time and one of those people who never forgot a name. He had a romantic side too. When I was pregnant with Katie and feeling like I was too clumsy to even put on my own shoes, he'd read Shakespeare to me and paint my toenails. He would sometimes brush my hair, capturing my eyes in the mirror and kissing my neck in a way that sent thousands of tiny silver shivers down my neck. My Oliver." She sighs. I hear her head shift on the pillow as she turns towards me. "So, I'll ask you again. Tell me about your young man."

I feel myself blush, never having expected quite such a vivid view into my grandparents love life. It seems weird thinking about them as young adults in love, even though logic points to that very conclusion. Talking in this way is unfamiliar, considering my distant relationship with my adoptive parents and my few close friends. It's as if my grandma is reading poetry, as though she has taken her feelings and put them poignantly into words. I know only one way to go to that place within myself. Like melding with a painting, I turn inward, exploring feelings rather than facts.

"Hmm... well, he is very handsome, kind of a cross between Tom Cruise and the young doctor on Everwood. He is funny..."

Again Grandma interrupts me. "Okay, so I see you need some help. Let's start with his neck. Tell me about his neck."

Surely I can do this. I mentally shake out my muscles and try another answer. "I have to agree that a man's neck is heavenly. I particularly like Scott's when it's the weekend, and he skips shaving for the day, everything bristly and rough down under his chin. He is very relaxed... his best look is a casual one, like when he is wearing an old t-shirt and faded jeans, usually with a bit of chalk or paint smudged underneath his neatly trimmed fingernails." I look to her for approval. She smiles and nods. I continue. "I like that he is hard where I am soft, that he has a green thumb and I don't, and that he reads the sports section while I read the arts. And I love his dimple. It's like a small new moon that makes an appearance to light up my day, a sort of childish trait that looks particularly sexy

on a grown man. And he has this way of looking at me sometimes that is both reverent and like he can see through my
clothes, all at the same time. I love that look." I feel Grandma
touch my arm and I stop, slightly embarrassed by my own
temerity, surprised how immersed I became in such a short,
first try.

"Amen!" Grandma smiles at me, squeezing my arm, "You
are not bad once you get going! He sounds just *yummy*."

I am too embarrassed to speak.

Grandma chuckles, "Oh honey, it's good for you to be more
in touch with how you feel. It's not embarrassing – *never* embarrassing. In fact it's healthy." She rubs my arm briskly for a
moment. "So… do you like him?"

We look at each other for a long moment as I wonder if words
are required, considering the heat of another major blush is
working its way up and across my entire face. Grandma simply
graces me with her finely-tuned all-knowing look and inhales
deeply. "Just one more thing on this subject," he says. "You
mustn't let the whole orexis thing get in the way of really getting to know each other, getting to know yourself. Sure, it may
end up being enough to keep you together, but you can have so
much more." Appearing to be at battle with her emotions, she
swallows hard, then says softly, "You can have it *all*." I close my
eyes, giving her privacy, time to regain her composure.

"Want to hear my idea?" she is smiling again, wiping errant tears from her cheeks.

I nod. Absolutely.

"Well. The other day I was listening to my classical music CD – you know, the one with that theme song from 'Portrait of a Lady—I just love that song! Well, I was listening and
reading my book and all of the sudden a song came on that
was louder, more discordant to me than the others, and it totally distracted me. I couldn't read and listen to it at the same
time."

She is looking at me expectantly, but I am not yet in the same mind-space.

"Don't you see?" she asks. "If we can find the right music, and play it at the right volume, maybe you could listen to it while you are looking at art and it would keep you from getting absorbed. You could use that little iPod of yours and just tune in when you need to."

I sit up, total realization dawning. "That's a great idea!" I imagine myself back at the art museum, something like country twang, not my favorite by a long shot, pumping into my ears, keeping me engulfed in a perpetual stream of disruptive background noise. Sure, I would have a difficult time hearing people, and I couldn't really meld with art until no one else was around, but I would be seen as a run-of-the-mill music junkie as opposed to something worse. "It just might work. I am going to try it out tomorrow at the art center."

"Hmm, Teddy," Grandma warns.

"Oh yeah," I say, weighing my options. "Oh! I know. I can take in some of the art at the Boom Day booths tomorrow." The annual Boom Day festivities always included a pretty well-rounded collection of vendor booths, a good place to test out Grandma's theory. I would just have to find something that really intrigued me.

"Sounds good," says Grandma. "Try to find someplace nice and quiet. That'll be a better test."

'Grandma?"

"Yes?"

"Do you think I can do it? You know, make a relationship work with my gift and Ella's to contend with?" I watch as she considers, not wanting her to temper her answer, yet wanting to hear that it will all work out.

"Well, I don't know for sure sweetie, but you had that vision in his art, which is as strong a sign as I know. And then there is the very strong orexis, and the fact that he seems committed to spending his free time with you." She nudges my foot with hers, "I think that destiny takes a hand in things when he's the right one, so why worry? It'll be okay."

I decide to cling to these words, to mentally tuck them away as talismans from a wise and gifted woman whose conviction I trust more than my own.

$\sim 25 \sim$

It was late. Lucy had gone to bed, but Grace was not yet alone. And this was a visitor she hadn't seen in quite some time; not this close anyway. Lying in bed, stretched out under the fresh-smelling bedcovers, she shut her eyes, letting herself feel the vibrations, the skittish movement of another's presence, brushing up next to her, but not quite locking in.

I'm not angry with you. Please, talk to me. Grace broadcast her own message, waiting for a response. She was, in truth, a little bit angry, but time had tempered most of her anger into a healthy curiosity, and she was ready for some answers. Plus, truth be told, it had simply been far too long since they'd talked, and she really needed to reconnect. But she was worried that no joining would take place tonight unless she conceded a little ground.

Finally the familiar, delicate scent grew closer, the air rippling as the presence slowly sought to join with her, tentatively easing into a single, shared space. *Mom.*

Grace felt the pores in her skin tingle, the surface of her body coming alive, reaching out to her only child, this prodigal daughter she had missed desperately, even as she had wanted to wring her proverbial neck. As she had done many times before, Grace offered up a prayer of thanks that she could still communicate with her daughter, a blessing that far outweighed the many darker sides of her gift.

Conversation during a joining was very different than simply talking to one another, the palette of available communication mediums richer, more crystalline, more whole. Emotions, information, scents and memories were exchanged, everything going on at once. It was hard to hide anything during such an intense dialog, and Grace wondered how Katie had managed to do it for so long. But tonight she was open, exposing parts of herself previously concealed, allowing Grace to see – see it *all*.

The image of Lucy's birth; Katie examining each tiny, pink finger and toe, tears spilling down her face, the nurse watching alongside, mesmerized by the outpouring of human emotion. Lucy's first steps, her adoptive parents beaming, cheering her on, the tall grass of the back lawn impeding the progress of her small, spindly legs as the delicate smells of the nearby flower garden drifted over it all. Kindergarten, Lucy's adoptive mother looking on with an expression of worry, the small girl looking up at her, whispering *I promise I'll be good.* The smell of lemons strong in the background, Lucy's adoptive mother's hand shooting out to slap the girl hard across the face, the presence of anger – raw, intense – and hate, so much hate. Then the unthinkable – Lucy raped and huddled on the bed, her head in her lap, her shoulders shaking with the force of her sobs. Ella, being presented to Lucy for the first time, the shiny, white umbilical cord still attached to the tiny, pink squirming infant, Lucy smiling through her tears, reaching for her daughter, undaunted by the blood and mucus still covering her small form. Lucy and Ella, huddled together on a cot in a small, plain room, a worn pale blue flannel blanket, mother singing daughter to sleep with Twinkle, Twinkle Little Star.

Katie had certainly not missed the events of her daughter's

life, even if her presence had been a bit unconventional and certainly virtually invisible to those here in physical form. Her love for Lucy was evident, the same type of strong bond that Grace felt with Katie. So then why?

What she found surprised her. It was horrible, yet so utterly plain that Grace couldn't believe she hadn't figured it out herself. As soon as she and Lucy had an opportune night, it would be time to read the journal.

~

Grace lay awake long after Katie left, replaying the memories and emotions in her head. Like the delicate pages of a cherished album, each vignette was so special, she worried she would mar them, afraid rushing through them would cause her to lose important details or recall facts incorrectly. So instead she painstakingly retraced each one, sifting through the collage of emotions, images and scents, carefully cataloguing them away for later.

The joining had been longer than any she'd experienced before, even though both she and Katie knew it would take its toll. While the intense sensory realm of a joining was all-consuming, and the temptation to stay locked-in strong, she was well aware of its physical impact, and knew better than to linger too long. Joinings were something to be savored in small doses, not long episodes like tonight, especially for old women with rather dicey health. Her heart was racing, and the all too familiar fluttering was more than a little disconcerting. She concentrated on her breathing, watching the flow of energy across the night sky, the brilliant lights forming beautiful patterns amongst the stars. She started to lift her arm to smooth her hair back from her temples and moaned as she found the effort almost more than she could manage. Her arm was shaking violently, so she simply let it drop to its former position atop the bed.

Damn! This was a fine mess. Now a tingling sensation moved through her arm, as though her limb had been asleep and was just now awakening. Figuring that couldn't possibly be a good sign, Grace lay perfectly still, petitioning her maker with fervent prayers asking for more time. *She is doing so well... she's almost there, almost ready to fly. I know you let me linger to be here for her... for them... just a little more time and she'll be through discernment. Please...*

A calm settled in around Grace, the fluttering in her chest tapering to a halt, replaced by a reassuring rhythmic beat. Sighing, she let go and allowed her exhausted body to sink further into the flannel-encased mattress, confident that she would be blessed with another opportunity to greet the morning sun. *Thank you* she mouthed, before drifting off to sleep.

~26~

It was a breathtaking sunrise, the glowing yellow orb slowly rising above the eastern peaks, gilding the wispy clouds in mellow shades of pink and orange. With a blanket around her to insulate her from the crisp morning air, her feet propped on the coffee table and Chloe by her side, Em sat watching the display, as she often did, from the cozy confines of the deck. Armed with a cup of stiff coffee and the Leadville Herald Democrat, she was well into her morning ritual, having already taken a shower, put in a load of laundry and started a quiche baking for breakfast. She still had a good half hour to sit and read the paper before anyone else ventured downstairs, although she was rarely able to sit in one place for that long.

She was a bit more tired than usual today, what with all the pitter-patter going on last night. Did they think she didn't hear them when they held their late night tête-à-têtes? The hushed conversations, punctuated by occasional outbursts of laughter or tears; the strange creaking, rustling and hissing noises that leaked out from under the door, quietly floating along the hallway. More than once she'd considered joining them, her curiosity almost getting the better of her, but hadn't she tried years before to no avail?

Sighing, she simply let the paper lie limply in her lap,

her thoughts elsewhere this morning. Because in truth, these sounds, while unfamiliar in the everyday world, were not unfamiliar to Em. She'd grown up with them. She remembered, as a very young girl, hearing the same kind of nighttime sounds emanating from her mother's room. And she remembered as well knocking on her door, only to be greeted by her Grandmother and gently, but resolutely, carried back to her own room and returned to her canopied bed. She'd assumed it was just that she was the younger daughter, and that when she grew old enough, she, too, would get to share in the activities. But she'd been wrong.

The closest she ever got was late one night a few years later when she'd followed the hushed sounds to the attic and discovered something she would never forget. She remembered the night clearly, a warm autumn eve during her ninth year. She'd been awakened by something – not so much a noise but a feeling; the overwhelming sense that something significant was afoot in the inky dark cover of night. Inching along the upstairs hallway in her bare feet, her soft, white lawn nightdress whispering as it brushed along her legs and ankles, she followed the invisible fluttering strain along the upstairs hallway. Goose bumps erupted on her skin, and when she saw the pull-down stairs leading up to the attic extending down towards the hallway, and the gently glowing mist spilling out and floating down the steps, she knew that she had found its source.

Holding her breath, she'd lifted her gown, slowly walking along the sides of the steps, mindful not to emit a creak or a thud that might alert anyone to her presence. The unfamiliar sensation of the mist along her shins was warm and pleasant, with a clean, delicate scent. When she reached the top, her eyes adjusting to the soft light of candles and mist, she simply stared at the scene before her, stunned.

Her mother was seated in the old wooden rocking chair

across the room, Em's sister Grace, at age thirteen almost the same size as her mother, lying across her lap. Grace was crying softly, her body twitching and convulsing, her face covered in a damp sheen, her hair moist. Em's mother was wiping her brow with a cloth, whispering words of comfort along with what sounded like instructions; *it's okay dear, be stern and force them away.*

As she continued to watch Grace, she became aware of subtly visible colors – ephemeral pulses of energy – throughout the room, the most discernible a vibrant blue coming from what looked to be an old hardbound book laying spread open on a low table in front of the rocking chair. The obvious source of the mist, the book looked alive, throbbing, its hum reverberating even louder now.

Her attention jerked back to her sister who, as she watched, was overtaken by another violent convulsion. The glow surrounding her, its aura a greenish-brown, seemed to suddenly burst out, a strong blue light emerging from underneath it, pushing and straining against it. Her sister whimpered, her beautiful face contorted in apparent pain. Em gasped, and she quickly covered her mouth to contain the sound.

She was sure the only reason no one heard her was that her sister was by this time in the throes of some kind of fit, her moans and cries filling the small room. The blue and brownish lights were shooting about the attic, bouncing off the bare wood walls and scattering dust as they bombarded with the boxes and old furniture stacked along the floor. Her mother's arms and legs were wrapped around her sister from behind, tears streaming down her face as she was as battered by the violent tossing and turning as the daughter she was trying to protect. Just as Em was about to run towards her mother, Grace flexed, her body rigid and her back arched. The brownish light shot forth from her body, hovering above her a few moments before quickly moving across the room, and seemingly withdrawing, with a long subtle hiss, out the nearby window.

The room was immediately quiet. Grace lay quiet in her mother's arms, her face turned into her shoulder, her quiet sobs muffled against the soft fabric of her robe. *It's okay sweetie.* Her Mother smoothed Grace's hair, talking softly in reassuring tones. *It isn't always like that. Don't worry, we'll practice and make sure you are ready to handle it next time.*

Finally a board moaned, giving Em away, now that all was silent. Her mother's vivid blue eyes darted across the room, immediately registering her presence. Shifting and settling Grace into the rocker, she placed a hand on her cheek and whispered in her ear before heading towards Em.

She didn't say anything, but simply took Em's hand, walking alongside her, escorting her back to her room. Tucking her back within the flannel layers of her bedclothes, she placed a cool, rose-scented hand along Em's cheek, searching her eyes, a pensive look on her face. Em still remembered her exact words that night, words from her beautiful mother, whose love and acceptance she wanted more than anything. "Emily dear. I know what you saw doesn't make much sense. And as much as I'd like, I can't explain it to you. But please know that Grace is special in a different sort of way. And even though she is your big sister, she will always need you to watch out for her, care for her." She leaned close, pulling Em into her embrace, her cheeks moist. "You are my dear, dear girl," she whispered close to her ear. "I love you so much – you must always know that. What Grace is doing is very important. Promise me you'll watch out for her, and keep her secret?" Em had promised, willing to do anything for the red-haired angel that was her mother.

The next day dawned with two inches of snow covering the lawn. To spite her lack of sleep, Em had eagerly hurried through her morning preparations, impatient to finish breakfast and steal away some time alone with Grace as they walked to school. But Grace stayed in her room and didn't come down to breakfast. Sick, her father had said, as he read the morning paper and drank his first cup of coffee alongside Em at the large kitchen table.

She remembered the big school clock seemed to move in slow motion that day, her mind back home, replaying the scene in the attic last night. "Emily Carlson. Are you going to answer the question, or not? Ms. Carlson!" She could still hear Mr. Hunter's harried tone when he asked her to solve the multiplication problem neatly outlined in chalk on the board, his red cheeks a result of his growing irritation. She'd been reprimanded in French class as well. When the final bell rang, she practically leapt from her desk, donning her boots, mittens, coat and hat so fast that she didn't realize her mittens were on the wrong hands until she was halfway home.

Home. The familiar sight of it, a long lazy stream of smoke coming from the chimney, was extra sweet that day. She was so anxious to see her sister – assure herself she was fine, share what happened – that she raced in the house, dumping her belongings in a heap by the front door, and taking the steps to Grace's room two at a time. Not bothering to knock, she clutched the door knob in both hands, turning it. Locked. The door was locked. Knocking, she called Grace's name, waiting for a reply, sure that when she knew who it was, she'd come to let her in. Silence.

She stared at the dark oak door for some time, refusing to believe that no one was coming. She and Grace had always been close, the two sharing tea parties in the sunlit living room, playing checkers on the patio and swimming in the pond behind the house. Giggling late at night under the covers, sneaking cookie dough when their mother wasn't looking; hadn't they been close? But sometime about a year before the scene in the attic, Grace had become more reserved, distant.

Just last week she had rejected Em's invitation to go skating on the pond, informing her that she'd rather go to the movies with some girls from school.

Dragging her feet, Em had surveyed each room from its threshold, unsurprised when she'd found one after another empty, save for the usual familial touches: the collection of family portraits on the polished grand piano, a beautifully pieced velvet quilt stretched out on her mother's quilting rack, the family's whites hanging from the drying stand in the utility room and a sundry of cooking utensils piled near the kitchen sink. Pulling on her wool coat and walking out to the pond, she hunched down along its edge, watching its silent surface, the brisk bite of the cold air comfortably numbing as it stung her cheeks and tousled her hair about her cap. The sun was already starting to set, its last rays setting the icy crust on fire. Looking back towards the house, she saw the warm glow from her sister's window cutting through the gray, two figures moving about. The distance to the house seemed endless, permanent.

At dinner that night, it had just been Em, Grace and her mother. Em had sat in her usual chair, across from Grace, and eyed her sister as she went through the motions of eating the pot roast, vegetables and potatoes that her mother had made. Her normally beautiful sister had bruises beneath her eyes, her vibrant hair hastily pulled back into a long ponytail. Em remembered their conversation as if it were yesterday.

"How was school today, dear?" her mother asked.

"Good, I guess." Em replied.

"Any tests?"

She shook her head.

"Homework all done?"

She nodded.

Her mother had smiled, satisfied.

It seemed as good a time as any. "That was really something last night, wasn't it?"

Grace's vibrant blue eyes shot up, piercing through Em.

"Emily." Her mother commanded her attention in a quiet, crisp, forceful voice. "Perhaps I wasn't clear last night. We will not discuss this topic. Not ever. Do you understand?"

Gulping hard, chin quivering, Em had nodded, trying to hold the tears at bay that were threatening to pour forth at any moment. She gripped the edges of her wooden chair in both hands, trying to find an outlet for the onslaught of hurt and rejection that were rushing through her. Finally, she'd fled from the table, running to the solace of her bedroom, protecting herself by locking the hurt securely on the other side of her formidable oak door.

The coffee had grown cold.

Briskly rubbing her hands over her face, Em pulled herself back to the present. Despite everything – the secrets, the rejection – she loved her sister. When Oliver had died she hadn't hesitated for a moment, packing up her belongings and moving here to be with her. She'd made a promise, those many years ago, and it had been time to honor it. And she'd grown much closer to her sister in the last few years. Until Lucy. And Ella. With their arrival, the secret society had burst forth with renewed vigor. Em sighed, briskly patting Chloe's back and stretching up out of the chair, picking up her coffee cup and paper before heading back into the kitchen.

Turning on the sink, she vigorously washed out her coffee cup, staring absentmindedly out the window. Em didn't know why she was so impulsive about cleaning, or about cooking, or volunteering, or all the other things that she did to fill her life. Everyone always said they never saw her sit down and while she always joked about just having excess energy, deep down she knew it was partly because as long as she kept busy, always in motion, then she didn't have to think about things.

Like Henry, the love of her life that she lost at a young age to the Korean War. Or the fact that she'd never had a family. Or the fact that even her faithful dog appeared to be a member of the inner circle that she herself could not join.

She set some glasses in the sink, the mass clattering in protest at their abrupt treatment. Grasping the counter with both hands and holding on tight, she gripped hard to help vent the painful feelings that were welling up inside her. She hadn't dwelled on all these lifelong frustrations since the episode in the living room some weeks before – in fact, she'd been working very hard to avoid them. But last night, with the late night girl talk and all, it had turned her thoughts inward again to melancholy things. It was bad enough that she'd spent her whole childhood feeling like she was playing second fiddle to Grace, knowing there was a bond between she and their mother that excluded Em, but now that same bond existed between Grace and Lucy, again leaving Em out. Why?

Didn't she take care of them all? Didn't she, even now, have breakfast cooking and a load of laundry running in the wash? Hadn't she taken care of Grace more than once after one of her 'attacks,' never asking for explanations? And more and more lately, didn't she pretend not to notice all their nightly activities, not to mention whatever was up with Ella and that horse of hers? She was loyal to all of them, damn it, and what did she get in return?

The tears began to flow and Em began washing glasses with a vengeance, resorting, as always, to constant activity in her search for comfort. And the more intense the emotions, the more intense the activity required to vanquish them. Water splashed and glasses chimed as she relentlessly worked through the stack. Eventually, the inevitable happened, a wine glass stem broke, cutting her finger and drawing her attention to the cut quickly welling up with bright red blood.

"Damn," Em put her finger to her mouth as she fumbled

to find a napkin to wrap around it. She plopped down in the nearest kitchen chair, laying her head on her arm and sobbing in earnest. What was wrong with her? Was she unlovable? Couldn't they just finally let her into their inner circle? She tried so hard to please everyone, trying to be an essential part of their life by being indispensable, and still who did Lucy always turn to? Who did Grace turn to?

She sat in misery, the therapeutic effect of a good cry dulling the pain. She felt a soft pressure on her knee and, lifting her head to look, saw that Chloe had come in and was standing on her back legs, rising up to see what was wrong. As soon as Em's face was exposed, Chloe began licking her cheeks, seeming to understand that comforting was required.

Em reached down and scooped her up, setting her in her lap. She rubbed her face against her fur, finding great comfort in the unconditional love of her dear, furry friend. "I know you must look out for little Ella, but please always be mine too," said Em holding the little white dog tight, drawing comfort from her small form, so warm, so loving, so dear. She knew today would bring the same frustrations. She simply had to believe that, just like the characters in her books, she had a role in this life, that she touched lives in meaningful ways. She had to.

~27~

July is fading into August, and I swear the summer heat is affecting everybody's brains. Aunt Em, usually such a dear – the perfect blend of the pre-criminal Martha Stewart and Aunt Bea from Mayberry RFD – has been moody and quiet, definitely not her usual self. She's avoiding Grandma and I, preferring to spend all her time alone in the kitchen, embarking on some kind of baking marathon. Every day she heads over to The Drip to drop off excess loaves of bread and entire batches of cookies; rumor has it that the regular baker has so much extra time on his hands he is now a familiar sight on the Arkansas River, fishing each afternoon.

At this exact moment, I can see her from my upstairs window, taking a break from today's banana bread crusade and walking with Ella and Chloe in the meadow, collecting wildflowers and admiring all the small treasures that Ella finds. Hopefully the fresh air will do them both some good, considering Ella's been moody too, even for a four-year-old, since Cindy has gone on vacation, leaving her without a riding coach for two weeks. The last two mornings she has drug me out of bed, begging to go riding, only to become melancholy after the first half hour when she starts to miss Cindy. None of us are comfortable letting her practice jumps in her trainer's absence, and posting around the ring is evidently a little too tame for my spirited child.

And then there is Grandma.

Clearly something isn't right, but she refuses to talk about it, and while she continues to try and reassure me that she's okay, I'm unconvinced. I'm sure our late night talks aren't helping, but when else can we do it? She is even avoiding writing anything down, so, unlike with Margie, I have absolutely no clues.

I can hear the buzz of activity over on Harrison, everybody getting set up for today's Boom Day festivities. An annual highlight for locals and tourists alike, Boom Days is a weekend filled with activities centering around the towns roots: mining. There will be booths along the streets selling all kinds of crafts, live entertainment, mining skill competitions, a burro race – better known as the Get Your Ass Over the Pass race – and of course, the popular pancake breakfast. I find myself smiling, thinking that Aunt Em could probably oversee the entire breakfast by herself, if only given the chance.

The kitchen screen door swings closed as the trio return from the meadow.

"Mommy," Ella bellows through the house. " It's time to go! Moooommmm!" I hear my daughter running up the stairs, her sandals clapping harshly against the wood floors. She rounds the corner into my room, running and diving onto my bed. Scooting along on her back, she hangs her head over the side, looking at me upside down as I sit in my desk chair. "You look funny," she grins, her teeth a startling white compared to her tan face and sun-pink cheeks.

"Yeah, I know. That's what they all tell me."

She giggles, her dark ponytail hanging to the floor, the red streaks even more noticeable than usual given her time outdoors. Her legs are stuck up in the air, long and spindly, her toddler form changing into a more coltish look, everything lean and lanky.

"*C'mon Mom*. Let's go see Shasty," she says, rolling over on her belly, resting her chin on her hands. "Don't you want to see her before the race?"

Shasty is a pretty white burro who lives in a pasture bordering the meadow, a friend of Ella and Chloe's. Her owner, Edwin, a frequent customer at The Drip, has regaled Ella with stories of Shasty's past races, and encouraged her to come and cheer her, and her human partner Mary, on at this year's competition. I sigh loudly for effect, then rise slowly from my chair before heading towards the door. "Okay, okay. Let's go."

We weave through the active streets, making our four-block journey to the bank parking lot where burros and human racers are gathering. Fuzzy beasts of all colors and sizes are being carefully brushed and groomed by their owners, their human running partners dressed in bright sports attire, stretching and limbering up before the half-marathon. Ella's eyes dart amongst the crowd, looking for the familiar fuzzy white face of her buddy. Spotting her, she pulls her hand from mine, running towards her target, a wide grin on her face, "Shasty!"

The burro turns her head, her ears perking up at the sound of her name. Relaxed, she stands still while Edwin places her saddle on her back with its regulation supplies, including a pick, shovel and gold pan. All the entrants have to carry the same items, and a minimum thirty-five pound weight requirement is set to ensure equity amongst the teams. Looking at Ella from underneath Shasty's fuzzy belly as he tightens the girth around her middle, Edwin smiles, his crooked front teeth somehow endearing, everything about him silvery from the top of his head covered in short tufts of white hair to his bristly chin covered in grey whiskers. Dressed in a white t-shirt that looked like it started the day clean, and loose tan trousers, he looks staid and ordinary compared to the sea of vibrant lycra running wear surrounding him.

"Treats?" Ella asks Edwin, used to having the privilege of feeding Shasty treats of one kind or another during our visits.

Edwin shakes his head, "No treats for our girl today. She might get an upset stomach once she gets to running." Ella ponders this and, after silently conferring with Shasty, appears content to accept Edwin's explanation.

"Water?" Ella asks next.

Edwin shakes his head and patiently explains, "Nope. Too much water and it'll be sloshing around in her gut. Not good, I'm afraid." Ella again leans close to Shasty, who lowers her head close to the ground. The pair stand unmoving, Ella's hand on one side of the burro's long fuzzy nose, her cheek alongside the other. This time, instead of being placated, Ella shakes her head at Edwin, who looks down from his vantage point far above. "No. Shasty wants water. Please?"

Edwin, looking a bit bemused, rubs his chin as Ella nods vigorously, insisting Shasty needs some water. Evidently deciding that arguing is futile, he relents and agrees to a little bit of water, Ella looking vastly relieved at his decision. I help her fetch it in a shiny galvanized steel pail, and Ella watches with interest as Shasty drinks, the child's hands on her hips, like a small personal trainer. At about the halfway point, Ella takes the pail in both hands, dragging it out of reach of her fuzzy white friend, the water sloshing over the sides in all directions.

Squatting down, my daughter looks up at the burro, her eyebrows knitted together in deep concentration. Shasty meets her stare with gentle brown eyes, occasionally tossing her head, only to have Ella respond by appearing even more stern. I try not to laugh, wondering what in the world is passing between the two. Eventually Ella looks satisfied, a smile on her face, as she stands back up, lifting her arms for me to hoist her up next to Shasty's face. Cradling her furry nose in both hands, she gives her a big resounding kiss, followed by several pats on her forelock.

Edwin laughs, "Those two have a relationship I just don't understand."

I manufacture what I hope is a normal sounding laugh, even as I find myself looking around, hoping no curious on-lookers are giving us much attention.

Ella beams proudly at Edwin, "Shasty is really smart. Just like Tali. She says she has a rock in that hoof." Ella points to her back left foot. "She says if you get it out, she will win!"

Edwin scratches his shorn head, looking at me for some kind of explanation. Having none, I simply shrug. Hesitant-ly, he walks over and lifts the burro's hoof, searching within the grooves, his eyes widening when he indeed finds a small, round black rock. "Well, I'll be..." He offers the rock for me to examine, and I roll the thing around in my palm.

"Huh. Good guess?" I can feel my cheeks beginning to glow and wonder what the heck she said to that burro, wor-ried what unnatural feats she has encouraged Shasty to try in her race for victory. It could have just been your standard pep talk, but it's doubtful. I catch Ella's eye and she simply smiles, eyes wide. *Sigh.*

It's time for the racers to gather at the starting line, Shasty's partner Mary finally coming over and giving her four-legged partner some affectionate pats. Looking to be about my age, Mary is tanned and taut, her calf muscles flexing as she walks. I can't help but feel a twinge of envy at the way her brief run-ning attire manages to look custom-made for her perfect, buffed physique. Gathering up Shasty's rope lead, she guides her towards the starting line, which consists of a six-inch white mark drawn neatly across the entire width of Harrison Avenue.

Some of the other burros look anxious, their partners walking them in circles to keep them from fidgeting at the starting line. Others look tired, like they long to return home for a good healthy nap. But Shasty, well, she simply stands quietly at the starting line, her gaze directed forward, a calm look of purpose on her face.

The master of ceremonies describes the course over the loud speaker, explaining that the teams will be running fifteen miles, ending up right back at their starting point, where they must cross the white line together. Raising the obligatory pistol overhead, he lets off a single shot, the mob bolting forward, racers holding onto their leads for dear life as most of the Burros burst into a dead run down Harrison, heading North past The Drip. A few of the fuzzy racers, looking confused, head backwards, or sideways, or simply stand still, evidently assessing the situation, at least until swatted in the rear with their lead ropes. For those going pell-mell down the street, the women try in vain to quickly slow their burro's speed, since it's important to pace themselves, working together with their burro to balance their limits, ensuring they both can make it the whole way.

The racers turn up Seventh Street, and I know from experience they will quickly be on the dirt road that leads over Mosquito Pass, out of view until they return to the finish line. There are, however, trail-watchers who will radio in the news as runners and burros pass their post. So taking Ella's hand, I start towards The Drip.

"Hey, you two! Over here," Margie beckons us from the tall main counter where she is watching Noah make three lattes. "What do you want to drink? The usual?" I nod, and Noah adds a mocha and a hot chocolate to the order.

Margie, her face tan and healthy looking below her short crop of white hair, leans across the counter and points out Grandma and Aunt Em, sitting at a table near the window, a prime place to watch the festivities. "Your Grandma and Aunt are holding down the fort over there. Head on over and I'll bring your caffeine fix as soon as my baby boy finishes our order," she says, playfully squeezing Noah's whiskery cheek while he groans and rolls his eyes. Her lilting laugh follows us to the table, the sound evidence of her improving health.

Over the course of the next hour, we nurse our espresso drinks while we listen to the voice over the loud speaker announcing the racers' progress, Shasty and Mary always somewhere in the top three spots. Edwin, who has also made his way to The Drip, is grinning from ear-to-ear. "The little girl hasn't done this good in years," he declares proudly, "It's damn amazing!" Jack and Noah agree, slapping him on the back and congratulating him on his good fortune.

Turning towards us, Edwin points to Ella, his grin broadening even further. "And little Ella, well, she found a rock in Shasty's hoof, and told me if I removed it Shasty'd win the race! The two of em had a regular conversation-like, and the little Miss told her to win! What-do-ya think of them apples?" he says, slapping his knee and laughing to himself, evidently not noticing that the general hum of conversation had suddenly disappeared, and that a table of three ladies on our left and a couple seated across the way are suddenly staring at us, two of the ladies whispering to each other, and the third shaking her head. *Great.*

Margie leans across the table in Edwin's direction, "Well, she better have. I coached her on exactly what to say. If this works, I'm taking her to the track next week." She sits back, resting her elbows on the table and smiling as Edwin lifts his espresso towards her in acknowledgement.

Laughter and conversation pick back up everywhere except at our small table, where Grandma, Aunt Em and I simply gape at the proprietress, who coolly returns our stares as she takes a sip of her coffee.

"What? Can't I do something unpredictable for once?" She leans forward towards me, a conspiratorial look in her eyes. "Just giving them different gossip to chew on," she says. "I hear the ridiculous things they say – and the stuff is just plain stupid. That Teddy Hemmings needs a good smack alongside the head. Why squelch what little magic there is in the world by forcing a spirited child to conform to societal norms?" Turning towards Ella, she puts a hand alongside her sticky cheek, "Right, my sweetheart?"

Ella nods, smiling. "And I did tell Shasty to win. And she will, too," she predicts.

"That's right, sweetie! If we believe, anything can happen," Margie beams, proud of her young protégée. Did she possibly have a glimmer of Ella's bequest, or was this simply no more than it seemed?

I turn to find Grandma, her beautiful blue eyes open wide, a slight smile on her lips, staring off into the distance. With anyone else, I'd assume they were simply daydreaming, but with Grandma, I'm never quite sure. And then, as I watch, her eyes flutter and the color drains from her face. I suddenly realize there is a luminous look about her, one that I have seen only once before.

"Grandma?" I whisper, tentatively touching her arm.

"Hmm?"

"Are you okay?"

Her eyes still vacant, she answers, trancelike, "Mm-hmm."

Not sure of my options, I pinch her, hard.

"Hey!" She turns towards me abruptly, blinking rapidly, trying to focus.

We have the attention of the whole table now. "I was asking you," I speak loudly for the benefit of our spectators, "if we should take Ella to see the booths." Capturing her gaze, I look to my right, indicating the door.

She works to regain her composure. "Oh, yes, of course. Let's go."

"Yes!" shouts Ella, as she quickly squirms to extract herself from her chair, nearly tipping the thing over in her rush.

Holding the door open, I find myself squinting as we trade the comfortable filtered lighting of The Drip for the intense Colorado afternoon sun. Dozens of tourists fill the streets, women gazing into shop windows, grasping their handbags at the ready; men communing on benches, waiting while their wives look for that perfect souvenir; and children scampering in and around them, waving newly acquired toys and gobbling ice cream cones. In the distance I can hear an occasional bang, as the contestants in the mining competitions successfully demonstrate their drilling abilities in the Singlejack and Doublejack events.

Once we are a comfortable distance from the Drip, I ask, "So what was going on back there? Were you in a joining?"

"It was the most amazing thing," she takes my arm and leans in close, "it's the first joining I've had in public. And that's not all. It's the first joining I've had with… *me*."

I jerk to a stop. Looking around, I spot a nearby alcove and pull her and Ella in along with me "*What?*"

"I know, its sounds far out, but I just had a visit with myself."

Ella impatiently jerks up and down on my hand. 'Mooommm! Let's go to the finger painting booth! You promised!"

"Just a minute, sweetie. I'm talking to Grandma," I say in a cheerful voice. "This conversation isn't over," I whisper over my daughter's head, steering us back onto the street, into the flow of pedestrians.

Five minutes later Ella is settled at one of the tables, happily smearing blobs of orange and purple paint onto a shiny piece of butcher paper. Veering diagonally across the street,

I head back to the bench where Grandma is sitting and plop down beside her. "Okay. Now start from the beginning."

She turns towards me, her hand to her lips. "Well, I was simply sitting there, and I felt a presence floating nearby. I could tell it was friendly, so I figured it would leave, head back on its way. After all," she quickly adds "I've never had a spirit actually initiate contact when I was with others – or at least people from outside the trust. This was different, though." Her brow furrows as she struggles to find words, "Have you ever been sitting out in the summertime when there's no breeze, and the temperature is just right, and you feel like you are absolutely one with everything around you? Whoever it was felt like that… completely familiar, comfortable. So I let my guard down, and she drifted in."

"She?"

"Mmm-hmm. Once we were joined, I got this peculiar feeling… everything I saw in her thoughts and memories seemed familiar," she smiles. "That's when I realized, it was *me*."

"But… how can that be?"

She sighs, "I don't know really. But it was amazing. I had glimpses of experiences I'd forgotten, and others that, well…"

"Well, what?"

"Oh, nothing really. It was more a sensation than anything, not concrete images."

"What do you make of it?"

She squeezes my hand and sits back, closing her eyes and lifting her face to the sun. "Believe it or not, I have no guidebook for some things. You and I see glimpses of mystical things that others don't, so we, of all people, know there is so much more to the world than what we can comprehend with the five senses we know how to use. And I'm pretty sure we are just scratching the surface with those. Maybe it was me from another time, or… well, who knows? Maybe it's what people without my gift would call a premonition, or deja vu, but for me, the experience is recognizable as something more. I think a more interesting question is why now? If this is possible, why haven't I met myself before, so to speak?"

Running my hands over my face, I try to take in the weighty thoughts she has just shared. "Do you think she – you – was trying to tell you something? Maybe she wanted to warn you, or give you advice. I mean, if it's a premonition, then doesn't that imply some kind of foresight into the future?"

"Maybe," says Grandma, continuing to sit with her eyes closed, her silver hair falling gracefully back from her face.

"Is she – you – still around?"

Grandma lifts her head and scans the air. Her eyes grow round, "Yes, she is."

"Mommy, Mommy look! They're coming!" says Ella, who has left her painting post and is now pulling vigorously on my arm. She is a mess, splotches of every color imaginable on her face, arms and t-shirt. I look down the street in the direction of her gaze and see what look like small black dots coming towards us from down the highway. Slowly they begin to take form, two humans and two burros indeed heading our way. Ella is practically climbing on top of me, bobbing her head around to get a better look.

"It's Shasty and Mary! It's Shasty and Mary!" Ella is jumping up and down, one of her shoes making a slight sloshing sound I hadn't noticed before. "Look! Look!"

Shasty and Mary are neck-and-neck with another team, Rufus and Kim, now visible a short distance behind them. Ella is gripping my arm with both hands, her eyes glued on the racers. Grandma leans forward alongside me. "Maybe you should try and talk to her again – see what she is trying to tell you." I suggest, trying to be heard above the chaos.

"Yes, I guess I could find a quiet spot and see if I can find out anything more." Grandma replies. "I'll head over to that bench," she says, pointing to a spot about a block away, out of the current mob of spectators.

"Okay," I say, my words trailing off into nothing as the sound of hoofbeats grows louder, the crowd beginning to cheer. I nod instead, and she heads off down the block, Ella and I battling through the crowd for a closer view of the action. Shasty and Mary are now only a block away, the perspiration on both human and beast glistening in the sun. Shasty's white hair is rippling in wet ridges, shiny drops of sweat spraying off around her. Ears back, her head bobbing in a powerful rhythm, her hoofs pound the pavement, driving her forward. Suddenly, Ella leaps up from my side, running towards the finish line.

The burro is thundering towards her. Ella beckons to it, tummy sticking out beneath her color-splotched shirt, her smile expectant. Shasty responds, picking up her pace, galloping hard. Ella squeals. She stands, her feet atop the white line, arms raised high above her head, calling Shasty's name.

Holding onto the end of the taunt lead rope, Mary struggles to keep up. Shasty is running straight for Ella, her face determined, despite the fatigue beginning to show in her dark eyes, and the fact that her mouth is gaping open as she gulps in lungfuls of crisp, mountain air. When she is only a few feet away from the finish line, looking as if she will career straight into the small, dark-haired girl, the burro begins to skid to a stop, bringing Mary to her knees on the rough pavement as she pulls hard on the lead, and eliciting a gasp from the crowd. But the burro comes to a dead stop directly in front of the child, the two virtually nose-to-nose, one nose albeit a bit lower than the other.

Knees bloody, her face a pasty white except for the flush of her cheeks, Mary scrambles to pick herself up, walking around to the front of the burro. Tugging on the lead line, she commands in a hoarse voice, "Come *on*, you stubborn thing!

We have to *cross* the line! Come on!" Shasty, standing directly over the line, seems exhausted and content just as she is, her face held by two small hands, kisses of adoration being deposited on her wet muzzle. "Damn if you are going to put me through all that for second place." says Mary, swooping up a startled Ella and carrying her backwards a few paces. The burro follows, unhurriedly moseying towards Ella, completely clearing the finish line only seconds before the next pair of runners come barreling over it on the far side of the street.

Mary bends over, her hands on her thighs, breathing in raspy gasps of air. Blood trickles down her shins from the scrapes on her knees. Letting loose of the lead rope, she plops down on the pavement, laying back, her eyes closed, her breathing labored.

Ella rushes over, kneeling behind her head, her face directly over the exhausted runner. "You okay?" she asks.

Mary sighs and opens her eyes, her body jerking for a moment, the sight of a small face so near her own evidently startling her. Ella reaches down and pats her face, tucking back the stray strands of sweaty hair plastered to her cheeks and forehead.

Standing behind my daughter, I look down at Mary's limp form. "Water?" I ask.

She nods. I turn around to get it, and find Aunt Em right beside me, water in hand. As I offer her the cup, Mary struggles to sit up, her cheeks flushed and her eyes a bit glassy. She gulps down the contents, using the back of her hand to wipe away the excess. Then she sits in silence for a few minutes, her small guardian squatting in front of her, leaning her face on her palms, and gazing at her with an expression far too insightful for a toddler.

"I'm okay now." says Mary, winking at Ella.

"Your knees hurt?"

Noticing them for the first time, Mary grimaces as she

pulls a piece of gravel from the scrapped skin. "Yeah," she says. "It looks worse than it feels." Ella smiles, scooting over and turning around so that she can sit down between Mary's outstretched legs.

"Ella," I say, horrified that my daughter is imposing on a poor woman who has just run fifteen miles, half of it uphill no less.

"It's all right," she assures me. Leaning back on her hands, she lets her head fall back, her face lifted towards the sky. "As long as I can just sit here, I'm good."

"You gave us quite a scare there." Edwin is kneeling beside her, his brows still furrowed in concern.

"No worries," says Mary. "But man, what got into that little thing? She has never run that fast for that long before – never! It was like she was on a mission from God or something. I could barely keep up!"

Edwin grins, "You know, you two came in right under two hours. That's gotta be the record!"

Mary looks up at her racing partner, raising a hand and petting her face which is bent low and within reach. "No wonder I feel like this! It'll take my body a good week to recover."

Ella jumps up, turning around towards me, "*I* told her to win," she says, her eyes beginning to tear up, her little face crumpling. "*I* hurt Mary." Her head bowed, she begins to cry in earnest, so I scoop her up and make my way to the side of the street, a short distance away from the small group.

Running my hand soothingly over her small head, I talk quietly in her ear, "Ella honey, its okay. Shhhhh. You didn't do anything bad and Mary's fine. She's just tired, that's all." I rub her back as her tears run their course. "You know honey, this is what Grandma and I keep talking to you about," I remind her. "You must be careful with your special gift." Her arms tighten around my neck.

The next thing I know, another nose nudges in between

Ella and me, a fuzzy white one, a bit damp with sweat. Shasty snorts, bringing forth peals of laughter from Ella, and as is often the case with the young, all the sadness and worry of the last few minutes is forgotten, her attention captured by the joys of the here and now.

"Aunt Em, will you take Ella for a minute while I go get Grandma?" I set Ella back on the pavement and await Aunt Em's nod before heading off quickly through the crowd. The street is packed with well-wishers, yet as I spot her, her bearing regal, her gaze turned away, I sense she is in a world of her own, a place far from the chaos on Harrison Avenue. As I draw near, I see her hands gripped tightly in her lap, her knuckles white. And when she turns to me, the perplexed look in her eyes frightens me. "What is it?" I ask.

"It was a premonition, I suppose. One message was fairly clear, but the other was a bit hazy," she takes a deep breath. "The first message was that you must go away on a trip, something overseas, something important to your future. I sensed it was coming soon."

"And the other?" My stomach feels tight, my senses warning me the second message is ominous. "It wasn't something about your health, was it?"

"Actually, no," she says, "It was about loss... I sensed I would lose something... *someone*. I don't know exactly. It was as if I was being given cryptic instructions to help me locate someone. Let's see," her eyes clenched tight, she extracts the words from her memory, "A situation dire, heed the night's choir, seek a starless lass, and no ill will come to pass."

Always, the joinings are accompanied by light. Light seems to materialize as if from the friction of the atoms themselves, the collision of souls from this world with those from the next. I saw it first hand when Grandma joined with Grandpa that night out on her deck; a warm glow radiating from her skin, long wisps of it floating out around her. I saw it again in the restaurant yesterday, when Grandma experienced her premonition. And I see a similar glow now. Only this time, instead of coming from her, it seems to be hovering around her, like a halo.

"It's time," she says. I instantly grasp her meaning and a sudden shiver jolts through me, rapidly followed by a prickly rash of goosebumps. I grasp my arms, briskly rubbing the pimply flesh, the warmth of my hands familiar and calming. Geez. If I'm reacting like this just thinking about reading my Mother's writing, how will I manage to deal with the truth, if I find it?

We are ensconced in my bedroom tonight, the hour customarily late and the room alive with energy, a suspicion on my part that Grandma has confirmed. She is radiant tonight; connected with whatever – or whomever – is in the room. She is an elemental strand of the interwoven network of life force, her entire being illuminated from within, her skin and thick snowy hair alive with a luminous glow. I sense that perhaps my mother is nearby, but I don't ask, since knowing will only add additional tension to the situation, and I'll probably need all my reserves for whatever lies ahead.

"Your journal is under the bed." says Grandma. "I put it there earlier today while you were at the stables with Ella." She extends her pale blue silk-encased arm and points to the nearest corner of the bed.

I lift up the bed skirt to expose the leather bound book, its familiar cover reassuring. Setting it carefully on my lap, I run my hand across it, examining it for change, and, finding none, hug it to my chest for a moment, fortifying myself before uncovering its secrets.

Grandma pats the spot beside her, beckoning me to return to her side. "And you're sure this is a good idea?" I ask, pulling my robe over my legs and settling the book atop my thighs.

She nods. Reaching out and gently tucking a strand of hair behind my ear, she says softly "Its time, dear. I think you are ready, and its one of the major steps left in your discernment."

"How does it relate to my discernment?" I ask.

Her lips curve into a subtle smile. "I wasn't talking about the discernment related to understanding your gift. I am talking about the process of discovering *you*."

Ah. I see. Like a swimmer poised, intensely alert yet unmoving, above the water, I find myself holding tight, hesitant to dive head-first into the unknown. My ears register the ticking of the nearby clock, its endless procession doggedly nudging me along.

Well, here goes nothing. Weeks ago I picked the page to analyze; the edges frayed and the words smudged, it contains a carefully scripted note addressed to me, a note I've read hundreds of times before. I turn to the well worn page and read the familiar words, or maybe I just retrieve them from memory, the page in front of me really just confirming what I memorized long ago.

Lucy –

I am writing this to you a week before you are due to be born, worried that if something ever happens to me you will not know the true story of how you came into this world, and how much you are loved – and you are VERY loved!

You are about to be born Lucy May Harrison, and will be the adoptive daughter of Janet and Carl Harrison. I have selected them especially for you, and I trust that they will adore and take care of you, as all true parents should. I will, however, always be your birth mother, and plan to be a part of your life, in whatever way I can. My name is Kathleen May Stafford-Carlson, Katie for short. At the time I am writing this, I am a law student at Duke University, and am 23 years old. I am letting the Harrison's raise you through an open adoption arrangement, and will be able to see you on regular visits.

I know your first question has to be why I would let someone else raise you, especially if I care about you as I say I do. Well, it's because I want for you everything that a girl should have from a normal childhood: two loving parents, a solid home, a good education, and a solid foundation for life. I feel very badly that I can not provide this kind of life for you, but there are things about me that I can not easily write, that I will hopefully get to explain to you in person someday.

Lucy, I do love you, and hopefully you will come to know that long before you read this letter. You may not have been planned, but remember, sweet girl, that life's surprises often far outweigh our plans. I know you have a special purpose, and I know no other child is coming into this world more loved than you.

I will keep this journal for you, adding pages as the years go by, to give to you someday in the future. I want you to know where you come from, to know your birth family. I have given you roots, and hope the Harrisons will be able to give you wings.

One final note – and this is very important – there is something I must tell you one day, and you will recognize when I have. If I am not able to pass down this special information with you, you must seek out your Grandmother and she will know what to do. This is very important. And no matter what, never think you are anything but perfect.

Reading these words inevitably evokes strong emotions in me; exactly *which* emotions is always the surprise. Tonight I feel neither happy nor sad, but rather just anxious to read what is hidden underneath. I look at Grandma and take a deep breath, "Here goes nothing." She hugs me for reassurance and then places her hand on the small of my back, her familiar scent of lavender surrounding me as she leans close.

There will be no tricks tonight. I am going for full impact, refusing to miss one iota of information. I blur my vision, the page swimming below, the words floating up towards me, exposing the layer of feelings, thoughts and images tucked neatly underneath. It takes awhile, but finally I reach the second stage, the words gently dissolving, the small black dots slowly drifting out of the way, leaving nothing between me and my mother but a thin layer of air. I move in.

She is sitting at a desk, the well-worn wood a rich walnut color, with a smattering of books, papers and pencils strewn on top of it. The Tiffany desk lamp is lit, casting a warm glow across everything, the inky darkness across the room suggesting it is nighttime. I turn around and find myself face-to-face with my mother.

I have had images of her before, but not like this. She is only inches in front of my face and I can feel the warmth of her breath, smell the floral scent of her perfume. Her eyes are hidden, her gaze cast downward, only two half-moons of dark eyelashes visible above her cheeks, a faint spattering of reddish freckles traversing along her nose. There is a sheen on her forehead, a slight glistening that is picking up the light of the lamp and bathing her in a mystical hue. Bracing her hands on the armrests, the chair squeaks in protest as she shifts back, gradually reclining, legs extending out in front of her, her hand resting atop her enormous belly. Atop of *me*.

A small series of rolling waves push outward against the taunt rosebud fabric of her maternity top, her hand slowly following their progression. Mesmerized, I watch the display, remembering back to my pregnancy with Ella, reliving the sensation of life straining to explore its boundaries. From somewhere behind me, I am conscious of a bracing support, a hard contact, as if I am being steadied in some way. I hover in the moment, readying myself to explore further when... *she looks directly at me*! I freeze, arrested in my invisible flight. Her gaze is focused on me – not past me, or in my general direction, but directly at me, as if she is *seeing* me. But how can that be? This isn't the here and now! It's a memory, a snapshot of the past... isn't it?

"Lucy," she speaks to me, her voice soft.

My mother is talking to me. Katie Carlson is taking to *me*. In 3-D living color, right now, right here.

"Lucy, it's okay. I know why you are here," she leans slightly forward, a look of purpose about her. "Are you ready? There isn't much time." She looks steadily at me, one hand still resting atop her belly, the other reaching out, touching me. Actually *touching* me!

I nod my swimming head, trying to absorb it all.

She sits for a moment, her moist eyes never leaving mine, and then begins to speak, the sheer sound of her voice pure heaven. "How I became pregnant is really not the most important part. I loved your father – he was a wonderful man – but we really weren't at a permanent place yet, you know? I didn't tell him I was pregnant because, well, I guess I was scared. And the reason I was scared is the important part," she runs her tongue across her lips, pausing before continuing on.

"Ever since I was young, I have had dreams about you as a child. And all the dreams started out happy – you and I at the playground, you and I at the beach, you and I making cookies. But every time, the dream turned dark, and you and I would be in a car, and the car would crash, and both of us," she covers her belly protectively now, staring quietly into the darkness, "would die." I hold my breath, waiting for her to continue.

"So. I vowed never to have a daughter. But by now you know that our family genes have a mind of their own," she chuckles dryly, "The family line always manages to continue, so of course, in spite of my best efforts, you came into being."

She sifts in her chair, her girth obviously making her uncomfortable. "The discovery that I was pregnant was thrilling and terrifying at the same time. And the dreams intensified, becoming more and more real. I would work though different scenarios in my head, like having mother raise you. But then the dream only changed to all three of us dying in the car accident. I imagined having Aunt Emily raising you, and still the nightmares persisted." She looks up at me again, her eyes pleading with me. "Please understand. I have had many visions of people dying, and they have always come true," she gulps, turning away.

"So. I tried to imagine a scenario where someone else raised you – not a relative or a friend. And finally, the nightmares went away. They went away so long that I thought maybe it was all okay. But the minute I let my guard down, the minute I entertained thoughts of us together, the visions would become so intense that I would wake up screaming and sobbing, my sheets ripped into ribbons. And that's when I knew I had to find adoptive parents for you."

She is looking at me expectantly, yet I have no idea what to say. It's not like this makes everything okay instantly, like a quick kiss on a child's scrape or a sappy card with well-intentioned prose. And the sight of her, alive, or at least appearing that way, directly in front of me, is a moment surpassed only by that of my daughter being born.

I simply hover, taking it all in. Her face is so real, so soft, like I could reach out and touch it. I try, but somehow, even though she was able to touch me, I can't seem to manage it. Just like in all my other experiences, I can see, hear and smell everything around me, but I seem to exist only in essence, no skin or bones to use as I see fit. She seems to be able to decipher my thoughts though. Damn! She knows everything I am thinking.

She smiles sadly, in a kind of Mona Lisa way. Her look is one of knowing, one of control. I have neither.

"Lucy. I feel as overwhelmed as you do. I have been able to watch you all your life, but I've never been able to interact with you, like we are now. You are so dear to me," she raises her hand to touch me, and after brief contact, quickly withdraws. "I want to stay and talk, to touch you. But we can only stay this way a short time. It is taking a toll on you even now that you don't realize." She looks behind me and nods. "This isn't it yet, is it?" she says to something behind me. I turn, but see nothing.

"This form of communication is so slow, so primitive," she says frowning, her hands wrapped around the chair arms so tightly that her knuckles are white. "Lucy. I am so sorry about the Harrisons. I thought they were good people. I didn't sense anything but kindness at the time. I am sorry I was so wrong." Again she looks behind me, saying "Okay. I understand."

She smiles, her eyes soft. "I love you my girl. I must go"

No! I am shouting it in my head, willing her to stay with all my might. But still her image begins to dissolve, the warmth, the pleasant scent, all of it drawing quietly away. "No!" This time I hear the words actually come from my mouth, filling the room. A hand quickly covers my lower face, a voice in my ear urging me to be quiet. "Shhhh sweetie. Shhhh."

Grandma. She is holding me tightly from behind, her legs stretching out on either side of me. "Oh sweetie, let it out, just quietly," she says.

And then, with no warning, I am crying, tears streaming down my face, my hands balled into fists on top of the journal. My heart is racing and my limbs are heavy. I lay my head against Grandma's shoulder and rest. The room feels suddenly as inert as an old engraving.

"She wanted to stay longer, but she couldn't. I'm not even sure this isn't more than is good for you." Grandma slowly runs her hands up and down my arms, pausing every now and then to check my pulse. "I know it was only a short time, but do you understand more now?"

Do I understand? Will I ever understand this family I belong to, with all its mysteries and secrets? But I can appreciate protecting my child, and while I can't condone what she did as a daughter, there might be a possibility of comprehending it someday as a mother.

"I understand more now, but I don't know, emotionally, if I'll ever really feel okay about it." I stare at the stars visible out my window, wondering if my mother is amongst them. "Is she still here?" I ask.

Grandma shakes her head, "No. She is overwrought, just like you. She has gone for now."

A bitter thought passes through my head before I can control it, the resentment that she can now, just like she did then, choose to flit away at a moments notice, leaving me here to deal with things without her.

The pain is more intense now, the resentment stronger. I feel cheated; the familiar ache inside of me growing larger than ever before, slowly gnawing at my belly. I have seen her now, almost touched her. Now, more than ever, I know exactly what I have missed. And she has mentioned my father. Is he out there somewhere?

Discernment

~29~

An eclectic group, the three mailboxes owned by the residents of AL huddle close together near the end of the block. Fern and Gus's box is designed like a large trout, its silver-lipped mouth shut tight since their mail is usually forwarded to the main branch. Margie and Jack's is the more classic model, an oversized metal box with weathered red paint, mounted on an old wooden ski to add a bit of flair. Ours, thanks to Aunt Em, is a lovely white birdhouse-looking thing, with carefully painted blue wisteria winding its way up the sides. It's here amongst this silent trio that the first of Grandma's premonitions arrives quietly in a small, letter-sized envelope, with a smudged purple Boulder Colorado postmark.

Walking back to the house, I carefully slit open the packet, pulling out an official looking letter with the University of Colorado letterhead.

Ms. Lucy Harrison,
  We are writing to inquire one last time if you would like to accept our invitation to interview for the 2005 Art Abroad program. We have not received a response from you, and would like to encourage you to reconsider applying for this valuable learning opportunity. Your application has been approved by the faculty, and we believe you would be a wonderful

representative for our university. Enclosed is the confirmation form. All final acceptance letters must be postmarked no later than August 20th. Candidates will fly to New York City for interviews with the selection committee…

The Art Abroad program! I don't know why I applied – I never thought I'd be selected anyway. But for some reason, when my professor had encouraged me to fill out the application form last spring, I'd quickly scrawled out the necessary information and handed it in. I didn't think anything would come of it. But then I received a missive about two months ago, confirming I'd made it to the interview round. I hadn't really given it serious consideration. The thought of going to study art in some of the most famous museums in the world had been dizzying, surreal, but not something for someone like me, someone who had a child, a grandmother with a heart condition and a gift to master. After reading and re-reading the thing, I'd finally tucked the limp, creased piece of paper in my underwear drawer underneath a silk nightie.

Then the second letter had arrived, again asking if I'd be interested in interviewing for the program. That time I just shoved it underneath the first, having only barely skimmed its contents. Why entertain dreams and fantasies that belong to other people? I have responsibilities, people other than myself to consider. Sure, its great fodder for daydreaming and late night fantasies, but I know my place, my responsibilities.

And now another letter. I suppose this one will end up sliding unobtrusively underneath the other two. Throwing away the whole lot of them is probably the most practical measure, but somehow, I can't quite bring myself to do it. It's like holding onto a promise; a lottery ticket with a one-in-a-billion chance of paying off, or a Willy Wonka golden ticket.

Scuffing along on the dirt lane, I look around, the vistas surrounding Leadville no less breathtaking to me than the first day I arrived. This is what they call Fourteener land, the Sawatch range following along the highway to the north and south and boasting fifteen of the state's fifty-four towering, fourteen-thousand foot giants. And while it is nothing like the low-lying, lush land of my youth, a place dense with trees and mild temperatures, I have come to claim this rocky, majestic, harsh world as my own. Europe, with its rich history and picturesque cities – not to mention its bounty of original art by famous masters – would certainly be fabulous, but I can be content with this for now. I have to be. I tuck the paper back into its envelope, sliding it underneath a glossy ad for big screen televisions.

Walking around to the west side of the porch, I find Grandma arranging wild flowers in a vase. "Lucy," she says, without turning around, "did it come?"

I stop dead in my tracks. "Did what come?"

"You know," she turns, smiling, "something for you, something to do with travel."

"*How* did you know?"

"Honestly, I've just had a feeling all day. So what is it?"

Leaning against the railing next to her, I reluctantly hand her the letter, watching her face as she reads it.

"You received something on this already?"

"Yeah," I shrug, "a couple letters."

"But you never said anything... why?"

"Because it isn't for me. I belong *here*." Turning away, I look out across the meadow.

"Luce. Look at me. What do you think I want? For you to stick around, putting your life on hold? To watch out for me until I die?"

"Don't say that," my voice catches on a sob, "you aren't going to die!"

"Yes, I am. Deep down you *know* that." She puts a hand over mine, "Dearheart, it's okay."

"It's not okay! I need you," I say, lunging forward, embracing her.

"Oh sweetie."

"I've only gotten to spend a little time with you... it's not fair."

"No, it's not fair," she agrees, pulling back, brushing the hair away from my cheeks. "But at least we got to have this time together."

"It's not enough."

"It's more than I ever dreamed I had left," she says as she pulls me over to the nearby loveseat. "Luce, I really thought my time was nearing a while ago. And then you came into our lives, and, well, it was like I got a second wind, an extension on life. I've always thought it was so that I could help you through your discernment, get your feet firmly planted."

"But I'm not ready... I haven't completely mastered my gift, and I'm not through with my discernment, am I?"

She sighs, "No, but you're awfully close."

"No," I say softly, shaking my head. "Not yet."

"No, not yet," she agrees softly, wiping a tear from my eye and pasting on a bright smile. "So. Tell me about this program." She waits for me to answer as I sit fingering the envelope. "Hey," her shoulder gently collides with mine, "talk to me."

"Well... I'd be studying art in Paris, and then in Florence, for the year. You know, studying the art, reading up on the history, learning the various styles. And this program is a little harder to get into than some of the others because it's smaller, and you get to spend time with the museum curators, actually shadowing them and doing some hands-on work." I settle my chin on my hand, "I don't even know why I applied, really."

"Yes, you do."

"Okay, maybe I do, but I never thought I'd get it, and I never planned on actually going."

"You know what this is. It's the first premonition. Remember? You need to travel across the ocean."

"So I need to travel across the ocean. I can always do it later."

"No. That's the point of the premonition. You need to do it *now*."

Leaping up and pacing up and down the deck, my brain shatters into a million thoughts. "I can't do it now! It's crazy. There's you, and Aunt Em, and Scott and Ella. And let's not forget Margie – Something could still go wrong with her, and-"

"Lucy, sweetie, this is an incredible opportunity! It's the ultimate way to use your gift in normal society – as long as you're careful. Not only that, but we had a *sign*."

"But I still don't-"

"No more buts," she says, arms crossed, eyebrows raised. "Just promise me you'll fill out that acceptance letter and get it in the mail by morning. We'll just see what happens after that. Okay?" Her blue eyes pierce through me until I agree.

We stand in silence, the only sound the evening breeze and the trill of a nearby hummingbird. Already I can feel a slight change in the air, a difference in the light; the transition of seasons slowly beginning. "Look there," says Grandma. I raise my gaze towards the meadow and see Aunt Em, Ella and Margie coming towards us, the trio returning from their walk. Chloe scampers along beside them, never wandering far from Ella. "Do you see the sisters around them?"

Squinting my eyes, I search for something more, but see nothing. "No. Is that unusual?"

"Very. I noticed it first when Ella had the run-in with that dog on Harrison. And since then I've seen them more and more. It's curious…"

I turn and watch her, waiting for her to continue, but she does not. Idly leaning against one of the smooth, varnished logs that support the porch eaves, her beautiful face lit by the late afternoon sun, she looks utterly at ease; one would never guess she was peering out at a host of spiritual creatures. "Why are they here?" I ask.

"I don't know," she muses, as the others approach the porch.

"Mom! Guess what I found!" Ella is skipping towards me, one hand lightly fisted, held close to her breast. "A lady bug without spots! Not a single one!"

"Really? How special!" I lean down to inspect her find. She opens her fingers to expose the small insect, its pale red shell indeed devoid of spots. "She is very pretty."

Ella giggles, "It's a *boy*, Mommy! You are so silly!"

I sigh and shrug my shoulders. "Well, how was I supposed to know?"

"You *ask* him," my daughter informs me, "That's how I knew."

Ah.

"Tell them your news, Lucy," Grandma prompts.

"Ooh, news," Margie rubs her hand together. "I just love news. What is it?"

"Well, I've been invited to interview for an opportunity to participate in the Art Abroad program for a year." Saying it out loud almost makes it feel real, almost possible.

"Oh! That's fantastic Lucy!" Aunt Em embraces me, everything about her soft and warm.

"Wow," Margie says, dropping her voice low for effect. "How many final candidates are there?"

I release Aunt Em and hold the letter up for them to see. "I don't know, really."

Huddling close, they scan the note. "My, my, my. Isn't this something? I'll get a pen so you can fill this out right now," says Aunt Em, scurrying off towards the kitchen.

"This is, well, *huge!*" Margie grins from ear to ear. "I think we should celebrate."

"Shouldn't we wait until – or rather *if* – I get picked?" I ask.

"Heck no. Celebrate well, celebrate often. That's my motto." The gleam in her bright eyes brings a smile to my face. As if on cue, Aunt Em returns with not only a pen, but a bottle of champagne and an opener.

"Lucy, you start writing. Margie, you pop the cork on this thing. Grace, you and I are getting glasses."

"What do I do?" Ella asks, her face expectant.

"Well, Ms. Roo, you and Chloe run to the kitchen and grab us some cookies, of course," says Aunt Em, giving her Great Niece a high five as she runs past, the small terrier at her heels.

I sit down in the nearby oversized wicker chair, the plush cushions expelling a heavy sigh as my weight sinks down into their depths. The distractions surrounding me wreak havoc on my concentration, the words on the page dancing before me. Forcing myself to focus, I start to script the curling letter of my first name.

Pop!

"Ah!" I jerk backwards as a cork goes sailing past my nose. "Margie!"

She grimaces, "Sorry, Luce. Bad aim."

Tucking my hair behind my ears, I start again. I've barely managed to finish my last name when two white, furry paws land smack dab in the middle of the paper. Sigh. Petting the small dog, I turn and see my daughter, her hands full with a plate of treats, scurrying through the doorway.

"Mommy look! Aunt Em and me made chocolate chip and cherry cookies. Aren't they pretty?"

"Yes, they are," I say, grabbing one as she passes by.

"Coming through," Grandma glides past right behind her,

glasses in hand. A soft gurgling sound comes from behind me, a tall fluted glass with bubbling amber liquid appearing from over my shoulder.

"A toast," says Aunt Em, raising her glass high. "To good luck in New York."

"Good luck in New York," the gathering repeats, everyone taking a sip.

~30~

"Did you bring the dice?" asked Grace. "I can't remember if I told you Margie said we should bring our dice." She turned to watch Em's profile as her sister maneuvered the SUV down the dusky mountain road, the last rays of sunlight illuminating her. It was rare for the two of them to be out in the evening, especially as Lucy was in New York, and it involved a babysitter for Ella, but they'd been invited to the first Bunko night of the season, and so duty called.

Without turning, Em answered, "Yep. I put all six sets in my bag." Em glanced at her briefly. "I popped a couple of your pills in there too, just in case."

"Thanks Em." Grace tried to put as much appreciation as she could in those two words and was thrilled to be rewarded by a small smile. She missed the jovial Em, the sister that she'd seldom been privileged to see the last few months. But no matter what, Em cared for her with the precision and thoroughness of a professional nurse.

They pulled up in front of a neatly kept white and black Victorian house shadowed by two tall pines, the brightly lit porch light illuminating a small, oval brass plaque that read "The Tolls." Several cars were parked in the driveway already, and Grace sighed to herself, frustrated that she always seemed to be a bit tardy lately, no matter how hard she tired.

And she knew it was hard for Em too, the two of them having been raised to consider punctuality one of the basic tenets of civilized society, a show of respect for other's time. But now, well, everything took longer, the simple act of getting dressed sometimes taking upwards of an hour, and farewells with Ella another good fifteen minutes.

Em grabbed a brightly colored tote bag from the backseat, and they headed up the long, straight gravel drive, Grace readily accepting her sister's arm for support. "We haven't been called on as alternates for Bunko night in over a year. I believe I'm actually looking forward to this." said Grace.

Em laughed, "As long as Noah survives Ella, I believe we will have a good time." She leaned her head against her sister's shoulder and squeezed her arm.

When they reached the front porch, Em rang the bell, barely getting a chance to lift her finger from the small button before the door swung wide.

"Hell... o," said Teddy, surprised to see the latest arrivals.

A feeling of unease permeated through Grace. This was just what they didn't need! "Hello Teddy," she smiled, holding her head high, and walking ahead of Em into the bustling front room. "Where shall we put our wraps?" Grace slowly took off her elegant black wool coat, the nighttime mountain air chilly, even this time of year.

Teddy simply stood eying the garment as if it might jump out and bite her, hands hanging limply at her sides.

"Oh for the love of Pete," Em moaned, as she stepped forward and deftly swept up the coat. "I know where Helen puts them." And smiling brightly at Teddy, she headed off towards a nearby closet.

Grace turned back towards the room, women milling about everywhere, grazing lightly on the hors d'oeuvres and chatting in small groups. She headed into the fray, smoothing her black velvet pants and running a finger along the neckline of her black silk blouse to ensure her turquoise necklace was hanging straight.

"Grace! Em!" Margie was motioning to them from across the way. Even without her hand waggling high in the air, she was taller than most women in the room, and to Grace, she was like a lighthouse in a storm.

Shuffling through the mob, she met Margie halfway, and was immediately enveloped in a hug. Margie whispered in her ear, "I'm so glad to see you. If one more person eyes me with that *oh, you poor thing* look, and then whispers something quietly to her friend, I swear I'll scream."

Grace laughed, "Well, I'll probably be the next victim of pity, so maybe you're off the hook." She leaned close. "Plus there's Teddy, who is still gaping at me from over by the front door."

Margie turned to look, and sure enough, there was Theodora, her white hair primly piled high atop her head, standing on her tip-toes and craning her neck to follow their every move. Margie snorted, quickly covering her mouth with her hand, her eyes large with mirth.

"What's so funny?" asked Em, joining their group, offering a cup of punch to Grace.

"Well, we are just wondering how long it'll take for Teddy's eyeballs to completely pop out of their sockets," Margie explained in a stage whisper.

Em chuckled dryly. "So long as that's all she does."

Grace nodded her agreement, picking the decorative toothpick out of her drink, and extracting the maraschino cherry with her teeth. She eyed the crowd while Em and Margie talked, the living room practically throbbing with female conversation and laughter. Unlike Margie, she was fairly unfazed by the occasional curious look, and simply returned their glances with a graceful smile and a regal incline of her head. She figured if they actually knew, that at that exact moment, she could see several spirits hovering above their stylishly coifed little heads, that they'd probably all fall over from shock, and a perfectly good bunko evening would be ruined. And Em deserved it so.

"What are you smiling about? You look like the cat who caught the canary." Margie, ever insightful, was eying her, eyebrow raised. But before Grace had time to conjure up an answer, they were swept away by their hostess, herded to their starting positions. Grace found herself teamed with Em, the two seated across from each other at table three. The room grew still as everyone eyed their hostess, Helen, at the head table, a sense of alertness pervasive throughout the room as the players waited for her to ring the bell that would signal the start of the first round of play.

At the tingling of the small instrument, the game abruptly began. Em grinned as she shook the three dice and tossed them onto the table, getting a pair of twos on her first throw, the targeted number for the round. The volume in the room begin to rise to a fevered pitch as dice were frantically flung across the tables, each team trying to roll as many twos as they could before the sound of the bell ended the round.

It was a microcosm of adult insanity, a place to be giddy and child-like for a couple hours while someone babysat your child, or perhaps your husband took care of cleaning up the dinner dishes. A chance to spend time with the girls, to connect with friends and catch up on the town news while at the same time surrendering to your competitive tendencies and enjoying the fun of winning, and the inevitable harassment of the losers. But all in good fun.

Grace found herself moving about the room, staying at a table for a few rounds when her luck was low, moving up to new tables as she won, and occasionally crossing paths with Margie or Em. She cheered along with everyone else when Stacy yelled Bunko during round five, becoming the proud keeper of the traditional large white stuffed rabbit; a prize she would keep until the next Bunko was called, indicating that in a single throw, the player had rolled three of the selected number for that round.

They were well into the second game when Grace finally ended up at the same table as Teddy. Unlikely partners, they eyed each other cautiously across the expanse of the wooden folding table. The bell signaled the start of play, and Teddy rolled for fives. Rolling none, she passed the three dice to a member of the opposing team. After accumulating three points, the other team relinquished the dice to Grace. On her first toss, she managed to roll two fives.

She grinned, not yet noticing her partner's quiet frown. "Hey! Looky there! Maybe this is my lucky number." She shook the dice in her palms before tossing them out again, this time getting three fives.

Clasping her hands together, she smiled as her tablemates hollered out for her, "Bunko! Grace has a Bunko!" The collective cheered, as the prized white rabbit, affectionately known as Bunky, was passed hand-to-hand until it reached Grace's lap. The Bunko officially ended the round, and Grace and Teddy, as the winning team, won the right to move to the next table.

Per the rules, Grace and Teddy were now on opposing teams, each pairing up with one of the women already seated at their new table. Rigidly seated next to Grace, her lips puckered into a tight knot, Teddy looked anything but excited to have progressed due to Grace's good fortune. The bell tinkled, and play began.

"Com'n sixes," chimed out someone in the room.

The dice migrated around the table to Grace. She shook them hard before tossing them out onto the table, the small ivory blocks settling into place, three sixes showing. "Oh! Oh," gasped Grace, amazed to throw two Bunkos back-to-back. "Bunko!" she shouted, everyone rushing over to see the amazing feat; a double bunko a first for the Two-Mile-High Ladies Bunko club.

"It's amazing!"

"I've never seen it happen before!"

"Wowzers!"

Teddy stood up abruptly, her chair toppling over behind her. "*What* is wrong with all you people! Don't you see? Of *course* she's winning at Bunko. But it's not luck, its *witchcraft*," she hissed the last word, hands on her hips, her hard, small eyes riveted on Grace. "The whole lot of them! Witches!"

Grace stared, slack-jawed, over the top of Bunky's stuffed white ears. With a long exhalation of air, she relaxed her shoulders, the beautiful black silk of her blouse rustling softly. "Teddy, that's ridiculous, and you know it," she said.

"Oh, I don't think so. You and your granddaughter, talking about how to read people's minds through their art! All kinds of strange shaking spells and gibberish talk about melding with spirits." She looked around the room at her audience, gathering steam, "And then there is her great-granddaughter, the one who talks to animals and tries to get them to attack people." Her small bony finger pointed squarely at Grace, "She is a freak, I tell you. She could cast a spell on any of us here if she wanted to."

Grace sat silent, her eyes calmly returning Teddy's stare. She could hear nothing in the room except her accuser's angry breathing. She didn't avert her eyes, refusing to defend herself against such claims, and in no hurry to read the expressions around the room. Finally the silence was broken by footsteps behind her, someone shuffling towards her through the crowd. She followed Teddy's eyes and found her sister standing alongside her.

Eyes sparking, Em put her hand on Grace's shoulder, staring down Teddy all the while. "Theodora Hemmings. You should be *ashamed* of yourself. What the hell are you thinking? Attacking my sister, who has never done *anything* to you," she turned to scan the room, "to any of you! The very woman who helped out when Jean's daughter needed surgery, and when Helen's husband asked for donations for a new school gym!" She clenched her fists at her sides. "Is it because, Theodora Hemmings, she is more beautiful, graceful and kind than you could ever *hope* to be?"

In the glacial silence that ensued, she urged Grace from her chair, setting the white rabbit on the table and making a path for her through the crowd. Margie joined them, taking up the rear, the three of them forming a wedge, heading towards the door. As Margie retrieved their coats, Em turned back towards the group. "And by the way, what *if* my sister were magical?" She let the quiet question hang in the air. "Would it be such a bad thing to have a little magic in this world? I mean, isn't that why there is a little piece in each of us that still believes in fairy tales?" Her face flushed, she turned to put on her jacket.

Speechless, Grace took her coat and simply laid it over her arm. She looked across at Helen, their hostess, and saw an expression of confused curiosity on her face. Stacy, the young Bunko winner, simply appeared stunned. Willa, the local florist, had the roused expression of someone watching the Jerry Springer show, eager to catch every last bit of dirt. And Teddy, well, she looked self righteous, and unbending and... small.

A single clap reverberated across the room, directly on Grace's left, where Margie was standing. It was followed by another and another. Soon, a fourth and fifth woman took it up, and not long after, the majority of women in the room were smiling and clapping. Several women came forward, offering hugs and words of encouragement. Others hung back looking uncomfortable and out-of-place, unprepared to take sides in the matter. Teddy stayed as she was, standing alone alongside Bunky, resolutely maintaining her post.

Helen began earnestly pleading with Grace, Em and Margie to stay, but they all declined, stating politely that they were ready to call it a night. As she was leaving, Grace cast one last look across the room and froze, blinking her eye lids to make sure she was seeing clearly. As she watched, several bright orbs materialized abruptly in the air around Teddy and began hovering and twitching in a strangely aggressive way. With an odd, nettled expression on her face, Teddy suddenly jerked in place. She was in the process of scowling at Grace, when a particularly feisty orb gave her a quick poke in her backside, evoking a squeal as she leaped forward.

Looking on calmly, Grace shook her head, half to herself, and then turned and left. As she passed through the front door, she could swear something white and furry went sailing past her and hit the wall by the door with a soft thud.

"What's up with *her*?" asked Margie, walking quickly to catch up with them at the end of the drive. "She was still jerking all over and mumbling gibberish when I followed you out."

"Who knows. Once you get that crazy, it's bound to start having some kind of outward, physical effect," said Em, pulling herself up into the driver's seat, slipping the key into the ignition.

By now it was pitch black outside, an awning of a million tiny twinkling stars high overhead. Em chauffeured them competently through the Leadville streets, the tires eventually crunching along the familiar gravel surface of AL. After letting Margie off, and waiting until she was safely inside, Em steered the car into the familiar white garage at 15 ½, and turned off the ignition. But rather than opening her door, she simply sat as she was, the dim glow of the overhead garage light bathing everything in eerie shadows.

Grace waited, finding she was holding her breath. Em was

different, the look on her face unfamiliar. And the air felt funny, heavier somehow.

Her gaze directed straight ahead, Em began to speak in a faraway voice. "Grace. I've had enough. Really and truly enough." She took a deep breath and turned towards her sister. "I have been patient. I haven't complained. I've always known something, of course. But I thought someday, when I was older, when I was good enough, someone would let me in on it too. But no one ever has." She reached out and placed a finger on Grace's lips when her sister opened her mouth to speak, shaking her head. "No. Listen," she inhaled deeply and continued on, "Mother made me promise when I was just a girl that I would always look out for you. And I promised her that I would. And I'll always love you, because you are my beautiful, enchanting sister." She composed her features as a wave of emotion passed across her face. "But I swear," her voice was only a whisper now, "until you choose to tell me what the secret has been all these years, I will take care of you, but nothing more. Just leave me be." With that, she turned and slid down out of the car, her door closing with a finality that darkened Grace's heart.

~31~

Manhattan is a world far away from my quiet mountain meadow at home, my peaceful microcosm of nature suspended high in the mountains under a canopy of crystal blue sky. Here humanity is king, the city a bustling, living thing. All around me are fast-paced moving objects and people; lots and lots of people. Looking up, I catch only glimpses of the hazy, grey sky, the bulk of my view interrupted by skyscrapers. And yet I feel a vitality, an energy that calls to me, beckoning me to match the rhythm of the city. The feel of my feet clapping firmly against the pavement, I am swept along with this mass of strangers, all of us moving forward with a sense of purpose.

Walking along Fifth Avenue, I spot the Metropolitan Art Museum only about a block away. An imposing, weathered-grey building with stately columns and classic lines, it looks graceful and elegant, nestled along the edge of Central Park, a sea of green foliage framing it from behind. And while everything behind me – the busy, traffic-lined street and fast-paced city dwellers – seems to be moving at warp speed, the scene in front of me is one of quiet, enduring strength. Pausing at the base of the long rise of stairs, I soak up the aura of my surroundings. The delectable whiff of hot dogs grilling at a nearby vendor stand. A scattering of pigeons pecking along the steps, savoring bread crumbs and scraps left over from previous visitors. The colorful banners advertising the current exhibits billowing gently in the breeze, high above my head. Looking at my watch, I see that it is time, and will my feet up the steps.

"Welcome to the Met. Can I help you?" asks the efficient-looking woman behind the ticket counter.

"Yes. I am here to interview for the apprentice abroad program." Simply standing in the high-ceilinged entryway, I feel the whispers, the humming, the tumbling currents of vibrations reaching out to me from the art hidden beyond the near wall.

"Of course. And you are?"

"Lucy. Lucy Harrison."

"I'll let them know you are here." As she turns her attention towards her phone, I rummage through my shoulder bag, searching for my iPod.

"If you'd like to take a seat, Lindsay will be down for you shortly," she says, her voice slightly muffled by the time it passes through the microphones wedged in my ears. Sitting on a hard wooden bench, I thumb through a brochure advertising the bright, bold sculptures currently on display by a modern-day artist. I wonder what kinds of vibrations they will arouse – happy, dark, brooding. My palms begin to sweat, just thinking about what I am entertaining; the anticipation, the thrill of being surrounded by small, personal realms that only I can enter, magical worlds of other people's lives with their doors wide open, literally beckoning me in. But along with it all, there is the fear of going through one of those doors and not coming back, of being swallowed up into a place where I am nothing but a perpetual visitor. Eventually someone would pull me out, but the whole scene would probably jeopardize my spot in the program, and what about the knowledge and experiences that could possibly haunt me forever, dark, unspeakable things that no one should uncover?

"Are you ready, Miss Harrison?" I look up to find a dark-haired young woman, professionally dressed in a white blouse, navy blazer and tan trousers, looking down at me expectantly.

Following her through the first floor, I turn up the volume on my player, the voices coming towards me somewhat subdued. A beautiful Matisse painting, the colors rich, the fabric textures outlined in intricate detail, is on my right. Dragging my eyes along it as I pass by, I see the piece become a bit fragmented, the colors starting to lift off the canvas. Snapping my head forward, diverting my eyes, I look straight ahead to the steep staircase before us.

"You must be excited about this opportunity," says my escort, looking back towards me, a slightly appraising look in her eyes.

"Oh yes, absolutely. I can hardly imagine getting a chance like this." We turn down a hallway, our feet echoing along the well-polished floor of the long corridor. Looking down, I see my reflection, and wonder if I've dressed right for the part. Black leather strapped shoes, a patterned handkerchief skirt with an uneven hem, and a pretty, deep rose summer sweater. Margie has loaned me her lucky earrings, a pair of small black pearl studs, and Aunt Em insisted I wear her gold baby ring on a chain around my neck. Grandma had simply hugged me tight and assured me that a sister or two would no doubt be hovering close by to check in on the proceedings.

"Here we are. Go on in." We have stopped at the entrance to a long narrow room, a large, dark rectangular wooden table inhabiting the center of it.

"Do come in, young lady," says a deep voice from within. Slowly entering the room, I see a large, bearded man rising from his chair. My first impression is that of a grey, bespectacled teddy bear dressed in a suit and bow tie. As he draws near and extends his hand, I see merry, dancing blue eyes and a ready smile. "You must be Lucy. I am Dr. Calvin, head of the selection committee." he says, encasing my hand in a firm, warm grip. Turning slightly to his left, he continues, "and this is Dr. Gottlieb and Miss Randall, my colleagues.

"It's nice to meet you all." I say, smiling and expanding my gaze to include the tall, scholarly-looking man and petite, silver-haired woman already seated at the table. And as he lets go of my hand, I rush to remove my ear buds, stuffing them into my satchel. I hear the door close behind me with a firm click as my escort leaves the room.

"Please take a seat," he says, extending his hands towards a lone wooden chair set about halfway down the table. Setting my things on the floor beside me, the thud of my backpack reverberating through the room, I sit listening to the ticking of the antique wall clock, waiting for the questions to begin.

"So. Your professors speak highly of you, Miss Harrison," says the woman. "Considering you are only a Sophomore this year, that says quite a lot. Why do you suppose they picked *you*?"

Gripping my hands below the table, I consider her unexpected question. "Well, I suppose because I have done well in my studies and shown a great interest in art."

"Did you ask to be considered? I mean, beyond filling out the application." she probes further, her lips tight.

"No."

"Then I submit there is something more." She and the other committee members quietly watch me.

"Why would *you* pick you?" asks Dr. Gottlieb patiently, laying his glasses down on the large writing pad in front of him.

"I don't know..." I stumble, caught off guard, "because I love art. Very much." Scanning their faces as I talk, I see bland looks of indifference, of apathy. I take a deep breath, knowing that in this defining moment, I must dig deeper, expose to them some of my passion, while still hiding my bequest. And as I do, my heart beating wildly, I realize how desperately I want this. "Its more than that really," my voice grows with conviction, "I have something that can't be taught, something that I was born with. A passion, a connection with art that is unique." Building steam, I lean forward, my hands on the table, "Maybe it sounds hokey, but I *feel* art. Sure, at school I am learning about the great artists, about technique, how to recognize styles and one artist's work from another. But I can look at art and know more. I can feel its moods, its meaning, its *soul*." I look around and see sparks of real interest in their faces. "I didn't go out of my way to ask my professors to recommend me for the program because I felt there were others more deserving. But I *want* this opportunity… more than any of them."

"And what do you have to offer this program?" Dr. Calvin poses.

"One hundred percent commitment, hard work and possibly a fresh look on things. I know I can handle whatever you ask of me." I wait, as the committee sits quietly, their pencils scratching noisily against their writing pads. The woman, Miss Randall, watches me, a considering look on her face.

"I am curious Ms. Harrison. You say you can connect with art, understand its soul. Would you be willing to demonstrate?"

I swallow hard, "Yes. Of course."

She leans towards the others, conferring in a low voice. Dr. Calvin nods, and they straighten, directing their gazes back towards me. "We have a piece in the next room that we recently received for restoration," she says. "Would you be willing to take a look at it, tell us what you think?"

I nod.

We all rise from our chairs. I feel a moment of panic as I realize that bringing my iPod is not an option. My knees feel unsteady as I follow the others through a large doorway, the small, adjoining room filled with filtered sunlight, small particles of dust shimmering, suspended in the muted streamers of pale light. The source of the light, an immense paned window, the wooden blinds covering it tilted to half-mast, takes up almost the entire wall on our left. The expanse with the doorway cut into it is lined with dark wooden shelves and cupboards, as is the adjacent wall on our right. A worktable sits only a few paces in front of us, bottles, brushes and rags on one end, a picture, covered with a white cloth, in the middle. Dr Calvin walks towards it, removing its covering and propping the painting against the wall. "Well, Lucy, tell us what you see," he says.

I immediately pick up a wave of vibrations, the sound reminding me of the high-pitched tone I used to create by running my wet finger around the rim of a wine glass. The strange, haunting current leaves me feeling naked and vulnerable, without any protection against its force. Unable to heed common sense, I slowly walk towards it, finally stopping when I am but a foot away.

Seemingly similar to many works I've studied, the picture shows a celestial display, angels hovering over what appears to be Christ, with many other animals and objects woven in, symbols of themes and hidden meanings. The artist is listed as unknown, but as I look at the piece, I see clues to his identity everywhere. I haven't seen his paintings before, and I wonder why. Captivated by its spell and unable to retreat, I let go, seeing the usual haze before the real essence of the art is revealed. Layer upon layer of colors lift, the objects floating, discreetly separate, the symbolism easily identifiable. The drone from the piece is heavy and compelling, reaching inside me and whispering to me in a sweet, haunting voice, inviting me in. Then the floodgates open and a stream of facts flow towards me.

The artist is a man, young, in his late twenties. He has completed only practice attempts, small pieces, before undertaking this. Having studied with Da Vinci, he is a student with enormous potential, this piece intended to be his first for prominent public display. But something has gone wrong... the images are becoming darker, and a chill is engulfing me... the chant turns deep, harsh. He doesn't believe in Christ... many of the symbols hidden in the painting are demonic, a distinctly evil undercurrent lurking beneath the seemingly angelic scene. He is mocking it; Christianity, love, beauty. Twisted inside, he is a bastard son raised by an unholy priest, a priest who'd raped him, beat him... he'd killed the priest. I sense rather than feel bile rising up in my throat, the horror of the imagery shocking. I try to pull away, but the painting has me tightly in its grip, its magnetism stronger than any I've encountered before. Pure hatred, drawing me in, tearing away at me.

The struggle is intense, like drawing inward and trying to climb out of my own skin. I've never been able to pull out of something this strong without help, and now I feel like my life depends on it. The evil is wretched, a barrage of images, feelings and thoughts that I can't even comprehend or put names to, even if I wanted to. My contact with the outside world is gone – no sound, no Grandma – there is nothing left with which to anchor myself. I must draw from within, find something to combat the painting before it consumes me.

But my eyes are riveted, locked. I try to close them, but I can't. If I can just break the visual connection... suddenly, some kind of instinct sets in, and I focus all my strength in my hands, the weight of them like stones, willing them, raising them inch by inch until they cover my eyes. The whirling mass of images abruptly stop, but the eerie chill persists, interfering with my ability to breathe. I divert my eyes to the floor. Like a black ooze, the picture is still with me, gripping me. I quickly turn around, and for the first time, remember my audience of three.

"Are you okay, my dear?" Dr. Calvin is peering at me with a look of worry and concern as he takes my arm to steady me.

Nodding, I try to find my voice, "Yeah, I'm okay. It's just so... vivid. And dark." I scan their faces, their eyes wide. "Please don't worry about me, I'm fine. The painting is just so... evil."

"I'm surprised you would say that. After all, it's a very religious work," says Miss Randall, eyeing me with a quiet intensity.

"Perhaps. But I don't think the artist who painted it was religious at all. I think he was, in fact, mocking Christianity. I don't profess to be an expert, but I think the symbolism seems pagan, some of it even satanic. And it has some subtle differences from other works created around that same time period." Unable to shake my mood, I hug my arms around my self as a shiver runs through me, "I believe the artist was quite disturbed, quite dark."

"That's a very interesting analysis. And when would you say the work was done?" asks Dr. Gottlieb, his brow furrowed.

"Around 1500 I would guess," I say. "I see elements of Da Vinci's style, and would guess he either studied with him, or was copying his technique." And while the painting is behind me, out of sight, I can still see every brush stroke, still feel every foul whisper from it.

"Bravo. I'm with you, Miss Harrison." I look up and find a smile emerging on Miss Randall's lips as she speaks. "I also believe that there is much more to this picture than what others have taken the time to notice in all these years. Very perceptive work indeed."

"Shall we move back into the other room to conclude our

interview?" suggests Dr. Calvin, extending an arm and motioning us forward. "Nice job," he whispers as I pass by.

~

A half-hour later, the interview concluded, I make my way back towards the main entrance. Feeling confident, having managed to extract myself from the forceful piece upstairs without completely falling apart, I allow myself to pause briefly to admire some more of the Matisse paintings near the door. Squinting at the detail, I will the paint to stay on the canvas, to let me look at the piece like any other art lover.

"Hey." says a familiar voice behind me, two warm hands covering my eyes. I twirl around, thrilled to find Scott standing there, a leather duffel bag thrown over one shoulder.

'Hey yourself! What are you doing *here*?"

He gives me one of his lopsided grins, "Well, your Grandma thought you might be lonely, so she overnighted me a plane ticket and sent me out here to keep you company for the rest of the weekend. She thought we could take in New York."

I narrow my eyes, "Oh really."

"Yes really." He takes me in his arms. "The thought of you and me alone in a hotel room with room service… lets just say it took very little persuasion on her part."

I laugh, "Yeah, we haven't been alone together for almost two weeks." Pulling back, I scan his face, the feel of him igniting sparks throughout my body. I am struck by the emotions I see displayed on his face, some of it the raw passion I have come to recognize, but there is something else, something tender.

"So, how long does it take to get to the Ritz?" he says in a low voice that makes my knees weak. Taking his hand, we head towards the entrance and down the long collection of concrete steps. Walking with a purpose surpassing even that of the native New Yorkers, we head south along the fringe of Central Park, a heady mixture of sensations passing between us. "Just so you don't think I'm a total letch," he reaches in his pocket, pulling out two bright tickets, "I got us tickets to *The Producers*."

"Oh, well, good to know you came for more than just my body," I laugh.

"Absolutely." He tucks my arm tight against him, asking "How did the interview go?"

"Good, I think… oh, I don't know, it's hard to say," I moan. "There were some questions where I could see them positively responding – you know, nodding their heads, smiling, that sort of thing. But other times they were quiet, just writing stuff down."

He looks at me and smiles, squeezing my hand. "I'm sure you did great."

"I don't know. The waiting is going to be torture, that's for sure. Oh, and they had me analyze a painting – which I think was a spur of the moment idea on their part – and it seemed to go okay."

We sidestep a jogger. "Well hey, that seems good, doesn't it?" he says. "You're pretty insightful with that kind of thing – I'm sure you impressed them." He tugs playfully on my hand, "Is this as fast as you can walk?"

Rolling my eyes, I groan, "Yes, any faster and I'll lift off the sidewalk." We deftly maneuver ourselves around a group of teenagers. "You know, the more this whole thing – the art program I mean – becomes a real possibility, the more I find my heart set on going. Do you really think I have a chance? I mean, like they mentioned, I am one of the youngest, least experienced candidates."

He slows his pace a bit. "Luce, you are very talented. And smart. I am sure you have *more* than a decent chance."

"And what about leaving everyone? My family, you... Oh, I just don't know!"

"Luce," he turns towards me as we wait for the elevator, "it'll be okay. Things like this work themselves out somehow. Just take it one step at a time." We walk into the elevator, an elderly woman standing primly next to us.

"That's what Grandma said," I whisper. "But she really couldn't say how."

"Trust me?" he asks.

"Yes."

"Then don't worry about it. If you get this chance, we'll figure out a way to be together." The doors open and we step out onto our floor.

"Really?" I stop and turn to him, needing to see his face at this moment.

"I promise."

Taking his head in my hands, I throw caution to the wind and kiss him soundly. Unable to pull away, we continue slowly down the hallway, devouring each other's mouths as we go. I vaguely notice the woman in the elevator craning her neck out into the hallway, her eyes as wide as saucers. Fumbling with one hand through my purse, I manage to locate the flat, rectangular room key moments before we make it to the door. Pulling away from Scott, I swipe it in the lock, pushing open our final barrier to solitude.

Tossing his bag to the floor, he pulls me towards the center of the room, motioning for me to sit down in one of the plush chairs. Kneeling before me, he looks earnestly into my face, both of us catching our breath. "Luce. We've known each other for almost two months now. Because of this, well, *thing* between us, the physical side of our relationship has moved incredibly fast. But I want you to know that there is more to it than that for me. A whole lot more."

"Me too." I say, revealing in the warm look I find in his

eyes. I run my hand across his warm cheek and through his hair, loving the feel of him. "It's a lot more for me too."

He doesn't waste anymore time. Capturing my mouth with his, the two of us are instantly consumed in each other, conscious only of feelings and sensations, our reality limited to each other and the confines of this quaint room nestled in the heart of the bustling city surrounding us.

~32~

"I knew it! Ever since you met us at the airport today, I knew something was up," I say, plopping into the oversized floral chintz chair near Grandma's bed. "So she isn't talking to you at *all*?"

Grandma rubs her eyes, "Well, no, not really. I mean, she talks to me when she has to, but it's more like living with a caregiver than a sister." She plops her head back against the chair. "She's been this way all weekend, ever since Bunko on Friday."

"What happened at Bunko night?" I ask, noticing the brackets of new wrinkles on her face.

She groans, "What didn't happen? Basically Teddy accused me of being a witch in front of everyone, threw a stuffed, white rabbit at me, and Em defended me.

"Wh..aat?" I stutter.

"Oh, it's not really all that interesting. The really bad part is that Em is tired of being on the outside. You know, tired of not knowing what the big secret is."

Somehow I suspect the story of last week's Bunko night is *more* than a little bit interesting, but I stay on the topic at hand. "This is bad."

"Clearly." Grandma runs her hand across her forehead while she rapidly taps her left foot, obviously distraught over the whole situation. "The thing is…" she swallows hard, obviously close to tears, "the thing is, Em has been putting up with this her whole life. It was like Mother, Grandmother and I had a secret club that Em knew about, but could never join. So many nights, we would lock ourselves in Mother's bedroom, or go up to the attic in the middle of the night." She stops to dab her eyes with a tissue. "And then there'd be Em the next morning, getting up early to make pancakes, or picking daisies for the vase on the kitchen table. Except for one night at dinner that I'll never forget, she never said a word. Sometimes she looked pale and, well, miserable, but she never said anything." Grandma looks at me, tears streaming down her face. "She just loved us anyway."

"Just like she does now," I say quietly.

Grandma, head bowed, nods. "It's just that I owe her so much. I should have told her after Katie died. I mean, I didn't know about you yet, so I would have only been sacrificing my own gift." She looks up, her eyes full of pain. "But I couldn't do it. I wanted to be able to talk to Oliver and Katie. And, well, I didn't want to lose something like that, something that had been mine from birth." As tears stream down her face, she says "I should've done it then, but I chose not to."

"Grandma, its okay." I rise from my chair to embrace her. "You took an oath and were trained your whole life that the sacred trust must not be broken," I say, speaking softly against her shoulder. "I think you did the only thing you could."

"Did I?"

"I think so." I pull away and sit back down across from her. "Maybe there's another way around all this – without telling her outright, I mean."

Grandma shakes her head, "We can't lie to her. Whatever we do, it has to have dignity."

"If we tell her outright," I ask, "are we absolutely sure we will lose our gifts?" Truth is, I am constantly worrying about seeing Ella on the ten o'clock news, some hard-hitting news journalist standing out in front of our house with a cameraman in tow reporting "scientists want to study the young girl who just today orchestrated a bird choir in Leadville's city park." On the other hand, do I want to lose that gift which is the deepest, most powerful thing I own?

"Well, no. It's always been felt that it is a secret that must be closely guarded, so I don't really know what would happen." Grandma has picked up the journal and is looking through its pages for answers. "I've read every single entry in here a hundred times, but maybe I missed something." Positioning her reading glasses low on her nose, she runs her finger across the page as she reads. "I've never come across anyone who actually divulged the secret, simply reminders that the secret must remain within the trust, the trust being only firstborn daughters."

She carefully lifts a large section of pages to jump ahead. "And there are ideas on how to keep the journal safe, but I've never worried much about that." She looks at me over the rims of her spectacles. "Em isn't all that nosey, and I've always kept it in a cardboard box labeled "Letters from Oliver.""

An idea begins to formulate in my head. "I have a thought," I say. Grandma gives me her full attention. "What if we don't *tell* her, but she simply figures it out!"

"And how might she do that?" asks Grandma, skeptically.

"What if someone were to leave something out, something like a book perhaps, that might lead her to a logical conclusion."

Grandma looks thoughtful. "I don't know. I mean, the secret would still be out, and does it matter how it happens?"

"I don't know," I groan. "Honestly Grandma, I don't want to wreck the whole trust thing either, but I can't help but wonder if Aunt Em is more important. And frankly, I find it hard to imagine that no one – not a sister, or friend, or husband

– has ever run across this book before in all this time. Don't you?"

Grandma appears to be mulling my question over in her head. "Well, it does seem plausible that *someone* may have seen it at sometime or another. I just don't know."

I realize, as I watch her, that the stakes are higher for Grandma than they are for Ella and I. After all, her gift allows her to communicate with her dead husband and daughter. To lose that would be devastating. Perhaps we shouldn't take the risk. Maybe we can smooth it over another way.

"Grandma, the more I think about this, the more I think I've changed my mind. I don't think you should risk this. I mean, there are Grandpa and Mom to consider…"

Grandma wipes a tear from her eye, "yes, it's truly a family decision, isn't it. But you know, I am not going to be here forever." She puts a hand up to stop me from protesting. "You know it is true dear, and its okay – and I would hate for Em to be left thinking she wasn't special, wasn't a real part of the family. I owe her so much… I *need* to set things right"

Grandma carefully places that large book on the chair and moves to the bed, lying down. I scoot across the bed to lie beside her. Reaching for her hand, I wonder how many more nights we have like this, the two of us lying here at midnight, sharing secrets in the dim glow from the side lamp, our silk robes floating out on the bedcovers around us, my pale yellow one overlapping with the edges of her baby blue version. "I don't know, Grandma. Maybe we should sleep on it," I suggest.

"Ha," she says, turning her eyes towards me. "I've had to try and sleep on it all weekend, and its making me nuts. Em isn't talking to me, and I just can't bear it. No, we must decide tonight." We gaze at the ceiling, perhaps for divine guidance.

My thoughts oscillate, so much to think about lately. "Is Mom around?" I ask.

"Mmm, no. There are a couple sisters of the trust hovering overhead," she points towards the middle of the ceiling, "but that's about it. If I had enough energy for a joining, we'd ask their opinion."

I scrunch my eyes, trying to see something other than white paint and plaster, but fail. Then a thought occurs to me. 'Grandma, did you ever tell Grandpa about your gift? No, right?" I answer my own question, building steam. "But I bet he had his suspicions, didn't he?"

Grace thinks about it, nodding, as it is all true. "Yes, Oliver always did wonder about my *lollygagging*, as he called it. I remember him catching me in a joining once, the whole thing very upsetting as it was a young man who had died only hours before in a climbing accident. I had a devil of a time explaining *that* one. I think I blamed my mood on a book I was reading at the time – I remember he took it from the bedroom and immediately gave it to Goodwill." She smiles, "he was pretty nervous when he saw me reading after that, always trying to make sure I was sticking to light, romantic themes."

I pressed forward, "and now that he has passed on, he definitely knows, right?"

"Yes," Grandma looks at me curiously, "he does."

"Well, so Grandpa knows. So what if he is in one world and Aunt Em is in another. Other people know eventually, don't they? And we are dealing with the mystical and unseen anyway, so perhaps that diminishes the importance of the distinction between this world and the next." My thoughts are swirling, the black and white of absolutes dimming and a light emerging gradually at the end of the tunnel.

"Yes, I suppose you are right." Grandma pushes herself up on the bed until her back is resting against the headboard. "With all that I've experienced, I would count myself an authority on the topic of life continuing after death, and the next life is no less real, perhaps more so, than this one," she says.

I nod, sitting up beside her. We certainly know more about the unseen than most folks, and what we do know might just be the tip of the iceberg. "We don't even know if the rules are real, or who made them," I say. "Plus, I *still* can't imagine a secret like this could have been kept completely within the trust for this long. I mean, think about it. A jeweled book staying unseen by others since before the birth of Christ?"

"It is hard to imagine, I admit," she says, her hands spread. "But I *do* believe it is possible. The jewels on the front protect it, help keep it hidden. Plus, only someone from the sisterhood can breathe into the box, make the Diurnus visible. Without that, it just looks like an empty box."

"True," I say hesitantly, seeing possible flaws in my argument, "but they had to notice the odd behaviors, like your joinings, or Ella talking to bugs – things like that."

"You know, as far as some of that goes," she looks at me, her eyes twinkling, "I think most of it gets chalked up to normal, run-of-the-mill weird human behavior. I mean honestly, there are some pretty odd folks running around."

I sigh, "Fine, so you may be right. Maybe no one here on earth has figured the whole thing out, but certainly those in the spiritual world know."

"You're right, of course. They absolutely do."

"Well, is that so different? I don't know," I readjust on the bed, working the kinks out of my limbs, "maybe I'm reaching too far trying to find a way, but its Aunt Em…"

"It is Em," Grandma says quietly. "And that's the heart of the matter. I owe her everything… I certainly owe her this." She sits quietly, folding her tissue. "So what it comes down to is this: are we willing to take the risk? The risk of losing our gifts, and future generations losing theirs? It's that, weighed against Aunt Em, and her finally understanding what has been going on all these years." She offers me her hand, "I'm in."

Swallowing hard, I think about what my life will be like if I lose my gift, moving forward in the world of art with only what I can learn in books. I think of Ella, losing her ability to communicate with Chloe, Tali. And I picture the withdrawn, disappointed look that I have seen so much lately on Aunt Em's face, even as she bustles around the house doing the bulk of the chores and spends her days with Ella, patiently showering her with love as they bake, take walks in the meadow, play dolls. It dawns on me that if Ella were given a choice in the matter, she would not hesitate. I have my reservations, but know what I must do. I grasp Grandma's hand firmly in my own. "I'm in too."

"Then it is done. Tomorrow we will leave the Diurnus out where Em will find it."

~33~

Em didn't put much stock in horoscopes, but found herself reading them in the daily Rocky Mountain News anyway, just for fun. You never knew what kind of crazy thing they'd have to say. And, if nothing else, it was constantly entertaining. Usually they spoke in abstract generalities, but today's was different: "You will receive life altering news today" the astrologer declared.

Making her oh-what-nonsense chuckle to herself, she gathered up the paper and stored it in the recycling bin. Not long after, her morning quiet time was shattered by a four-year-old demanding cinnamon toast, and then the other women of the house wandered down to the kitchen for their first round of coffee. Lucy's warm embrace, a bit stronger and longer than usual, was especially welcome, given the aloofness that seemed to have crept into the atmosphere lately. Leaving them to their breakfast, Chloe opting to stay behind too, sitting beneath Ella's chair waiting for tidbits of sugary, buttery bread, Em proceeded upstairs to gather the first load of laundry for the day.

She always found something comforting in doing the laundry, the steady hum of the machines and the warm smell of fabric softener almost therapeutic. Plus sorting through the clothes they had worn during the prior week sparked fond memories, like getting to replay the events over again in her head. And once the bins had been emptied, and everything hung neatly back in the closets, they were prepared for whatever new adventures lie ahead.

She started in Grace's bedroom, heading through the large airy chamber towards the oversized closet where Grace's dirty clothes would be waiting in her new-fangled two-sided, rolling hamper. Grabbing the handle to roll the contraption towards the laundry chute, she noticed something sitting on the nearby chair. Bending closer, she reached out a hand to inspect the large, square object, almost immediately jerking it back when she felt a strange, warm pulsating sensation, as if the object were in fact quite alive.

More cautiously this time, she leaned down, studying the thing from a couple feet away. It appeared to be some kind of book, bound with leather straps. At least three inches thick, the book looked bulky and heavy, the rough textured paper worn and yellowed on the edges, its entire appearance suggesting that it was an antique of some kind. Had Lucy bought this for Ella's school play?

Sitting next to it, Em slowly extended a finger, resting it on one of the pretty gems – surely paste – that studded its surface. She experienced the same quivering sensation as before. But instead of backing away, she simply remained as she was, slowly extending contact fingertip by fingertip, then lightly touching down her palm, familiarizing herself with the strange, near cardiac throbbing. Supporting it with both hands, she carefully lifted it onto her lap, the feel of it strange, the vibration penetrating straight through her navy cotton slacks to her thighs.

While it boasted a beautiful brass lock, it had been left unsecured, the weighty cover crackling slightly as she opened the volume, a low humming sound escaping from its depths. Hands shaking, Em continued to gradually open the cover until the book was fully exposed. With only the dim glow from the closet light overhead and no reading glasses, she squinted a bit, trying to bring the first page into focus.

The inside cover contained a few short lines, the text looking to be Latin. Em's grasp of the language a bit rusty, she was only able to pick out a few words, just enough to understand that the numbered lines were a list of three rules, or laws, one of them having something to do with selfish gain. At the bottom was one sentence that appeared to be a reminder to never do something... confess? Reveal? She wasn't sure and moved on to the first actual parchment page, which contained a list of names, each having a date next to it, the first one marked 150BC. Startled by the date, she paused a moment before scanning the rest of the page, intrigued by the unusual, and as of yet, unfamiliar names. A history account of some kind, she wondered? Surely this was a reproduction of some kind. Turning the page, she continued down the entries, her heart learching when she read the name of her Great Grandmother, her Grandmother, her Mother and, most surprisingly, Grace, Katie, Lucy and Ella. But where was she? And why had she never heard of this book if it somehow contained a family genealogy?

Turning the page again, Em found smudges of color, each with a name next to it. The tints gradually deepening in tone, it looked like a color palette for lipstick, or makeup of some kind. At the bottom there was a star, its size and shape reminding her of the odd birthmark she'd seen on Ella, the mark positioned precisely in the middle of her chest. Her hand shot to her mouth. Grace had one too! She was sure of it! She hadn't seen it since they were children, but it was hard to forget such a distinct imprint. Her curiosity growing, she excitedly turned the heavy, crackling page. She found a handwritten account of something, the script and language not familiar to her. The top of the page was blazoned with what seemed to be a name and a year, and a quick check backwards confirmed the information matched the first entry in the list at the front of the book. Turning a large section of pages, she jumped ahead, getting to a portion that, while written in old English, was in a tongue she could understand.

From what she could decipher, it was an account of a woman's life, or more precisely, certain aspects of it that related to what she referred to as her "bequest." It was all still terribly cryptic, but she had now deduced that there was a page or so for each woman listed in the front. She turned to the back, seeking out information about the women in her immediate family.

Finding a page with her mother's name at the top, the flowing script familiar, she folded her arms across herself to stop the shaking in her limbs and looked away, struggling for self control. What was going on? Why was this large book suddenly sitting in the closet as if a part of the ancient world had fallen from the sky? And why was she getting hot and cold flashes, the thing practically primeval with its constant throbbing? And yet, despite its apparent age, it contained information about people in her immediate family. Everybody except, of course, herself. But despite the raging torrent of conflicting emotions swelling through her, Em took a deep breath, turned her eyes back to the familiar script, and began to read.

My name is Elizabeth Lea Heck, born 1912, first born daughter of Iris and Forrest Heck. My gift is that of sustenance telesthesia, or the ability to understand every element in food, in addition to understanding what utensils and processes were used in preparing it.

My mother first noticed my gift when I was a toddler, and I refused to eat a bowl of my favorite porridge at breakfast one morning, tossing the bowl off my highchair. The rest of the family contracted food poisoning by mid-morning, and it was then she suspected that perhaps I had sensed something irregular about the food."

The entry went on describing how her mother had been able to break down any food dish into its most basic ingredients and how she had used this gift in different situations, such as when she had detected salmonella in the fried chicken at the church picnic and had buried the lot of it under a bush, or how she'd deconstructed the ingredients for a French chef's famous chocolate chip cookies, and won herself a blue ribbon in a magazine contest. Some of the experiences were funny, but others were harsh, like the account of the time she'd been suspended from school after yelling in the cafeteria that there were maggot eggs in the bread pudding. And while many of the stories were surreal, the passages also rang of truth, Em recalling many times in her life when she had been amazed by her mother's cooking, her creations a medley of tastes that seemed somehow reflective of her emotions and moods. And the birthday cakes she had made for Em! She remembered back, an unbidden smile curving her lips. Her favorite had been a mermaid confection that she'd requested when she'd turned ten. The beautiful red-haired maiden, complete with her shiny emerald tail, had somehow even tasted a bit like the sea, as if Em had sat out on a dock with seagulls flying overhead while she'd eaten it. "I made it just for you, Emmy. It has all my love for you baked right in," her mother had told her. Em had never thought she'd meant it literally – until now.

Directing her attention back to the book, Em slowly turned the page, knowing she would find her sister's name next. Grace Lea Carlson. She gently ran her hand over the page, over the scrolling lines of her sister's script. She could see an evolution in the handwriting, the first of it childlike, with large loops and wobbly letters, while that near the end was a more confident script, the letters even and neat. Breathing in deeply, she began to read.

My name is Grace Lea Carlson, born 1933, first born daughter of Elizabeth and Howard Carlson. My gift is that of Inner-body Communication. I have the ability to communicate with spirits via something called a joining, or a melding of selves that creates a two-way parallel dialogue within me, without the need for words. This gift first manifested itself as an ability to predict the weather, and to see light, in the forms of beams and orbs, in the sky (I later discovered this energy was spirits). By the time I was thirteen, I found that spirits were able to enter my body and communicate with me. Unlike a back and forth conversation, this is more like a free-flow current of information passing both ways simultaneously. All of the spirit's thoughts, memories and feelings are visible to me.

Em scrunched her eyes tight and sat back, her mind replaying events in her head. Grace in the attic, convulsing. Grace sitting in her bedroom window seat, staring out across the pond, a faraway look on her face. Grace coming down to breakfast, pale with dark rings under her eyes. She could remember running up to her sister on a hot summer day, Grace sitting on the swing that hung from the big oak tree, idly pushing herself back and forth. Em had been in her new red swimsuit, a fluffy white towel under her arm.

Grace, come out and swim in the pond with me!

No, not today Em. I'm kind of tired.

Cmon! How tired can you be? You're acting like an old Grandma!

Em, you just don't understand! You're such a baby!

Grace had stomped off, leaving the swing twisting wildly, and Em standing alone.

So what did she see in these beams of light? Did they look like angels floating about? Did they shoot through the sky, or simply hover aloft with the clouds? And who were these people who traveled to see her sister? Why did they come?

She started reading again.

Some of the spirits that visit me are friendly, very lively sorts that simply seem lonely. They all seem to be traveling somewhere, usually to check in one loved ones still here on earth. Others are wicked and evil. These ones always seem to have recently passed over, and are on their way to hell. These are the joinings I hate, and try hard to avoid, but sometimes I can not.

All joinings take a toll on me, leaving me feeling weak, and causing my heart to palpitate. I know it will eventually be the end of me, and yet I still am so very happy when my husband, Oliver, or daughter, Katie, come to visit. Other members of my family visit as well, as do the sisters of the Sodalicium. So far, all joinings have happened only when I've been by myself, or with those of the trust.

All in all, my gift has been a blessing. But having to keep it a secret from my husband, and especially from my sister Emily, has been very hard. It doesn't feel right that I may be helping those in the spirit world, helping myself, but hurting those around me. But as I am bound not to speak of the trust while I am here in this life, I look forward to the day when all is revealed in the next.

Em blew out a long breath. Grace had added the last paragraph recently, possibly just in time for her to see it today. She was apologetic, but she couldn't share that she was having regular conversations with Oliver and Katie, and probably with Mother and Father? *She's* talking to dead relatives while

I am off making breakfast and taking out the trash? Is this for real?

But even as she asked herself that question, Em knew it was. *This* was the big secret, the thing they'd hidden from her all these years. They had stars on their chest. She didn't. They had special 'bequests' as they called them. She didn't. Why not? Lucy's name was in the book, and so was Ella's. Why not hers?

Turning the page, she felt tears well up in her eyes as she read Katie's entry, only a small portion written in her own hand, the remainder written by Grace and Lucy.

My name is Kathleen May Carlson-Stafford, born 1962, first born daughter of Grace Carlson-Stafford and Oliver Stafford. My gift is that of truth. I have the ability to know, when anyone speaks, if they are telling the truth or a falsehood. Also, as I am a cerise star, I can foresee the deaths of those around me, and I am told that I will see my own.

Em felt the blood drain from her face. She could remember it as clearly as if it were yesterday; Katie running up to Grace in tears, tugging on her sleeve and saying that Grandpa was going to stop breathing during the night, that his heart would give up. Grace had scooped her up and taken her inside, trying to sooth the child. And while she hadn't thought it odd at the time, Em realized she never tried to reassure the child by telling her it was just a nightmare, or that everything would be okay. No, tears had filled Grace's eyes as well, and she'd watched over Father like a hawk for the rest of the day. And he did die, of a heart attack, that very night.

And what was a cerise star? Turning back to the colored smudges, Em tried to make sense of it. Did the colors stand for different kinds of gifts? The pages had smudges too. What did it mean?

Heavy. Em suddenly felt like her limbs were weighed down with bowling balls and her head was filled with rocks. Where was she when all this was going on? Of course she'd been there physically – living in the same house, eating the same food, singing along with everyone else at the piano on Christmas Eve – but she existed in a different realm, lived a different life than everybody else. They'd had whole other experiences, secrets – like a private club. And it wasn't fair. Damn it, it just *wasn't fair*!

When the tears came, they came with a vengeance. Em covered her face in her hands, her body convulsing from the force of her sobs. Why them and not her? Why couldn't they tell her? Did they think she was a fool? She grabbed a flow-ered towel from the laundry basket and used it to wipe her face, to muffle her cries. And when the tears finally subsided, she felt spent, drained. Laying back she reclined on the couch, closing her eyes, blocking it all out. With knowing came some comfort, but there was pain too, a hell of a lot of pain. Who was this family she belonged to? Did she really know any of them? She pushed it away, tried to slow things down. In, out, in, out. She concentrated on her breathing. The heavy journal on her lap kept pulsing, its regular rhythm becoming almost familiar, hypnotic. Before long, from sheer mental exhaustion, she fell asleep.

~

Almost an hour later, she was blinking hard, trying to drag herself back to consciousness. Adjusting her eyes to the light, she pressed a hand against her forehead, her head literally ringing from too much thinking. But despite her headache, despite however long she'd been in this closet so far, she was going to at least read Lucy and Ella's pages, at least under-stand all she could. She knew, without a doubt, that this was the first and last time she'd see this book. And that it would not be a welcome topic of conversation, just like when she'd been young. No, she needed to glean everything she could now.

Scooting up against the chair, she turned the page again, this time to Lucy's page. The bulk of the paper still a wide expanse of unmarred ivory parchment, there was a brief paragraph at the top, written in Grace's hand.

> *My name is Lucy Rae Harrison, born 1984, first born daughter of Kathleen May Stafford-Carlson and _____ ___. My gift is that of Art Telesthesia. When I look at anything done by hand – handwriting or art – I can merge with the art, understanding things about the artist and the art itself.*

More pieces to the puzzle fell into place. No wonder Lucy was so passionate about art, often staring at a piece for minutes at a time. She wondered what had taken place at the art gallery, what had gotten Teddy so wound up. And Em noticed a pattern: every daughter was listed as the firstborn. She flipped through previous pages, reading the first line of each page. Without exception, they were all firstborn daughters. Em realized that as far back as she could remember , on her mother's side of the family tree, there had never been a son. Not one. She heaved a sigh. One entry to go. She plunged ahead to the last, populated page. What was there had obviously been written by Grace as well.

> *My name is Ella Rae Harrison, born 2001, first born daughter of Lucy Rae Harrison. My gift is that of Animal Telesthesia.*

Animal Telesthesia? Did that mean she could read animal's minds? The vivid memory of Ella's first day at the stables replayed in her head. And her walks with Chloe, always chattering to her and showing her bugs. *Of course.* For the first time since coming into the closet, a smile tugged at her lips. The child talked to everything that walked, crawled, swam or flew! Em had always thought she was just imaginative, fond of animals. But this… well, it explained a lot. Her Ella, able to talk to animals. Incredible.

Putting the book aside, Em sat numbly, trying to make it all real in her mind. Obviously these "bequests" were not to be shared. Her mother's stern talk long ago, the privacy with which Grace had kept the album, the locked cover, all suggested secrecy, an exclusive club whose members were selected by virtue of their birthright. She was odd woman out. She got to watch it all, spend her life wondering what the hell was going on, but she couldn't join the club.

So she was worthy enough to carry the burden of caring for Grace, the promise her mother had extracted from her so long ago, but she wasn't fit to know about something like this? They didn't feel the need to tell her that they were talking to ghosts and animals and… and… ooooh! Her hands balled into tight fists, her jaw clenched, tears streaming down her face, Em felt herself tremble. And while she couldn't quite put a name to the dark feeling clutching her heart, she doubted it was forgiveness.

~34~

She always liked going on special adventures with Mommy, especially when it was just the two of them, like today. Ella held onto her Mommy's hand as they lay on the bristly grass in the meadow. "I think that one looks like a piggy – see his curly tail?" said her Mommy, pointing overhead, indicating which white, puffy cloud formation she was talking about. Ella giggled next to her, snuggling closer. From their cozy little spot, laying flat on their backs, they were all but hidden from sight, the tall grasses forming a protective wall around them, the infinite blue sky with its scattering of clouds the only thing visible. It was late afternoon, and they soaked in the sun's warmth, an occasional breeze fluttering the grasses surrounding them.

"See that one there?" Ella's small finger, its nail painted a vivid pink, pointed to the right. "It's a hippo." Her Mommy looked with her, nodding as she saw the shape. Except for the sound of nearby insects, it was quiet. Mountain quiet. A plane passed overhead, its long white vapor trail streaming behind it and its faraway hum joining with the insect's medley. Then a loud noise erupted – Ella's tummy grumbling – sounding particularly abrupt in the tranquil setting.

Her Mommy laughed, sitting up and stretching. "We better head back and get you a snack. We've been out here a good long time." Ella reached up to take her outstretched hand, skipping along beside her as they made their way back across the meadow. "I think a little sunscreen might have been-"

Ella jerked to a stop, looking at the rustling grasses nearby. "Look, Mommy," she said in a loud, stage whisper. Sure enough, there was a raccoon standing only two feet away, watching them with his masked bandit eyes. Ella stood gazing back at him, her head cocked to one side. Slowly, she shook her head no, looking apologetic.

"Mommy," she said matter-of-factly, "he wants to know if I've seen a little green frog." She paused, looking at her feet, her next words spoken quietly towards the ground. "I told him no, but I sort of lied." She motioned for her Mommy to lean down so that she could whisper in her ear, "I know where the frog is, but I don't want the raccoon to eat him."

Her Mommy smiled, one of her bright smiles that turned her into the prettiest Mommy in the world. "It's okay honey. I understand." Relieved, Ella started back off towards the house, waving behind her at her fuzzy friend.

They were just nearing the house when Auntie came rushing out onto the porch, "Lucy! Lucy dear! There is a phone call for you from the Dean!" Ella looked at her Mommy, wondering if this was good or bad, but she couldn't really tell from her face – it was like she was wondering the very same thing. And she was glad to see Auntie Em because she'd been in her room most of yesterday, and whenever Ella had asked to go up and play with her, Mommy and Nana had said no.

Her Mommy picked up her pace, and Ella had to skip faster to keep up. They climbed up onto the deck by way of the North steps, coming in the living room door. Her Mommy picked up the phone next to Great-Grandma's chair.

"Hello? Yes, this is Lucy Harrison... Oh, its nice to talk to you too, Dean Reynolds... Really... No, you're kidding... me? Are you sure? Yes, I can hold a minute." Her Mommy placed her hand over the receiver and screamed. Ella raced to her, standing alongside her leg as she sat down on the couch. Her face looked kind of funny, like she just swallowed an icky brussel sprout whole.

"Grandma," her Mommy whispered towards Nana, "it's the Dean of the arts school. He says I've made it into the art program! In Europe! Me!" Suddenly she took her hand off the receiver and started talking to whomever the Dean was. "Yes… It certainly is an honor… Yes… Yes… Okay… I'll think about it until then… Thank you very much… Good bye."

Her Mommy hung up the phone, letting out another squeal, "Ahhhhh! This is incredible! I can't believe I'm in!"

Nana laughed. "So, what did he say, dear? Auntie had come in too and was standing alongside Nana's chair.

"He says I have been offered a spot in the program, I have one week to confirm acceptance, and they want me to fly out by September twentieth. Can you imagine! The Louvre! And Italy," said her Mommy, as she danced around the room, twirling with her arms outstretched. The next thing Ella knew, she was swooped up, twirling around along with her. Auntie and Nana just grinned, at least they looked like they were grinning when she caught sight of them for a brief moment during each twirl.

"Miss Ella Roo, isn't this exciting?" said her Mommy. Ella nodded, not really understanding anything other than that Mommy was radiantly happy, and whatever made Mommy happy made her happy too. When she set her back down, Ella had to grab the coffee table for support, since the living room was spinning around like a blur of colors. Auntie laughed and came to stand by her, a steady hand smoothing her hair.

"I've got to tell Scott! He'll be so excited!" Her Mommy ran up the stairs, taking them two at a time.

"Well, that is certainly something, isn't it," said Auntie, who was sitting in the chair nearest Ella. She leaned down and pulled the girl into her lap. Auntie smelled really good, like pancakes and flowers and soap.

"Yes, it certainly is," said Nana smiling, but her eyes looked big and empty, like they did sometimes when she was thinking. She thought a lot. Auntie was watching her, probably trying to figure out what she was thinking too.

"Are you all right, sister?" asked Auntie, her voice quiet.

Nana sighed, "Yes, I'm fine. I'm just... watching the meadow."

"Any wild life today?" asked Auntie in a funny voice.

Nana smiled, her eyes twinkling. "As a matter of fact, there is quite a bit of wildlife today."

Ella ran to the window, excited to see the animals, and was disappointed when she saw nothing. She couldn't even hear the elk or deer talking, which she could normally do if they were nearby. "Grandma, there aren't any animals. At least not the big kind."

"Ah, well, they must have run off," said Nana.

Skeptical, Ella decided to go upstairs and see what her Mommy was doing. Climbing the big stairs slowly, clutching the hand rail for support, she could hear Nana and Auntie talking in soft voices, even over the clicking of Chloe's toenails on the wood. And from up above on the second floor, she could her Mommy talking fast and happy on her phone. Pushing open the door, she saw her standing across the room, so she lay down on the bed with Chloe to listen.

"I don't know what to think. I know everyone says I should do this, that it's a great opportunity. But it's so far. And there's Ella... somehow she has to come too." Her Mommy sat down at her desk, running her free hand through her pretty hair and listening into the phone. "I don't know though, I mean Grandma isn't doing so hot, and there is Aunt Em... and lets not forget Tali and Chloe. I just don't know about leaving everybody right now and flitting off to France. I know you can make it over for big chunks of time, but what about everybody else? They can't up and fly whenever they want."

Ella's little ears perked up at her last statement. What did that mean? Who was leaving Nana, Auntie, Tali and Chloe? No! What was her Mommy talking about? And none of them knew how to fly!

Ella backed out of the doorway, racing downstairs as fast as she was able.

"Nana, where is France?"

Nana turned to look at her as she ran over. "Why, it's in Europe. You fly there in an airplane, over the ocean."

Ella felt terror rising up and taking hold of her body. Her Mommy had told her about the airplane she'd taken to New York City. She'd told her about the tiny little seats and the oversized man who'd sat next to her and how he'd barely been able to squeeze into the chair.

"Nana, is France further away than New York?" Ella asked.

"Yes, sweetie. It's much further actually. But in a plane, it only takes a day."

France was on the other side of an o-shin, a place far, far away where you have to sit in a tiny seat and ride for a long, long time? Well, she wasn't going. And if she *was* going, she'd make Auntie and Nana go too. And Chloe, she was small enough to fit in one of those seats. And… Tali! What about Tali? He was much too big! He was bigger than a person, even a *big* person. He couldn't ride in the airplane! No! No, no, no! She was not going anywhere without Tali. Nu-huh. No. This was bad, very bad. She must do something to keep Mommy from going. She'd have to hide until she figured this out. Mommy couldn't go anywhere without her, could she? She couldn't leave without her, which meant no one could leave Tali. No, no, no.

She decided to talk to her small white friend. *Chloe, Mommy wants to fly over the water to France! We have to stop her. I can't go because I can't take Tali.* Ella sat looking at Chloe, who cocked her head to one side, taking in all in.

Why? asked Chloe.

Because he is too big to fit on the airplane! And he can't sit either. If he could jump the water, like a magic horse, then he could go. She suddenly felt scared, the prospect of her future uncertain, important people and animals in her life missing.

Stay here then, suggested Chloe.

Maybe… but I don't want Mommy to go without me either. I love her.

Suddenly the kitchen door opened, and she heard G-ma Margie's voice, "Yoo-Hoo, we're here." She and G-pa Jack came into the living room and immediately everyone began talking about Mommy and Europe.

Ella felt miserable. Everything was out of control. She wanted to go see Tali desperately, but everyone seemed busy at the moment. Chloe, *do you know how to get to the stables*?

No, but I know the car drives off that way. The white terrier looked off to the north.

Ella set her chin on her hands, realizing the Chloe had never come to the stables to visit Tali. Everyone always said she'd get stepped on, but Ella knew that she had much more sense than that. She could her them talking in the background, everyone excited for her Mommy, everyone saying she surely must take this chance and go to Europe. She thought of Tali and another wave of terror ran through her, jerking her into action. *Chloe, let's go find it – I think I can find the way. We have to get to Tali. We can't leave him behind.*

Chloe rose up, walking over to her and licking her knee. Not wanting to take time to get Chloe's leash, and thinking it silly anyway, Ella headed out towards the kitchen door, Chloe on her heels. They clattered down the steps, still unnoticed in all the chaos. *Okay, let's go through the meadow, cuz there aren't any cars that way, and we would have to hold someone's hand if we went across the street.*

Heading off to the North, swishing through the meadow, the pair quickly disappeared into the tall grasses, making their way towards the stables.

~35~

Everyone was talking at once, the mood festive. But their words were unintelligible to Grace, a jumbled cacophony of sounds. Pressing her hand against her chest, her legs unsteady, she quietly sat down in her chair, unnoticed by the others. The fluttering was worse today, the familiar palpitations having started long before sunrise. And the sisters... they were everywhere. More of them than she'd seen since her own discernment – at least thirty or so – were hovering about the room and just outside on the deck. What could it mean? She'd been worried that after showing Em the Diurnus she'd lose her bequest – which she obviously had not – but now that particular worry had been superceded by a different one, a familiar one.

She'd known it was finally time for Lucy's discernment ceremony for the last couple weeks, but she'd been stalling, putting off the event because of everything going on with Em, not to mention Lucy's interview for the art program. Surely no one could expect her to crossover before that – it would be unheard of, unprecedented. No sister in the trust had ever been cheated of the all-important discernment event. Was that why the sisters were close? And what about the second premonition?

"Sister," asked Em, pulling her out of her reverie, "would

you like some of the special carrot cake Margie brought over?" Her eyes were curious, questioning.

"Before dinner?" said Grace, raising an eyebrow. "Oh why not. That sounds wonderful."

Her gaze lingering, Em turned slowly towards the kitchen, heading off in the same direction everyone else had gone. Halfway there she turned, quietly looking back at Grace. "Are you well?"

"Not as well as I'd like." admitted Grace ruefully. Softly raising her hand to her chest, she added "a bit weaker today than others."

Her sister lingered hesitantly. "Do you need anything?"

Grace shook her head. "Just time. I'm more interested in you," her voice softened, "how are *you* today?"

Em stood as she was, halfway across the room. "Well, I certainly have a lot to think about." She rubbed her hands together, inclining her head towards the kitchen, "I suppose I should get in there and help with the celebration... unless, of course, you need me."

"I'll always need you, but I am fine for now," said Grace motioning towards the kitchen. "You go ahead. I want to sit for a spell."

The happy voices and laughter from the kitchen seemed to bounce off the glossy wood floor and float like bubbles through the air. Even the meadow was active today; beams of energy crisscrossing every which way, pinpoints of light shooting about here and there, other glowing orbs hovering quietly. All around her there was a feeling of anticipation, a certain alertness that was almost palpable in the air. Sitting in the midst of all the activity, Grace felt like a dull rock, immovable, confined, and most definitely old.

Lucy popped her head around the corner, "Grandma, have you seen Ella?"

"No. Have you tried upstairs?"

"I'll go check. She's probably up there with Chloe." Lucy started towards Ella's bedroom, her long, graceful legs taking the stairs two at a time. "I can't believe she's missing out on cake," Lucy's voice floated down from above. "Ella?" Grace could hear her calling into rooms, doors opening and closing. "Ella, you in there?"

Thinking back to when she'd last seen the girl and terrier, Grace realized it had been at least a half-hour ago, when Ella and Lucy had arrived home from their walk.

"She's not up there." Lucy was coming down more slowly than she'd gone up, her face pensive. "Where could she be?"

Grace began to feel a small knot of worry forming in her chest. "Try the porch," she suggested.

"Good idea... the porch."

Grace watched the worried mother as she passed by each of the long, floor-to-ceiling windows throughout the house, checking first on the west side of the wraparound porch, then moving onto the north, and then to the east. As she moved out of Grace's line of sight, Grace found herself clutching the arms of her chair, waiting for the sound of small feet to come running into the kitchen. But there was no sound. And when Lucy returned, her eyes huge dark circles in her pale face, the knot in Grace's chest took hold and began to grow.

"She's not there," said Lucy, her voice timorous. "Where could she be?"

Em was coming from the doorway behind her, wiping her hands on a kitchen towel. "What's going on?" She looked from Lucy to Grace, the color suddenly draining from her face. "Where's Ella?"

"We can't find her!" cried Lucy. "I've looked all through the house and I can't find her or Chloe anywhere!"

Em swallowed hard, her eyes darting about the room. "Well then, we'll spread out and check again," she said. "They have to be somewhere. Have you checked the garage?"

Lucy shook her head.

"Okay. You go look there and the rest of us will check the house again. Grace, you stay right where you are."

Their voices rang through the house, alternately calling first Ella, then Chloe. In the beginning, their tone was cheerful, hopeful. But as time passed, the timbre of their voices changed to one of desperation. They resorted to looking in cupboards, the laundry chute and the crawl space. They checked boxes, under the beds, and beneath the deck. For good measure, they even looked in the washing machine. When they didn't find Ella or Chloe anywhere inside, they moved outside, spreading out and combing the nearby meadow. Grace got up and moved to the deck, frustrated at being useless and consumed with dread. Where could the girl have run off to? And it would be dark in a couple hours, the temperature rapidly dropping.

The premonition.

Grace crossed her arms and shivered. How did that little ditty go? *A situation dire, heed the night choir, seek a starless lass, and no ill will come to pass.* Well, this was rapidly becoming a dire situation. Heed the night choir... what could it mean?

"Grace," said Em, having come up behind her. "I think we need to call search and rescue."

"Yes. Let's do it now."

Em's face tense with worry, she looked Grace square in the eye. "And maybe I'm not supposed to say anything, but wouldn't *now* be a good time to use your gift? Isn't *this* when it could matter the most?"

"Yes," Grace leaned forward, pulling Em close, the tears starting to run down her face. "Yes Em, this is the *perfect* time." Pulling away they smiled at each other tentatively before quickly heading off in different directions. Awkwardly maneuvering the stairs, Grace made her way to her balcony, a place far away from the hubbub below and safe from curious eyes. Leaning against the railing, out towards the meadow, she could see the others, their urgent cries rising up towards her. Jack and Margie walked west in straight lines, the two of them spread about twenty feet apart, both of them calling Ella's name. Lucy was running helter-skelter now, sifting through grasses and looking under rocks. But from her vantage point high above, Grace could confirm what was beginning to become plain in her heart: the child was nowhere in the nearby meadow.

There were no orbs in Grace's immediate vicinity. She closed her eyes, standing perfectly still, seeking out a helpful spirit. But other than the cool breeze against her skin, she felt nothing, no one. Sighing, she looked out into the beautiful pink and orange sunset, the peaks in the distance turning purple as the sun dropped behind them. But no spirits were close enough to communicate with, no one was even moving in her direction. She tried again, this time trying her breathing exercise in an effort to slow things down, center herself. Holding her temples, her eyes closed, she broadcast her plea for help, straining outward, seeking.

"Grandma!" Grace turned around to find Lucy behind her, panting for breath. "She isn't anywhere! Where could she be? Oh God, it's like she's vanished!" Tears sprang from her eyes, her slender shoulders trembling.

"It's going to be okay." Grace stepped forward and took her face in her hands, keeping her eyes strong, commanding Lucy to return her gaze. "Now *listen* to me, dear. You *must* get a hold of yourself. I know its terrifying, but it will be all right, really. Do you trust me?" she asked her frantic granddaughter. Lucy quickly nodded. "Do you trust your gift?" Her granddaughter hesitated, finally nodding again.

Keeping eye contact, Grace spoke slowly and calmly, "Lucy. I am terrified too. But if we work together, if we use our gifts, we can find her. I know we can." Even though her own knees were shaking, she knew she had to lend whatever strength she had to her Granddaughter, help her keep going. "Plus we have the poem from my premonition, remember? A situation dire, heed the night choir, seek a starless lass, no ill will come to pass. I feel sure that the clues have to do with this, with Ella. We just have to sort through them and use our gifts however we can. Okay?"

Wiping the tears away from underneath her eyes, Lucy nodded absently.

"Okay. The night's choir. What can that mean?"

Lucy stared out across the meadow, her eyes frantically searching, probing.

"Luce!" Grace grabbed the girl's arms hard. "Focus! You're no good to me like this! Think! Night's choir… what might it mean?"

Lucy swallowed hard, "I don't know… probably you talking to the spirits I guess – Oh God! That means we aren't going to find her before it gets dark!" Her eyes wide with terror, Lucy leaned out over the railing, a wretched sob erupting from somewhere deep inside her. Then, in a sudden fluid movement, she collapsed down to her knees, head bowed, hands clutching the railing. "Oh God… please…"

Grace knelt beside her, holding tight to her quaking shoulders. "Honey… we'll find her." Looking out over her head, Grace saw the searchers now, the twilight illuminating their colorful orange jackets. The bright beams from their lanterns bounced about like massive fireflies, some of them in the meadow, some starting into the forest and others bobbing along the river bank. The river… for a moment Grace thought her knees might give out as well.

"Mmm-mm" Em cleared her throat, walking up slowly behind them. Sinking down onto a lounge chair, she sat silent, eyes bright, her lips pressed together, her chin quivering. "Any ideas?"

"Well, other than seeking the advice of others," she tilted her head towards the meadow, "no."

"We should be searching for her!" Lucy scrambled up. "I mean, what are we doing standing here?"

Struggling to her feet with the help of the railing, Grace stood beside her. "Well first off, we need to know where to look. *That's* what we need to figure out."

"And how in the *hell* are we supposed to know that?" Lucy buried her face into her hands, "Oh Grandma, I'm so sorry…"

"Look, we are all upset. We have to think." Em drummed her fingers on her thigh. "So the last I talked to her she was asking Grace questions about Europe – you know, where it was, how you got there."

Grace nodded, "Yes, that's right. She seemed a bit… anxious."

"Yes… yes that's right. And I remember her and Chloe, well, you know, talking after that." Em looked thoughtful, staring off into the distance.

"Starless… what the heck?" Brows furrowed, Lucy was pacing, chewing distractedly on her fingernail. Grace watched her as she traveled the length of the deck twice, muttering as she went. "A starless lass… *Aunt Em!*" she swirled around, mouth open. "Aunt Em knows where she is!"

Startled, Em simply looked to Grace for guidance. "Ah, yes," whispered Grace, "but of course."

"Tell her," said Lucy urgently, "Explain."

Turning towards her sister, Grace's struggled to find words. "Em, I had sort of a vision – the day of the burro race – and based on that vision, I think you're the one who can best find Ella." Grace cast a sideways glance at Lucy, "I know it sounds weird, but I think Lucy's right."

"Me?"

Lucy rushed forward, bending down in front of Em, her

eyes entreating. "Aunt Em, it makes total sense. Who spends more time talking to Ella than you? You understand her... *think*... where would she go?"

Closing her eyes, Em sat. Leaning her chin on her hands, she remained perfectly still, the silvery curls on her head jiggling slightly in the breeze. With nothing to do but wait, Lucy began pacing again, and Grace turned back towards the meadow, searching for help. Night had descended in earnest now, the shimmering globes of energy even more visible than before. But still they kept their distance, as if an invisible barrier had been erected around the balcony. Had she done something wrong? Was she being punished for showing Em the journal? Searching among them she looked for Katie, but her daughter was not a member of the gathered assembly.

"Grandma," Lucy said softly, standing next to her, unfolding something she'd just pulled out of her pocket, "Ella drew this just this morning." Grace could make out only vague images given the limited glow available from the porch light. "It's a picture of Tali," her granddaughter continued, gingerly touching the paper, "she was thinking about what it would be like if Tali could live in her bedroom with her, whether or not she could sneak him up the stairs, feed him peanut butter and jelly sandwiches."

"Tali... *Tali!*" Em leapt up off the lounger. "That's *it*, don't you see?" Impatiently, she looked from one woman to the other, "She is going to the stables to Tali. She thinks you are going to take her away on a plane, and she doesn't want to leave him behind!" When no one moved, Em began pushing them towards the doorway. "Come on, you two! We know where to look!"

Racing down the stairs, Grace followed behind Lucy, leaning heavily on the handrail. "It's almost five miles... does she even know the way?"

"I don't know," said Lucy running towards the command center set up in front of the house, "but she might."

"I'll grab your jacket for you," said Em, heading off towards the coat rack in the kitchen.

Grace watched through the screen door as Lucy excitedly talked to the man in charge, her hands moving in large gestures. The pair moved quickly to a folding table that had been set up with various supplies, spreading out a large map and tracing along it with a red marking pen. The tall man in the orange jacket with "coordinator" on the back began nodding. He reached for his walkie-talkie, rattling off commands and coordinates to the searchers in the field. Stepping out onto the porch, Grace suddenly paused, lifting her forearm in front of her eyes, warding off two beams of glaring light suddenly coming down AL in their direction.

"Grandma, it's Scott," burst Lucy over her shoulder as she raced towards the car.

"Well, thank the Lord." Em was standing beside Grace, a bundle of supplies in her arms. "He can help her look, keep her calm."

"The pink sweater?" asked Grace.

"Yes. And her fleece hat." Em started towards Lucy and Scott who were talking next to the Prius. She handed Scott her soft heap of clothing as Lucy turned to take two flashlights and a walkie-talkie from the coordinator. Waving, Lucy ran towards the passenger side of the car. "I've got my cell phone – call me if you find out anything from, um, the choir!" and with that, she disappeared into the sleek little car, gravel crunching as she and Scott headed off to join the search party.

"The choir?" asked Em, eyebrow raised.

Grace looked around and realized that the bright spheres of energy were suddenly all around her, some so close she could reach out and touch them if she wanted to. "Yes. You have done the hard part, Em." She smiled, squeezing her sister's arm. "I think I'll head up to my room and... see if I can help."

~36~

Ella shivered, her short-sleeved top and shorts insufficient covering against the cold, night air. She and Chloe had walked for what seemed like forever, stopping only to investigate interesting bugs and talk to an occasional big-eyed rabbit or fidgety squirrel. She hadn't found anyone yet who knew where the stables were, but one of the rabbits explained she'd seen horses come this way, and had been happy to show them the path. They'd been walking on that very path now for a long time – her feet felt scrunched in her new sandals – and they still couldn't see Tali's stables.

Tired and hungry, Ella sat down beside a big, grey rock, the grass prickly on her bare legs. Leaning against her, Chloe felt warm and fuzzy – very reassuring at the moment. Ella had not realized it would get dark, and by the time it had happened, they were too from the house to go back. Leaning against the rock, she looked up at the sky, the stars bright and hopeful in the purple dome overhead – like the fairy lights in her room. They did not, however, lend much light for walking, mountain nights being some of the darkest around.

Shivering some more, Ella snuggled closer to Chloe, pulling the small terrier tight against her. *I love you Chloe dog.* She was rewarded by a quick lick on her arm. *Do you think the stars are angels?*

Her buddy looked too, then told her she didn't know, but perhaps so. Satisfied that they could be, Ella gazed at them, figuring that if they were angels, maybe they would look out for her and Chloe.

Closing her eyes, Ella let her mind float off to comforting images. Aspen trees, tall and slender, their pale green leaves fluttering in the crisp mountain breeze, the dappled sunlight filtering through the canopy of shade. Clusters of columbine growing along the forest floor, interspersed with old tree trunks, long meadow grasses and discarded leaves creating a cushiony floor that feels light and springy to one's feet. Faces, familiar, comfortable, weathered and wrinkled, full of character and patience, smelling of old spice and lavender, welcoming, the essence of warmth, love and acceptance. And the faces of animals, deer, bear, moose and a small white terrier, ears perked and nose quivering, always on the alert. Tall peaked roofs, Victorian gingerbread trim, wrought iron fences and rooms full of warmth and charm. The feel of long meadow grasses, the cool water of a mountain stream, the squish of dark mud between your toes.

She was just drifting into a happy sleep when off in the distance, they heard the howl of a wolf. Ella shivered again, this time for an entirely different reason. She was not afraid of animals in the same way as other children. No, she was afraid because she *understood* them, and like the dog that had raced down Main Street, she knew that these fanged and predatory creatures were to be feared.

It'll be okay, Ella told herself and Chloe. She listened in the night, sensing rather than hearing that other more friendly animals were nearby. She focused, her nose scrunched and her brows furrowed, as she made 'the bridge' again, sending the fizzing energy in her head outward, like someone flinging seed. She and Chloe could use all the friends they could find right now. It'll be okay, she said to herself again. Won't it?

Somewhere nearby, concealed in the night, she heard animals answering her call, rustling the grass as they moved towards them. She opened her eyes, but could see nothing, not even her own hand as she lifted it in front of her face. Intercepting the nearby currents, she sifted through them, finding two curious deer and the rabbit she'd met earlier, all standing just beyond arm's reach. They, too, had heard the wolves, and were feeling a general sense of unrest. At least it wasn't just she and Chloe, and that was reassuring. She beckoned them closer, closer, finally satisfied when she could feel the deer's hard hooves, the rabbit's nose tickling her as it sniffed her toes.

There it was again, the howling! But it was closer this time. She covered her ears with her hands, blocking out their eerie cries. Ella sensed the animals were frightened, one of the deer darting off, the grasses rustling in its wake. *Chloe, I'm really scared.* She hugged her friend, shivering violently now. She had kept them at bay as long as she could, but the warm tears fell freely now, into Chloe's soft white coat as she buried her face in fur.

Mommy is going to be sooo mad at me. And if I get eaten, she is really going to be mad. I wish she were here right now. I wish we were home in my own room, with the pretty glass fireflies. More howling. This was bad, very bad! She could try talking to them if they came really close, but she wasn't sure she could stop them from hurting her and Chloe. Their howling sent shivers up her spine, the same kind of feeling she got when she ran her fingers down her play chalkboard, but lots more scary than that.

They could try to keep moving towards Tali – he would save them – but they couldn't see anything. They couldn't even see each other. *Do you think Mommy has missed us yet? Do you think she will try to come find us?*

Chloe wasn't sure, and didn't know how Lucy would find

them in the dark when they couldn't see themselves. Good point, thought Ella. They were probably going to have to sleep here. But it was cold, so cold.

More howling. Ella could feel her heart beating, almost like a drum that was slowly getting louder. She placed her hand on her chest, feeling the rhythm, curious why it was so loud, so loud she could almost hear it.

Light emerged, a little at a time, illuminating Chloe and the one deer that still remained. She could see again! She looked this way and that, trying to decipher its source. Ah. The full moon had risen up over the peaks and was bathing the meadow and forest in a silvery glow. Ella grinned, the danger lurking nearby seeming at least a bit more manageable when you could actually see. The horse trail, a minute before invisible, now lay distinct before her, a dark swath through the grasses. Tali. They would run to Tali.

Our lanterns seem to be at odds with the moonshine, lighting up everything close by, but casting the rest of the horizon in total darkness. We decide to flip them off, then elect
to stand for a moment, letting our eyes adjust. My voice is
already hoarse, and I am fighting off the relentless waves of
terror that threaten to overtake me. We are almost four miles
from the house, there is no sign of Ella, and only a single worried call from Grandma, wondering if we'd found any clues.
Now even Grandma has lost her confidence. This just can't be
good.

"Ready?" Scott asks. I nod, and we set out again, calling
Ella and Chloe's names and then stopping to listen for any
possible reply. Nothing. I am yelling as loud as I can, hearing my voice picked up and carried by the wind, along the
meadow, into the blackness.

"Do you really think she could have made it this far?" says
Scott, stopping and turning towards me. "I mean, it's a really
long way for a four year old."

I run my fingers through my hair, finding the pressure
against my scalp soothing, as if it is keeping my frayed nerves
from popping out. "Yeah, I know. But she's been gone for
hours now, so if she kept walking, if she was heading in a
constant direction, I think she could. I don't know, I just don't

know," my voice cracks on the last word. Suddenly, the hair on my arm rises, as off to the right, we hear the eerie howling of wolves.

"Oh my God! Did you hear that? Oh God!" My insides are churning and my lungs are suddenly devoid of air. I wrap my arms around myself, gripping my sides.

Scott pulls me close, "Okay now, let's not panic. We can do this, we can find her. Come on."

I can hear the hysteria in my voice now as I call Ella's name, a harsh discord in the silent night. Damn the darkness! Where was it hiding my daughter? Scanning the meadow, I am disheartened to find this section looks depressingly similar to the rest. But as I turn to my right I gasp – standing right in front of me, blocking my path, is a buck. The tips of his fur glistening in the moonlight, the shadows of his antlers extending along the grass in long eerie fingers – he stands regal and still, and I wonder if we have stepped into the presence of the majestic meadow prince. Keeping my gaze forward, I grope for Scott's arm, and silently pull him alongside. "What the…" he utters before I can squeeze hard on his arm.

"Shhh," I say, continuing to maintain eye contact, knowing somehow this is a sign. But what is he here to tell me? I can't talk to him. I concentrate, hoping for a miracle, but sense nothing. The Buck's dark eyes continue to gaze at me intently, his magnificent rack perfectly still. Unable to simply stand in one place, I decide to turn around, thinking that perhaps the deer is blocking our path to the west for a reason. Taking Scott's hand, I slowly head east, seeing what the deer will do.

With sudden, graceful movements, the buck quickly barricades our path again. *Ah, so now we are getting somewhere.* I turn to my right, starting back to the south, back towards the house. The animal trots around in front of us again, not more than two feet from where we are standing. Out of the corner of my eye, I can feel Scott sending questioning looks my way, but I am focused and desperate, so I stay the course.

"Okay buddy, only one more way to go." I turn around, facing north. I wait, but the buck doesn't move. Tentatively, I take a few steps and wait. Nothing... ouch! I feel a sudden jab in my backside! The deer has just given me a rather abrupt push with his nose!

"All right already, I get the picture!" I grin at Scott, buoyed by the first positive sign since Aunt Em's revelation. "She's this way!" Tugging on his hand, I pull him into a near run, hopeful we won't trip over anything along the way. The buck follows behind, evidently escorting us to ensure we keep heading in the right direction.

"I suppose I should ask later?"

"Yes, later."

We resume our calling now, I with renewed hope. We are covering territory rather quickly now, but with the buck to guide us, I am confident we won't accidentally pass her without noticing. My cell phone rings shrilly from my pocket. I stop, yanking it from my pocket and flipping it open.

"Hello? Grandma?" I listen as she reports on news from the spirit world. "Got it." Flipping the phone shut, I relay the news to Scott. "She says she has word Ella is past the pond, which is about a quarter mile further. She is following the horse trail."

"Who told her that?" asks Scott, obviously confused.

I simply shrug and smile.

"I know, trust you for now, answers later," Scott says, shaking his head.

I nod, and then find myself jerking forward into Scott's chest, my pesky friend growing impatient again. I roll my eyes and pick up the pace, thrilled to have an actual destination in mind. We stop calling and simply run down the trail, intent in getting to the pond. The sound of hooves following along behind us is just one more peculiar thing in this odd night.

As we approach, I see the water of the pond rippling slightly, a gentle lapping sound as it pushes against the shore. Scott shines his lantern, but the beam picks up only a tranquil mountain setting, no small child, no white terrier. Calling their names, we listen, wondering if they are still nearby. Instead, we are greeted again by the unnatural howling, the predators seeming much closer than they had before. Grabbing Scott's hand, we continue to move north, and I can't shake the feeling that we are now in a race with the predators. A race to get to Ella.

Off in the distance, I can see lights – from what, I do not know. But it is civilization, which, despite its name, may or may not be safer than the dark meadow and wolves. My feet are temporarily stuck, thoughts of Ella chasing Chloe in front of a car's headlights, Ella getting into a stranger's warm car, Ella's battered body lying alongside the road. I scream out my daughter's name, listening, praying. Resolute, I break into a run, the sheer exertion a relief from the film clips playing in my head.

The grass slashes against my shins, the brittle strands breaking under my weight. Scott is right behind me, his breath warm on my neck. On my right, I see the buck is coming up alongside us, quickly moving to block our path and veering us to the left. Slowing, I gulp air into my lungs, wiping the tears from my face with the back of my hand. "What!? What are you trying to tell me?"

As if in answer to my question, I hear an unnatural cry, not far in front of us. I push aside the long grasses, frantically scanning the ground. Then I hear the sound I've been searching for, my daughter. Ella is crying, the sobs sounding muffled and indistinct from here. "Ella! Where are you?" I cry. "Mommy is here!"

"Mommy!" Ella shrieks, the single word overwhelming me with its intense tone of terror.

"I'm coming sweetie!" I grapple with the grass, practically ripping it out of the ground, making my way towards the sound of Ella's voice as quickly as I can. Scott flips on the lantern and I gasp in shock, staggering backwards. Ten feet away is a scene I will never forget. A large wolf is crouching low, growling, menacingly stepping slowly toward his prey: the small white terrier that is bravely standing between him and my Ella. The hair on Chloe's back is raised as she valiantly tries to stand her ground in the face of certain death. The sheer terror on Ella's face takes my breath away – she sits on the ground, crying, pleading with the wolf and reaching her hand towards Chloe. She is shaking violently, either from cold or fear or both, tears streaming down her face.

"Oh God!" I say, clamping my teeth down on my fist and sinking to the ground.

Coming up behind me, Scott quickly takes in the situation and throws his lantern, the only thing he has, in the Wolf's direction. The beast yelps and jumps back, reassessing his situation given the arrival of two more humans and a buck.

"Chloe!" Ella cries, beckoning the terrier. Reluctant to withdraw, Chloe slowly backs away from her foe, her hair raised and her eyes locked with his. Good versus evil, David and Goliath. Ella whimpers, reaching, reaching, until finally her tiny fingers can encircle a fuzzy rear leg. Pulling the dog towards her, she gathers the terrier close in her arms, scooting along on her backside away from the dangerous predator. The trance is broken. As quickly as possible, I slowly edge my way towards the pair, the wolf still eying us, but retreating nonetheless. When I reach my daughter, I quickly scoop her up, canine included, and back up quickly towards Scott. The wolf pivots and runs off into the night, evidently deciding the odds are against him.

"Oh my gosh! Ella!" I hug her tight, kissing the top of her head as she sobs, touching her everywhere, assuring myself that she is okay. Collapsing down to the ground, I hold the two close, rocking back and forth until my tremors subside. Finally, with the help of my lantern, I inspect my daughter, finding scratches crisscrossing up and down her legs, a purplish welt on her left arm, and smudges of dirt all over her tearstained face. Bits of weeds and sticks are tangled in her beautiful dark hair, the auburn strands shimmering like blood in the harsh glow. Laying my hand atop Chloe's head, I run my fingers through her fur, my heart welling up with love for this loyal friend. My lips pressed against her, I whisper words of thanks; her ear twitches in response. A sudden cocoon of warmth surrounds me as Scott sits down behind me, enfolding me with his arms and legs. My head lying back against his shoulder, I capture his eyes.

"It's okay," he says. "We made it in time. It's okay."

"But it could have happened," I say, my voice hoarse.

"But it didn't."

The initial wave of relief subsiding, I realize Ella is shaking like a leaf. "Oh honey, are you cold?" I ask. She nods, snuggling closer. A rather large sniffle rings out next to my ear. Scott takes off his coat, quickly wrapping it around her and Chloe. He is tucking the ends tight when I look up and realize the deer is still standing nearby.

Well, here goes nothing. "Ella, will you tell the deer that Mommy says thank you for helping us find you?" I ask.

Scott's head jerks up and he looks on quizzically as Ella nods and seems to comply with the strange request, turning to look intently at the deer, holding his gaze for several seconds. For a moment, all is still. Then the large buck inclines his regal head, tapping the dirt briefly with his front right hoof, before cantering off into the veil of darkness.

"Mommy?"

"Mmm?"

"I have to potty."

~

A short while later we are at the stables, the source of the bright light on the horizon. By the time the rescue crew, Aunt Em and Grandma arrive, Scott and I are outside Tali's stall, watching over our small clan, child and dog now contentedly sleeping with the large black stallion. He lays on his side, with Ella curled up against his front legs, her head resting on his girth. Chloe is nestled between them, all but hidden by Scott's coat and the surrounding hay.

"You were right, Aunt Em." I say, as I sense her coming up behind me. "She was going to find Tali."

Her cool hand rests on my shoulder as she steps beside me and peers into the stall. "Well, it really wasn't that hard to figure out. She adores that horse."

"True, but it took someone with a cool head, someone who loves her enough to understand that to figure the whole thing out."

She sighs. "That's one thing I know how to do – love her that is. She's really something, isn't she?"

The rescue crew wanders over, quietly marveling over the intelligence and persistence required of a small four-year-old to travel the almost five miles from her home to her horse's stall. For those who understand her gift, it is a no less miraculous feat, and one that I fervently hope will never be repeated. I wish I could capture this moment in time, when all those I care about are safe and close by, the younger set peacefully resting. I have a few words for my daughter, but they can wait until later, after everyone had experienced a sound night's sleep and the terror of this night has faded a bit.

But even as I enjoy my moment of peace, I turn towards

my Grandma and notice her face for the first time – her skin is pasty and she looks more than a bit unsteady on her feet. A splotch of pallid grey in the midst of orange jackets. Rushing towards her, I unlock her fingers from the stall door, which she is clutching so hard her fingernails have made indentations in the wood, and help her to a seat on the nearby bench.

"Grandma, what's wrong? You don't look well." I take in her features, wondering how I could have missed her wan appearance. Her breathing labored, she looks weak and, for the first time since I've known her, more than a little afraid.

She lifts her hand with what appears to be a large amount of effort, and places it against my cheek. Cold, so cold. Clasping it with my own, holding it in place, I suddenly know, without being told, that the evening has taken quite a toll on Grandma, perhaps more than she'd had left to give. Despite the fact that I thought I'd used up my reservoir of tears for the night, I feel them slowly welling up again, spilling over onto my cheeks. I shake my head slowly from side to side. "No, Grandma, no."

Her smile is weak, fragile. "Dearheart, take me *home*."

Settled comfortably in her bed, the blankets tucked in around her, Grandma appears smaller somehow, fragile, like a delicate china doll. The flush of her cheeks in sharp contrast with her pale complexion, she looks as if Ella has decorated her with the contents of a rouge pot. Aunt Em and I sit at the foot of her bed as Doctor Evers checks her over, his eyes solemn under his bushy silver brows, belying the pleasant smile he keeps painted on his lips. When he is finished, he loops his stethoscope around his neck and covers her hands with his. He says nothing, but rather looks steadily into her eyes, wordless communication passing between the two; both doctor and patient understand the state of things.

The black leather bag clamps shut with a quiet finality. Dr. Evers quietly rises and heads out into the hallway, Aunt Em and I following close behind. Once the door is firmly shut, he turns to give us the news. "Emily, Lucy, I know you both understand the state of Grace's heart." He waits until we nod. "Well, I think it is finally too tired to keep going and needs to give up the fight."

Aunt Em bows her head, concealing her face in her crumpled white tissue. A single great sob wracks her body. "Em, she is ready." says Doctor Evers, resting a hand on her back. "But I know how hard this is for both of you, being left behind. I doubt she will make it through the night, so you must spend what remaining time you have with her, okay?"

Without looking up, Aunt Em nods. I take her hand, squeezing hard, no words to dull the sting, for me or for her. Standing quietly, we huddle in the hall, trying to take in the impact of the Doctor's words. Suddenly, Aunt Em unbends her limbs, straightening, and letting out a quick sniffle.

"You go back in with Grace, and I'll show Doctor Evers out." Despite her glittery eyes, Aunt Em looks focused and in charge. "Since Ella has already kissed her goodnight and is sleeping, I'll send Margie and Jack up next," she says. I nod numbly, retracing my steps back into Grandma's bedroom.

"Lucy? Is that you?" Grandma asks, struggling to turn her head towards the door. I quickly rush forward, sitting close on the bed so that she can see me without straining. Brushing the hair from her cheek, I savor the warmth, the life that I feel beneath my fingertips. "Luce. We have something to finish. Something big… important." She rests for a moment, running her tongue across her lips. "Are the others coming up?"

I nod. "Yes. Aunt Em is sending up Margie and Jack to… see you."

"Stay nearby, okay?" She clutches my hand. "We have things to do once we are alone. Promise?" she asks, looking worried.

Without hesitation, I nod briskly, biting my lip to ward off the rush of feelings threatening to overtake me. Her vivid blue eyes, weathered a bit recently, seem to be taking in every detail of my features, storing them away. Afraid to blink, afraid if I do, she'll leave me, I do the same. A quiet knock sounds at the door. "Come in," I say. Margie peers around through the opening, slowly pushing open the large oak door and entering the room, Jack close behind.

"Oh sweetie." Margie rushes forward and hugs me. "How are you, honey? You okay?" she whispers in my ear. I force a weak smile and nod, backing away as I hold her hands. With a quick smile, she turns towards the bed. The mood in the room is heavy and intimate; I open the French doors leading out onto the deck, and rejoin the night.

The rough wood of the railing feels harsh and unyielding as I grip it with both hands, leaning back and staring at the twinkling lights overhead. Under Grandma's tutelage, I have learned to detect when spirits are present, the feeling usually akin to a slight tingling sensation, or a cold feeling on the back of my neck or arms. But tonight, well, it's as if I am standing in the path of lightning, my hair eerily rising up around me, the air crackling when I move. The intensity has been steadily increasing, ever since we brought Grandma home from the stables a couple of hours ago, but out here now, well, it's like standing in an electrical storm!

Closing my eyes, I feel the energy probing around me. Whispers, strange and haunting, fill the air, the din so loud I put my hands over my ears. It doesn't help. I can still hear them, all of them. But instead of seeking my grandma, they seem to be seeking out... *me*.

"Aaargh," I whisper loudly. "Stop! I have enough to deal with tonight!" I stomp my foot and stride across the deck to the dark west corner. The whispers are still audible, but quieter now. I can hear myself think. Hugging my arms across my waist, I try to imagine all of this without her, the feeling akin to a body without its heart. Everything about her is so spiritual, so whole. How will we continue? How will I?

Roughly wiping the back of my hand across my eyes, I remove the latest film of tears. I can see the occupants of the bedroom through the window, Margie lying alongside Grandma and Jack on the other side, holding her hand. Margie talks for a bit, then gives Grandma a big kiss on the cheek, she and Jack heading out of the room. I know without being told that Aunt

Em is next, and lean against the railing, waiting for her. But to my surprise, it's Scott who appears.

I start forward and then stop, realizing that whatever they are discussing is none of my business. So instead I watch. Sitting alongside her on the bed, he holds her hand, listening, as one receiving instruction. Occasionally he nods, or voices a brief reply, but mainly he sits patiently, a warm, solemn expression on his face.

He has seen us at the height of our eccentricity tonight and still he is here, taking time to listen to an old woman's last wishes, or perhaps some advice and instructions. What is she telling him? Just as I move closer, intending to eavesdrop, he smiles, patting her hand and standing up to leave. As if sensing me from across the room, he looks up and smiles for a long moment before turning towards the door.

Aunt Em, evidently having been waiting just outside the door, enters the room as he leaves. The sight of her, pale, distraught, her hair standing up on end where she's been running her fingers through it – it tears at my spirit. I want to turn away, but am riveted to the spot, watching through the constant haze of tears, as she sits tentatively on the bed, and then, as Grandma lifts her arms towards her in invitation, lunges forward, the two embracing. This is how it should be with them. No secrets. No barriers. This is how it should be. I move in closer, listening at the door.

"I'm so sorry, Em."

"Shhh. It's okay. It's not important now."

"Not important? It's everything! I should have said screw the whole gift thing a long time ago and just told you. It was never more important than you, Em. Never."

I watch as Aunt Em pulls back slightly, looking lovingly into Grandma's face. "You are my sister," she wipes away a tear, lower lip quivering, "there are no apologies needed between sisters."

Grandma whispers, "Sometimes there are, Em." With a sob, Aunt Em hugs her tight, scooting up alongside her on the bed. They lie in silence for a spell. "And you know what else?"

"What?"

"Who would have known you had the most powerful gift of all."

Puzzled, Em watches her sister's face. "What do you mean?"

Grandma closes her eyes, her cheek pressed against Aunt Em's. "Love. You have the gift of Love, Em." Feeling like an intruder, I back away, the soft murmur of their voices drifting out into the night.

The night breeze strokes my exposed skin, the sound of the air gently bending the trees limbs to its will a stirring melody, all of it heightening the mystical, haunting mood of this night. Finally, as I watch, the long embrace ends, and Aunt Em gathers supplies from the bathroom, gently bathing Grandma's face with a damp cloth and smoothing her hair back with her fingers. She plumps her pillows and straightens her bedcovers. She brings her a glass of cool water. And then, her ministrations complete, she settles back down beside her sister, the two talking softly. When her watery eyes rise and gaze directly at me, I know it is time.

Walking towards the light of the door, I meet Aunt Em's gaze. She solemnly nods. The hum is growing louder now, the air taking on strange, luminous quality. Stepping into the room, it's as if I am enveloped in a warm, living mass, the surface of my skin tingling in response, the pores visibly opening. Aunt Em smiles, sad, yet whole, pulling me into the warmest hug we've shared since my return. And then, with one more tight embrace for Grandma, she departs.

"*Lucy.*"

My name sounds foreign to my ears, her voice weak and breathy.

"Come here. It's time," Grandma says, raising her hand towards me. I heed her request, joining her on the side of the bed.

"Luce. I have a few things I want to tell you, practical matters that must be taken care of."

I nod, waiting for her instructions, ready to carry them out, no matter the request.

"First, I am worth rather a large bit of money – enough for you and Em to live quite comfortably for the remainder of your lives. So I want you to take that horse of Ella's with you to Europe – Chloe too." She pauses, waiting for an answer and gathering her strength. I squeeze her hand.

"Also, I want you to take your Aunt Em with you when you go. She needs you and Ella, and you need her – who else is qualified to look after our little monkey?"

I manage a weak smile, "Of course I will, Grandma. I promise."

"Okay then. Onto the matter at hand," she says, a smile spreading across her face. "Its time for your discernment." She stops, working hard to pull in her next lungful of air, the wheezing sound scaring me. "Usually, we start the discernment ceremony by having you write in the Diurnus. But given the circumstances, I think we'll waive that part for now. But it's important to know for Ella – have her write a few sentences, okay?" I nod.

"And next, you must recite the percepta-orum. Do you remember them?"

Honing my thoughts to answer takes a minute, my mind more focused on my Grandma's short tenure left on this earth. "Um… Don't use your gift for evil, don't use it selfishly and… oh, I know, don't use it to manipulate love."

Grandma raises her eyebrow. "Yes. Don't forget that last one, okay?"

I feel a blush coming on as I realize that deciphering Scott's note in the ice cream parlor probably falls under that third rule. I nod.

"Okay." She folds her hands together atop her chest. "When you take Ella through her discernment process one day, you must do all of this with a bit more flair. You must impress upon her the duties that come with belonging to the trust." She pauses a moment, gathering strength. "And you will know when the time is right. She must have made significant strides towards mastering her gift and must show enough maturity to truly grasp the responsibility she carries. Do you think you can judge her readiness?"

"I suppose so," I say. "I wish you were going to be here to help me, Grandma."

She reaches out to touch me. "So do I, child. But I think the good Lord gave me extra time simply to make sure I could take *you* through it. We must consider *this* our blessing. Right here, right now." She struggles with another deep breath, and smoothes the covers atop her. "Okay. Now is the time for the Orbis. Usually, I would recite your duties before this part, but I am going to have the others help me, as I fear its more than I can manage." She chuckles at my bemused expression and pats my hand. "Now. You must lay down next to me, and hold on to me tight."

Sliding to the other side of the bed, where there is more room, I recline down next to her, resting my head on the pillow alongside her, grasping her in a firm embrace. Our noses almost touching, she whispers, "Lucy, always remember that I love you, yes?" Her beautiful blue eyes are shiny with moisture, her expression solemn.

"I love you too," I say.

"Do it just like this with Ella one day, okay?" she says.

"They'll come, even though it's not your gift, they will come. You can feel them, all around us, can't you?"

She must mean the energy, the humming. "Yes," I say.

"Good. They are here. All of them." She squeezes me tight, giving me a kiss on my cheek and looking lovingly into my eyes. "Let's go," she whispers. And with that, she breathes in through her mouth, her eyes fluttering shut as she sinks back farther into the pillows. "Close your eyes," she instructs in a hushed tone.

I do.

At first, it is simply dark – the barrage of tonight's emotions hammering in my chest, Grandma's heartbeat pulsing reassuringly beside me, but the space inside my head empty. I wait, not knowing for what, the velvety void full of portents. Gradually, the blackness begins to develop shades, strains and currents running through it, rich tones of color that are felt rather than seen. The space I am in feels fluid; it caresses me, warm and inviting. From somewhere in my head, I feel whispers, quiet murmurings coming in through my pores, my skin no longer forming a protective shell around me. And as with the others, the delineation between Grandma and I fades, the two of us melding, sharing a single space. Whether the universe has suddenly reached down inside of me and pulled me in, or if it is all simply within me, within my grasp, I am not certain.

I begin to make out shapes. They start out initially as spots of hazy light, but eventually they take form, the entities far more than just physical beings. Swirling around me at various speeds, eagerly communicating with each other, their auras each perfect and distinct, they are women; many, many women. In this private chamber of my mind and soul, this place that I thought was mine alone, I now find that I am in the company of the Sodalicium.

They are greeting me, beckoning to me.

Lucy, welcome.

Dearest Sister, we come to join you.

You are one of us.

Lucy. We are here with you, says my Mother. *We will take you through your discernment, darling. Just let go.* She hovers aloft and I can see her plainly, her beautiful face, all of its forms from infancy to womanhood visible simultaneously, her presence intense, heady. She is visible in a way previously unknown to me, everything about her – her physical, emotional, spiritual and mental elements – is present, intermixing and discernable.

Another voice, *You must be careful to always keep the trust.* The speaker is another sister, the dark red family hair floating around her alabaster features as if she swims underwater, her lips curving into a smile. It is my Great-Grandmother! *Never tell another.* I feel her, an embrace of sorts, a mixing of selves.

Protect the Diurnus. This sister, elfin-like with her pert chin and freckled face, states her instructions with an impish grin. Waggling her finger in front of me, she adds, *Hide it well and keep its secrets. Pass it down to Ella when it is time.* Giggling, she darts away, a delightful minnow on a pond, her tinkling laughter dissolving into a glittery spray of embers.

Raise your daughter in our ways. Teach her to respect her bequest, using it to mark the world with good, not evil. Three ladies chant in unison, yet their mouths are still. Hovering with their heads close together, the small band is intertwined, their gay attire, full dresses of rich fabrics and trims, floating around them. Throwing me kisses, they float on their way, the spicy scent of musk lingering in their wake.

The next sister is more somber, her prevailing presence gentle and wise. *We have prepared him. He will always suspect, but will never know. We will protect you both.* Spreading her arms wide, her lips arch into a smile, her curling tresses drifting out behind her. *Lucy, he is enchanted with you. He is the one.*

It's Grandma!

But she is so different than the Grandma I have known, or rather she has so many more dimensions to her than I've ever seen. She is young, beautiful, gentle and strong. She appears before me in a long white gown, so white it almost hurts to gaze upon it, the translucent garment looking as if it was sewn from the delicate threads of dandelion wisps, right before they are carried away by the wind. Her beautiful blue eyes are familiar, but they are no longer weary, but rather vibrant and alive.

She stays before me, watching me intently as the other sisters begin to gather round, forming a circle, me at its core.

It is time for the Orbis Lucy. Once we begin, we can only stay in the Orbis for a short time, as mortal hearts can only withstand true love, true communion for a short while. But one day, you will be with us always. She looks to her left, and then to her right, silently ensuring that everyone is ready. *Carry this moment in your heart forever. We will always be near, dearheart.*

And with that, I am pulled into a swirling vortex of riotous color. Everywhere I turn, there are foreign sensations and emotions pouring towards me, through me. I am conscious of voices and communication everywhere, but I can't extract any single thought long enough to make sense of it.

Lucy. Let go.

I mentally jerk backwards as I hear, or feel, Grandma. It's as if she is now the voice in my head, as if they are *all* the voices in my head. I try to let go of my focus, just like I do when I look at art. And the most amazing things start to happen.

It's like I am having a wordless conversation, my thoughts simply flowing outward and others' flowing in. And not just one at a time, but thousands, in many directions, all the same time, backwards and forwards. More than mere words, the exchanges are riddled with feelings, some transfers simply remembrances of scents or sensations of touch, others motion pictures of fond memories or physical sensations of pain or desire.

The lives of these women are melding within me, each of us wholly exposed, our communication effortless as it is simply the essence of who we are, the richness of it needing no further embellishment or explanation. These are my ancestors, my sisters, for as far back as we go, each of us unique, each of us connected. This is who I am, where I come from. They are passing to me their wisdom, memories of sublime joy and utter sorrow, instruction for the years that lie ahead.

The feel of Gertie's daughter, the reassurance of her small form, the smell of milk and the soft feel of flannel, everything savored within a mellowed glowing memory. Elizabeth misses her human form, having always wanted to be a ballet dancer, the fluid flow of the perfected movements satisfying, the physical exertion invigorating. Elsie smells of roses, a climbing vine of yellow blooms surrounding her, engulfing her, her very limbs branches extending outward, twisting and straining towards light. Mary wants me to remember joy comes with sorrow, her memory of losing her kitten vivid, her gut wrenching in despair as her father, dressed in rough work clothes and bending down on one knee, holds her close, explaining death. My mother, her memories of me as fresh as if they had happened yesterday, my father's face visible to me for the first time. A tall man, his face full of angles, with dark, curling chestnut hair to soften his features. His name, Ben Richards, flies by.

And they pick through my memories and feelings as well. Their commiserations are a balm to my heart, their carefully chosen words of advice appreciated. Some of them simply absorb me, conveying back a general sensation of well-being, of acceptance. Others ask questions, wanting to understand further, petitioning me to explore deeper, to understand my thoughts. I try to let them in even further, and am surprised to find that as I expand, exposing more of myself, I am rewarded by even more information flowing towards me. And through it all, Grandma simply stays beside me, holding me, watching.

It's time to say our goodbyes, says my Mother, probing me, looking for something. Hovering directly in front of me, she closes her eyes, a beam bursting forth, hundreds of bright memories flowing towards me, her life, herself. I barely get to start sorting through the memories, when she speaks again. *We must leave you now... to stay longer is not safe.*

Not safe? But it all feels glorious, stupendous! *I don't want you to go! Please stay!*

She loses a bit of her glow. *I'm so sorry, sweetie, but we must... it's for your own good.*

The bright fairy-like creatures who are my family transmit farewells, some of them happy, some of them melancholy. Their beautiful spirits begin to float outward, as one by one, they start to exit, the dark void quickly losing its luster, their small orbs of light becoming more and more distant. Soon only Grandma and Mother remain.

We love you, they say. Reluctant to go, they tarry, and I greedily soak up their warm messages, gathering them close to store away for the years ahead. *We will be near you always*, they reassure me.

I love you too, I say. My heart begins to ache as I feel them retreat. *Please! Please don't go!*

The wave of emotions I am feeling from them tells me that they have no choice, that this is the way it must be. I strain upwards as they rise, trying to reach up, trying to hold on. But they continue onward, and as they leave me, I feel the separation, the emptiness of being alone again. I slowly open my eyes, and find I have barely enough strength for the task, my eyelids feeling weighty and awkward. My Grandma lies beside me, but her heart is still, and I can no longer feel her warm breath on my cheek. She has gone with them.

A tinkling sound drifts down from above me. I turn my gaze upwards, detecting a subtle disturbance in the air, like bubbling water spinning and dancing, suspended overhead. As I watch it, twirling near the ceiling, it stretches out and flows towards the French doors, slowly extending out over the deck and disappearing into the meadow beyond. She is with them now, in good company, traveling somewhere that for now, I can not go. And for the first time, my memories, and those that have been entrusted to me by my mother and the others, are in color. Bright, vivid, glorious color!

~

Ella, with her dark auburn hair and pale yellow sundress fluttering behind her in the breeze, held her mother's hand as they stood in the long, golden meadow grasses, looking across to the tall snow-capped peaks. Em stood by their side, all of them forming a chain of women, each link unique, secure.

The eldest of the remaining clan had been forged from an enduring, translucent gemstone of quiet beauty, able to effortlessly support and care for her own. The next was woven from long, limber jade grasses, the mass intricately fashioned for beauty as well as for substance, age deepening its hue and strengthening its roots. The smallest link was boldly crafted from butterfly wings and soft, wispy bunny tails, the creation held together with cords of tangy pepper-root and sprinkled with twinkling stardust. Together, they had brought the ashes of one of their own, ready to let the wind gently lift her, spreading her across the meadow and into the sky; the places she alone understood.

Opening the painted urn, they watched together as the dull grey ashes began to shimmer, slowly swirling, gaining energy, before gently rising, reaching up and dancing with the sky. The tears on the women's cheeks rose too, the glistening droplets lifting upwards, shiny, crystalline beads of love.

Margie and Jack stood back, along with Scott, wanting to share this moment, but yet respectful of the bond that belonged to this house of women alone. And when the ashes didn't immediately scatter into the air, but rather were lifted by the wind, carried high in a long, wavering stream, up over the meadow and across the tops of the highest peaks, no one was surprised. They expected nothing less. The rare and extraordinary was commonplace at 15 ½, and in this meadow.

ISBN 1412092280-0

9 781412 092289